Copyright © 2024 Kate Hill

Cover design by Kate Hill & Tanner Gordon
Edited by B.K. Bass

ISBN 979-8-9914809-0-1
First Edition, 2024
Published by Kate Hill

 *@itskatehill*

For all the places I'd rather be.

And for Stephen King.

Without his words and inspiration,

this book would not exist.

Under the Same Sky

Year One

Chapter 1

Seren wished she could explode out of her skin and become someone less complicated. She was beyond tired, her eyes at half-mast, gloomily surveying the rows of snow-painted pine trees passing by the bus window. Soon, the late January light would fade, and darkness would bathe the landscape. Her head swam with too much information. Her thoughts tread water, so she could not feel. It had been an awful couple of days, and nothing made her feel better. Her fight-or-flight response had been jammed into overdrive since the prior evening, and she hadn't slept in thirty-six hours. She realized she was running away, but for once, she didn't care. She knew she had to get out of the city.

She shifted in her seat, unable to get comfortable. Her black city-slicker coat was too warm. Beads of sweat formed on her lower back, causing her shirt to stick to her skin. She was dressed as she usually would not—without care and sloppily. None of that mattered now. No one knew her where she was going, and she wouldn't have it any other way. She was glad to be anonymous, a mysterious figure in a new place, and she hoped her presence in Adytown would be just that. Whispers.

As the bus rounded a corner, one of the rear wheels hit a pothole, and the entire vehicle undulated and creaked. *This bus is so old*, Seren thought, grimacing. It was unlike the ones in the city. It made sense that Adytown wouldn't have the resources for newer transport, but she wasn't used to older buses. She liked comfort and ease, but where she was headed was not bound to be comfortable or easy.

When her grandfather passed away, it wasn't a shock. He was old and had lived a long and fulfilled life. Seren hadn't seen him in some time because she was usually busy trying to make something of herself in the city. The love of her grandfather's life was his farm, which he named Hiraeth.

Seren and her grandfather could not have been more different. He was like an oak tree—strong, rooted, and constant. She was like the wind—inconstant, changing, and untied. One could say Seren had little control over her life, much to her dismay. Her life path wasn't obvious, and the uncertainty was unbearable. She was constantly searching, but for what she could not say. Her inconstancy seemed to stain every aspect of her life. No place was home for long. Her worldview evolved with each passing day. She did not long to be one person; she wanted to be many.

Could the next person she encountered have all the answers to her questions? Could they know better? Maybe the right information would undam a tidal wave of golden answers, and everything would make sense, and then she could be happy. But that never happened, and Seren was not happy.

After her grandfather passed, a will was discovered deep in one of his bureau drawers. It read: *To my granddaughter, I give you Hiraeth Farm. Take care of her, and she will take care of you.* It was a shock to receive Hiraeth. Why her? Initially, she didn't know whether she would accept. She hadn't been there since she was a child and didn't remember it well. The only thing she remembered was the peach tree that grew in the western field. It grew the most delicious pink peaches Seren had ever eaten.

She smiled at the memory. She could almost feel the juices running down her chin, and in that moment, she wanted to sob. Her throat tightened, threatening to strangle her, and a familiar sensation crept up her neck. As her chin began to quiver and the slightest wetness reached her eyes, she stamped her foot. *No*, she demanded. *Not now.*

"Arriving in Adytown in ten minutes!"

The bus driver's voice startled Seren, and she flinched. They were so close. She was so close. The hour-and-a-half trip felt like a dream. Had it really been nearly two days since she slept? Yes, it had. Her body was still, but her heart fluttered in her chest as frantically as a caged bird. Her skin was cool, but she felt warm. She wondered if she had a fever. It wouldn't be out of the realm of possibilities, considering how much adrenaline was coursing through her veins. She closed her eyes, hoping to breathe or that maybe her body would allow her to sleep, even for a few minutes. She laid her forehead against the cold windowpane, grateful for the relief from the heat.

When sleep did not come, she opened her eyes. The dim yellow lighting on the bus made her feel as though she were in a submarine. Despite her best efforts, she couldn't sleep or relax.

This is torture, she thought.

She wanted to collapse, shatter, melt, or disappear. She longed for someone to comfort her, or rather that *he* would comfort her. Her throat tightened again, and tears readied to burst through the dams of her eyelids. She would not let them. Seren looked at the gray ceiling, imploring the space to anchor her. She squirmed in her seat, wanting to lift herself out of her body so she would not feel the icy pool of despair growing in her chest.

Seren opened her coat as far as she could and shook its sides, hoping to fan some cooler air onto herself.

Just a little longer, she thought. *It's going to be okay.*

As they approached their destination, it all felt so final. Everything had changed, and Seren hadn't had the time to make

3

sense of it. She felt like she was walking a tightrope, and it took all the focus she could muster to get to the ledge at the end. There wasn't time for logic. There wasn't time for feelings or self-reflection. Only one goal was clear: *get out.*

What if he took me back? The thought flashed across Seren's mind. *No,* she continued. *No, this is exactly how you shouldn't be thinking. He doesn't want you. He made that abundantly clear.* Her eyebrows knit together, and the back of her head pulsated.

"I have to get off this bus," she said under her breath, her voice scratchy and thin. As if in answer to her prayers, the bus slowed and pulled off to the side of the road.

"Adytown!" the bus driver called.

Seren sighed. *Thank God.*

To her surprise, the bus driver turned off the ignition and pocketed the keys. Without asking questions, Seren grabbed her duffle bag and made her way down the rows of empty bus seats. She hadn't realized she was the only person traveling tonight.

As she stepped down the stairs, an icy chill cut through her like blue fire. It must've been twenty degrees colder here than it was in the city. Her teeth chattered. She wrapped her coat around her and fastened its gold buttons, begging the heat she once despised to stay with her.

"Welcome to Adytown, kid," the driver said as she opened the side door to retrieve Seren's suitcase.

"Oh, th—thank you," Seren stammered as she shuffled over to her, still reeling from the cold.

The driver was a stout and gruff woman with short, sandy-colored hair. Her bright pink and green windbreaker shifted and screeched with every movement. In the darkness, Seren could barely make out an obnoxious baby doll shade of lipstick and pale blue eye shadow. Everything about the woman screamed 1980s Jazzercise. She hauled Seren's massive, wheeled suitcase out of the compartment as if it were a bag of feathers. It was impressive, considering how short the woman was.

"Name's Faye, by the way."

Seren looked at Faye as if she didn't speak English. "Y—yes. Thank you," Seren began, handing Faye a five-dollar bill. "I'm Seren."

"You look as though you've seen a ghost," Faye chortled.

Not knowing how to respond, Seren offered a weak smile in return. She reached for her suitcase and pulled it to her side. Beyond a single streetlamp at the bus stop, it was dark. Seren's stomach sank as she realized she had no idea where she was going.

"All I have to say is good luck with that suitcase. This ain't the city. The roads ain't paved out here. They are in the town square, but otherwise, it's nothin' but dirt."

"Do…" Seren began tentatively, "Do you happen to know where Hiraeth Farm is located?"

Faye's lips parted. "Oh, yeah, of course. Uh, when you get to the path through the trees down there, take a right. I can't say I know for sure how far down, but it can't be more'n five minutes' walk."

"Thank you," Seren said.

"No problem, kid. Alright then, if you don't need nothin' else from me, I'm gonna go get me a drink."

Seren nodded. Faye closed the luggage hold and walked off into the night.

Shit, Seren thought. The roads were certainly not paved, much less cleared of the fresh, untouched snow. Thankfully, no more than four inches were on the ground, which was some relief, though it was just enough to make Seren wish she had paid Faye more to help carry her bag.

Alright. Let's go.

It was a struggle to balance her duffle bag on her shoulder and drag her stuffed suitcase through the snow. Making her way to the path, she gazed toward town, where Faye had gone. A short distance away, she saw a few buildings, their forms revealed by the faint glow of iron street lamps. It must've been around 7:30 p.m., but Seren saw no one. In her haziness, she doubted she could commit anything of Adytown to memory. Seeing the town would have to happen another time. Shifting her duffle bag, she turned down the dark path through the woods that supposedly led to Hiraeth.

5

Snow bunched under the wheels of her suitcase, slowing her down. Feeling it get stuck, she mustered all her strength to pull it as hard as she could. In doing so, her duffle bag fell into the fresh snow, sending a cloud of powder into the air, which tickled her exposed skin. Her foot slipped in the struggle, and she fell backward.

"Damn it!" Seren snarled as her back hit the ground.

As she gazed up at the sky, her breath billowed in front of her like a steam engine. She could just make out a smattering of stars beyond the thick, gray clouds that moved through the air like cruise ships. She stayed there for a moment, then another. It was remarkably peaceful, staring at the sky like this.

Somewhere in the thick woods, a tree branch snapped. Panic rose in Seren's chest, hasting her to her feet as quickly as she could. She investigated the thick forest, trying to make out any shapes or moving figures, but saw nothing. It was too dark. She grabbed her duffle bag, slung it over her shoulder, and reached out to grasp her suitcase.

Please, she thought.

She wanted to cry. Her imagination assumed the worst, that it must be a bear or wolf or something that would tear her apart and leave her for dead. Kicking snow away from her suitcase, she forced it to her side. Her heart pounded as she labored to get her footing. Ahead, the pathway opened and gave way to what she assumed must be the farm. A small porch light flickered in the darkness, beckoning Seren closer.

She felt exposed as she entered the clearing with the thick blanket of trees behind her. Her fingertips were numb, and her hands struggled to keep a firm grasp on her luggage.

At last, she reached the cabin stairs. She threw her duffle bag onto the wooden porch and gripped her suitcase handle with both hands. Grunting, she forced it up a stair at a time, the sound of scraping wood assaulting her ears. Breathing heavily, she fished into her coat pocket for the keys. Grasping them, she fondled each key and tried to remember which opened the front door. She jammed a larger one into the keyhole first, but it didn't budge. She inserted a second key, and thankfully, it worked.

6

She snatched her duffle and hurled it into the dark room. Returning to the porch as quickly as she could, she dragged her suitcase across the threshold and slammed the door behind her. Finally, after everything that happened in the last forty-eight hours, Seren's legs could hold her weight no longer, and she sank to the floor.

Chapter 2

When Seren opened her eyes, she didn't remember where she was. Blinking a few times, her eyes slowly adjusted to the gray light filtering through the cabin windows. She stared at the ceiling, her mind completely blank. Her body felt like a dead weight, and she wasn't sure she could force herself to move even if she tried. The old sheets were scratchy and needed to be changed. She became aware of layers and layers of clothing piled on top of her. She was confused for a few moments, and then she remembered the prior day's events: the agonizing bus ride, her dalliance with the perceived monsters in the forest, deliriously nesting in bed under a pile of clothing to keep warm, and finally, the image of *him*.

Tears exploded from Seren's eyes. Her small frame wracked and heaved with unrelenting sobs. She grabbed fistfuls of the sheets and pulled the rough fabric close to her chest. Her nose quickly clogged, making it harder to breathe. She rocked back and forth, then slammed her hands against the mattress as another guttural sob filled the empty room.

She sat up and brought her trembling hands to her drowned face. Her heart gave a resounding thump, and she panicked. With her breath caught in her chest, she flung the covers and clothing away from her. Her foot tangled in the sheet, and she stumbled onto the hardwood floor. She sat down and propped her back against the creaky bed frame, her arms and legs shaking. How pathetic she must look. What a sniveling, stupid mess.

"*Why?*" she demanded. "I don't understand why! Why have you done this to me?"

The cold room provided no counsel, no resolution for her cries. She wanted to break everything she saw, but even in grief, she still had incomprehensible control over herself.

Misty white clouds filled the space as she breathed in and out. The longer she sat, the number the tips of her fingers and toes became. It was like an icebox in the small cabin, threatening to freeze her tears in their tracks. Regardless of how much she could keep crying and let every ounce of grief and rage spill out, she would likely succumb to hypothermia unless she figured out how to heat the place.

Seren took a shaky breath, wiped her face with the backs of her hands, and stood. Before she could cross the bedroom threshold and enter the living room, she stubbed her toe on her suitcase.

"*Fuck you!*" she yelled at the large, inanimate rectangle, giving it a defiant kick.

When she arrived the night before, she hadn't bothered to look around for light switches, a fireplace, or anything else. She didn't know whether her grandfather's cabin had running water, heat, food, or anything. As she stood, shivering, she realized that would have been valuable information to know before her impromptu exodus to the country.

Seren surveyed the one-room cabin. It was quaint and decorated to her grandfather's taste: simple and rustic. Given its size, at least cleaning the place would be easy.

9

The cold winter air permeated the floorboards, seeping through Seren's socks, and her skin pimpled from the chill. She looked around the room for a thermostat, but there wasn't one.

"Shit."

Rocking back and forth, she pondered what to do. Then her eyes fell on what appeared to be a stoveoven. *Is that what that thing is called? No. A wood-burning stove. That's it.*

"Oh, no..."

The stalwart contraption waited for her to make the first move.

She assumed two adjustable vents controlled the airflow, plus a door on the top of the structure and another on the front. Next to the stove were bundles of twigs, birch bark, sticks, logs, and a carton of matches.

"I guess let's just... start burning stuff."

She opened the door, arranged twigs and bark in a neat pile, and then picked up the box of matches. Her fingers shook as she attempted to strike a match against the grain. After a couple of attempts, a flame ignited, and she held it to the earthy mixture. It took immediately.

"Yes!" she cried. "Okay, now what?"

She looked back at the organized woodpiles. Following her instincts, she added more kindling to the fire. As it grew, smoke billowed into the small room.

"Ah!"

Seren turned a silver knob on the smokestack and hoped for the best. Gradually, the smoke subsided. Relieved, Seren continued her fire quest. She added a couple of smaller logs to the fire and prayed they would ignite.

"I suppose it'll take time."

The excitement of figuring out the wood-burning stove diminished, and the heaviness in her chest returned. Sitting down in front of the growing fire, she propped an arm on her knee and rested her chin against her palm.

Warm, stinging tears came again, but with less violence. Staring at the flames, her throat raw with grief, Seren wondered how long she would feel this way, how many more tears she would cry, and most importantly, if she'd ever find what she was looking for. Of course, she didn't know what that was, but she felt there had to be something. At least, that was what she told herself over the years. One day, it was bound to show up, whatever 'it' was. She wished she didn't have to be strong. People loved to call her resilient, and she came to resent the word. Why did her life constantly require her to be resilient? She'd grown tired of it long ago, but her fate seemed fixed, and there was no other recourse. Her life offered an endless stream of things to 'handle,' where being soft or taken care of wasn't an option. The only thing that kept Seren going was hope. Hope that one day, things would be different.

The fire crackled. She added a log to it, and then another. It would be okay on its own.

Seren stood, grabbed a quilted blanket from the back of the couch, and wrapped it around herself. She walked to one of the windows and gazed outside. It was snowing, and she couldn't see much of the landscape.

"Snow day," she croaked as she wiped her cheek.

She walked to the worn leather couch and sat down. It was warm against the back of her legs, the heat from the fire already filling the room. Exhaustion washed over her as she lay her head on one of two red pillows and gazed at the fire. She adjusted the quilt to cover her legs and got comfortable. With snow falling steadily outside, the warm fire, and exhaustion setting in, she drifted off to sleep.

The cabin was much warmer. Seren's eyes fluttered open, and she looked up to the clock on the wall, which read 4:30 p.m. The quilt fell to the floor as she stood to add a few more logs to the fire.

This isn't so bad. Who needs a thermostat when you've got a wood stove? she thought as she lovingly wiped some dust off it.

Seren walked to the front door and opened it. The cold air rushed through her body, but it felt refreshing. A light wintry breeze

11

tousled her hair. Leaning on the porch banister, she gazed over her grandfather's land. It stopped snowing during her nap, and all was still. On the far end of the farmland, a thickly populated grove of trees sagged under the weight of the freshly fallen snow. Something about them called to her, but she wasn't sure why.

Ducking inside for a moment, she grabbed her black coat and slipped on her snow boots. Stepping back out, she closed the front door behind her and took a few steps in the fresh powder. She felt an undeniable delight in completely undisturbed snow.

Seren made her way toward the grove, kicking snow as she walked. Spindly branches of dormant trees reached toward the gray sky, reminding Seren of a Tim Burton film. She didn't know what kinds of trees they were. Fruit trees, perhaps? The late winter day was too dim to see what her grandfather had left of his farm, a task she would have to tackle in the spring if she were still there.

As little as Seren knew about Hiraeth, she knew it was at least ten acres. She doubted she had any neighbors, or if she did, they must not be close by. The thought comforted her. If she wished to run naked through the fields, she could very well do so without prying eyes. In the city, there was seldom space for her to do anything. Here, she could take up as much space as she desired.

As Seren approached the forest, she hesitated. The late winter light was fading, and she didn't know if she'd be able to find her way back in the dark. Nevertheless, the tall trees beckoned her inside.

Snow crunched under her boots with each step. Otherwise, it was dead silent. Nothing rustled, no animals stirred, and not even a slight breeze dared to whistle. The pine trees towered over her, making her feel safe. She laughed at herself, remembering how she'd acted the night before. It was unlikely any dangerous animals lived in these woods, or if there were, they were hibernating.

Seren stopped and breathed the crisp winter air. She crouched on the forest floor, sat, and finally lay down in the snow. Fine speckles of powder fanned over her face, tickling her cold skin. She felt she could stay here forever. At least here, she knew peace. At least here, things made sense. It was foolish to cry, but Seren couldn't stop herself.

Remember who you are.

Sitting upright, Seren looked around the trees. She heard someone, a voice, utter those words. She was sure of it. But there was no one.

"Hello?"

Silence.

Seren stood up slowly. Unsure what to do next, she wiped the snow from the back of her legs and stuffed her hands into her coat pockets.

She shivered. The temperature had dropped significantly, making the outing much less enjoyable. With the sun dipping below the horizon, Seren decided to head back to the cabin.

As she stepped out of the woods, a crescent moon rose over the outline of the cabin, the chimney trailing light puffs of smoke into the air.

Closing the cabin door behind her, Seren ran her hand along the wall until she found a light switch and flicked it on. She exhaled as a small light on the ceiling glowed to life. *At least there's electricity*, she thought. That mystery solved, she realized how badly she needed a hot shower. She grabbed some clean clothes from her suitcase and headed to the bathroom. She was delighted to find a white clawfoot tub with a long showerhead attached. Nothing sounded more perfect than a warm, luxurious bath, and she prayed the cabin's water supply hadn't been shut off.

Seren turned the white, cross-handled knobs and held her breath. Water dripped out of the faucet tentatively, and then the pipes roared to life. She turned the hot water knob as far as it would go and was delighted to discover that not only did her grandfather's cabin have running water, but it also had hot water. She plugged the tub and undressed.

To Seren's pleasure, she discovered a couple of candles below the sink and lined them up on the windowsill. Soft orange light reflected off the windowpane as she submerged herself in the hot water. If heaven existed, Seren was sure it was a warm bath.

As her tense muscles relaxed, she thought of the voice she heard in the forest. She knew she was alone, but where had it come from?

13

Too tired to come up with an answer, she nestled deeper into the water and decided to find out another day.

Remember who you are.

Chapter 3

A loud growl woke Seren the next morning. Strong pangs of hunger rocked her stomach. Food. How could she have forgotten?

Did I not eat yesterday? she thought.

Her stomach growled again, demanding sustenance. Throwing the covers off herself, she beelined to the kitchen pantry and yanked it open. There were some canned beans and bagged rice. The beans were still good for a few more months. She closed the pantry and opened the fridge. There was nothing inside.

I guess someone must've cleaned it out after Grandpa passed. Unless she wanted to subsist on rice and beans for a few days, she would have to get groceries. The thought of going into town so soon filled her with anxiety. She already missed the city's convenience and its many delivery services, which would have saved her at that moment. There was no way Adytown would have a delivery service. Seren shut the fridge door and tapped her nails on the kitchen counter.

Well… I guess I don't have much of a choice.

Maybe she could slip into town without anyone noticing, and if they did, maybe they'd have no interest in her. In the back of her mind, she knew that was wishful thinking, but she could pretend. She was good at pretending. She could slip past them all, not receive a second glance, and get back to the warmth and safety of the cabin in no time.

"Yeah, I can do that."

She threw a couple of logs into the wood-burning stove and pulled on an olive-green Henley, a pair of thick wool socks, and her favorite pair of worn Levi's. She threw her hair into a quick messy bun in the bathroom. Her face was puffy and red, and her eyes were rimmed with purple, but she couldn't bring herself to care. Instead, she splashed a handful of cold water on her face, dried off, and walked to her bedside table to tap her phone screen. It was 11:35 a.m.

The path into town was far less spooky in the daytime. The snow-covered ground told the story of her obvious struggle from the night before. Her eyes stung from crying, and she realized it was a mistake not to bring her sunglasses for added anonymity, but she was far too hungry to turn back.

How the hell did I forget to eat?

On some level, she understood that her raging hunger must mean she was feeling better. "Better," in her case, of course, meant being on the upper deck of hell rather than the lower, but better was better. It was as if her brain numbed the pain enough for a blissful few hours so she could eat and disassociate.

As she drew closer to the town center, she bowed her head and surveyed her surroundings. It was beautiful, as only a small town could be. A three-tiered, cast stone fountain stood in the middle of the square, dormant under the gray winter sky. Seren wondered what it would look like come springtime. It seemed a lovely place to sit and talk. To the south was another pathway with a stone bridge which, to Seren's surprise, led to the ocean. Next to the bridge were what Seren assumed were houses. Immediately to her left were two businesses that were conjoined. The larger of the two had a bulletin board affixed to its wooden paneling and a red-bordered white sign that read *Perry's Home & Groceries*. The smaller structure had a red cross and read *Adytown Clinic*.

Farther down was a single building with worn brick and wooden trimming with the words *The Rusty Fig*. It was tempting to skip grocery shopping altogether and visit the Fig instead. Maybe Seren could get some food to go and bring it home. That seemed the fastest way to get in and out of the square without being noticed. Seren checked her phone again. 11:50 a.m. She decided to go with the quick exit strategy.

The door to the Rusty Fig was locked. In her hastiness to get out of sight, the denied entry took her aback.

What? she thought, her anxiety growing. *Oh, come on!*

Feeling exposed, Seren considered what to do and resolved to go to the grocery store. Just then, footsteps echoed from inside the establishment. She froze.

After a light click, the door opened. A stocky man wearing a chef's apron stepped out, rested his eyes on Seren, and smiled. "Oh, hi there! I thought I heard someone out here. You must be Seren."

"Y-yes. How did you...?" she stammered.

The man chuckled. "Oh, that's Faye for you. But it's cold out! Come on inside." The man gestured for Seren to join him.

I don't understand, Seren thought. *What does he mean, 'That's Faye for you?'* Deciding there was no other recourse, Seren followed the man inside.

It was clear the place was not yet open for business. Only a few lights were switched on, and there were no patrons. The place reminded Seren of something out of the old west. She pictured cowboys and gunslingers slumped over the dark wooden tables, brooding over a glass of whiskey, sore from a hard day's ride. Seren had seen no cowboys in Adytown, so she assumed it was an aesthetic choice. In the corner was a brilliantly colored, 1950s-style jukebox, and a pair of swinging doors that led to the kitchen. To the right was a green felt pool table and a couple of arcade games. There were a few tables and chairs throughout the space that could easily be moved aside to make room for a dance floor. A large, polished bar framed the back of the room, with a decent collection of red wine, beers on tap, and liquor. Altogether, it seemed a fun place to spend a Friday night.

"Come on in. Have a seat," the man said.

Seren pulled out a bar stool and sat, feeling self-conscious. "I'm sorry to have barged in. I didn't know when you were open."

"Don't worry about that," he said as he made his way behind the bar. "I was just about to open, as a matter of fact, so really, you were just in time."

There was something genuinely friendly about him, which put her at ease. He seemed to be in his mid-forties and had a thick head of brunette hair with speckles of gray at his temples. He wore a mustard yellow blouson jacket over a simple white button-up and brown corduroy pants. His nose was large and round, and he had a smile so genuine Seren imagined he must put everyone at ease.

"That's good to know," Seren began, then paused for a moment. "What was it you said about Faye?"

"Oh, yes! She came in last night for her usual and told us all about the new farmer."

Seren grimaced. *Farmer?* "Us?"

"Just a few regulars and myself. Jake usually comes in for a beer every happy hour and stays till late. Oh, and Emelia. She works here sometimes as a waitress."

Seren's face fell. She hoped the few people who heard of her presence in Adytown would keep it to themselves, though she had a sinking feeling the damage was already done.

"I know just what you need," the man said as he lightly smacked the counter and made his way to the swinging double doors. "I'll be right back."

Seren laced her fingers together and sank against the counter. How many more people knew her name? News certainly seemed to spread quickly. She couldn't say she was surprised. In a small town like this, everyone had to know everyone and everything about each other. Clearly, she wasn't as anonymous as she wished, but she held onto a faint hope that she would be left alone.

Behind Seren, the front door opened. She looked over her shoulder at a disheveled-looking man with dark hair, a five-o'clock shadow, and dark gray eyes. He had his hands in his pants pockets and a distinct look of contempt on his face. Though it was winter, he was dressed for spring in a blue hoodie, faded jeans, and sneakers.

He looked directly at Seren. "What?"

Seren turned away from him and said nothing. He walked to the end of the bar near the fireplace and plopped on one of the stools. Seren shifted her focus to the wine bottles and read the labels.

The stranger snickered.

She turned to look at him out of the corner of her eye.

He stared back, his expression a peculiar mix of intrigue and disdain. "What kind of person goes to an empty bar just to sit there?"

Seren parted her lips. His lack of social boundaries took her aback. She looked him up and down and raised her eyebrows.

He laughed. "Yeah, alright. Where's Otis?"

Seren assumed that was the barkeeper and said, "He went to the back." She looked away from him, hoping that inattention would end the conversation.

"So, you're Seren, huh?"

"Alright, what—does *everyone* know my name around here?"

The man raised his eyebrows and smirked. "Relax, okay? You're not that special."

"Thanks, I'll remember that," Seren muttered, clenching and unclenching her hands as she looked at the swinging doors, hoping Otis—if that was his name—would rescue her.

"Just so you know, I don't care who you are."

"Are you always this rude, or do I just bring it out of you for some reason?"

"Jake!" the barkeeper's voice filled the room. "I hope you've been welcoming our newest addition to the valley."

Seren turned to look at him, grateful for his return. He walked behind the bar and placed a steaming plate of spaghetti and meatballs in front of her. The delicious aroma of garlic, parmesan, and tomato sauce filled her senses. He ducked behind the bar and retrieved a bundle of silverware. "Here you are. My famous spaghetti made fresh this morning." He smiled at her before turning to the stranger, who must be Jake.

"Yeah, Otis, sure I have," Jake said, still smirking.

Seren wanted to wipe that smirk clean off his smug face.

"Good. She's a very lovely lady," Otis said as he poured an amber-colored beer into a pint glass and delivered it to Jake.

Seren's face burned, feeling embarrassed by Otis's words. She smiled timidly and unraveled the silverware.

Jake shrugged and gulped half of his beer.

Otis reached for a wine glass and placed it in front of Seren, then turned and picked up a bottle of wine with a light blue label. "This is an amazing pinot noir, made just a few miles from here. It pairs well with the tomato sauce."

Seren normally wouldn't drink so early, but she couldn't say no. In fact, she felt she may need the whole bottle just to put up with Jake. "Thank you, Otis," she said, excited to dig in.

She picked up her fork and spiraled a big helping of spaghetti, perfectly coated with thick, garlicky tomato sauce, and took a bite. It was the most delicious spaghetti she'd ever tasted. The tomato sauce was robust, flavorful, and full of complexity. She speared a meatball and took a bite. She didn't think it was possible they could be even better than the sauce, but they were.

"Wow, this is amazing," Seren said through full bites of food.

"I'm glad you like it! The secret is in the breadcrumbs. I use a special sourdough I bake myself, but don't tell anyone." Otis winked at Seren.

He filled a second glass with amber beer and delivered it to Jake, who immediately downed half of it. Seren sipped her wine. Rich berry and oak flavors danced around her tongue, making her mouth water. Otis was right. It paired perfectly.

Without realizing it, Seren had wolfed down most of her meal. The wine warmed her stomach, and her tense shoulders relaxed. A slight nausea crept in when she finished eating, but she ignored it.

Just the anxiety, she thought.

Jake tapped his beer glass, which, to Seren's amazement, was empty again. Otis picked up the empty glass and replaced it with a filled one.

"We're thirsty today, huh?" Seren teased.

"It's my day off. I can have a drink or two if I please," he said.

"Or three or five?"

Otis glanced at Seren, his expression implying caution.

Jake glared at his pint. Seren felt she may have overstepped, though she meant no harm. Jake picked up his pint and surveyed it, sloshing the liquid around the glass. He seemed to reach a conclusion and promptly downed his beer before rising. "Otis, put this on my tab. I'll be back later."

Otis nodded and waved goodbye. He seemed to sense the awkward moment but maintained his pleasant disposition.

Jake left through the front door, which closed with a thud.

"I—"

"Don't even worry about it," Otis cut her off. "Jake is, well, he's a troubled guy. We've all learned not to ask questions."

"Troubled?"

Otis raised his hands and shrugged. "I wouldn't worry yourself about it too much. Jake seems to have problems with everyone. I believe deep down he's an honest, good-hearted guy, but he's too stubborn to let us see it."

Seren's wineglass was empty. Otis moved to refill it, but she politely declined. "Thank you, but I should probably get back."

"You know, I knew your grandfather well."

Seren's eyes widened as she looked at him. "You did?"

Otis nodded. "Yes, he was a good man. Very hardworking, but I'm sure I don't need to tell you that." He chuckled. "We were good friends. He'd come in here some nights and grab a plate of food or a bourbon. Sometimes, he'd bring in fresh produce after a harvest, and I'd cook whatever he brought me. It really added diversity and freshness to my dishes. I know he'd be so proud to see that you're taking over the farm."

There it was again, 'taking over the farm.' Seren didn't come to Adytown to become a farmer. She didn't think herself capable of becoming one and knew nothing about it or where to start, even if she somehow talked herself into it. However, letting the expansive farmland waste away seemed a terrible fate. It was, at one time, fertile and teeming with life. Though Seren hadn't seen it in its heyday, her grandfather regularly wrote to her about it. He'd been so excited for pumpkin season a few years back. Apparently, he grew several pumpkins the size of a large doghouse, and he couldn't wait to share them with the town.

"I'm not sure I could," she said. "I… don't really know what I'm doing."

Otis's gaze softened. "You will know what is right for you at the right time. Just be gentle with yourself."

His understanding made Seren want to cry. She cleared her throat and nodded.

"Is there anything else I can get you?" Otis asked.

"This was delicious. I don't have much food back at the house, so could I order some food to go?"

"Absolutely! I've got a creamy mushroom risotto, some vegetable stew, and more of the spaghetti if you'd like."

"All of the above. It all sounds amazing, thank you."

She reached for her wallet, but Otis stopped her.

"It's on the house," he said.

"Oh, no, I couldn't possibly—"

Otis waved his hand. "Think of it as my way of welcoming you to town."

It was hard to argue with him. He was sincere, so she didn't persist. He disappeared into the back to pack up her meals. After the doors swung shut, Seren pulled a ten-dollar bill from her wallet and placed it under her empty wine glass. If he would not let her pay for her meal, perhaps he'd accept a tip. It was the very least she could do to repay him for his kindness.

Chapter 4

Otis's words crossed Seren's mind often over the next day. *'I know he'd be so proud to see that you're taking over the farm.'* Otis seemed to assume that's why she came to the valley, but she didn't have the heart to tell him he was wrong.

I came here because… because… there wasn't an end to that sentence.

Seren lay on the couch, thinking about Otis and how she hated to let him down. Seren craned her neck to see the clock on the wall. *3:02 p.m.* She lounged on the couch for a few hours, unable to find a reason to get up. In the city, she always found something to keep herself occupied. There was always somewhere to go, work to attend to, a new tv show to watch, and so on. From what she could tell so far, other than the Fig, there wasn't much to do in Adytown. Her grandfather's cabin was hardly party-central either. It had an old tv with a VHS slot and a long silver antenna on the back. It was from another age that did not include streaming or internet. Seren wondered if the cabin could even get internet.

'*I hope you've been welcoming our newest addition to the valley.*' There were Otis's words again.

Seren willed herself to sit up, hoping a change of position would drown him out. She stretched her arms and felt her back pop. She looked around and saw a small closet next to the bathroom she hadn't noticed before. Curious, she walked over and opened the door. Inside were built-in shelves containing a few board games, clean towels, and a couple decks of cards. On the bottom shelf was a tattered orange leather book. Unsure of what it was, Seren picked it up and brought it to the kitchen table. She didn't want to damage it, so she carefully opened the cover.

Inside was a yellowed photo of her grandfather, who must've been in his mid-forties, standing in a field of tomatoes. He was absolutely brimming with pride. His sweet smile made her heart swell. He looked so happy to be surrounded by the fruits of his labor. Turning the page, she was greeted by a menagerie of unfamiliar faces. They were hard to keep up with. In one photo, her grandfather stood with a shorter man who had slightly bushy eyebrows and a gray goatee. He wore a plaid newsboy hat and was giving the camera a thumbs-up. Her grandfather had an arm around the man's shoulder and looked to be mid-laugh when the photo was taken. There were younger people, older people, and children, all of whom looked happy and familiar with her grandfather. There was picture after picture of harvests throughout the years, with brilliant shades of green, red, orange, purple, and yellow filling the scrapbook's pages.

Seren's eyes fell on one person she recognized. Otis was holding a pint of beer next to her grandfather inside the Rusty Fig.

The next page showed a picture of a beautiful young woman with blonde hair and hazel eyes. She wore a stunning white lace gown and a long white veil that reached the ground. She held a bouquet of pink peonies and baby's breath. Slowly Seren realized who it was and rested her fingertips on the picture.

"Hi, Mom," she whispered.

There were multiple photos of her mother on that day. Another photo showed rows of white folding chairs with a large, flower-woven archway at the end of an aisle. Guests arrived in formal attire. Again, Seren saw the man in the plaid newsboy hat, and Otis, looking spiffy in a bowtie and brown suit. It was bizarre because Seren didn't know her mother was married at Hiraeth Farm. Looking over the photos was like an out-of-body experience. They revealed such a rich history, a whole other life, which Seren knew nothing about. She blinked away tears welling in her eyes and took a deep breath. How could she not know her mother was married here? Why hadn't anyone mentioned it?

Another slightly ripped picture showed a man standing at the end of the rose-petal-covered aisle. It was a man she wished to forget: her father. She had to admit he looked dashing in his suit, but that was all the credit she was willing to give him.

Mercifully, there were no other photos of her father, nor were there any more of her mother in Adytown. The wedding was clearly the only time they spent here.

The final photo in the scrapbook was a group shot. Her grandfather stood at the center, with the residents of Adytown spread around him. It was a gorgeous, sunny day, with blue skies and a few clouds overhead. Seren stared at the photo for a long while but couldn't ascertain when it was taken. She chuckled when her eyes landed on Jake. He was closer to the end of the lineup, sporting a tight-lipped smile—if you could call it that.

Even Jake is part of the family, huh?

Just as her eyes landed on a tall, broad figure in a green dress jacket standing next to her grandfather, there was a knock at the door.

Seren paused for a moment, wanting to pretend no one was home. Whoever it was knocked again.

"Er... coming," she called as she slowly stood and ran a hand through her hair. Thankfully she was already dressed. She walked to the door and opened it.

An older man with a gray goatee stood on her porch. His plaid newsboy hat immediately gave him away. "Ah, hello! You must be Seren."

"Yes, hello," she replied.

"I'm Franklin Doney, Mayor of Adytown, but you can call me Frank. Pleased to meet you." He stuck out his palm with conviction to shake Seren's hand. "I wanted to come here to welcome you to town, and to say that we're all so very excited to know Hiraeth Farm is in good, no—*great* hands!" His cadence seemed genuine, but there was something fundamentally cheesy about the man. He played the part of mayor with such gusto.

"Yes, well, I—thank you," she said, deciding the best course of action was to be polite. "It's funny, I... recognized you from my grandfather's scrapbook."

"Did you now? Oh my, might I have a look?"

Despite feeling self-conscious about the state of the cabin, Seren decided to allow him inside. She walked to the kitchen table, picked up the scrapbook, and opened it to the picture of him with her grandfather.

"Ah, yes, I remember this well. We were celebrating a prosperous harvest. Your grandfather ran this town then; I was just a figurehead," Frank said with an infectious laugh. "At the time, a major corporation wanted to move into the valley, some kind of mega grocery store, soul-sucking conglomerate. *Pah!* Your grandfather kept them out of town."

"And now?" Seren asked.

"Oh, well, they've moved in now that there isn't stiff competition. Poor Perry, he really does try, but he can't beat their prices."

Seren remembered the sign in the town square that read *Perry's Home & Groceries*. His shop looked small, but as far as she could tell, he was still in business. "I'm sorry to hear that," she said.

"Yes, well, won't they be shaking in their boots when they hear good ol' Harold's granddaughter moved in," he said, lightly tapping her shoulder with his fist.

"I'm sorry, Mayor Doney—Frank, people seem to have the wrong impression about me. Truthfully, I don't know where they've gotten it. I've hardly spoken two words to anyone here. I didn't... I didn't come here to take over the farm. I came here because..."

Mayor Doney looked at her expectantly.

Seren decided to lie to him. "I came here to, um, to get the place in order. Y'know, see what needs to be done in case I sell the land."

Mayor Doney looked as if she had slapped him. "Oh. That's a shame."

Seren felt embarrassed, but she didn't see any point in entertaining his wishes, not when he was so excited to believe that a carbon copy of his old buddy was there to save the day, and she had no intention of doing so. It felt cruel to allow him to build his castles in the air.

"Well, if you decide to stay, I know everyone here would be delighted. And, if I may, I know Harold would be too." Frank tapped his leg a few times and then made his way to the porch. "Oh, also, I know Harold didn't have much time... you know, at the end, to keep up the place. It was hard for him to be active. If you decide to stay, you should meet Rita. She lives just up the hill from Perry's. She'd do a swell job fixing up the place."

"Thank you, May—Frank. I will give it some thought."

This seemed to brighten Mayor Doney's mood, and a smile returned to his face. "Excellent! Yes, yes, very good."

He walked down the stairs, and Seren came to lean against the porch banister.

"Welcome to Adytown," he said, tipping his newsboy hat to her.

Seren watched him leave, knowing he meant well, but she couldn't help but feel he anticipated her staying. She shook her head at the sky, scanning the fluffy white clouds as if her grandfather had heard their conversation. *You had some interesting friends, Grandpa,* she thought. She slid her hand down the banister, which she instantly regretted, yelping as a sizeable wooden splinter lodged itself into her palm. A single drop of blood fell onto the slowly melting snow.

"*Damn,*" she cursed.

27

Seren examined the wood that was deeply lodged under her skin, then walked into the cabin and closed the door. Opting to sit at the kitchen table, she attempted to pinch the tiny end of the splinter with her fingernails. She tried once, twice, and three times, but couldn't dislodge it. She wasn't sure if she had tweezers. If she did, they were lost somewhere in the giant mess of clothes and toiletries she hadn't bothered to put away.

"You're such a mess."

Her eyes landed on the scrapbook once more, and all the happy smiling faces looking back at her. She'd had enough of memory lane for one day, so she closed the scrapbook, returned it to the shelf in the linen closet, and shut the door. She looked at the splinter again. It didn't hurt, so for the time being, Seren decided to ignore it. She figured, one way or another, it would dislodge itself.

Chapter 5

The following few days were unseasonably warm. By midday, temperatures reached the lower fifties, and the snow-covered landscape quickly transformed into swaths of muted green and brown. Spring was still a few weeks away, but Mother Nature had other plans.

There wasn't much need for the wood-burning stove, so Seren stoked the flames less often. She even opened the windows occasionally. She didn't mind the cold, even preferred it, though the warmer weather was a nice break from the bleak stagnancy of winter.

Seren sat on the porch in an old rocking chair. She laughed, thinking of her grandfather unknowingly participating in an old cliché. It was a fine choice though, and a lovely place to sit on a nice day. She leaned back in the chair, rocking slightly with a steaming cup of Earl Grey tea in her hand, and gazed at her grandfather's land.

Most of the snow had melted, revealing cultivated fields. She imagined brilliant red tomatoes in one, green-striped watermelons in another, and the satisfaction of knowing it was her hard work that brought them to life. Then she'd walk up the stairs, wipe her forehead with the back of her gloved hand, and be—well, alone. Perhaps that was okay. She could get used to being alone, maybe even come to prefer it. All she knew was that it would take someone extraordinary to change her mind.

Seren took a sip of her tea from one of her favorite new mugs. It was white with painted red strawberries and little green stems. It seemed too dainty to have belonged to her grandfather, but the thought of him using it made her smile. She imagined his thick, dirt-stained hands grasping the cup, being extra careful not to drop it. Then he'd take a sip with one hand, extending a pinky for show. Seren laughed.

The more time she spent at Hiraeth Farm, the more she felt she knew her grandfather. The simple and well-used furniture, the old, banged-up teakettle, and the sturdy bed all made her think of him as a straight-to-the-point, efficient man who made use of everything. However, the strawberry mug made her think of him as someone who had a soft side, and would greet everyone he met with a hug instead of a handshake.

She wished she had visited and called him more often. She hoped he knew she loved him and wanted to spend more time with him. When one is young, one tries so hard to make something of oneself, and Seren was no exception. But Seren had made little of herself, and the feeling of being a failure made the reality of lost time sting even more.

"I miss you, Grandpa. I hope wherever you are, you're happy and know you lived a fulfilled, amazing life."

Her grandfather knew his purpose, a concept upon which Seren had often ruminated. What was her purpose? What was the purpose of life? It seemed pointless to ask, especially when no one seemed to know the answer, but she couldn't help but think about it. She wished to know her purpose. She wished to know where she belonged. If she never got the answer, she would think about it until the day she died.

"What do I do, Grandpa? Please, show me."

Seren thought of the voice she heard in the forest. She heard those words plain as day, she was sure of it, though she didn't understand their meaning. She thought she knew who she was: a woman with all the potential, brains, and beauty in the world, but she never lived up to that potential. It seemed whatever she tried wasn't enough. She never measured up to the impossible standards and ideals she imposed upon herself. What would happen if she let those standards go? She would shatter into a million pieces, no doubt. Maybe that was exactly what she should do.

"I need a drink."

Seren entered the cabin and opened the liquor cabinet. It only contained a half-drunk bottle of Jim Beam. She had to be in the right mood for bourbon, and today was not that day. She closed the cabinet, placed her hands on the tile kitchen counter, and pondered what to do. The Perry's Home & Groceries sign popped into her head.

Seren checked herself in the bathroom mirror. Her long hair looked fine enough, and today seemed to be a good skin day. She swiped mascara through her eyelashes and applied a little blush before giving her hair a slight tousle. Her complementary gray sweater made her gray eyes pop.

Good enough.

Seren took off her drawstring sweatpants and put on jeans that were much looser than a few weeks prior. She slipped her purse strap over her head, walked to the front door, and stuffed her feet into her boots. Grabbing the keys off the wall, she opened the front door, stepped through, and locked it behind her.

Perry's shop wasn't what Seren expected. Mayor Doney's description made it sound like the shop was on its last legs. It was a far cry from the mega stores Seren was used to in the city, but it seemed to have all the essentials, plus some odds and ends. The produce looked a little sad but edible.

Seren rounded a corner to find a small red and white wine selection.

Jackpot.

Most of the selection were big-name brands. She had expected to have difficulty choosing just one from a fine array of local wines. Regardless, she settled for two bottles of a popular Malbec, and concluded that at least Perry's had some selection.

"Disappointing, isn't it?"

The voice seemed to appear out of nowhere. Seren shuddered and spun around. A man with slicked black hair and a sycophantic grin stood much too close to her, and she recoiled. The scent of too much peppercorn and bergamot wafted off his deep purple suit and assaulted her nose. His manner reminded Seren of a used car salesman preying on her like a vulture, trying to convince her to purchase a beat-up Pontiac with stripped tires.

"I can tell just by the look on your face you want more to choose from. After all, variety is the spice of life," he said.

Seren didn't trust him, so she took a step back. He was determined to hold her attention, so he stepped with her.

"Name's Myron. I run the Wares & More Grocery Store just over the river. Stop by sometime. We have a fine selection of wines that'll keep you browsing for hours, plus anything else you may need. That's the Wares & More promise!"

"Thanks," Seren said, taking the business card he folded into her hand.

Just as quickly as he arrived, he turned and left Perry's. Seren grimaced. He was like sludge personified, and the encounter left her feeling in need of a shower.

The checkout counter was empty. She tapped a small gold bell next to an old, gray register, and shortly after, a man with dark red hair and a surprised expression emerged from a side door.

"Oh! Hello. Welcome to Perry's. Did you find everything you were looking for?" he asked.

"Yes," Seren replied.

As she placed the bottles of Malbec on the counter, Myron's business card slipped out of her hand and fell to the ground. The man picked up the card and sighed as he stared at it. "Oh, was Myron here?"

"Yes, he pretty much forced me to take it," Seren said.

"Ah, well, just the same." He looked at Seren, and something dawned on him. "I'm sorry, I don't believe I've had the pleasure...Oh, yes! You must be the late great Harold's granddaughter." He reached out his hand.

"Yes, Seren. Nice to meet you—"

"Perry, very nice to meet you, too," he said, shaking her hand a little too vigorously. "Oh, what I'd give to have your grandfather here now. I've just about had it with that damned Myron coming in here and stealing my customers. Harold would know what to do. He'd say, 'Perry...' Well, that's the thing, I don't know what he'd say because he's not here!" Perry snorted as he laughed. He had a look of desperation in his eyes that said, *Please. Buy something.*

"But I know he'd come up with something. Harold used to stock these shelves with just about anything you could ask for. I tell you, those were the days. Those were the days... Anyway! What can I do for you?"

"Just the wine, thanks," Seren said.

"Right away, right away."

Perry got to work, displaying a level of showmanship not usually seen in a supermarket. He snapped open a brown paper bag with a *thwack* and fanned it until it stayed open on its own on the counter. Then, he cradled the wine bottles and nestled them inside as if they were made from fine crystal. The shit-eating grin he shot at Seren was comically exaggerated.

"Well then, that'll be thirty-five forty-seven," he said.

"What?" Seren asked.

"Thirty-five forty-seven," Perry said again.

Seren knew she was being had. The price of the two bottles of wine was much more than they were worth, but just this once, she'd let it slide. She took out her debit card and attempted to hand it to him.

"Oh... I'm sorry, we only accept cash."

Really? she thought.

33

Times might have been tough, but Perry was partly to blame for keeping his store in the dark ages. Myron's store probably accepted all kinds of payment methods, no questions asked. Still, she didn't like the man. Perry seemed nice enough, albeit a bit eccentric, but with all his customers seemingly opting for more convenience and lower prices, how could she blame him?

Putting her debit card away, she took out two twenty-dollar bills and handed them over.

He looked a little embarrassed and asked, "Ah, do you have change for a five?"

"It's alright, just keep the change," she said, not in the mood to spend any more time with the shop owner.

"Oh, thank you, thank you." He handed over her purchase. "Oh, and…" He held out Myron's business card.

"I don't need it. If you'd like to toss it, that'd be fine."

"Excellent, ha-ha! Down with capitalism," he said as he dramatically spiked the card into the wastebasket. What a peculiar man he was.

"Thank you," she said as she turned to leave.

"Do come again!" Perry said, that tinge of desperation still coloring every word he spoke.

If Seren had not met Myron, she would have undoubtedly looked elsewhere for her groceries. Her experience with Perry's store was abysmal—comical, even, and paying forty bucks for two bottles of cheap wine that would not have cost more than seven dollars each in the city was ridiculous.

Outside Perry's shop, Seren paused. The faint glow emanating from the Fig's windows made it look incredibly inviting. She wondered if she should stop by and pick up some food, but after spending almost all her cash on mediocre wine, she decided against it. She remembered she had a plate of mushroom risotto at home, which she planned to wash down with a bottle of Malbec. The events of her evening decided, she turned to head home.

Seren was so deep in thought she didn't hear the clinic door open and close, and she ran full force into a tall, broad figure in a

34

green dress jacket. The wine bottles clanked against each other, and she nearly dropped them.

"Oh! Excuse me," the man said.

Seren gazed up at him, meeting concerned green eyes that towered at least a foot above hers. He wore a white button-down shirt tucked neatly into brown dress pants under his jacket. His well-kept oxfords shone as if they had been recently polished. His tie was slightly undone, and the top button of his shirt was open, revealing a hint of chest hair. Seren hadn't seen many men with mustaches, but his suited him. A stray strand of his otherwise well-kept brunette hair fell in front of his scholarly-style glasses, which had slipped down the bridge of his nose.

"Are you alright?" he asked, his hands bracing her forearms.

"Y—yes. I'm sorry I wasn't paying attention." Seren repositioned the wine bottles and pushed her hair out of her face.

The man laughed and let go of her arms. "That's alright," he said. He appeared to be close to her age, if not maybe a few years older. It didn't matter, however, because Seren realized, to her horror, that she found him attractive. Refusing to acknowledge the thought, she tried to focus on holding the brown paper bag with both hands so the bottles would stop clinking.

"Dr. Harlan," he said, offering his hand.

"Seren," she said, wincing as she pressed her palm to his.

Concern shadowed his handsome face. "What happened to your hand?"

The splinter hadn't dislodged itself, and she couldn't find her tweezers for the life of her. It was red and swollen, a sure sign of a growing infection. "Oh, I—it was silly. I slid my hand down my banister, but it's nothing."

"I'd be happy to take a look at it if you'd like. I just wrapped up for the day, so I've got time."

Seren slightly parted her lips and stared at him. "Okay," she found herself saying.

Dr. Harlan took out the clinic keys and unlocked the door. Seren followed him inside, feeling completely out of place. The tidy waiting room had a few simple chairs, a coffee table, and surprisingly up-to-date magazines. The place could have used some color, but for a clinic, the atmosphere made sense.

He clicked on the fluorescent lights and beckoned Seren to follow him. She swallowed hard as they entered a sterile examination room, her hands growing clammy.

"Please make yourself comfortable. If you'd like to place your bag on the counter, that'd be fine," he said, looking over his shoulder to smile at her.

She did as she was told. The wine bottles made a racket as she placed them where Dr. Harlan instructed, and she cringed as she sensed him moving behind her. He removed his dress jacket and hung it on a hook on the back wall, then unbuttoned his cuffs and rolled up his sleeves. She backed up to sit on the hospital bed, suddenly feeling very aware of her body.

"I'm sorry," Seren said.

"For what?"

"Oh, I—just… I bought wine."

Dr. Harlan laughed. "Sounds like a great evening to me." He washed his hands, picked up a pair of tweezers from a small table next to the counter, then sat on a rolling stool and wheeled over to her. "May I?"

Seren nodded.

He held her injured hand and looked closely at the splinter. His hands were much larger and warmer than hers, and his palms easily enveloped them. He dragged the cold, hard tweezers over the wound. "I'm having trouble finding an entry point. Are you okay with needles?"

"I guess I'll have to be." She hated them, but she wasn't about to appear weak in front of him.

He wheeled back to the side table and picked up a needle, concealing it in his hand. "So, tell me, what kind of wine did you buy? It's been a while since I've gotten into a bottle myself."

"Oh, uh, malbec, I think. I haven't tried this one before, but the label was cool, so of course I had to get it," Seren said, attempting to sound lighthearted.

"I've done that before. There's this one chardonnay. I can't recall the name of it… It begins with an 'R,' I think," Dr. Harlan said, looking to the ceiling in thought.

Seren's eyes traced the curve of his neck. He must have shaved that morning, as his skin looked fresh and clean.

"Rombauer?" she asked.

"Yes! That's it. One of my absolute favorites."

"It's one of mine as well."

Dr. Harlan wheeled closer to her, the needle barely visible in his large hand. "You have good taste," he said, smiling at her.

She could only hold his gaze for a few moments before needing to look away, her cheeks warming with a sudden flush. *What is happening?* she wondered, stealing glances at him as if he'd have the answer.

"If you'll allow me, I promise I'll work quickly," he said.

His tone calmed her, and she nodded after a moment or two. She took a deep breath and extended her hand to Dr. Harlan, which he held ever so gently.

"Ready?" he asked.

"Yes."

He lightly pricked her skin with the needle at one end of the wooden sliver. Seren drew in a sharp breath, but his attention didn't falter. He pulled back the bit of punctured skin with the tip of the needle, hands steady, as Seren watched them do their work. She dared to drag her eyes up to look at him. His expression was all business, completely focused on the task at hand. He pinpointed the end of the splinter with the tweezers and removed it from her palm in one easy motion. He disposed of the nuisance into the trash bin beside the hospital bed and wheeled to the counter to place the needle and tweezers in blue liquid. He doused a cotton ball in solution and returned to her.

"This might burn a little," he said, then lightly dabbed the cotton on Seren's wound.

Her hand twitched as a sharp sting coursed through her palm.

"Sorry, almost done." He discarded the cotton ball and grabbed some antibiotic ointment, which he spread on her cut and covered with a Band-Aid. "All done! You were very brave."

His praise made her feel as though she were back in elementary school, where her favorite teacher had just awarded her a gold star.

Dr. Harlan rose from the stool and walked to the sink to wash up. With his back turned to her, she raked her eyes over the outline of his impressive figure. He looked strong and in shape, and his bedside manner was capable and attentive, all the things one hoped their doctor would be.

What is someone like him doing in Adytown? she wondered.

"If you'd like to meet me in the waiting room," Dr. Harlan said, "I'll just take a moment to clean up a few things here."

"Okay." She jumped off the bed, turned, and ran right into the door. As if literally running into Dr. Harlan wasn't mortifying enough, she concluded that she'd most likely have to spend the rest of her days in solitary confinement or avoid the clinic altogether. Looking at the floor, her legs wobbling, she turned the handle and left the room.

What is wrong with you? Get it together, she thought.

The stock images of men and women that lined the clinic hallway seemed to echo the sentiment. *Yeah, Seren, get it together!*

She glared at them. *Just hold your stupid clipboards and shut up.*

Pushing through another door, Seren entered the waiting room, then placed her hands over her face and shook her head. Pacing back and forth, she looked at the clinic door and wondered if it'd be rude to leave. She could have him send her the bill in the mail or something. He had gone out of his way to help her, however, so she felt she should stay to thank him. Looking at her bandaged hand, she could still feel where his skin had touched hers, and her skin prickled.

The hallway door swung open, and Dr. Harlan walked toward her, holding a clinking brown paper bag. He had changed back into his green dress jacket and straightened his tie, the top button of his shirt now closed. "Can't have you forget this."

"Oh, yes." Seren had completely forgotten about the wine. He handed her the bag, and as she took it, her hands lightly brushed his.

"So," she said a little too loudly, then cleared her throat. "What do I owe you?"

"Oh, no, don't worry about that. It was my pleasure," Dr. Harlan said.

"Is that a habit in this town?"

Dr. Harlan gave her an inquisitive look.

"Otis did the same thing when I first got here. He let me take home a bunch of meals for free the first time I met him."

"Oh, well, I'm sure we can figure something out if you'd like."

Seren's heart rate increased.

"A bottle of wine, perhaps?" he offered.

"Oh," Seren said, settling.

"I'm just joking," he said. "It'd be silly to charge you anything for this. I'm just happy I could help."

Seren smiled at him, and for a few brief moments, she felt she could talk to Dr. Harlan. She wondered if he had treated her grandfather. She wanted to know why he wanted to become a doctor and to ask him what other wines he enjoyed. They could talk about anything he wanted. She just wanted to talk to suppress the raging storm inside and quiet the thoughts of *him*. Maybe he could help her forget everything for a night.

Her musings were cut short when her phone vibrated in her jeans pocket. The screen lit up as she raised it, and to her horror, she saw the one name she hoped never to see again.

"Are you alright?" Dr. Harlan asked.

Seren stared at her phone screen, unable to compute what was happening. "I'm—" The room started spinning, and Seren knew she had to get out of the clinic. "I'm sorry Dr. Harlan, I—I have to go."

She turned on her heels and raced out of the clinic.

Chapter 6

Seren gripped the cabin keys in her shaking hands. As she attempted to unlock the door, she dropped them. She leaned over and scooped them up, feeling as though she might vomit. Finally, she managed to open the cabin door and shut it behind her. Breathing heavily, she grasped the two bottles of wine and threw the bag on the floor. Depositing the bottles onto the counter, she tried to gain her bearings.

She pulled out her phone to check the message to make sure she wasn't hallucinating. There was *his* name, and there was his simple question, splayed across the screen.

Can we talk?

The temperature in the cabin had reached a boiling point. Seren ripped off her sweater and threw it on the kitchen table, then walked into the bedroom and put on a white t-shirt. Dissatisfied, she raised every window as far as possible to get some fresh air. Lastly, she walked to the wood-burning stove and turned the top lever, allowing the hot air to be sucked out the chimney.

Sitting on the couch with her phone in hand, she stared at the screen. Whatever he had to say, she knew she couldn't put off hearing it forever. She hated this feeling, one that was all too familiar.

It was as if she were standing on the edge of a cliff, and hundreds of feet below, the ocean churned and smashed against jagged rocks. The crash of the salt spray cut through the air like hissing serpents that opened their mouths to devour her. She didn't want to go, but some unknowable force brought her there over and over again. She could only look forward, never backward, fearing that someday that force would push her over the edge.

As if another hand guided her own, she typed *yes* in response to his message, set the phone down, and waited. Her breath hitched in her throat as, almost immediately, the screen lit up with an incoming call. She answered.

"Hi, Adam."

"Seren," he said.

A long pause came after, making Seren feel as if her stomach would fall out.

"What do you want?" she finally asked.

"I, um… I wanted to say I'm sorry."

"You're sorry?"

"Yes. This won't change anything, but I am sorry."

"Is that it?"

"Yes."

"Why don't you love me anymore?"

"Seren—"

"No, really, I don't understand. What am I supposed to do—" her voice cracked. Seren's stomach muscles failed, and she couldn't keep herself from hyperventilating. "What am I supposed to do with all these memories?"

Adam was also crying on the other end of the phone, but she didn't believe him. She didn't believe he was capable of feeling pain, or grief, or remorse. His tears seemed fake, and she hated him for it.

41

She forced herself to continue. "What am I supposed to do with all those beautiful cards you made me? I brought them with me, you know. What about that? What am I supposed to do without hearing your voice? Or getting to hold you every day? I don't understand. Why?"

"I'm sorry. I wish I knew what to say to… to make it better, but I've had time since we last spoke to really think about everything, and… Seren, we're just not compatible."

"What the fuck does that mean?"

"You… You're not ambitious, and that worries me. I just don't see that drive in you. I know you're going through a difficult time, and you're confused, but I need that stability in a partner."

"So… what?" Seren asked. "You called me just to rub my face in it? It wasn't enough to end things the way you did. You just had to call and say—what? That you've made up your mind? That nothing has changed?"

"Nothing has changed. I'm sorry. I know this is… this is what needs to happen. I can't be with you without feeling selfish for needing you to change."

"But I… I love you."

"I've got to go, Seren. Please, take care of yourself."

The phone beeped three times. The call was over. Everything was over. Seren grabbed an empty water glass from the coffee table and threw it against the wall, shattering it into a thousand pieces. Hot blood gathered in her cheeks. This couldn't be happening. It just couldn't. All that had once been a dream but never came to be bubbled to the surface, too long dormant under the steel trap door Seren closed over her feelings, day in and day out, like a militant gatekeeper. It felt like all her life, everything she had hoped for, was going up in flames.

Unable to think straight, she stumbled toward the front door and threw it open, slamming it against the wall and rattling the windows in their frames. She lurched down the cabin steps and fell to her knees, then ran her throat raw as she let out a gut-wrenching cry that echoed far across the open fields. She looked up at the deep purple and blue sky, like a bruise in need of icing. The cold, hard ground offered no counsel, but steadfastly held her quivering bones. Slowly, she stood and looked around. A short distance from the cabin was a small shed, and Seren made her way toward it. She needed something, anything, to take these feelings away. She threw open the door and grabbed the first tool she laid eyes on, which was a broad metal hoe with a long wooden handle.

Seren wildly pummeled the ground again and again. She hacked away until her arms burned. Hot tears blinded her, yet she kept striking the silent earth until she couldn't any longer. Feeling lightheaded, she stopped to throw the tool hard on the ground. She panted from the exertion, yet she was not done. She returned to the shed and grabbed a small fire pit from the corner. There was plenty of bark and logs, so she added a few pieces to the pit. Then, she ran inside the cabin to get a box of matches, lit one, and threw it onto the logs. Bending down to pick up a bottle of firestarter, she squirted it directly onto the rubble, sending a fiery wall of flames into the sky, illuminating the darkening landscape.

Ducking inside the cabin once more, she grabbed everything she had brought from the city that reminded her of Adam. She grabbed every card he made her, his sweatshirt, and her favorite picture of the two of them. In a frenzy, she burned the cards one by one. Their sweet, sentimental phrases whizzed through the air and into the growing fire, which devoured every word. She grasped the picture between tense fingertips. They looked so happy. She loved this picture. Adam looked so handsome in a light blue button-down shirt and dark jeans. It had been an uphill battle to get him to use any product in his hair, but that night, the night of their two-year anniversary, she had convinced him. There was that big goofy smile, the one that made her melt since the first night she met him. His arm was wrapped around her waist. Seren's hair was shorter then, but still well-kept and shiny. She wore a pastel cocktail dress, perfect for springtime.

It was all a lie.

Taking one last look at the two of them, she placed the picture directly in the middle of the fire and watched it slowly disappear in a thick cloud of black smoke.

Chapter 7

The bleakness of winter gave way to spring, turning the ground into a thick mush of dead grass and mud. Birds gradually returned to the valley, their sweet song scoring the early morning stillness. The thick sheet of ice on the pond to the south side of the farm slowly melted, its inhabitants breathing a sigh of relief. With each passing day, the sky brightened from gray to light blue, ushering in a feeling of renewal.

Seren was bent over a wheelbarrow, depositing large handfuls of fallen tree branches, twigs, and rocks. Stray hairs from her haphazard ponytail pricked the back of her neck like thorns, and though it was a mere sixty degrees, she sweated as if she had dumped a bucket of water over her head. She took a moment to lift a fatigued arm to wipe her brow.

She had accomplished a lot in the past few days. After the snow melted, she was surprised to see how much debris littered the fields. It was hard work, but Seren had cleared a large portion of fallen branches and leaves. Using a pickaxe for the first time was dangerously exciting. She had only seen them in old gold rush films, where bearded men sang songs in dimly lit mines as their weathered hands swung hard against the rock walls, hoping to strike it big. Seren's lot wasn't quite as romantic. Her only use for it was to dig deep in the soil to clear away any sediment or rock that would obstruct growing crops.

Discarding one last bundle of debris, she moved the wheelbarrow toward the large pile of brush next to the shed. Eventually, she would organize the debris and keep what was useful.

The midday sun shone brightly overhead. Seren turned to allow its rays to warm her face. Her stomach growled, signifying that it was time for lunch. She discarded her grandfather's oversized gloves into the wheelbarrow and walked into the cabin. In the bathroom, she turned on the hot and cold taps to wash her hands. There was dirt under her fingernails, and small red blisters were forming on her palms and fingers. It was funny to see them in such a different light. Never in a million years would she have thought they'd look like this, and for a moment, she felt as though she were in a parallel universe. How funny life can be.

Dirt swirled inside the sink as it made its way down the drain. Seren did her best to clean under her fingernails until they were spotless, then splashed a handful of water on her sweat-ravaged face. She grabbed a clean towel to dry herself, then let her hair down to brush it through and throw it up into a quick bun.

When the door to Perry's didn't open, Seren was confused. Just to be sure, she jostled the handle again, but it didn't budge. She looked through the store window and confirmed that the shop was clearly closed. There was no one behind the counter, nor were there any customers—though for Perry's, not having any customers was just like any other day. Beside the store entrance was a list of store hours. Midway down the list, it said, *Closed on Tuesdays*. Seren sighed.

46

Everything about Perry and how he ran his store was becoming more and more inconvenient. She wanted to support local business owners, but he was making it impossible to do so.

Seren thought of the slimy, black-haired man she'd met, who had all but forced her to take his business card. She looked across the river to the outskirts of the town center. Not far away was a large modern-style building with sliding doors and a sizeable billboard on the roof that read *Wares & More*.

Unfortunately for Perry, he lost another customer. Adjusting her bag, Seren made her way toward the store.

Futuristic sliding doors welcomed Seren into Wares & More. Despite her reluctance, she could not deny how impressive it was. Everything seemed impossibly clean and well organized, as if Myron was expecting the King of England himself. The smell of fresh bread filled Seren's senses and made her mouth water. It reminded her of the impeccably stocked and efficient mega stores in the city. Perry's Home & Groceries had maybe two or three aisles, whereas Wares & More had at least ten. It would be quite easy to get lost between the rows and rows of richly colored produce and packaged goods.

Seren had only taken a few steps when she heard a familiar, slimy voice uncomfortably close to her ear.

"Ah, hello. Welcome. I knew you'd come to my side eventually," Myron said. He interlaced his fingers and smiled widely, his teeth glistening with spit. "Is there anything I can help you with today?"

"Yes, um, I'm just looking for seeds," Seren said.

"What kind of seeds, my dear?"

She really didn't like the way he said, 'my dear.' *Gross.* "I'm not sure. Maybe some tomato seeds, or whatever grows in the spring?"

"Ah, well, you see, agricultural needs are not my specialty, but I'm sure one of my fine workers could point you in the right direction. *Jake!*"

A slouched figure in a blue jumpsuit and a black baseball cap that said *W&M* on the brim stopped what he was doing and turned to them. He was carrying a clipboard and some collapsed cardboard.

"Yes, Mr. Fox?" Jake asked.

47

"Please assist our lovely customer with anything she desires. And, Jake…" Myron straightened his back, purposefully looked at him, and pointed toward the ceiling.

Jake did as he was told and straightened his back. "Yes, Mr. Fox."

"Very good. I am sure Jake will help you find whatever you need." With a flourish, Myron swept his arm in front of him in a half bow, half wave before departing toward the back of the store.

When Myron was out of sight, Jake glared at Seren and pushed his lips together. "What do you want?" he asked.

"Wow, what hospitality," Seren said.

"Look, tell me what you want, or don't. Either way, I've got a lot of work to do."

"I'm looking for seeds."

Jake impatiently raised an eyebrow. "And? What kind of seeds?"

"Look, I don't know. Just… whatever grows in the spring."

Jake rolled his eyes and walked away. He gave no indication for her to follow, but she did. Their shoes clattered against the finely polished floors as they made their way past the well-stocked aisles.

At last, they came upon a large display of hundreds of packets of seeds. Images of the perfect vegetables, fruits, and flowers made farming look easy. There were so many choices, and Seren didn't know where to begin.

"What do you want to grow?" Jake asked.

"Oh, well, I…"

He huffed and placed his clipboard and cardboard on the floor. "Everything we have displayed can all be grown this season. How well some of these grow will depend on the quality of the soil, the proper amount of sunlight and water, the right fertilizer, spacing, and of course, how large a scale you're operating. Do you have a compost pile?"

"A what?"

"Compost. To feed the soil."

Silence.

"How about mulch? Have you got that?"

Seren stared at him blankly.

48

He drew in an annoyed breath before continuing. "The most common crops this time of year are tomatoes, lettuce, spinach, potatoes, snow peas, cucumbers, peppers, green beans, carrots, beets, and radishes. You'll need trellises for most of those."

"Trellises?" she asked.

Jake looked at Seren as if she were the dumbest person on Earth. "You're hopeless."

"Look, Jake, I know we got off on the wrong foot, and I'm sorry for that. I never meant to offend you. But if you can't be patient with me, then I'll just… figure this out myself." Seren's reply didn't have the convincing gusto she had hoped for.

"Okay, then figure it out yourself," Jake parroted. Without another word, he picked up his materials and walked away.

Seren's lips tried to form some retort to chastise him, but nothing came out. Truthfully, she was disappointed he hadn't stayed to help her. He seemed to know considerably more about farming than she did.

She turned back to the seed display. Jake had rattled off all the most common crops so quickly she barely remembered what he said. He'd said tomatoes, that much she remembered, and there was something about trellises. Seren felt semi-confident that she knew what those were, but there was so much to learn.

Seren decided on tomatoes, beets, and potatoes. That seemed to be a good enough start. She grabbed five packets of each and walked to one of the many checkout counters to pay.

Seren was glad to be out of Wares & More. It was clearly far better managed, stocked, and maintained than Perry's, but she felt terrible for lining a big corporation's pockets. She had to convince herself that Perry was only doing it to himself. After all, his store was closed on a weekday; he was practically telling people to shop elsewhere. Seren promised herself that she would go back to Perry's the next time she needed something. Hopefully, he would value her loyalty.

Seren decided to walk a different way to the Rusty Fig. She didn't want to cut through the town center, especially during midday. The warmer weather would surely bring out more of the townspeople, and though Seren felt more comfortable conversing than when she first arrived, she still preferred to keep to herself.

The river flowing south toward the ocean babbled pleasantly as Seren strolled alongside its steady current. Water lapped and splashed over smooth stones, and the bright sun glistened on the water. As Seren walked with her small plastic bag in hand, she thought of the time to come. What she was attempting could lead to disaster, but she had to try. She thought about how much she had to learn and wondered if she was capable of succeeding. She wished she could talk to her grandfather, to ask him for advice. He knew what he was doing, and Seren hoped one day she could say the same.

As Seren came upon the stone bridge that led back to town, she noticed a dark green building to her left that she hadn't seen before. The roof looked like it could use some attention, and the flowerbeds needed weeding, but overall, the place looked inviting. There wasn't a sign or indication of what it was. She made a mental note to ask Otis about it.

The afternoon patrons had not yet arrived, so the Fig was empty. Seren preferred it that way so she could sit and chat with Otis and enjoy a good meal.

She made her way toward the bar as the doors at the back of the pub swung open, and Seren's favorite chef appeared, holding a fresh plate of spaghetti and meatballs.

"Seren! I knew it had to be you," Otis said.

His apron looked freshly laundered, despite red stains here and there, no doubt from the countless times he made his delicious marinara.

"Hi, Otis, good to see you," Seren said. She always enjoyed her time with him, no matter how brief. His unpretentious demeanor made him a wonderful friend, and she couldn't wait to tell him her news. She set her grocery bag on the bar and took a seat. She slowly and deliberately raised her arms above her head and stretched her sore muscles until the pleasure outweighed the discomfort.

He placed the plate of spaghetti, along with a bundle of silverware, in front of her. "So, will it be a glass of the pinot today? Or would you like something else?"

"I'll just take some water. Thanks, Otis."

Otis poured a glass of water from a metal pitcher, which was laden with condensation, and handed it to Seren. He noticed the obnoxiously large W&M label on her grocery bag and audibly snorted.

"What is it?" Seren asked.

"Wares & More, huh? Don't let Perry see you carrying that bag around town."

"He's closed today! I stopped by his place first, I swear. He did it to himself, really. Closed on a weekday? Who does that?"

Otis chuckled in agreement and shook his head. "Poor Perry."

There was a slight pause before Seren continued. "I got seeds."

Recognition played across Otis's face. "Seeds? Does that mean you're staying?"

"It does."

"Seren, that's wonderful!" His congratulatory tone was infectious, and she couldn't help but break into a wide smile. "That's truly, truly wonderful. What convinced you to stay?"

"It's just something I've got to do," said Seren.

"Well, forget the water. This calls for a celebration!" Otis opened a fridge under the bar and grabbed a bottle of champagne. He unclasped the cage and eased the cork out until it popped. He placed two champagne glasses between them and poured the bubbly golden liquid until it almost spilled over. "To your new venture, may it be bountiful and prosperous!"

They clinked their glasses together and took a sip. The bubbles tickled the roof of Seren's mouth. He placed the bottle inside a bucket of ice and left it on the counter.

"I really couldn't be more excited for you," Otis said.

"I'm excited too. Well, nervous, but also excited."

"You're Harold's granddaughter. If anyone could do it, it's you."

Seren scaled the cabin's porch steps and unlocked the front door. As always, Otis had insisted on not taking Seren's money, but with some effort, she persuaded him to let her pay for half. It was the least she could do, considering he'd also gifted her the rest of the champagne. They talked for much longer than usual, mostly about farming plans and the coming season. When customers started filing in, she took that as her cue to leave and quietly exited without much notice.

Setting the Wares & More bag on the kitchen table, she put the meals from Otis in the fridge. The light buzz from the champagne only elevated her mood, and despite her exhaustion, she couldn't wait to prep the fields for her newly purchased seeds in the morning. Her excitement grew as she retrieved a clean wineglass from the kitchen counter. There was no reason to stop drinking yet. Seren uncorked the half-full bottle of champagne and poured a hefty glass, unbuttoned her flannel, and draped it over the back of the dining table chair, revealing a thin white tank top underneath.

Turning to lean against the countertop, wineglass in hand, she looked over the now clean, well-organized cabin. Everything she brought was in its proper place, and she stowed her suitcase in the closet with the board games and the orange scrapbook. It was nice to walk freely through the bedroom door without getting her foot tangled on a sweater or pant leg, and to sleep on fresh, soft sheets. Every counter, panel of flooring, and bit of machinery shone, thanks to a fantastic array of cleaners from under the kitchen sink. The stagnant, stuffy energy in the cabin was cleared away, and the space felt rejuvenated.

Seren was proud of herself and all she had done. At least if Mayor Doney or anyone else decided to stop by, she would happily invite them inside.

There was still the matter of sanding the porch and making sure the cabin was structurally sound. Mayor Doney had mentioned a woman named Rita, who was the town carpenter. It wasn't a top priority, but Seren surmised that sometime soon, she would need to make the trek to find out what work should be done. Who knew how many more splinters she would accumulate if she did not?

An image of Dr. Harlan crossed her mind. Seren set her wineglass on the counter and trailed her thumb across where the splinter once was. She pictured how he looked bent over her hand, his legs splayed open in her direction. She remembered how his thighs looked pressed against his pants, and she wondered what they really looked like, free from all that fabric. Heat pooled in her stomach as she thought about taking them off herself, and then, a pair of green eyes slowly lifted to meet hers.

"Nope, uh-uh," she muttered as she shook her head and forced his image from her mind.

She quickly grabbed her wineglass and drank. Suddenly, her throat felt very dry, and the slightly acidic, fruity flavor did just the trick. She picked up the bottle to accompany her to the bathroom.

She set it and the glass on the bathroom sink and filled the bathtub. Her fingertips grasped the side of the cool ceramic tub as she looked outside. Though it was spring, the sun still set early, like a strengthening yellow ball dipping behind sparsely budding trees.

Seren peeled her dirty clothes off one by one and tossed them into a wicker hamper in the corner. It was a relief to be free from the day's sweat and toil. She hadn't brought many clothes fit for farm life, so what little she had took a beating. Her work had completely ruined a pair of running shoes, as she didn't own boots capable of handling copious amounts of dirt, mud, and grass stains. She would need to overhaul her closet soon. Her cocktail dresses and high heels, she could not part with, though she doubted she would have much use for them. She had placed them prominently in her bedroom closet, to not completely forget her previous life.

Seren connected her phone to a portable Bluetooth speaker that she'd placed on the bathroom floor and played her current favorite songs. Soft, melodic sounds reverberated against the bathroom walls and set the tone for the evening. She lit a few candles and placed them in a familiar pattern, mimicking the many nights she'd partaken in this ritual.

Picking up her wineglass, she sank into the steaming water. No matter how many baths she took in her lifetime, slowly sinking into warm, fresh water always felt like home. No matter how difficult a day was, or how anxious she felt, a hot bath always melted away the stress and strife of whatever was going on in her life. There, her imagination could run wild as curated music, always suitable for her mood, played in the background.

Tonight, as she sipped on champagne, she felt like a siren. She sat with her back propped against the smooth, sloped surface with one leg bent and the other playfully kicking the water with the tips of her toes. The warm water snaked down her legs in spidery tendrils, and the faint candlelight flickered against her soft skin.

"Maybe it was just the moonlight…" she sang along as she raised her glass of golden elixir into the air.

In the oasis of the cabin bathroom, all was well. Brief moments like this were worth living for. She wasn't sure what to call this feeling—carefree, relaxed, or maybe just happy. It was all she ever truly wanted, and she felt it now, happily swimming and rocking in her small ocean.

Seren often imagined life as one long train that never stopped. She was a solitary passenger, sitting and watching the world and her life go by. There were peaks and valleys, dark tunnels, and a never-ending mystery of where the train was headed. She wished she could stop it to get out and look around—absorb each moment of life, drink in the wild air, and experience the euphoria of being.

In times like tonight, when all was well, she felt she could get off the train, even for just a moment. This feeling, which was ephemeral and difficult to hold on to, was her ticket out. When the feeling passed, she would need to get back on the train. It was never permanent. It was never fully real.

Despite how quickly this feeling came and went, it was enough to escape. It was enough to dream. It was enough to hope.

Seren took another sip of her champagne and set it on the floor. It warmed her stomach, and the buzz that had been steadily building all afternoon reached a point of bliss. As she splashed warm water over her collarbone and shoulders, an idea came to her.

She unplugged the bath drain and dried her impeccably clean body. Without bothering to get dressed, she gathered all the remaining candles from beneath the bathroom sink and opened the door to the main room. One by one, she placed them throughout the space and lit them. The remaining champagne begged to be poured, and Seren happily obliged. She turned up the portable speaker and placed it on the coffee table.

The combined roar of the fire in the wood-burning stove and the soft candlelight gave the rustic cabin the ambiance of a Grecian temple. Champagne in hand, Seren swayed and spun joyously to the music. She freed her long hair from the tight bun she'd sported all day, which fell in thick waves over her shoulders.

The rest of the world melted away. All that remained was her, how she felt, and this moment. It was as if the music lived in her bones and directed her feet in perfect rhythm. Her arms flung out as if to embrace the whole of the universe, as if she could reach out and pluck a star from the night sky and bring it down to Earth. There is an inherent vulnerability in joy, and Seren only dared to feel it alone. She did not want to be alone, but just for tonight, she could let go and be content. She could abandon control and the need to know whether things could or would turn out. She could simply celebrate being alive.

For now, there was all the time in the world, and the train could wait.

Chapter 8

✐

"A dance?" Seren asked, horrified. "When?"

Otis chuckled. "Next Friday. And I better see you there, young lady."

"Oh no, no, no. I couldn't do that," she said, withdrawing her hands from the bar. The last of the vegetable stew she had for lunch sat in front of her, stone cold.

"Yes, you can. It'll be good for you," Otis said.

"For your information, I am perfectly happy to just stay at the farm."

"You can't do that indefinitely, you know," he said as he discarded the bowl in a bin beneath the counter.

Seren huffed and stared straight ahead. He was right. He always was. "What's so special about this dance, anyway?"

"Well, it happens every year to celebrate the coming of spring."

Seren snickered. "Sounds kind of hokey." But that wasn't true. She thought it sounded lovely, but she didn't want to admit that to herself or to Otis.

"It'll be a nice way for you to meet people. God knows they've asked enough about you!"

Seren's face turned ashen. "People have asked about me?" She wasn't sure she really wanted to hear the answer.

"Well, of course!" Otis said as he wiped down the counter with an old dishrag. "Who wouldn't ask about the pretty new farmer who mysteriously showed up in the middle of the night and has barely been seen or heard from weeks later? Stories get around."

"Who said I was pretty?" she asked.

Otis shook his head and stopped wiping the counter to look at Seren. "Listen, I understand you need to do things at your own pace, so I won't rush you, but I think you should come. Even for just a little while. And if you're uncomfortable, you can always come hang out with me at the buffet. I'm catering."

Otis's presence at the dance would be some relief, though it wasn't enough to convince her to go. After all, what would happen if he were busy? What if other people wanted to talk to him, too? She would stand next to the buffet table partnerless and mute while everyone else chatted away, thinking about how silly she looked. "Does she know we don't bite?" they'd ask.

"Is this a... like a *dance,* dance?" she asked.

Otis's perplexed expression prompted Seren to elaborate. "Will I be... dancing with anyone?"

"Well, I think that's entirely up to you!" he said, guffawing.

"No, Otis, I can't, I'm not—" Seren cut herself off, wringing her hands together.

Otis offered her a tender smile. "I understand, Seren. Whatever you decide is a-okay with me." Otis rested his palm atop Seren's forearm and gave it a light pat.

Seren looked up at him. "Thank you, Otis."

A mutual smile passed between them, and Seren stood up to put on her jean jacket.

"So! What have you got planned for the rest of the day?" Otis asked.

"Oh, I don't know," Seren said. "The seeds are in the ground, so that's a start. I guess we'll see if they grow. Really, I'm just sort of… following my instincts. I wish I could ask my grandfather about all this."

Otis nodded in sympathetic agreement. "If Harold and I had ever talked about how to be a farmer, I would not hesitate to tell you everything he told me."

Seren searched herself as if there were something else she meant to say or do, but she couldn't remember what it was. She slung her bag over her shoulder and pictured the walk back to Hiraeth. She saw the cobblestone path leading away from the Fig into the town square and the path that led across the river toward the—*Oh, that's right.*

"I meant to ask you. What's that dark green building over there?" Seren asked as she pointed across the river.

"Ah, that's the library. It has a surprisingly good selection. You should stop by sometime," Otis said.

Before either of them could say another word, the door to the Fig swung open, and a woman with long red hair, neatly swept to one side in a classic three-strand braid, quickly approached the bar.

"Otis! I think I've had a stroke of genius," the woman announced. "Could I please borrow a couple of tomatoes?"

Otis seemed chuffed by the woman's enthusiasm. "Of course, Jenna. You know, with the beets last week and the tomatoes this week, you're gonna put me out of business."

Jenna giggled and straightened her overalls, which were heavily stained with every color under the sun. It appeared that Jenna had sewn patches over small tears in the fabric with colorful thread. The woman seemed bright and cheerful, and she exuded confidence.

"Oh, hi!" Jenna exclaimed as her gaze came to rest on Seren.

"Jenna, have you met Seren?" Otis asked.

"The legend from the city herself? No, I haven't."

Jenna extended her hand. "I'm Jenna!"

"Seren."

"Nice to meet you, Seren!"

The pair shook hands, and Otis smiled at the two of them before disappearing into the back.

"So, tell me everything! How are you liking the valley?" Jenna asked as she pulled out a barstool. She rested her elbows on the bar and leaned forward, seeming intent on listening to Seren's every word.

"Oh, um, it's nice!" Seren tried to match her energy. She felt awkward standing, so she sat down once more.

"I'm sure it must've been a shock, coming from the city and all," Jenna said.

"Yes, definitely."

"I moved here from the city a few years ago too. It took me a long time to settle in, but once I did, I really grew to love it here."

Seren nodded and wished she felt more unbridled, like Jenna. Though Seren felt socially inept, Jenna seemed eager to talk and enjoyed the conversation.

"Oh! Are you going to the Aster?" Jenna asked.

"The Aster…?"

"The Aster Dance!"

Just then, Otis returned with three ripe tomatoes. "Maybe you can convince her, Jenna."

Seren tilted her head at Otis and drew her eyebrows together.

Otis simply winked and chuckled quietly under his breath as he placed the tomatoes before her.

"Yes! Oh, you must come," she said.

Clearly, the Aster Dance was one of her favorites. Or everything was Jenna's favorite. Either way, Seren was surprised that her mind was gradually being changed by the woman's exuberance. "Oh, I don't know…"

"If you don't have anything to wear, I can lend you one of my dresses. All the women wear white," Jenna explained.

"Why white?"

"Tradition, I guess. Oh, or florals. Florals are even better."

Both Jenna and Otis looked at Seren. They appeared to be waiting for her to respond. Otis gave her a knowing look and waved his hand absentmindedly.

Seren could tell he expected Jenna would convince her, but she couldn't bring herself to be annoyed at him. Still, she stalled. "Why is it called the Aster?"

"The Aster flower. They grow wild here in the valley," Jenna replied.

Otis and Jenna were still staring at her, clearly anticipating her response. She was all out of questions. *Damn.*

"Well… I guess it's decided then," Seren finally said.

Jenna clapped her hands together and bobbed up and down on the bar stool. "Perfect! Here, let me give you my number so we can coordinate on dresses and everything."

Seren opened a new contact on her phone and handed it to Jenna, who did the same. The last bit of hope that Seren would get out of going to the dance faded away into nothingness. Even though it was a week away, apprehension set in.

"Great! I'll text you," Jenna said as they exchanged phones. "I've got to get back. I have a canvas waiting for me. Thanks again for the tomatoes, Otis!" She placed the three tomatoes into a burlap tote bag and headed for the door.

"No problem, Jenna!" Otis called after her.

"Nice to meet you, Seren!" Jenna yelled from the entrance.

"You too, Jenna," Seren responded.

The door closed behind her, and Seren dropped her face onto her hands, her elbows propped on the bar. She could feel that Otis was grinning at her. She knew a total look of triumph was splayed across his face, so she delayed looking at him. He poured her a glass of water, which she immediately picked up and downed.

"Did you plan that?" she asked, finally daring to make eye contact with him.

Her intuition was right: he looked positively tickled. "Absolutely not."

Chapter 9

Seren opened her front door and found a large package propped against the frame. It was spattered with raindrops, as it had been storming all morning. Knowing exactly what was inside, she rescued it from the elements and placed it on the kitchen table. She retrieved a serrated knife from a kitchen drawer that squeaked when she closed it. The tape easily sliced apart, and Seren excitedly opened the box.

Long gone were the days of her toiling away in insufficient clothes and boots. No more would she ruin what little attire she had with dirt and grime. She laid out each item on the kitchen table and marveled at her new wardrobe. Before her were a pair of overalls, several simple t-shirts in varied colors, leggings, a new pair of jeans, a sunhat, garden gloves, two tubes of sunblock, a packet of white ankle socks, and her favorite piece of them all, a pair of canvas utility boots that screamed fashionable, yet functional. She would be a farmer, but she would do it in style.

Seren smiled and thought how much she'd like to try on every new piece, but if the rainy weather was any indication, she would most likely not be doing any work in the field that day.

Gathering the clothing in her arms, she moved toward the bedroom. She neatly folded each item and put them away. Her new boots were given special honors by being prominently placed at the foot of the bed. Chuckling to herself, Seren surmised they would never be that clean again. She ran a calloused hand through her hair, which was tangled from a night of fitful sleep.

The Aster Dance was in two days. Seren couldn't get the event out of her head since Otis and Jenna spoke to her about it, and her throat tightened at the thought of attending. It seemed rather embarrassing to go to a dance alone and without really knowing anyone. Seren imagined all the unkind words the townspeople might gossip behind her back, the feel of all their judgmental eyes fixed upon her like a sniper, and how she'd endure it all with a stomach full of butterflies.

Seren glanced at herself in the mirror and saw pure fear in her eyes, which, honestly, was a bit comical. Her hand froze with a bunch of hair clenched in her fist, and her lips pressed tightly together. Seren released her arms and crossed them in front of herself.

Maybe there was still a way out. She didn't have a white or floral dress, and she wasn't eager to seek one out. Perhaps Jenna had forgotten she'd volunteered one of her own.

As if on cue, Seren's phone buzzed on the bedside table. She picked it up and groaned when she saw Jenna's name on the screen.

Hey there farmer! I've got the perfect dress for you. Want me to bring it by today?

No. Seren didn't want that, but before she had time to think of a soft letdown, Jenna sent another message.

And you're coming! ;)

Jenna's enthusiasm was not to be overruled. Seren opened the text to reply.

Hi Jenna. Yeah, that would be ok, but it's raining pretty hard.

It seemed too stormy for Jenna to make the trek all the way to Hiraeth. Seren didn't know where Jenna lived, and she didn't want to inconvenience her.

Only a few seconds went by before another message came through.

Oh no I don't mind. I can come by around 4:30?

Seren sent back a thumbs up and accepted that her fate was sealed.

Sighing, she decided to start her day. She walked into the bathroom, brushed through her hair, threw on a fitted t-shirt and jeans, then headed into the kitchen to prepare a quick bowl of oatmeal.

Water spattered violently against the kitchen window as if the entire cabin was cycling through a car wash. In the city, Seren loved rainy days. They were a wonderful excuse to stay in and daydream. Though after consistently rising with the sun each morning to tend to the farm, it seemed unnatural to sit still. Her body desired to move, to sift through dirt, chop wood, or do something, anything, but sit on the couch.

Seren stared at the mediocre bowl of oatmeal in her hands. The mushed banana seemed slimier than usual, but it would have to do. Perry had forgiven her well enough for shopping at Wares & More when she stopped in for groceries the day before, and he relented that being closed on a weekday wasn't the best business strategy. He admitted that it was hard for him to divide time between his work and family life. Seren felt for him and recognized his desperation as fear. Fear that he could lose it all, and that his family would not be taken care of. Seren had empathy for Perry, no matter how ridiculous he seemed.

She leaned against the kitchen counter, absentmindedly swirling her spoon around the bowl as she ate her breakfast in silence. The rain seemed steadier than before, and much less intense. Perhaps it would even clear up before the day was over.

Seren made her way to the window that overlooked the field. Her homemade trellises seemed to be holding up well in the storm. She was proud of everything she had accomplished and hoped the rain hadn't washed away her hard work. She'd taken to farming much more readily than imagined, but there was still much to learn.

As she spooned the last bit of oatmeal into her mouth, she decided to visit the local library. There wasn't anything else to do, and she was curious to see what they had to offer. She walked to the kitchen and hand-washed the dirty bowl and spoon, then laid them on a beaten-up wire dish rack next to the sink to dry.

She slipped on her navy-colored rain boots and fetched an under-used umbrella from the closet. When she opened the front door, an orange tabby cat crouching under her grandfather's rocking chair startled her.

"Oh!" she exclaimed. The poor thing was drenched and stared up at her with wide eyes. It mewled, and Seren's heart melted.

"Hi, kitty, what're you doing here? Where'd you come from?"

The cat meowed as if to answer.

Seren wasn't sure what to do. She had no way of knowing if the cat belonged to a neighbor or if it was a stray that somehow found itself on her porch. Either way, she didn't want to leave it without water or something to eat, though she didn't have any cat food. Deciding water was enough for now, Seren ducked inside, filled a small bowl, and placed it next to the rocking chair. "Hey, I'm going to go into town for a bit, but I'll see if I can pick up some food for you, okay? If you're still here when I get back, that is."

The tabby meowed again and tentatively poked its nose around the water bowl before drinking. Satisfied the cat would be safe, Seren walked toward town.

The library was unassuming and simple. Someone had pulled the weeds since the last time she walked by, and the general upkeep of the place seemed good, though it wasn't much to look at. Years of weathering had chipped the green paint in places, and the roof seemed to be on its last legs. It was hard not to make assumptions about what might be inside, though Seren decided to give it the benefit of the doubt. She turned a brass handle and pressed the surprisingly heavy ornate door open. She peered around the frame, and her mouth fell open. Thousands of books packed the walls, along with intricate velvet tapestries and sliding mahogany ladders. Flickering lanterns hung from the ceiling and filled the room with a warm glow. A deep red Persian rug, which was slightly frayed at the edges, covered the dark hardwood floors.

A man in his early thirties with long auburn hair sat with his feet propped up on a large desk at the back of the room. He wore a red checkered flannel that was open in the front, a gray t-shirt underneath, and dark jeans with a worn brown belt. He seemed to have nodded off, so Seren padded into the room. She approached the first bookshelf and scanned over the titles. There was the *Collected Works of Thomas Troward,* a hefty book on the history of the Titanic, memoirs, Bram Stoker's *Dracula,* books on ancient astrology, Jane Austen's *Northanger Abbey…* There was no rhyme or reason to the groupings, which was intriguing yet confusing. Finding anything specific seemed daunting, though it added to the charm of the place.

"Oh!" The man awakened from his slumber and adjusted his shirt. He tucked his luxurious hair behind his ear and walked over to her. "Hello! Welcome to the Adytown Library. I'm Everett, and…" He stuck his hand out.

"Oh, Seren. Nice to meet you," she said, taking his hand and shaking it.

"Yes, of course. Jenna mentioned you the other night. Pleasure to meet you."

He withdrew his hand, which was uncommonly soft, as if he had never done a hard day's work in his life. He was also good-looking, in a tortured artist kind of way, though Seren guessed he knew that.

"Is there anything in particular you're looking for?" he asked.

"Well, I've taken up my grandfather's farm, and, well, I don't have a lot of resources to figure out what I'm doing. So, I came in to see if you have any books on farming or farming techniques. Anything like that?"

"Hmm," he hummed with a look of deep concentration on his face. "I have a few books by Michael Pollan, and plenty of works of fiction, though I don't believe those are what you're looking for."

Seren waited for Everett to finish pondering in silence. She laced her fingers together and eyed more of the random assortment of book titles.

She ran her fingers along the spine of a red colored book and pulled it off the shelf. "Oh. I've been meaning to read this."

"Ah, *The Alchemist*!" Everett exclaimed. "A classic, to be sure. 'To realize one's destiny is a person's only obligation.'"

Seren gave him a quizzical look.

"It's a quote from the book."

Seren nodded. "This place is quite impressive, very beautiful too."

"Thank you. I curated it myself. I have a bit of a passion for books, you might say," Everett said with a theatrical wave of his arms.

"Seems like it'd be a full-time job."

"Yes, it is, though thankfully, I have a room of my own in the back, so I don't have to part from this place for long."

Seren held the book reverently in her hands and considered what to say next.

"Will you be at the dance this Friday?" Everett asked.

"Oh, um, yes. Jenna… she sort of talked me into it."

Everett laughed. "I'll tell you what: why don't you go ahead and take that with you, and I'll look over the shelves to see if there's anything about farming. If I find something, I'll bring it to you at the Aster Dance."

"If it wouldn't be too much trouble."

"Oh, no, it would be my pleasure."

Chapter 10

By the time 4:30 p.m. rolled around, Seren wasn't in the mood for company. The tabby weaved around her legs beneath the kitchen table, purring softly as she rubbed her head against Seren's shins. Seren assumed it was a female cat, lacking evidence to the contrary.

"What are we going to call you?" she asked.

The cat lifted her head and chirped happily. She must have been famished because she devoured the food Seren brought home. Because she didn't know if the cat belonged to someone, she allowed her access to the outdoors, just in case the tabby decided to make her way home.

Seren looked out the window and spotted a rainbow-colored umbrella bobbing to the far south of the farm. It had to be Jenna, though Seren could see little of the person beneath it.

She looked around to make sure things were tidy and welcoming. She was nervous, though she was always nervous. It seemed nothing needed straightening or fluffing, and since she'd officially decommissioned the wood-burning stove until the fall, there were no embers to stoke. Unable to find some menial tasks to perform, Seren stood like a statue in the kitchen, lightly patting her hands against her thighs.

Short, peppy steps soon thumped up the cabin steps. Three quick knocks sent the cat running for the safety of the bedroom, and Seren made her way to open the front door.

"Hey, Seren!"

Jenna again sported her red hair in a side-swept braid that was somehow unbothered by the rain. She flashed a friendly smile, and her brown eyes shone with glee. Slumped over her shoulder was a stuffed tote bag, which Seren assumed must be carrying the dress Jenna had brought for her. She wore the same pair of overalls with colorfully threaded patchwork, but with a long-sleeved gray Henley underneath this time. Her rain boots were slick with rain and mud, which she courteously took off before entering the cabin.

"I think I have the perfect dress for you!" Jenna nearly shouted in her excitement. "What are you? A size two? Four?"

"I think so," Seren said. "It just depends on the brand, I guess."

"I knew we must've been the same size. I think we're the same height, too, so this should fit you perfectly." Jenna swung the tote bag off her shoulder and placed it on one of the kitchen table chairs.

Seren closed the cabin door behind them and took a few steps toward the table.

Jenna whipped out the dress with a flourish and held it up for Seren to see. "Ta-da!"

It was stunning. Seren stared at the dress, unable to comprehend that it was real. It was a bouffant-style pink dress with embroidered white roses and delicate, off-the-shoulder sleeves. The bottom flounced like a blooming peony that begged to be twirled. She wasn't sure what she expected, but it wasn't this.

"Wow, Jenna, it's gorgeous. Are you sure I can wear it?" Seren asked.

"Of course! Besides, I have a different dress Emelia made for me."

"Emelia… Oh, Emelia, who works with Otis at the Fig?"

"That's her. She's a very talented seamstress. She made this one too."

Adytown's inhabitants grew more and more interesting by the day. Emelia had a real talent for dressmaking, and Seren wondered how long it took her to make such a beautiful frock. Each embroidered rose must have taken hours if not days. Seren didn't think herself worthy of the dress, but Jenna held it out for her once more.

"Take it. And yes, I'm sure," Jenna said with a smirk.

Seren took the dress between reluctant fingertips. It was even more beautiful up close, better suited to be displayed in a gallery of haute couture than an afternoon of dancing, or rather an afternoon of hanging out at the buffet table, as was more likely.

"Here's this, too," Jenna said, retrieving a wooden hanger and handing it to Seren.

Seren made sure the sleeves spread over the hanger without snags or pulling and hung it on her bedroom door hook. It was like the final dress that Flora, Fauna, and Merriweather made for Princess Aurora in *Sleeping Beauty*, and as it sat and waited for Friday's dance, the dress dared Seren to feel excitement for the first time in a long time.

"So… you gonna ask anyone to dance?" Jenna asked.

Seren's cheeks grew pink with the slightest blush as she turned to face her. Why was she embarrassed? It was an obvious question to ask. "Oh, no, probably not," she said with a halfhearted laugh.

"Why not? You've been here, what, about a month and a half now? Surely there's someone who's caught your attention." Jenna leaned her elbows on the kitchen table.

Seren shook her head. "Nope, not one. But…what about you? You know everyone here far better than I do."

Jenna shifted in her seat to prop one foot on the edge of the chair. She seemed comfortable in Seren's home. "I think Everett might ask me. At least, I hope he will. It'd be about damn time."

The image of the long-haired, bohemian-style man crossed Seren's mind. Everett, the book purveyor with interesting taste and poor organization skills. The artist and the librarian. She could see it.

"He's a writer, you know," Jenna said as she twirled her braid around her fingers.

Seren nodded, suddenly aware she was still standing in her bedroom doorway. *You're being awkward,* she thought and walked to the kitchen table to sit across from Jenna. "What does he write?"

"Romance novels."

"Of course."

Jenna laughed heartily. "Right? He looks the part."

"He has some of the most amazing hair I've ever seen."

"Doesn't he? It's got to be a full-time job. He told me once that he uses a special kind of boar-bristle brush because his scalp is so sensitive."

"What?" Seren asked, trying not to laugh.

"I know, he's *so* fancy."

A bit of movement caught Seren's eye. The tabby was rubbing her face against the bedroom door frame, then meowed softly and eyed them both.

"Aw, hi kitty!" Jenna said as she placed her hand near the floor. "What's her name?"

"I don't know, actually," Seren said. "I found her on my porch this morning."

"She's adorable!" Jenna continued to hold her hand out for a few moments, but the cat showed more interest in the doorframe. Accepting defeat, Jenna sat up and crossed her legs.

"I think I might call her Mabon," Seren said.

"Mabon? I like that. After the autumn equinox, right?"

"Exactly!"

The day became night in no time at all. The wine and conversation flowed in a steady current, and Seren and Jenna talked for hours like old friends. Jenna had moved to the valley two years earlier and knew all about being a stranger in a new town. Although Jenna being Jenna, she fit in with grace and warmth. She knew how everything worked in town and everyone's names, history, jobs, and what made them tick. Everything Jenna knew seemed like it would take a lifetime for Seren to learn, but that was who Jenna was—she liked people.

They sat on the couch and sipped their wine while Jenna filled Seren in on everyone in the group photo from the orange scrapbook.

"That's Chessy," she said as she pointed to a sweet-looking woman in her late forties with a mass of shaggy brunette hair. "Some say she and Mayor Doney have a little thing on the side, but he's keeping it quiet because he's afraid it'll tarnish his reputation."

"I would've never guessed Mayor Doney was a ladies' man," Seren said, laughing through her light buzz.

"I know! As if anyone would care," Jenna said.

"Who's the woman with the long silver hair?"

"That's Corinne, Perry's wife. And this is Lenora, their daughter." Jenna pointed to a rebellious-looking young woman with striking lavender hair and black lipstick. "She's cool. You'll probably meet her at the dance. She's really into crystals and stuff like that. Corinne and Perry wish she was a little less wild, but Lenora would never listen to them, anyway."

"I like her already."

Jenna took a sip of her wine and continued down the line of people. "This is Rita, her husband Darius, her son Damien, and Darius's daughter Mira. Previous marriages and all that... You were saying you might want to do some renovations around here; this is the woman to go to. Rita's an amazing carpenter."

"Oh yeah, I remember Mayor Doney mentioned her. She's just up the hill from Perry's store?"

"Yeah. I'm sure she could figure out the Wi-Fi too."

Seren's eyes landed on Jake's grim outline. His hands were stuffed in his pockets, and a light five o'clock shadow made his demeanor seem even more dejected and unkempt. He was standing next to Chessy outside of a brick house, who had her hand lovingly placed on his shoulder.

"I've met Jake," Seren said.

"I'm sorry to hear that."

"Do you know him?"

"I think it's safe to say no one really knows Jake, except his aunt Chessy, I guess. I tried talking to him a bit when I first moved here—when I saw him at the Fig, which was basically all the time—but he always brushed me off."

"If he doesn't even like you, I guess there's no hope for anyone."

"He does it to himself. I wouldn't feel too bad for him."

Seren looked at the picture of Jake and saw pain in his eyes. He had been nothing but rude to her the few times they met, but there was something about him that earned her sympathy, and she hoped he was all right.

"This is Dr. Harlan."

Seren glanced at Jenna before staring at the image of the tall, broad-shouldered doctor. He was wearing the same green jacket from that day at the clinic, but his glasses were a different, wire-rimmed style. His hair was shorter than she remembered, so he must've recently cut it. He had his arm around her grandfather, who seemed thrilled to be standing with him. Seren involuntarily took a shaky breath in.

Jenna seemed to notice. "What is it?"

"What?" Seren asked, startled. "Oh, nothing. I've met him before."

"Oh, well then, I don't have to tell you he's a great doctor but such a mess."

"Is he?" Seren asked as she took another sip from her wine glass.

"Totally. Or, well, maybe not a mess, but he never seems to let himself have fun. He's always at the Fig alone at night with some medical journal or something. He usually has one drink and goes home no later than nine."

"Maybe he's just responsible," Seren suggested.

Jenna gave her a knowing look and leaned back on the couch. "You like him, don't you?"

Seren froze. "Wh—uh, no. No, I don't."

Jenna didn't look convinced. "Uh huh, okay. If you say so."

Seren cleared her throat and realized that her mouth was dry. She went to take another drink but found her glass was empty. "Um, do you want another?"

"Would love one," Jenna said.

Seren rose from the couch and pressed the backs of her hands to her warm cheeks. She shook her head and picked up the half-empty bottle of cabernet from the kitchen counter.

"He seems to like you well enough, anyway," Jenna said.

Seren felt her blood run cold. She gripped the bottle so tightly it was a wonder it didn't crack. Dumbfounded, she turned to Jenna. "What?"

"Yeah! I mean, I dunno. He was talking about you to Otis the other night."

"What did he say?" Seren asked as she walked back to Jenna.

"Are you sure you don't like him?" Jenna chuckled under her breath.

"No—I mean, yes? I don't really even know him. I… was just wondering," Seren said, trying very hard to appear natural.

"Why don't you ask him at the dance on Friday?" Jenna asked as she took the bottle from Seren and poured herself a half glass.

Seren wanted to change the topic of conversation. It seemed Jenna was trying to get her to admit to something she wasn't even sure she felt. Feigning composure, she poured the rest of the wine into her glass and returned to the couch. She chewed her lip and hoped Jenna wouldn't press her with any more questions about how she felt.

A light scratching noise broke the silence. Mabon was pawing at the front door.

"I think she wants to be let out," Seren said.

Jenna nodded and opened her phone as Seren got up to open the door. Mabon darted out into the dark night, perhaps never to be seen again. A light breeze tousled her hair and gave her pause. The cool night air felt good as it danced over her skin. She could make out the hazy outline of rustling trees against the waxing gibbous moon. It would most likely be full on the eve of the Aster Dance. A good omen, she hoped.

"Everetts at the Fig. Do you wanna go get a few more drinks?" Jenna asked.

Seren turned around. "Oh, I think I'm kind of tired. I might turn in early."

"You sure?"

"Yeah."

There was no reason not to go hang out with Jenna and Everett, but self-sabotage filled her head with nonsense. *Isolate and separate. They probably don't want you there, anyway. Perhaps another time. You suck.*

"Okay girl, get some rest," Jenna said. She polished off her drink, gathered her things from the kitchen table, and hugged Seren goodbye. "See you Friday!"

As Seren watched her leave, she felt happy. It was nice to have a friend. At least, she hoped she could call Jenna a friend. Their evening together made her feel as though some of the weight of the past few weeks had been lifted. She leaned against the doorframe and gazed at her growing tomatoes, beets, and potatoes. The soft glow of the porch light illuminated them enough to see their progress. Small green leaves were just beginning to snake up the trellis wires and poke through the tilled soil. Seren felt protective of their little lives as they reached for the sun. She imagined everything must be reaching for the light in some way.

He talked about me, she thought, *but that could mean absolutely nothing.* She tried to outwit her mind's insistence on squandering any sense of excitement or pleasure the thought of him gave her. Still, she couldn't deny she was happy he remembered her.

"It's too soon," she said. "Better to forget about it."

She gave her surroundings one last look before turning in. She was more tired than she thought and was glad she decided to stay home. Her copy of *The Alchemist* caught her eye. She picked it up and flipped through its pages a few times before landing on page eleven and reading the first passage she saw.

The secret of life, though, is to fall seven times and to get up eight.

It's all a process, she thought.

Chapter 11

Seren was a nervous wreck. The day of the Aster Dance had finally arrived, and no act of fate had saved her from having to attend. She'd been pacing back and forth for thirty minutes, the beautiful dress she had for the occasion staring back at her as it hung motionless on the bedroom door.

Jenna had given her directions to the dance a few hours earlier, which turned out to be just south of the farm. The dance would begin around 5:30 p.m. and go well into the night until the townspeople felt it was time to end the festivities. It was nearing five p.m., and Seren was running out of time.

Unable to put it off any longer, she took the dress off the hanger and undid the back zipper. The silky fabric felt good as it brushed against her freshly shaved and moisturized legs. She struggled with the clasp at the back of the dress and had to maneuver her arms into an uncomfortable contortion to close it. Then, she slipped on a pair of simple white shoes with a chunky heel, hoping they would withstand the grass and dirt on her trek to the event.

Fully dressed, she looked at herself in the mirror. Seren had styled her hair in loose curls that fell over her tense shoulders. She couldn't remember the last time she put any effort into her appearance. As she gave herself a once over, she felt somewhat satisfied with how she looked. Her hair paired well with the light English rose makeup she'd done for the occasion. Though not one to compliment herself, she decided she looked pretty good.

Startled by the sound of her phone ringing, she hurried to answer it.

"Hey, Jenna."

"Hey, girl! Are you sure you don't want me to meet you at your place to walk over?" Jenna asked.

"Oh, no, you're right by the dance, anyway. I wouldn't want you to have to walk all the way here and back."

"Okay. Well, I'll meet you there. See you soon!"

After they hung up, Seren slung a small golden handbag over her shoulder and walked to the front door. As ready as she ever would be, she pulled the door open as confidently as she could muster and closed it behind her with a thud.

It was the first time Seren had been to this part of the valley. The flatlands of the farm gave way to a sloping hillside with a clear path to the south. Tall, thick green bushes lined the pathway, which made Seren feel claustrophobic. Music played on the wind as she drew closer. Her heart rate quickened, and she clutched the thin handbag strap. It was like middle school all over again, and she was certain that in no time, she would see the boy she was crushing on slow dancing with another girl.

Everything became real when she noticed figures of the townspeople mingling and moving together. No one had noticed her yet, but it was only a matter of time before they did. From a distance, she searched for Jenna, but the bubbly redhead was nowhere to be seen. At the buffet table that was set up to the right of the clearing, Otis was happily serving an older couple plates of food.

Just beyond the pathway, the venue opened into a large, grassy clearing. To the left of the dance floor, a small DJ booth and stage hybrid was set up. A couple of guitars and a keyboard were on stage. Strings of patio lighting cabled between the trees, though they were not yet lit. The late afternoon sky cast beautiful swaths of pink and purple on the horizon as the sun made its slow descent into the underworld.

Seren stopped just short of the clearing and took a deep breath. It was now or never. She willed herself to move forward, taking one agonizing step at a time. Her head hung low, and her palms sweat with anticipation. Her plan was to make a beeline to the buffet table and hide out with Otis, though her plan was short-lived.

It seemed that almost everyone in the clearing turned to look at Seren at once. Her face grew hot, and she wished she could eject herself from her body.

It was as if some hidden stagehand had shone a bright spotlight on her so everyone could get a proper look. *Here she is!* a vaudevillian voice crooned over a loudspeaker. *The one you've all been waiting for... Seren Grinaker!* Instead of applause, there were chirping crickets, and instead of acceptance was a smattering of indifferent coughs and yawns.

She begged for something or someone to cut the tension, but their stares refused to release her.

"Seren!"

Jenna emerged from the crowd and ran toward her, immediately enveloping her in a big hug. Jenna's greeting turned off the vision like a light switch, and Seren silently thanked her.

"You look so beautiful! Emelia, look!" Jenna said.

A small woman with a short bob haircut walked over to them. If fairies were real, Seren imagined they looked just like Emelia. "Yes! That dress is totally working for you," Emelia said, her voice lilting.

"C'mon, let's get you a drink," Jenna said as she wrapped her arm around Seren's.

Emelia must have sewn bells into her dress because light pings rang and chimed with her every step. Seren peered around the clearing. The once scrutinizing faces of the townspeople were nowhere to be seen. All around her, people talked and laughed with ease, and she wondered if she'd imagined their intense stares. The general energy was relaxed and lighthearted.

"Well, look who it is! That was quite an entrance," Otis said as he greeted Seren and company.

Seren was happy to see another familiar face. "Hi, Otis," she said through a half smile.

"You look beautiful," he said. "What can I get you lovely ladies?"

"Three glasses of the midnight punch, please," Jenna said.

"Midnight punch?" Seren asked.

"Emelia made it."

The other woman flashed a proud smile. "It's my specialty."

Seren nodded. She didn't care what was in the drink; she just needed to drown herself with liquid comfort—and fast. Otis filled three plastic cups with a curious purple liquid that seemed to contain muddled blackberries and... glitter. *Is that glitter?* Seren had never seen anything like it.

"Here you are, ladies," Otis said as he handed them the strange concoctions.

Emelia and Jenna toasted each other, but Seren was already downing her drink. The girls laughed and rallied around her. The purple liquid hit Seren's tongue with a bizarre but pleasant mixture of flavors. It was fruity and sour, yet also a little spicy. The juice from the blackberries burst in her mouth, adding some needed freshness.

"Another, please, Otis," Seren said as she held out her cup.

"Alright. Just be careful with that. It's stronger than you think," he said as he gave her a refill.

Seren turned to Jenna and Emelia. She attempted a smile, which drew light laughter from the girls. "What?" she asked.

"Your teeth are purple," Jenna explained, then flashed her own violet grin.

"It's good," said Seren, giving a thumbs up to disguise the fresh rush of apprehension. She looked around the clearing again to see if anyone was looking at her. Thankfully, it seemed that, for the moment, she was off the hook. Seren tried not to think of what the crowd might be saying about her, but as more and more of the midnight punch seeped into her stomach, she cared less and less.

"Well, well, who do we have here?" a tall, lanky man with jet-black hair asked. He wore a tailored black suit with a silk shirt that was unbuttoned almost to his navel.

"Hey, Damien. This is Seren," Jenna said.

Seren took another sip of her punch and waved to Damien.

"Does Seren have a voice?" Damien asked.

Seren cleared her throat. "Oh, uh, yeah, sorry. Hi. Nice to meet you."

"Cool," Damien said.

A man with the spirit of a golden retriever bounded toward their group. He had wild blonde hair that looked as though he had spent hours styling it to get just the right volume and texture. "Dude, we have to get ready for our set!"

"Seth, meet Seren," Damien said.

Seth turned toward Seren, his eyes getting wide. "Oh, hi," he said as he shuffled his feet. "Um, you look really pretty."

Seren opened her mouth to respond, but Damien cut her off. "Dude, come on," he said as he slapped his hand to Seth's chest and dragged him toward the stage.

"Catch you later!" Seth said. He flashed her a goofy smile before following Damien.

"Ooh," Jenna teased.

Seren cocked an eyebrow at her. "What?"

"Seth thinks you look pretty," Jenna teased.

Seren laughed half-heartedly and took another sip of her punch.

It was bizarre to see the static faces of the townspeople Seren had only known from her grandfather's scrapbook come to life. Everyone seemed to be having a good time swaying and tapping their feet to the music. There must have been at least forty or fifty people there, and thanks to Jenna, Seren recognized almost everyone. Lenora was talking to Mira and another girl with short auburn hair. Perry, Corinne, Rita, and Darius were trading stories of the newest bed-making techniques and new additions to Perry's general store. A little girl named Gia, who was Jake's niece, ran gleefully with Theo, Seth's younger brother, a freckle-faced boy with untamed reddish hair. They laughed and tripped over their feet as they chased each other through the trees, pausing every so often to tap each other on the shoulder.

Chessy stood close by to watch the kids and occasionally stole flirty glances with Mayor Doney. Seren noticed that Jake was nowhere to be found. A dance hardly seemed like his scene.

Across the clearing, Dr. Harlan stood with Marty, an old seaman who brought fresh fish to Perry's general store every week. Marty rolled his shoulder and pointed to a specific spot that seemed to be giving him trouble. Dr. Harlan patiently listened and offered advice. Nodding eagerly, the old fisherman shook hands with the doctor and patted his arm before turning to strike up a conversation with Edna and Horace, an older couple who had lived in the valley all their lives.

Dr. Harlan must have sensed Seren's eyes on him because he looked at her, and unable to avert her gaze, she looked back.

"Seren! I was wondering when I was going to meet you."

She turned and saw a woman in her mid-forties with brunette hair pulled back in a simple ponytail. She was lively and eager to shake Seren's hand.

"Hello, Rita, right?" Seren asked.

"Yes. It's so nice to meet you! I don't know how much you've been told, but your grandfather and I were great friends. I worked on his cabin for him many times. He always spoke of building a chicken coop, or a barn, or updating that old shed of his, but he never got around to it, unfortunately. If you ever want to do some updates or anything on the farm, I'd be glad to help you out."

"Thank you. I'm sure there will be many things I'll need help with."

"Well, let me give you my card, and please, feel free to reach out anytime."

Seren slipped Rita's card into her bag and realized she was out of punch. She didn't dare glance across the clearing again, just in case a pair of green eyes met hers once more.

"Otis, more, please," Seren said as she held out her cup.

"I think you're doing great! What're you so keyed up about?" he asked.

"Nothing," she said. Otis hadn't lied about the punch being strong. Even after only two cups, she felt the effects of the strange potion setting in.

"What's in this?" she asked.

"You don't want to know."

Otis refilled her cup, then fixed his gaze on something, or someone, behind Seren. He motioned to her in ways she didn't understand until finally, she followed his gaze and saw Dr. Harlan walking towards her. *He's just a man,* she thought. He smiled and waved at her in that pleasant way of his, and Seren prepared herself. *A very good-looking man,* she thought before she could stop herself.

"Dr. Harlan," she said stiffly.

"Hello, Seren. I'm glad you're here." Unlike everyone else, the doctor had a cup of water in his hand.

"No midnight punch for you?" Seren asked.

"Oh, no," he said. "I'm on call tonight."

"On call?" Seren asked.

"The next town over sometimes calls me in for work, so I told them I'd be available to help if need be."

"Responsible," she said.

The doctor smiled at her as a piece of his thick brown hair fell in front of his glasses. "So, how are you? You left the clinic rather quickly the last time I saw you."

Seren shifted on her heels.

"It's none of my business, of course. I just wanted to make sure—"

"I'm fine," she said, much more coldly than she intended. *Why am I being rude to him?* She wondered. His eyes searched her face, and she scrambled to recover. "I just—I really hate hospitals... or, um, clinics."

81

Dr. Harlan nodded. "I completely understand. I used to hate them too before I went to medical school."

Seren fiddled with her full cup of midnight punch. It was her turn to talk, but she felt so agitated she didn't know how to continue the conversation. *Say something. Hello? Are you in there?*

A new, slower song came on, and Dr. Harlan looked toward the dance floor for a moment. "So, um…" He looked down at his feet and stuffed his free hand inside his pocket. Before Dr. Harlan could say another word, the overhead string lights turned on. They cast a beautiful yellow glow throughout the clearing and softly illuminated the trees. The remainder of the sun's light slowly faded. All that remained was a faint purple sky, and in the twilight, the realm of the moon took over.

"Pardon me, I hope I'm not interrupting," Everett said as he sidled up next to Seren and greeted Dr. Harlan. He wore a deep red vest with a gold pocket watch and a brown tweed suit. Perhaps the most distracting were his black service boots with metal studs on the toes. "I believe I may have found a book that can help you." He held out a tattered brown book with uneven edges and yellowed paper.

"Oh, thank you, Everett," she said as she took the volume. "I forgot you were bringing me something."

Dr. Harlan looked between Seren and Everett.

"Would you like to dance?" Everett asked.

Seren stared at him with her mouth agape. She heard the words leave his mouth but couldn't comprehend that he had said them. "Oh, um…"

Dr. Harlan shifted his weight beside her.

"I'm pretty sure Jenna is waiting for you to ask her," she finally said.

"The night is young," Everett said.

Seren froze. She didn't want to dance, though a nagging voice in the back of her head said she ought to. She was young, and she should have fun. Jenna caught her eye from a short distance away. She looked between Seren and Everett.

"I think you should ask Jenna," Seren suggested. "I know she would love to."

"If you're sure," he said.

Seren gave a slight nod.

Everett excused himself and made his way toward Jenna, whose face instantly lit up when she saw him. He took her hand and led her to the dance floor, where she eagerly placed her hands on his shoulders.

"That was a nice thing you did," Dr. Harlan said.

"I couldn't betray my friend like that."

From the south side of the clearing, a figure emerged, stumbling every other step. Seren recognized the blue hoodie and thick five o'clock shadow on the man's face. It was Jake. He took a few steps toward the dance floor and attempted a few sloppy dance moves before taking a hefty swig from a large can. Becoming bored with the dancing, he fixed his steely eyes on Seren. "Well, well, look who it is, the princess from the city," he slurred.

"You're drunk," Seren said.

"No shit, pretty thing." He stumbled closer to her.

Dr. Harlan extended a hand between the two of them. "Jake, that's enough."

"Hey-ey," Jake said, "don't worry, doc. I've got this under control. Well, don't you look pretty? The fuckin' bell of the ball, right?" he laughed.

Seren felt like he was mocking her. Her face burned as she touched the hem of her skirt and looked away from both men. If the ground could somehow swallow her whole at that moment, she would be grateful.

"Remember, like I said, you're not special." Jake took the last sip from his can of beer, crumpled it, and tossed it on the ground.

"Jake, maybe you should have some water," Dr. Harlan said.

Jake lurched forward and stuck an indignant finger inches away from the doctor's face. "I don't need you to tell me *anything!*"

A few people in the clearing noticed Jake's disruption and whispered to one another. The sky was clear, but it was as if Jake were a storm cloud, bringing all the rain and darkness with him.

"Jake… people are looking," Seren said.

"Oh, are they?" Jake asked. "Does that bother you, princess?"

"Jake, *enough*," said Dr. Harlan.

Seren's face grew hotter. The last thing she wanted from the dance was to draw more attention to herself. Though there Jake was, stinking of beer and insults, doing the job for her, his voice growing louder with every sentence.

He stepped toward her. "Well, get used to it."

His eyes were rimmed with red and black circles, and up close, he looked like he hadn't slept in days. He had clearly nicked himself a few times while shaving and had red bumps on his cheeks. The closer he got, Seren wanted to move backward, but she couldn't move.

Then, something in Jake shifted. He swallowed hard and opened his mouth, bringing a few fingers to his lips. His other hand held his stomach while his body contracted. It dawned too late on Seren what was happening. Jake heaved and threw up all over Seren's dress, covering her in stinking, bubbling liquid. She stumbled back and stared down at the dress.

"Jake!" Chessy said, appearing next to him. "What have you done?"

If everyone hadn't been looking before, they were after that. Time slowed as Seren looked around the clearing. Everyone saw what happened, and she couldn't help but notice the looks of shock and disgust on the townspeople's faces.

Jenna, still mid-dance with Everett, dropped her arms from his shoulders and ran toward her. "Oh my god, Seren, are you alright?"

"No, this is disgusting," Seren said. She wanted to puke also, but she tried to maintain her composure.

Otis came running from behind the buffet table with a roll of paper towels. "Let's clean this off." He meant well, but the vomit was seeping through her clothes and touching her skin underneath, and he gave up as soon as he started.

"I have to get out of here," she said.

Otis nodded. "Right, okay."

"I'll walk you back," Jenna said.

"No, Jenna, please stay. I don't want to ruin your night too. And I'm fine. I don't need any help."

"Are you kidding?" Jenna asked. "It's dark out, and you're covered in puke."

"I'm fine," Seren said. It took everything she had to keep from crying. She'd never felt as small as she did at that moment, covered in rancid beer and whatever half-digested food Jake had eaten that afternoon. *Kill me,* she thought. *Kill me now.* She hadn't hated anyone before, but in that moment, she hated Jake.

"I can take you home," Dr. Harlan offered.

She shrugged at him and didn't look to see if he followed her. The pathway opened to the south side of Hiraeth, and the pair made their way up the hill. Her feet were wet and sliding in her shoes for reasons she did not want to think about. The plastic straps rubbed blisters onto her cramping feet, making each step more painful than the last.

"*Agh,*" she said as she stopped for a moment to adjust the straps.

"Is there anything I can do to help?" Dr. Harlan asked.

"I'm fine," she replied.

"Here, let me hold your book."

Seren had completely forgotten about the book Everett brought her. Miraculously, it was vomit-free.

"Okay," she said as she handed it to him.

Seren could barely see Dr. Harlan in the darkness. The only light was the full moon overhead. She could see the porch light in the distance. It wasn't far, but she didn't know if she could make the rest of the journey without becoming barefoot. Deciding she didn't care anymore, Seren ripped off her shoes and tucked them under her arm.

"This is *so* embarrassing," she said, wiping her eyes.

"Are you alright?" he asked.

"Yes, I'm *fine,* just—please stop asking me if I'm alright."

Seren's words punched the still night air. *What is wrong with you? You're making this all so much worse.* She heard her blood thrumming in her ears, and she tried to calm herself as she stopped short to look at Dr. Harlan.

"I'm sorry, I just—look at this!" she said indignantly. "What the hell is wrong with him?"

"I've seen a lot worse if that helps."

"What?"

"In the ER. I worked there many years when I did my residency. I can't even tell you how many times I've seen vomit in weird places."

"Okay…"

"As for Jake, I'm sorry you were in the path of his destruction tonight. The things he was saying…and what he did, they are inexcusable."

"Thank you for saying that," Seren said. The moonlight glinted off his glasses, so she couldn't quite make out his face, but she felt that if she could, she might melt. "Uhm…we're almost to the cabin. Don't feel like you have to stay."

"You're not an imposition, Seren," Dr. Harlan said.

Seren's heart rate quickened. "I didn't say that I—I don't think I'm…" The sour, cheesy smell overwhelmed her, and she gagged. *Oh god,* she thought. If there was any hope of saving the dress, she would have to act soon. As they approached the cabin, a long green hose caught her eye.

"I need you to hose me down," she said.

"What?" Dr. Harlan asked.

Seren placed her purse on the porch steps, picked up the hose, and held it out to him. "Please, just do it." It might have been the buzz from the midnight punch or the bizarre circumstances, but either way, it was the only thing she could think to do.

He took the hose and stepped back as Seren turned on the water, which came shooting out moments later.

"If you're sure," he said.

Seren nodded.

He turned the stream of water on her.

"*Ah,* oh my god!" she screeched, instantly recoiling. The water was so frigid she was sure her blood had turned to ice.

Dr. Harlan stopped, looking concerned.

"No, keep going! It's the only way to save this dress."

Dr. Harlan hesitated at first, but then sprayed her with water again.

"Put your thumb in it. It'll spray harder."

Dr. Harlan did as he was told. He made quick work of washing as much of the vomit away as he could, soaking Seren to the bone. She held out her shoes as well, which he watered until they were clean. Even in the dead of winter, she had never been so cold. The fabric clung to her skin, and she hoped it wasn't transparent.

"Did you get it all?" she asked.

Dr. Harlan gave her a once-over and sprayed a little more water on the hem of the dress before looking satisfied. "I think so," he replied.

Seren turned off the water.

"Can I get you a towel?" he asked.

"Please. Um, I'll get you the keys," she said in between shivers. She retrieved them from her purse and handed them over. "There's a small closet next to the bathroom where I have clean towels."

In the doctor's absence, Seren had little to do but hold her shaking limbs and reflect on the absurdity of her life. At least the dress would hopefully dry by morning. Then she could give it a proper wash and return it in one piece to its rightful owner.

Dr. Harlan returned within moments and handed her a fresh, fluffy towel. "Here."

"Thank you," Seren said.

She sat on the porch steps and dried her arms and legs before standing up to wring out as much water from the dress as possible. If she had been alone, she would have stripped in the springtime air and hung it over the porch banister, but she didn't want to embarrass Dr. Harlan, no matter what he had seen in the ER.

She motioned inside. "I'm just gonna…"

"No problem," Dr. Harlan said.

Seren retrieved a pair of clean sweatpants, underwear, and a crew neck t-shirt, then walked into the bathroom and closed the door behind her. She pressed her back against the hard wood and took a deep breath. Chills ran through her body, making the skin on her arms pimple. Her nipples poked through the fabric of the dress, and she wondered if Dr. Harlan had noticed. She peeled off the soaked garment and hung it over the sink. She needed a warm shower to restore her. Quickly, she turned on the water and washed any remnants of stink and dirt from her body.

When Seren emerged from the bathroom, with the dress slung over one arm, she didn't see Dr. Harlan. *Did he leave?* she wondered. Then she noticed the front door was open. He was sitting on the porch steps, stroking Mabon.

He turned to her. "Feeling better?"

"Much," she said, smiling at him. "I'm sorry about all of that."

"Please, don't apologize. I was happy to help."

Seren hung the dress over the banister and sat on the porch steps. "There you are," she said to Mabon. "I was wondering where you were!"

"She's very sweet," Dr. Harlan said. "Or he?"

"She, yes." Seren smiled. "Her name is Mabon."

"Hi, Mabon."

"She likes you."

Mabon rubbed against his shins and purred happily into his outstretched hand, which he made readily available for pats and ear scratches.

"What a night," she said, sitting next to Dr. Harlan.

Mabon padded off into the fields as he shifted on the steps. "One for the books."

"Yeah. I mean, if you told me I'd be ending my night walking barefoot through farmland covered in dirt and vomit, then hosed off in my front yard by the town doctor, I'd say you have a bad sense of humor."

"I must admit, hosing someone down like that was a first for me," he said, laughing. Seren looked at him and had to try very hard not to let him in too much. It was maddening how easily he could disarm her.

"I'm sorry I was rude, too," she said.

"Like I said, I'm still open to a bottle of wine..." he replied.

"Okay, noted." They both laughed.

Seren wrapped her arms around her shins and looked out over the farmland. Maybe coming to Adytown was a mistake. It had caused her more trouble than anything else thus far, and tonight had been the cherry on top of it all. But there was nothing left for her in the city. It was full of ghosts.

Mabon headbutted her knee and broke her train of thought. Seren sighed. "I don't know how many of these people will want to get to know me now."

"What do you mean?"

"I'm sure I'll forever be known as the girl who got puked on."

"That wasn't your fault. Everyone in town… they're good people. I promise you it reflects far worse on Jake's character than yours."

"If you're sure," Seren said.

"I am."

Their eyes met without strain or difficulty. It was easy to pause with him and take in the moment. In a way, Seren was glad Jake had disrupted her night. If he hadn't, she wouldn't be there under the light of the full moon and thousands of stars gazing into a pair of kind, green eyes.

"You know, I recognize you," Seren said.

Dr. Harlan knitted his brows.

"I—um, here… I'll be right back." Seren grabbed the orange scrapbook from the closet and returned to the porch steps. She sat down and thumbed through the pages until she arrived at the group photo of the townspeople. "I found this when I first moved in. It belonged to my grandfather. You're here next to him in the photo."

Dr. Harlan looked at the photo, and a flash of clarity overcame him.

"*You're* Harold's granddaughter?" he asked.

"Guilty," Seren said.

"Oh, wow, what a pleasure. What a wonderful man he was."

"Yes, he was."

"I'm so sorry for your loss."

His words seemed to cut right through her walls and touched the most vulnerable parts of her. She failed to keep herself together, and her eyes grew watery.

"I didn't mean to…" He reached to touch her arm but hesitated.

"It's all right. It's been a really hard couple of weeks," she admitted, catching a tear with her index finger.

Dr. Harlan opened his mouth as if to say something but stopped. He sat in silence for a few moments, his face twisting through masks of concern and doubt. Finally, he asked, "Can I see your hand?"

"My hand?" She asked.

"I just want to see how it's healing up."

"Oh, of course."

Dr. Harlan gently clasped her hand in his. She felt a gnawing sense of déjà vu. Here he was once again holding her hand with more tenderness and care than anyone had before, and it was hard to withstand. Seren hoped that when he was done, he would look at her the way she expected all men would look at her: as a piece of meat, with indifference, or as something to be conquered. Anything but the way he looked at her.

"It looks like it has healed excellently," he said.

A loud, jarring ringing sounded from Dr. Harlan's pocket. He took out his phone and looked at the screen. "Sorry, I have to get this."

Seren nodded, and Dr. Harlan stood and walked a short distance away. She felt awkward listening to his conversation, so she tried to divert her attention to the photos in the scrapbook until he was finished.

"Okay, okay. Alright, I'll be there soon." He hung up the phone and walked back to Seren.

"Did they call you in?" she asked.

"Seems so. They almost never do, but tonight's my lucky night, I guess."

"Must be the moon."

Dr. Harlan tilted his head.

"Well, we're fifty-five percent water, or something, so whenever the moon is full, hospitals have an uptake in cases—or so I've heard."

"You know what? There is something to that," he said as he smiled at her.

"Thank you for helping me," Seren said as she stood.

"Of course. And, please, if you ever need anything, don't hesitate to come by the clinic."

"I won't," she said.

"Goodnight, Miss Grinaker."

"Night, Dr. Harlan."

Chapter 12

Seren ripped gnarled weeds out of the brown earth and tossed them over her shoulder. It was as if they took over the small patch of land overnight.

"Goddamn stupid motherfuckers," she muttered with each bunch she ripped from the ground. She kneeled beside the tilled soil and halfheartedly picked at bits of shredded fibers and roots and threw them toward a pile of rubbish.

The tomatoes were by far the biggest overachievers. In the few weeks they had been in the ground, their tiny green branches slowly crept up the trellises, but they seemed small and frail. The beets took almost no time at all to burst through the soil, but the potatoes were only just beginning to sprout.

The book Everett lent Seren from the library was an informative read, even though it put her to sleep. The author preached, above all else, to practice patience and perseverance. It was like a mantra she muttered all day until she burned the phrase into her mind. Still, even after all the patience and perseverance Seren could summon, and after all the sweat and tears she poured into the small plot of land, why did the return seem so miniscule?

The more Seren tried to get into a rhythm, the more the earth endeavored to reveal her mistakes, though she didn't know what they were. It didn't seem normal for weeds to sprout almost every day or for aphids to have already taken residence amongst the sprouting leaves. One of the tiny green bugs caught Seren's eye. It was munching on one of the beet leaves.

"You've eaten your last meal, buddy."

She grabbed the nozzle and sprayed the leaves with a hard stream of water, launching the tiny creature into oblivion. She wiped her brow with the back of her gloved hand and dropped the hose, a bit of the cold water dripping onto her pants' leg.

Seren took off her gloves and walked toward the porch. A loud flutter of wings behind her demanded her attention, and she turned to find a flock of crows had landed amongst her crops.

"Hey!"

Seren lurched toward the flock and shooed them away with flailing arms. It was the third time that day the crows had visited.

"You're supposed to help me with them!" she yelled at Mabon, who was grooming herself on the porch, clearly more interested in cleaning her ear than in chasing crows.

"You know you can't hide yourself out here forever," Jenna's familiar voice called.

"I may have bitten off more than I can chew," Seren said as she plopped herself onto the highest porch stair.

Jenna came upon the crop field and gasped. "Oh! Everything's growing so fast. It looks so good!"

"You don't have to lie to me," Seren said as she grabbed a glass of iced water and took a few large gulps.

Jenna snapped her head toward Seren. "I'm not! I'm serious. Really, you should be proud of yourself."

"Yeah, for sure."

"Cut yourself some slack. It's your first time. I know I couldn't pull this off no matter how hard I tried." Jenna sat next to her.

"These stupid crows keep showing up. I don't know what to do about them," Seren said. "Don't know why. It's not like there's much for them to pick at."

"Scarecrow?" Jenna offered. "I mean, those are supposed to work, right?"

"I guess."

"Chessy might have one she'd be willing to sell."

"Chessy... *Jake's* aunt Chessy? Yeah, I'll pass on that for now."

"But that's neither here nor there because..." Jenna grabbed Seren's hand and dragged her to her feet, "I'm taking you into town."

Seren let her body become a dead weight and pulled back on Jenna's enthusiastic reach as she groaned, "Jenna."

"It's Emelia's day off, so she and I are meeting Lenora at the Fig. Come on! It'll be fun."

Seren fell back against the porch boards and crossed her arms over her eyes.

"Emelia doesn't care a thing about the dress. Promise. If anything, she feels terrible about what happened. Jake is such an ass." Jenna rolled her eyes.

"Jenna, I can't."

"Come on. It's been weeks!"

"I know, it's not that—well, it is, but it's also not. I have to go to Rita's," Seren said as she sat up and rested an elbow on her knee.

"Why?" Jenna asked.

"Have you seen this place? It needs some TLC. And I still need to ask her about the wifi."

"Okay, but listen, the second you're done, text me. I'm pretty sure we'll still be there."

"Okay."

"I mean it!"

"Yes, okay, okay, I will."

"You better," Jenna said as she took a drink from Seren's water glass.

Seren half-heartedly saluted her red-headed friend as she set off toward town. Jenna had been trying to get Seren to come out more often, but she always declined. She figured one day her friend would give up, but she never did.

The afternoon sun hung lazily in the sky. The days were getting longer, which only meant there was more work to do.

Seren gathered the weeds in a wheelbarrow and wheeled it toward the western field. As she walked, she noticed a beautiful sight she hadn't seen in years. The peach tree she loved so much was about to bloom. Brilliant pink flower buds covered its branches. Seren left the wheelbarrow and placed a hand on the tree's sturdy trunk. She could almost feel the years of joy the tree had brought her, her grandfather, and anyone who ate its delicious fruit.

"I'm happy you're still here," Seren said. A light breeze swept through the field and tussled its pink leaves.

Seren brought the wheelbarrow to the edge of the woods and dumped the weeds. The birds could use the fibers for their nests.

After stowing the wheelbarrow in the shed, Seren closed the door and gazed over the expansive farmland. She didn't want to acknowledge it, but the feeling came anyway. Somehow, over the past few weeks, it was beginning to feel more like home.

Chapter 13

"Yes. That should be no trouble at all," Rita said, her voice echoing through the high vaulted ceilings of her home. "I could get started tomorrow if that works for you?"

"That would be great, thank you," Seren said.

Rita took out a paper calendar from the large wooden desk she stood behind and scribbled in the next day's schedule.

Seren knew Rita was the town carpenter, but it was comical how *much* she had managed to make out of wood. The floors, the walls, the ceilings, and the general décor, including a wooden chess board with carved wooden game pieces that were polished to a fine sheen.

"Did you make all of this?" Seren asked.

"I sure did. We bought the house in 1995, and I've been working on it ever since." Rita stored the calendar and clapped her hands together. "My hourly rate is usually around thirty, but for you, I'll make it twenty-five."

"That's very kind."

"So, did it take forever to wash the dress?" Rita asked, the slightest sliver of pity in her eyes. Her question caught Seren off guard, and her face betrayed her surprise.

"Oh, uh…"

"I don't mean to remind you of any unpleasantness. I just can't believe that happened."

"Yeah, me too."

"Well, anyway, you made it all the way up here. I know it's a long walk. Can I get you anything? Some water, or we have some lentil soup leftover from last night."

"Thank you for the offer, but I'd better be getting back," Seren said, straightening her purse strap over her shoulder.

"I'll see you bright and early tomorrow," Rita said.

"See you then," Seren said before heading outside. Rita's house had a beautiful view of the town square and the ocean beyond. Seren could just make out the slim foam-lined waves that crashed onto the sandy beach as the sun set. As she walked the pathway into town, the world was quiet other than a faint chirping of crickets amongst the grass.

Seren took out her phone and opened her conversation with Jenna. She wasn't sure if she wanted to go out tonight. From up there, the still mountain air seemed much more pleasing than socializing.

I told her I'd text her, she thought.

Seren huffed a small sigh and sat on a bench overlooking the town. She drafted up a quick message to Jenna and pressed send.

Seren looked down at the fountain in the square. The lone spout atop the structure poured a stream of clear blue water that cascaded lazily over the stone tiers. It reminded Seren of her childhood. When she was thirteen, she lived in a small seaside town on the East Coast. On the east side of town, in the middle of Prescott Park, was a blue-painted fountain. On summer days, she would wander through the pathways and small grassy fields to throw in a penny or two. Then she would run her hand through the cool water and wipe it against her forehead to relieve herself from the midday sun. Portsmouth hadn't been home for long, but it had been a home.

Seren's phone buzzed almost instantly.

Come! We have a seat saved for you, Jenna replied.

Seren clicked off her phone. Jenna was peculiarly good at twisting her arm. Still, a few more minutes up there probably wouldn't put her off too much.

Seren heard footsteps approaching from down the path. She instinctively reached for her bag to ready her pepper spray but immediately felt foolish. "Hi, Dr. Harlan."

"Hello, Seren. I didn't expect to see anyone up here this time of night." He had loosened his tie and folded his green dress jacket over his arm. His hair was slightly disheveled, and he'd rolled his shirt sleeves to his elbows. "May I?" he asked, gesturing toward the bench.

"Please," she replied.

Dr. Harlan sighed as he sat. It seemed he was glad to be off his feet.

"Long day?" Seren asked.

"Oh, nothing too bad." He removed his glasses to rub them with a small gray cloth from his shirt pocket. "Sometimes there's just too much paperwork to file. I like to come up here to clear my head after work." He briefly rubbed his eyes and replaced his glasses. "How have you been?"

"Good. I just left Rita's. She's going to help me fix up the cabin and maybe even install internet."

"That's exciting."

"No more run-ins with splinters," Seren joked.

"Even if you do, you're always welcome at the clinic." Dr. Harlan smiled at her.

He told her that before, and she'd expect the repetition to annoy her, but nothing in his delivery implied he was disingenuous. She regarded him momentarily, then looked at her laced hands. "I... wanted to thank you, again, for helping me after the Aster Dance. There were many ways that night could have gone after what happened, but you made it better. Thank you."

Dr. Harlan seemed touched by her thanks, and he smiled at her in that same agreeable way he always did.

Just then, Seren's phone buzzed again with another message from Jenna. *Are you coming?!* it said.

Seren chuckled. Jenna was nothing if not persistent. She wasn't sure what would be worse: enduring several more weeks of badgering or relenting and meeting with Jenna and the girls at the Fig, possibly facing more questions about the ill-fated Aster Dance. She glanced at Dr. Harlan before typing out her reply. *Yes, I'm coming. I just got momentarily held up.* She then shoved her phone in her pocket.

"So, what're you up to tonight?" he asked.

"Uhm, well, Jenna and a few people are waiting for me at the Fig."

"Don't let me keep you. It was good to see you again."

"Do you want to come?" The question slipped out before she could stop it.

Dr. Harlan seemed surprised, yet not unhappy to be included. "I wouldn't want to impose."

Seren's heart rate quickened. "You wouldn't be. I—we'd love to have you."

"I would love to," he said.

The front door seemed heavier than usual when Seren pushed it open. Dr. Harlan extended a hand to help her. "Thank you," she said. Though it was a Tuesday night, the Fig was packed. A loud mixture of people were talking, and *Tennessee Whiskey* by Chris Stapleton played on the jukebox.

"Hey!" Otis yelled out as they entered.

Seren turned to the bar to wave at him.

"Come on in, Seren. Good evening, Dr. Harlan," Otis said.

Jenna, Emelia, and Lenora whooped at them both from their seats in the corner.

"I'm sorry. I hope they're not too drunk," Seren said as she gazed up at Dr. Harlan.

He smiled at her and said, "I'm sure we can handle them. Go ahead and join them. I'll get us drinks."

Seren nodded and walked toward the rowdy group of women. She made eye contact with Jenna, who gave her a sly, knowing look. Seren said hello to everyone and sat in an empty chair next to Jenna.

"Held up, huh?" Jenna said as she sipped on a darkly colored beer.

"Jenna—"

"Well," Jenna cut her off, snorting with laughter as she nudged her, "I hope he didn't hold you up too hard."

"It's not like that. I just ran into him."

"I'm sure you did," Jenna said, cackling.

Thankfully, Emelia and Lenora were too busy discussing a stitch pattern that Emelia was showing off on her phone to notice the ribbing.

"Stop, he's coming," Seren said.

"Okay, okay, but you gotta tell me later," Jenna conceded.

Dr. Harlan made his way to their table with two glasses of red wine. His capable hands deftly held them by their stems. Seren couldn't help but be impressed by his small attention to etiquette. A small lock of auburn hair fell in front of his glasses as he set a glass down in front of her.

"Otis tells me this is one of your favorites," he said.

"It is," Seren confirmed, still distracted by his hair.

"Heya, Dr. Harlan! Didn't know you were allowed out after hours," Jenna said.

He laughed as he pulled up a seat next to Seren. "Well, how could I turn down the invitation? It's nice to get out of my cage once in a while." Jenna laughed at that and eyed Seren.

"He's got jokes! Who knew?" Jenna said.

Emelia nudged her and motioned for them all to toast, and the five of them clinked their glasses together.

After a few more glasses of wine and conversation, Seren was glad she came. Otis had supplied them with a big platter of spaghetti and meatballs, and he occasionally stopped by to see how they were getting on. Dr. Harlan remained relatively straight-edged most of the night. *A limitation of being a doctor*, she figured. It probably wouldn't do well for his reputation to be publicly drunk in front of all his patients. Still, she wished she could see a looser, more casual version of him. He was delightfully funny when he allowed himself to be, and there was an unmistakable spark in his eye when he got to speak about things he cared about.

"A pilot?" Seren asked.

"Yeah," he said, "but it turns out you have to have excellent vision to be one, so off to medical school I went." He took another sip of his wine.

Seren's knee lightly brushed his as she asked him another question. "You aren't afraid of flying?"

"Well, that was the other issue. I'm also deathly afraid of heights," he deadpanned.

Seren broke into a fit of laughter and leaned her cheek on her palm, beaming at him.

"I'm serious!" he said. "I would've made a terrible pilot."

"You really are afraid of heights?"

"Oh, yes, terribly. Thankfully heights aren't really something that come into play as a physician." Dr. Harlan smiled over the rim of his wineglass.

"Unless there's a helicopter rescue… or something," Seren offered.

"Helicopter rescue?"

"Yeah! Like… someone is stranded on a mountain, and they call you to assist because they're badly injured. Wolves got 'em."

"It's always the wolves," said Dr. Harlan.

"A whole pack. They lost an arm, but that's where you swoop in on the helicopter to save the day." Dr. Harlan shook his head, clearly amused.

"I think," he said, his arm lightly brushing hers as he retracted it from the table, "I'll stick with non-helicopter rescues. For now, at least."

"Work your way up to it and all that," said Seren.

"Absolutely." Dr. Harlan smiled and gestured toward her empty glass. "Can I get you anything else? I think they'll be closing soon."

101

Seren hadn't realized it was so late. "I better not, but thanks."

Dr. Harlan stood, brought both their empty wine glasses to the bar, and closed out his tab with Otis.

Seren checked her phone for the time. *11:30 p.m.* She stood, and the room spun around her. "Oh."

"You headed home?" Emelia asked. Jenna was passed out on the table, and Lenora had left an hour earlier, saying she had some level to beat in a video game or something.

"Y—yeah," Seren said, attempting to steady herself. "What about Jenna?"

"I'll get her home. Don't worry," Emelia lilted.

Seren gave a thumbs up and sloppily dragged her hand over her purse strap, scraping it off the table to get it over her shoulder.

"Seren!" Otis called to her. "Bring this home with you. It'll help you tomorrow." He held a white to-go box.

She walked to the bar, took the box, and saluted him.

"Can I walk you back?" Dr. Harlan asked. "That path is dark at night."

"Yes, please," Seren said as she cradled the warm takeout box and swayed to the music, which wasn't as loud as before.

"Goodnight, Otis," Dr. Harlan said as they exited the Fig.

"Have a good night, you two," Otis replied with a smirk.

Dr. Harlan reached out to steady Seren, placing a hand under her arm as she stumbled over something unseen, probably a stray root or rock. *Good thing I came with her*, he thought. He wouldn't have minded having her as a patient again, but would rather she avoid hurting herself. He had been right—the pathway was dark. That night was a new moon, so only the stars lit their way.

Without a moment's acknowledgment of her near fall, Seren asked, "Do you… think there are monsters in these woods?"

"Hmm. I would say I don't think so, but I guess anything is possible. Why?" Dr. Harlan asked, carrying the takeout box. He

102

wanted to make it as easy for her to walk as possible, and he made sure to keep an arm open to catch her if needed.

"I think there are," she said. "I heard one."

"You heard one?"

"Yep. When I first got here. I lay in the snow in the woods, and I heard one. It said—what did it say? Oh yeah, it said to 'remember who I am,' or something." Seren twirled on the balls of her feet.

"Are you sure it was a monster?" he asked.

"No, but then again, I'm not sure of anything."

That was one of the most honest statements Dr. Harlan had heard in a long time. He could relate, though he didn't think Seren was capable of expounding upon what she meant in her current state.

"But I am sure of one thing," Seren said, turning to look at him.

"What is that?"

"I can't tell you," she said, spinning again. "In fact, I can't tell anyone, because I've got to keep it locked inside." She pantomimed a lock and key in her chest. "But maybe, one day, when you're older."

Dr. Harlan laughed. "Okay, I'll hold you to it."

The porch steps proved a challenge for Seren. She stumbled on the first one, so Dr. Harlan wrapped his free arm around hers to guide her. He was patient and made sure she safely made her way to the door. It took her a while to find the right key, but when she did, she threw it open and beelined inside. Dr. Harlan wasn't sure how appropriate it was to follow her, but didn't have much time to think it over because Seren loudly told him to come in.

"I'm just going to put the leftovers in the fridge," he said as he peered around the door.

He was about to say his goodbyes when Seren slumped onto the couch and laid her head against the cool leather. Dr. Harlan wondered if he should let her pass out there, but he wasn't entirely comfortable with the idea. She could fall off and hit her head on the corner of the coffee table or miss the comfort and warmth of her bed. He decided it was better to get her safely into the bedroom, so he made his way to her and lightly patted her arm.

"Seren?"

"Hmm?" she grumbled.

"I think I should help you to the bed, okay?"

Seren didn't say a word but lifted her arm for him to help her to her feet. Her heavy head thumped against his chest as he wrapped his arm around her waist, careful to make sure she didn't trip on the rug. He brought her to the edge of the bed and threw back the covers. Like a small child, she sat and waited for him to tell her what to do next. He kneeled to take off her shoes and told her to lie back. She wasn't far enough down on the bed, so she almost collided with the headboard. He reacted in time and cradled her head down onto the pillow. When he pulled the covers over her, she opened her eyes to look at him. A surprised sound escaped from him as she grabbed his tie and pulled him in close. Her hot breath fanned over his lips as she closed the distance and kissed him. Before he could think not to, he slightly parted his lips and kissed her back.

"You're so handsome," she said as she pulled away, his face inches from hers. "That's what I wanted to tell you."

The kiss left Dr. Harlan breathless. He opened his mouth to speak, but Seren closed her eyes and fell into a deep sleep. He stood upright and adjusted his tie. A slow stream of heat snaked up his spine like warm honey and pooled in his cheeks and ears. Checking himself, he turned to leave the room. He left the door ajar and gazed at her. He ran his hand over his mouth and felt as though he were lost in a dreamy stupor. A yellow notepad and a pen were on the coffee table. She had scribbled a few words on the top sheet, but he didn't read them. He tore a sheet from the pad and jotted a quick note.

Leftovers are in the fridge. Be sure to have them in the morning, he wrote.

He capped the pen and left the note on the kitchen table. Then, he took one more glance toward her bedroom. Seren was sleeping peacefully, so he closed the cabin door softly behind him.

Chapter 14

Seren was floating in a deep lake with her eyes closed. The surrounding trees stretched taller than normal as if they were made of putty. She stared at the purple sky, her ears submerged in the tepid water. She had jumped in from a long dock that extended to the lake's center. Her toes hit the wood softly with each push and pull of the current. The energy shifted, and she opened her eyes. The figure of her grandfather stared down at her, and Seren abruptly thrashed in the water.

"I'm here," he said.

Seren couldn't speak because her mouth was numb.

"But I cannot stay forever," he continued.

Seren ascended metal steps affixed to the side of the dock and stared at him. A large ship wheel appeared next to him. He stood aside, motioning her forward. She stepped up to the wheel and held out her hand but stopped short of touching it. Her lips were beginning to fill with blood. She paused. "I—"

"You are waking up," he said.

She felt a gnawing, horrible pounding in her head. The image of her grandfather, the lake, and the wheel faded into nothingness as she catapulted through time and arrived back in her body, aching. She opened her eyes to a knocking on the cabin door. The sound echoed through her bruised brain. She shielded her eyes from the morning sunlight, unable to stomach its harsh glow.

"Hello in there! It's Rita!"

Oh my god, she thought. She had forgotten Rita was coming to work on the cabin. Seren forced herself to sit up and threw the covers off. Her stomach lurched.

"Oh—"

Seren held her mouth and ran to the toilet to purge. Her horrible retching echoed in the small bathroom, making her vomit again. Throwing up had to be one of the worst things a human being could experience, but she was thankful to feel better once it stopped.

"Coming," she called to Rita as loudly as she could. She spit in the sink on her way to open the front door.

"Ooh, what happened to you?" Rita asked.

"I, uh… had a little too much to drink last night," Seren replied.

Rita chuckled. "I'll say! Well, at least by the end of today, you'll have a prettier cabin, and hopefully internet." She held up her tools and what appeared to be an old modem.

Seren hoped it would work. She gestured toward the interior and said, "Have at it. If you need anything, please just help yourself, I've got to—"

"Feel better."

"Yeah."

Seren returned to the bathroom and shut the door. She turned on the cold tap in the shower and stripped naked. Her hands felt hot against the cool ceramic sink. She grabbed a bottle of Advil from the bathroom cabinet and popped the lid. The pills probably wouldn't help much, but she hoped some kind of placebo effect would kick in and relieve her pounding head. She popped two in her mouth and downed them with a handful of sink water. The bitter, acidic taste of vomit lingered in her mouth. It was enough to make her want to puke again, but she didn't. Instead, she quickly brushed her teeth and rinsed twice with mouthwash before stepping into the cold shower stream.

When Seren emerged from the bathroom, hair wet and wearing fresh clothes, Rita was hard at work sanding the porch steps. The high-pitched whir of her neon yellow machine only made Seren's head ache more.

"Sorry," Rita yelled over the noise.

"I'll live," Seren yelled back.

She considered returning to bed for a moment but spotted a folded piece of paper on the kitchen table. She walked closer and found it had writing on it.

Leftovers are in the fridge. Be sure to have them in the morning.

Seren read the message a few times but was no less confused than the first time she read it. She barely remembered the night before and didn't recall if anyone had come home with her. She read the message again and opened the fridge to reveal a white to-go box. Inside was a hefty helping of Otis's spaghetti and meatballs. She wasn't hungry, but the message seemed to be an order rather than a request, so she placed the food in the microwave and did as she was told. Whether it was the spaghetti, the Advil, or the large glass of water she forced herself to chug, she felt better, though not enough to stay awake. She deposited the empty box in the trash and went back to bed.

When Seren awoke, she felt much better. The incessant whirring of the sanding machine had stopped, and her headache had reduced from a hard pounding to a light throb. She wanted to remain in bed but couldn't if she wanted her crops to live. When she stepped out of her bedroom, Rita was crouched by the tv.

"Hey! How're you feeling?" Rita asked.

"Better, thanks," Seren said. "How's it going out here?"

"Very well. I got a lot of work done on the porch, so it's just smooth wood from here on out. I'm working on the internet now. I had some issues at first, but I think I can figure it out."

Seren looked at the clock on the wall. *2:30 p.m.* "Can I get you anything?" she asked as she rubbed her forehead.

"Don't worry about me. Do whatever you need to do."

Seren stepped onto the porch, and its transformation delighted her. Somehow, Rita had made the old wood look new again. She ran her hand down the banister, which was as smooth as a worn rock on the beach. Mabon seemed to like it too. The tabby rubbed her head against the railing and purred.

For the rest of the afternoon, Seren divided her time between refilling her water glass and shooing away more crows from her crops. They came less frequently but were still as much of a nuisance as the weeds. As the afternoon drew on, most of her work centered around ripping the latter from the ground and depositing them at the edge of the forest. The birds seemed thankful for the weeds and fibers, as each time she brought more, the previous batch was gone.

Seren sat on the porch rocking chair, feeling more relaxed after working her stiff muscles. To the south side of the farm, a peculiar double figure appeared. One had a stiff, cross-like body, and a thick head of medium-length brunette hair obscured the other. Flashes of color swirled around the crossed one, which scrambled Seren's recovering brain.

What is that?

"Rita?" she called. "Could you come out here?"

"What's up?" Rita asked as she came outside.

"Do you see that?"

Rita placed a hand over her eyes and gazed toward the two figures.

"Oh, that's Chessy," Rita said. "I'm almost done with the setup, so I'm gonna get back to it. Should be done in a few."

As the two figures neared, Seren recognized the face that, just weeks prior, was contorted in embarrassment and anger at what her nephew had done at the Aster Dance. She looked pleasant, and Seren hoped that if the matter was brought up, she could address anything Chessy might have to say quickly and put it to rest.

"Hi there," Chessy said. The other figure was a scarecrow, and the flashes of color were ribbons festooned all over it. "I don't think we were properly introduced, but I'm so happy to finally meet you! My name's Chessy."

Seren shook her outstretched hand and welcomed her to Hiraeth Farm.

"Jenna came by yesterday and told me you could use some help keeping pests at bay," Chessy said. "I had this ol' guy in the back of my barn, and he wasn't being put to good use—I don't really grow much anymore, you see, it's too hard on my knees—so I thought I'd give him to you."

"Thank you," Seren said. "These crows have been coming by pretty much every day. I thought I would never get rid of them."

"Yeah, but see, this guy's got ribbons on 'im. That's a little trick for ya. Stationary scarecrows do okay on their own, but birds respond more to movement."

Seren and Chessy drove the scarecrow's stake into the ground just shy of the crop field and piled a few rocks around the base to keep it steady.

"That should do it," Chessy said as she wiped her hands on her gingham blouse. "Oh, and one more thing. I wanted to say how sorry I am about my nephew. I really don't know what to do with him sometimes."

The sadness in her big brown eyes made Seren feel for the woman.

Chessy brushed her shaggy brown bangs out of her eyes and continued. "I talked to him about it, and, well, it's harder to get Jake to open up than it is to shuck an oyster with your bare hands, but I hope he will apologize."

"Thank you for saying that," Seren said.

She thought about asking Chessy more questions about Jake and telling her about the other run-ins she'd had with him but decided against it. The woman seemed to be the type of person who saw the good in everyone, and the darkness in Jake appeared to drain her. Seren didn't want to trouble her more.

"Also, you looked beautiful, dear. The valley is lucky to have you," Chessy gushed.

Seren looked over at the gifted scarecrow. "You said you don't grow much anymore? You have a farm, too?"

"Oh my, yes. Luckily, I can still do what needs done short of getting down in the dirt. I keep some livestock—easy stuff like sheep, goats, and chickens—which I sell, along with related equipment and supplies." She paused and looked around, seeming to ponder for a moment. "You know what, in the future, should you expand, I'd love to help you in any way I can."

"That'd be nice." Seren broke the tension by kicking a rock toward a lingering crow, which seemed fascinated by the scarecrow. The bird hopped back a few steps but didn't fly off.

"Well, now." Chessy clicked her tongue. "Stubborn fellow. I better let you get back to it. I need to see Mayor Doney, anyway. Volunteered to help with some tax issues. Don't be a stranger, now!"

"I won't," Seren promised as the woman turned to leave with a broad smile and an enthusiastic wave. She thought it was strange for Chessy to volunteer with something like taxes, but then she remembered the rumor that she and Mayor Doney were an item. After meeting them both, they seemed an unlikely but sweet pair.

"Okay!" Rita called out from the doorway of the cabin. "We're in luck. Come on inside and see if this thing works."

She gave Seren the network name and passcode, which was a bunch of random jumbled letters.

After entering the information on her laptop, Seren opened a new page.

"Moment of truth," Rita said.

At first, nothing happened, but after a few seconds, it worked.

"Yes!" Rita shouted. "I'm not even sure how I did it, but here we are."

Seren tore her eyes from the screen to look up at her savior. "Thank you so much."

"Aw, no problem, dear. Glad I could figure it out. Here…" she fished a folded piece of glossy paper from her pocket. "That says how to change the network name and password. I'll come back tomorrow morning to finish the structural work on the cabin."

"Hopefully," Seren said, "I'll be in much better form to receive you then."

"Ha! No worries. I've tied a few on myself in my time." With that and a wink, Rita collected her tools and headed for the door. "See you tomorrow."

Shortly after Rita's departure, Jenna called. She was full of questions about Seren and Dr. Harlan arriving together at the Fig. Seren explained it again, trying to convince her nothing happened before they arrived.

"Well, how'd you get home last night?" Jenna asked.

Seren glanced at the handwritten note on the table. "I was hoping you could tell me that."

"Last thing I remember was Emelia telling me about how annoying and desperate Craig is, and you were still there, so I have less of a clue than you do."

"Hm, well, I've never been more hungover in my life than I was today. I can't do that again."

"Well, did you have fun at least?" Jenna asked.

"Very much so." Seren traced her fingers over the dark ink. "Anyway, I've got to have dinner and go to bed. I'm exhausted."

After Seren hung up, a faint memory struck her of a hand wrapped around her waist under a moonless, starry sky and talk of monsters in the woods. It felt real, though she couldn't place it, so she assumed it must've been a dream. Maybe Otis had written her the note, and it fell off the box when she walked to the fridge. Either way, after the busy day, she decided she'd had enough thoughts and settled in for an evening of warm soup and an early night's sleep.

Chapter 15

Dr. Harlan was a man of routine. Every morning, he awoke at the same time, turned off the same alarm clock, drank the same cup of home-brewed, bitter coffee, ate the same simple oatmeal with walnuts and blueberries, and wore the same clothes. Over the years, he discovered buying multiple copies of the same button-down shirts and pants was easier than agonizing each morning over his attire. The one way he shook things up was with his socks. That day, he wore dark green ones with little paper airplanes. He kept his apartment clean and orderly, with limited décor. He had little reason to decorate. The last time he had company was years ago when Mira had stopped by to deliver paperwork.

He lived atop the clinic in a studio that was too cramped for his stature, but it worked for him. It was convenient to live above the clinic, especially if there were an emergency—not that many happened in Adytown.

Dr. Harlan finished shaving and patted his face with a small dab of aftershave. He rubbed his eyes for a moment and put on his tortoiseshell glasses. He still had a few minutes, so he clipped the small edges of his fingernails and filed them until they were smooth. A crisp white shirt he had ironed a few days prior hung on the closet door, with a red tie on the hilt. As he removed his gray t-shirt, he caught a glimpse of himself in the mirror. Dr. Harlan had always taken good care of himself, but he had to admit that he wasn't as in shape as he used to be. His arms were still strong, and his chest broad and toned, but he couldn't help but notice the small belly he had developed over the past few months. He was getting older, and if he wanted longevity, he would have to be consistent.

Thirty-four, he thought.

He told himself he still had time, but it was disconcerting to realize he was entering his mid-thirties in a few months. He decided he had more important things to worry about, so he donned his white shirt and tie, fastened the buttons, and tied a simple oriental knot, as he had on hundreds of days before.

When he unlocked the door that separated the clinic hallway from his apartment, it was dead quiet, and the lights were off. Some mornings, Mira came in early to set up for the day, but that day, the task was up to him. He flipped on the lights and checked the schedule at the front desk. Most days were quiet in the clinic. Adytown only had around fifty inhabitants, and they could only be sick so often. Other patients came to him from neighboring towns, which sustained the clinic enough to stay open.

Some days, he felt redundant. It didn't seem Adytown needed a clinic, yet he was happy to have the job. He had worked in the trauma center in the city when he first graduated from medical school, but over time, it wore on him. There were only so many nights he could stay up late and treat the unspeakable horrors he routinely saw in those operating rooms. Somewhere around twenty-seven, he decided he needed peace. When a job listing opened in Adytown, he didn't hesitate to submit his resume. Not long after, Mayor Doney called him, elated that an experienced, well-liked, and respected physician was interested in downsizing. Still, when days turned into weeks with little to do, he missed the fast-paced

113

environment of the ER. He had lived in town for seven years, and it turned out time went by just as quickly, no matter where he was.

Dr. Harlan sipped his dwindling coffee. There was probably some busy work he could attend to, but for the moment, he sat at the front desk and rested his eyes.

The clinic doorbell chimed, and Dr. Harlan opened his eyes.

"Sorry I'm late, Dr. Harlan," Mira said.

She was struggling to cradle a couple of cups of coffee and a large blue binder. He appreciated how seriously she took her job, but her anguished regrets for being five minutes late never failed to amuse him.

"Has Horace come in yet?" she asked as she set down the binder and gave Dr. Harlan another cup of coffee.

"No, his appointment is in about ten minutes," Dr. Harlan said, looking at his watch.

"Hmm."

Dr. Harlan could tell she had more to say about Horace, but she bit her tongue. He decided long ago it wouldn't be in good faith to speak ill of their patients, no matter how frustrating their treatment may be.

Mira picked up the blue binder and walked to the back room. She was a useful and much-needed addition to the clinic. She attended nursing school in the city and had intended on staying, but eventually moved back to the valley after she decided city life wasn't for her. Her father, Darius, was an astronomer who followed a similar pattern when he was her age. He had come out to the valley to observe the aurora borealis, an exceptionally rare occurrence in North America, which was visible that year in November. That night, he not only got to have the experience of a lifetime, but he also met Rita. They got married three months later. The valley had that kind of magic to it, and Dr. Harlan wondered if one day he might be so lucky to experience it.

Outside, a pair of muffled voices neared the clinic. Dr. Harlan glanced at his watch, which read *8:15 a.m.*

"Right on schedule," he said.

"And another thing, if he tells me one more time—" The clinic doorbell chimed, and Edna and Horace entered the waiting room.

"Good morning, Mr. Fielder," Dr. Harlan said.

Horace grunted and waited for Edna to wheel him to the consultation room.

"Good morning, doctor," Edna replied. Her countenance never soured from Horace's ill-tempered nature.

"Right this way," Dr. Harlan said as he held open the hallway door.

The three of them entered the patient consultation room. Edna sat in the visitor's chair and took out a pair of knitting needles from her purse. She was working on a pair of lilac-colored gloves. Horace begrudgingly stood from his chair, leaned against the hospital bed, and crossed his arms. He almost never sat on the bed, no matter how often Dr. Harlan told him he'd be more comfortable.

"How are you feeling today?" Dr. Harlan asked. He opened a gray file cabinet with a small key from his pocket and took out Horace's file.

"Fine. I don't know why I have to keep coming here," Horace replied, sounding annoyed.

"Well, Mr. Fielder, your wife has expressed some concerns about your weight. In your age bracket, there is a higher probability of heart complications from a sedentary lifestyle. Have you been incorporating more walks, as we discussed?"

"No. Ain't no reason to."

"Are you still feeling out of breath from any physical exertion?"

"Yes, which is another reason I shouldn't have to keep coming to this damn clinic."

"Now, now, dear," Edna said.

"You two are conspiring against me, I tell ya," Horace muttered.

"How about diet?" Dr. Harlan asked, unphased by Horace's outburst. "Last we spoke, we mentioned incorporating less red meat and dairy and implementing more vegetables and whole foods."

Horace glared at his wife. "She made some god-awful Brussels sprouts last night. Damn near put me right off my appetite."

"I understand that any change in lifestyle can take time, but it is essential that we get you walking more and sticking to a healthier meal plan," Dr. Harlan said.

"See! There it is again. I told you!"

"He's just trying to help you, dear," Edna said, her voice unchangingly sweet and understanding.

Dr. Harlan put away Horace's file and laced his fingers together. "How is your nephew?"

"He's fine." Horace looked surprised by the change of conversation.

"His name is Zach if I remember correctly. He'll be coming to live with you both in a few weeks' time?"

Horace nodded and seemed to settle down some. "He's a fine boy."

Dr. Harlan nodded and leaned forward in his chair, placing his hands in his lap. "Listen, I understand this is all very difficult. Working on ourselves is hard work, but you owe it to Zach. We're talking about longevity here, Mr. Fielder. I know you want to be around to see him grow up, maybe teach him a bit about football, or watch tv shows together as a family. If you can't convince yourself to do it for yourself, do it for Zach."

Horace cleared his throat and shifted his weight. He fixed his eyes on some unperceivable spot on the floor and grew silent for a moment. He then looked Dr. Harlan square in the face and said, "I'll give it some thought."

"Good, that's all I ask. If there is anything I can do to help you, don't hesitate to call or come in for another visit."

Dr. Harlan waited for Horace to make a move to indicate he was done for the day. When he finally did, Edna put her knitting away and held onto his arm. They had been married for over fifty years, and no matter how crotchety Horace behaved, Edna was always there by his side, and he hers.

"Thank you, doctor. You're a fine young man," she said, patting his arm.

By two in the afternoon, the day was winding down. The day's schedule had been very light, with only Horace's visit that morning

116

and one other patient from the next town over. Dr. Harlan sat in his office and leaned back in his desk chair, reading the latest edition of *Plane and Pilot.*

"I finished filing the rest of the paperwork," Mira said as she entered the office. "Do you think I could head home early today? Rita wants me to help with some housework dad didn't have time to get to."

"Yes, you can," Dr. Harlan replied.

"Thank you," Mira said before turning to leave, then she spun back on her heels. "Oh, also, I printed more of the patient intake forms. Where do you want them?"

"I suppose the top drawer of reception would work just fine."

"Has that new girl been in to fill one out yet?" Mira asked.

Seren, he thought. "Oh, um…" he began, clearing his throat. "No, I don't believe she has."

"Should we send her one?"

"I'll take care of it."

"Okay. See you bright and early tomorrow," Mira said as she walked down the hallway to leave for the day.

Dr. Harlan put down his magazine and loosened his tie. He remembered how Seren's lips felt pressed against his. He had walked back to town, unable to comprehend that she had kissed him. When he arrived home, he went straight to bed and pushed the fact that he had kissed her back out of his mind.

It all came flooding back.

He was reticent about sending her an invitation to the clinic to fill out an intake form, but he didn't know why. It was only right that she be in the system in case of an emergency. She also lived here now, so it made sense. If it all was so rational, then why did he not move to make it happen?

He remembered her head thudding against his chest and placing an arm around her waist, so she didn't trip over herself. He'd had such a nice night with Seren and her friends. Dr. Harlan hadn't gone out with anyone in a long time, and even longer since he remembered having such pleasant conversation. It was hard being the only town physician, as it made dating an interesting minefield. There was little room for it. Everyone was his patient, and he was their doctor. It would be a gross violation of trust.

She thinks I'm handsome, he thought. *But she was drunk. She probably doesn't remember anything.*

Adjusting his glasses, he stood to retrieve Harold Grinaker's file. Atop the form, it read, *619 Roseleaf Way.* He would invite her to the clinic and endeavor to put what happened out of his mind.

Chapter 16

It was a dream to have an internet connection to the outside world once more. Rita's AirCard router, using a sim card for a spare cell line she wasn't using, was the solution. Luckily, her family plan didn't have a data limit, and she told Seren not to worry about the bill since it was a package deal. Seren was grateful for the book Everett had lent her, but it couldn't compare with the wealth of knowledge available online.

By the time Rita arrived the next morning, Seren had spent an inordinate amount of time watching YouTube videos and Netflix, so much so that she almost forgot she had a job to do.

Rita finished sanding the porch at record speed and even gave the revived wood a much-needed, rich walnut stain finish. She told Seren not to walk on it for at least twenty-four hours so the stain could dry. In doing so, it was Rita's fault Seren spent the next few days staring at her laptop screen.

When she at last ventured outside and comically shielded her face from the sun like a vampire emerging from a tomb, her crops weren't too worse for wear. They were just a little dry, so Seren concluded she could forgive her minor negligence.

It was too easy to hide from the world. Seren could feel herself slipping back to the cave she once delighted in inhabiting. Farming, as she found out not only from the pages of the snore-inducing book but also from hands-on experience, was inextricably linked to time and perseverance. It was not a craft for those whose great love was instant gratification. So, as time droned on and days passed with few results to speak of, the waiting wore on Seren. Though she loved the small green leaves sprouting from the ground and knew one day they would hopefully grow to something grander; she felt they taunted her at times.

You can't do this. This is a waste of time. You really thought you could become a farmer, just like that?

Those uncomfortable, intrusive thoughts were, of course, manifestations of Seren's lack of faith in herself. Still, she tried. She tried to follow whatever the old book Everett gave her said. She watered and weeded and tended until her fingers were raw. She wiped her forehead every time sweat trickled down her temples. She listened to the peculiar sense of intuition she seemed to have. Most of all, when she wanted to quit, she did not.

Still, the allure of the cave was always there. She could let the crops die and shell up in the cabin for the next few years and do nothing else. Money wasn't an immediate concern. She *could* do it. It would be just like every other time things turned over on a hairpin and took her by surprise. Anyway, Seren felt that if her life up to then were a saved file, she would've deleted it. How could she not? She had little to look forward to. What she did look forward to would likely never come to be, or change, or wouldn't be as sweet as she imagined. There was always the nagging question: *What have I accomplished?* A few sprouting leaves were hardly an answer. It was difficult to stay grounded when every cell in her body felt restless— restless for what? She did not know, and that frightened her.

By mid-April, Seren spent half her time working outside and the other half drinking soda and watching a new book vlogger she found on YouTube. Jenna and Otis texted or called her from time to time, but she almost never reached out first, and she visited town only when she needed something.

Jenna was fast working on a new art piece she called *Dalliance with the Sky*. It was an experiment on the use of as many shades of blue as she could find. From time to time, she would get self-conscious and threaten to throw the piece away. Luckily, Seren was always there to talk her off that ledge. Her friend was peculiar at times. She had a fiery countenance but would easily decide to shut down her artistry and hide away whatever she created in her little home. Jenna talked a lot about needing an artist's inspiration to unleash her projects into the world, saying she just wasn't ready, and neither was the world. Though they had grown close, she still hadn't shared her art.

Must be a personal thing, Seren told herself.

Jenna was the only way she came to know anything about the goings on in town. Faye's daughter Penelope was tutoring Gia and Theo. Apparently, they walked past Jenna's home every day on their way to the library. Gia and Theo teased and poked each other every chance they got and seemed to really love coming up with fantastic stories about creatures in the ocean and how they'd come visit them in their dreams. Theo's mother, Joyce, loved to do aerobics with a few of the other moms in town in the town square on Tuesdays. Joyce's husband was always away, but to where, no one knew. Though she loved and missed him, she had grown used to his absence. Maybe even, as some townspeople gossiped, she had come to enjoy it.

Craig was still annoying Emelia, but she took it well. Emelia did not have a mean-spirited bone in her body and seemed to have endless patience and understanding for a man who was at least ten years older than she was. He was sort of a jack of all trades and was particularly skilled in motor repair and metal works. He lived alone and was understandably lonely. A few years back, he fixed his sights on Emelia, and hopelessly lusted for her ever since. *Like that will ever happen,* Jenna had said to Seren, her voice thick with scorn.

Perhaps one of the saddest rumors was that Perry was considering closing his shop. Competition from Wares & More and the greasy Myron was too stiff for him to keep up. Allegedly, he didn't know how long he had before he would have to close the General Shop's doors, but it couldn't be too far away.

"What'll happen to him?" Seren had asked Jenna.

"Who knows? But if he and Corinne don't do something fast, *poof,* goodbye. Maybe the clinic will expand," Jenna said.

"Could they do that with how few people there are out here?"

"Well, they certainly have more visitors than Perry, that's for sure."

Jenna was right. Somehow, the clinic brought in enough patients to stay open. Seren had not yet met everyone, but it was peculiar that Adytown even needed a clinic. It turned out that people from every town in the surrounding area came to Adytown for medical attention. According to Jenna, they came for Dr. Harlan.

"Why's that?" Seren asked.

"I mean, he's a good doctor. Plus, he's a catch, but he's much too modest to notice."

Seren's face had grown hot at that.

Seren got up from the couch to get a sparkling water from the fridge. She was midway through a March reading wrap-up video by Gabby, the book vlogger, who had somehow managed to read sixteen books in one month, and Seren envied her. It seemed impossible to read that fast. The copy of *The Alchemist* that Seren had gotten from the library was only a quarter finished, and Seren had had it for about a month.

She banged the refrigerator door shut as if in response to her own reading inadequacy and pulled the tab on a soda can, which opened with a hiss. She passed by the handwritten note on the kitchen table as she took a sip. For some reason, she couldn't bring herself to throw it away. Though it had been over a week since it inexplicably showed up on her table, it was her last tie to an unknown visitor or circumstance, and the mystery of it clutched her.

Leftovers are in the fridge. Be sure to have them in the morning.

Well, the leftovers were long gone, much like her memory of that night. She thought of Mrs. Jennings from *Sense & Sensibility* saying to Marianne in her colorful, high-class English accent, "*Come, Miss Marianne. Looking out at the weather will not bring him back!*"

But she was looking at a note, not the weather, and there was no *him* to bring back, or at least none that she remembered. Still, somebody had to have written it, and perhaps if she stared at it long enough and traced her fingers over the letters another hundred times, it would come to life and tell her what happened.

You were drunk, and there's nothing more to it, Seren thought.

As if thinking those words had broken the spell, she picked up the note. After a weeklong relationship she had built with the folded sheet of paper, she resolutely threw it into the trash.

The next morning, Seren rose early. It was one of those rare times her body felt rested. As if her feet had a compass of their own, she found herself on the porch. Through the misty dawn, she saw the little red flag on her mailbox was raised.

Chapter 17

"What's wrong with them?" Seren muttered.

The potatoes she unearthed were mushy and an unpleasant brownish-purple color. She'd been so excited for Jenna to try the potatoes that she invited her over before she dug them up. The beet harvest a month earlier was so perfect it was almost too good to be true. They came out of the ground a beautiful deep purple, firm, and ready to be eaten. There were sixteen—which was less than expected—but it didn't matter because that night, she feasted on food she had grown herself.

Seren picked up another potato. Without applying much pressure, her fingers sank into the soft brown skin and split the root in two.

"Maybe they're... supposed to do that," Jenna said.

Seren stared at Jenna incredulously. "Have you ever *had* a potato?"

"Well... yeah."

Seren threw the ugly Frankenstein creation back into the gaping hole in the ground and got a trash bag from the cabin.

"No, wait, you can still—"

"They're bad, Jenna. I don't know why, but they're bad."

That night, she and Jenna did not dine on double whipped mashed potatoes, baked lemon salmon, and beets as planned. Instead, Seren sat on the couch and stared into a small, flickering fire in the wood-burning stove. It was a cold night, and she needed the comfort. Jenna had invited her into town to cheer her mood, but Seren declined. Why should a failure like her have fun? She wiped a tear from her eye and leaned on her palm.

There was nothing to be done about the potatoes other than throw every one of them away. Three long months of hard work down the drain. The perfectionist in Seren wanted to pick up the book on gardening and open her laptop to research precisely what went wrong, but her arms felt like lead. She couldn't move. Defeat was a potent poison.

Mabon jumped onto the couch and nuzzled Seren's thigh. It was as if she knew something was eating at her. Seren petted Mabon as the cat placed a paw on her stomach and investigated her face. She purred, and though she could not speak, somehow Seren knew that Mabon was telling her it was going to be all right.

In the morning, Seren still felt the iron grip of defeat. She ate breakfast and got dressed but couldn't force herself to go about business as usual. She stood in the middle of the cabin, holding a lukewarm cup of tea.

The letter Adytown Clinic had sent her in April was on the kitchen table. It was June, and though Seren had avoided going, that she would eventually have to register with the clinic weighed on her. She hadn't lied when she told Dr. Harlan that she hated doctors' offices. Every physician who had treated her in the past knew she had full-blown white lab coat syndrome, and it didn't help that Dr. Harlan made her stomach do somersaults just by looking at her. *But we're done with that, remember?* she thought. It was just easier to stay home rather than face her fear. Once more, she was brought to the ledge, but this time, she pushed herself over.

Screw it, she thought as she grabbed the keys off the wall and headed into town.

"Adytown Clinic, this is Mira, how can I help you?"

Seren entered the waiting room as Mira was mid-sentence, a white, corded phone pressed to her ear. Seren gingerly took a step toward the front desk and waited.

"Of course. I will let the doctor know. Goodbye," Mira said, then hung up the phone. "Hello, how can I help you?" she asked.

"Uh, hi," Seren said. "I was sent a notice to come register with the clinic?"

"Oh, yes! No problem. Did you make an appointment?" Mira asked as Seren peered around the office.

"Ah, that probably would've been a good idea, wouldn't it?" Seren asked. *Idiot.*

"We can schedule you in, no problem."

"Y'know, I think I'll just come back another—" Seren's skin broke out in gooseflesh as the hallway door swung open.

"Dr. Harlan, we have a new patient," Mira said.

Dr. Harlan looked up from the journal he was intently scrutinizing. When his eyes landed on Seren, his demeanor changed. "Good morning, Miss Grinaker."

"Hi, Dr. Harlan. I don't have an appointment—I should've known to call."

"It's alright. I have some time now if you'd like."

"Okay," Seren said, her stomach mid somersault. *Yeah, you're definitely done with that.*

Dr. Harlan nodded and walked back through the door. He seemed different—cold, maybe. She thought she detected a terseness in his voice.

Mira interrupted her pondering. "If you'll just fill out these intake forms and have a seat, Dr. Harlan will be with you shortly. Do you have a driver's license?"

Seren handed over her license and received a purple plastic clipboard with two sheets of forms. After completing them, she returned the clipboard.

"Excellent. If you'll just follow me," Mira said before leading her to an examination room. "Just have a seat, and the doctor will be with you shortly," she said.

"Thank you."

Seren felt a gnawing sense of déjà vu as she sank onto the hospital bed. It was the same room she and Dr. Harlan had been in the day they met. Though the once punctured and sore skin had faded and healed, it felt like it was only yesterday.

There was a light knock on the door. Dr. Harlan entered with a manila file folder and ran a hand down the length of his tie. "Good morning, Miss Grinaker." He stared intently at the open file folder in his hands and avoided her gaze. "Let's get you set up here…" He grabbed a pen from his shirt pocket and clicked it. "It says here you do not smoke and have no preexisting conditions. Do you wear contacts or glasses?" he asked.

"No," Seren said.

"Okay, and you marked 'other' for medications. What would that be?"

"Just birth control."

"Is that pill form or something else?"

"IUD."

Dr. Harlan made notes on the page, and Seren got lost watching the tendons of his hands flex and shift as they pressed the pen to paper. His nails were well-manicured, and his skin looked impossibly soft. His fingers were well-proportioned, and in that moment, she had a desire to reach out and touch them.

"Do you drink, and if so, how often?" he asked.

"Ah, probably a few glasses of wine a week. It depends." *Except that one time…* she thought to herself, embarrassed.

"When was your last physical?" he asked, pushing his glasses up the bridge of his nose.

"Um, it's been a while. I guess… five years ago?"

"Okay, if you like, I can perform one now." He lifted his green eyes to look at her.

Seren's face felt warm. "Okay," she said, shrugging.

Dr. Harlan stood to grab a pair of white medical gloves and put them on with a thwack.

With his back turned to her, she couldn't shake the feeling that something was off. Wanting to cut the low-grade tension, she asked, "So, how have you been?"

"Oh, the usual. Can't complain," he said with his back still to her. "And you?"

"All right," she lied. "I had fun that night at the Fig. I think I got a little too drunk, though. I don't really remember how I got home." She tried to add a lighthearted tone to her voice.

Dr. Harlan donned a silver stethoscope and turned to face her, a half-smile on his face. "I walked you home."

"Oh!" Once more, the image of a moonless sky along the path to the farm came to her. "And the note?"

"I wrote that too."

Mystery solved.

Dr. Harlan walked to her, took the stethoscope off his neck, and put the black tips in his ears. "Do I have your permission to lift your shirt?"

Seren cleared her throat. "Yes."

"When I tell you to, take a nice, deep breath in and out," Dr. Harlan said.

Seren nodded.

He lifted the back of her blue crew neck shirt and pressed the cold steel drum to her left side. "Breathe in… and out."

Seren did as she was told, though her breaths were shallow. He moved the scope to her right side and had her do the same. As he lowered her shirt, his fingertips brushed her side—an accident, she figured. Again, she thought of a strong hand wrapped around her waist, not too low to indicate anything untoward, but not too high to render the gesture unhelpful. Her ears burned, and something more, something *else,* was just on the tip of her mind.

"If you pull down your shirt a little, I'll listen to your heart," Dr. Harlan said. "Breathe normally."

"Okay." She stared at him as he drew closer and pressed the cold steel to her chest. It was too quiet in the room, so quiet that Seren became hyper-focused on the sound of her breath going in and out of her nose and the rapid beating in her chest.

"Your pulse is a little high," Dr. Harlan said.

"Sorry, I… don't like hospitals."

"Ah, that's right," he said, smiling at her.

She would not meet his gaze. She couldn't. He was so close that she could feel the heat radiating off his body. Simultaneously, as if two worlds were collapsing in on themselves, she remembered her heavy head thumping against Dr. Harlan's strong chest. Mercifully, he had turned his back to her once more to get a tongue depressor and otoscope. He checked her throat, ears, and, lastly, her eyes.

"Look at me," he said.

He leaned in close. A light scent of vetiver and coffee lingered on his shirt collar. There was something else too, but Seren couldn't put her finger on it. Regardless, he smelled *good*. She loved his face. There was no other way to put it. She loved the freshly shaved curve of his jawline, his well-kept bit of facial hair, the slight creases in the corners of his eyes, his kind expression, and his deep green eyes.

He's so handsome, she thought. Then another wave collapsed, and Seren's blood ran cold.

"Well then, you seem perfectly healthy." Dr. Harlan took a second glance at her and asked, "Are you alright?"

The question thudded against Seren's ears. "Yes, um—sorry. I… just remembered I forgot something."

Dr. Harlan nodded, closed her file, and gestured for her to follow him to the front desk, where Mira sat reading a magazine. "Thanks for coming in," he said.

Seren said her goodbyes to Mira and stole one last glance at Dr. Harlan before exiting the clinic and hurrying toward the bridge on the south side of town.

Oh my god, she thought, bringing her hand to her lips.

Why had he agreed to see her? Had she imagined the whole thing? No. He told her he had walked her home and written the note, so everything else had to be true, too. *But then, why was he so…* She couldn't think of the right word. She was disappointed he didn't seem more flustered, or something. *What else did you expect? He had a job to do. He probably figured you didn't remember because you were drunk. So, so drunk.* Of course, he had walked her home. That's the sort of man he was. He was patient, and kind, and intelligent, and safe, and *she*—she didn't want to think of herself or her mortifying behavior.

A phantom of pressure on her lips struck her from somewhere deep in the alcohol-drenched shadows of that night.

She kissed him. She knew it, and she knew he knew it. He had to, unless he was also drunk, but he drank very little. Had he kissed her back? *No, it was me. It was only me,* she thought. Every image—the walk, the talk of monsters, the hand on her waist, her head on his chest, and finally, the kiss—all clicked together. He had been kind enough to walk her home, just as he had after the Aster Dance. A gentleman. He had walked her home both times because he was a gentleman, and she had taken advantage of him.

Another thought struck her. *Why do I care?* It wasn't as if that kind of thing didn't happen all the time. How many people in their lifetime have gotten drunk and kissed their fair share of random people? But he wasn't random, and she wasn't like that. She rarely ever got drunk, and certainly not *that* drunk, but on that night, she did, and he was there.

Do I like him? she wondered. Immediately, she scoffed at the idiocy of her question. *Of course, I like him. I can hardly stand to be around him without feeling flustered, or wanting to reach out and touch him, or thinking of him in other ways…*

Enough. She cut off the conversation she was having with herself. She hastened toward the roaring crash of the waves below. The beach was deserted. Her white-hot embarrassment and the warm summer day pulled her there, and she was going to walk directly into the water.

She didn't bother undressing. She knew her jeans would stick against her legs once she got out, but she didn't care. She dropped her bag on the sand, walked into the water, and dove under the blue abyss. Saltwater shot up her nose and burned her sinuses. The current was strong, and it threw her around like a sock in a dryer. Gaining her footing, she dug her toes into the paste-like sea floor and burst out of the water. She wiped her eyes and panted. The water was so cold she had to resist chattering her teeth. She scanned the horizon to look for ships. It would only take one blessed hull to take her far, far away from here.

"You *idiot*," she said as she slapped the surface of the water.

"Uh, what're you doing?"

Seren turned and saw Jake standing near the edge of the water, holding flip-flops in one hand and a six-pack of beer in the other. She gazed at the horizon once more, heaved a heavy sigh, and waded back to the shore, her jeans rubbing uncomfortably against her frigid skin.

He stood motionless as she grabbed her purse and strode past him.

"What the hell?" he called after her.

"Enjoy your beer," Seren said, venom in her voice.

"Alright, wait a minute—"

"Good*bye,* Jake."

"I'm sorry!"

Seren planted her feet, her wet shoes sinking into the sand. She turned to him, shaking. "What was that?"

Jake rolled his eyes. "Just... come here. Sit down for a second."

"You *humiliated* me, and now you want me to *sit down* with you?"

Jake just stood there, mute.

"There is nothing in the world that would make me want to spend another second with you," Seren said, accentuating every syllable with her hands. "And in case you haven't noticed, I'm sopping wet. I'm also freezing, so if you don't mind, say whatever you have to say so I can get home and take a hot shower before I die of hypothermia."

"Well, you kinda did that to yourself," he replied, nonplussed.

Seren turned on her heels to walk away.

"No. Just *wait* a second, please. A beer will warm you up."

She whirled around and grabbed a beer from Jake, who had an unmistakable look of bemused surprise on his face. She plopped down on the sand and opened the can. The hot June sun was already drying her clothes and warming her up.

"I hate beer," she said as she took several gulps of the hoppy liquid.

Jake snickered. He sat down a few feet away from her and placed the beer in between them. Overhead, a pair of seagulls flapped their wings and cawed before flying on.

Seren shook her head. "I don't know what I'm doing."

"I don't think anyone does." Jake opened a beer and took a few sips.

That wasn't what Seren wanted to hear. Surely, somewhere, someone must know what they were doing or where they were going. The world could not be pure chaos.

"I came here because I was heartbroken," she said as the walls she put up suddenly crumbled. "I've spent my life searching for meaning, for anything that would tell me I'm special. And finally, when my life was coming together, it fell apart. The man I loved, who I thought was my person, broke my heart. On top of that, I lost the only job I ever liked, my friends deserted me, and my grandfather—the only living family I cared about—died. So, I ran away. I came here. And maybe out of some sick sense of retribution, I wanted to show everyone, to show *him,* that I could prove them wrong. So, I started planting, just like my grandfather did, on the land that he gave *me* for some reason. Even though I was scared, I did it. The beets I grew were perfect. Too perfect. I should've known that was all the luck I would have because not long after, the potatoes rotted in my hands, and who knows how the damn tomatoes will turn out."

Seren took a long sip of her beer. "Anyway, I guess it doesn't matter because here I am drinking something I hate with the *asshole* who threw up on me."

"If I'm an asshole, then why are you telling me all this?" Jake asked.

"I don't know."

He held his beer between his legs and looked down at the sand. He gulped audibly and took a deep breath. "I'm… sorry for what I did."

Seren scowled at Jake, not believing a word he said.

"I'm an asshole, I know, but I mean it," he said. "Oh, and beets are probably one of the easiest vegetables you can grow. But potatoes? Those can take some finesse. When did you plant them?"

"Mid-March."

"That's where you fucked up. Should've waited until April. The ground was probably too damp."

"How do you know these things?" Seren asked.

He looked at her, an unmistakable hesitation pulling at the corners of his mouth. He looked out to sea once more before finally replying. "I used to help Harold out from time to time. Not often, mind you, but I learned a lot from him."

"Well then, help me," Seren said.

"What?"

"Come help me on the farm."

"Do I get a choice in the matter?"

"No. You say you're sorry for what you did. Well, then show me. You don't have to be there forever, just long enough to tell me what you know, and we'll call it even."

Jake rolled his eyes and took a long sip of his beer. His expression gave away nothing as he stared at the ocean. He scratched his stubbled cheeks, then turned to Seren. "Fine."

Chapter 18

Seren and Jake stared into the giant hole in the ground where the potatoes had been.

"They should only be buried about six to eight inches deep, and by the look of them…" Jake crouched on his heels to pick one up, completely unphased by its grotesque color and texture. "You planted too deep." He threw the potato back into the trash bag and wiped his hands on his jeans. When he stood up, he looked at Seren and shook his head.

"What, Jake? *What?*" Seren asked, readying herself to be made fun of once again.

"You have grit, I'll give you that, but this," he waved his hand at the cropland, "this is insane."

Seren fixed him with a stern, humorless look.

Jake seemed to understand her inference and said nothing more about insanity. Instead, he glanced at the tomatoes and gave an encouraging shrug. "The tomatoes are doing well. You did a good job with those."

"Good," Seren huffed.

Jake frowned and shot her a sideways glance. "Next time you plant potatoes, just don't bury them as deep and make sure the ground isn't too wet. It's cooler here, so you still have time to plant more. They'll be ready in September."

"What about raised beds?" Seren asked.

"I don't know anything about them."

"I read that they're more controllable than ground beds. Better drainage, crops can grow earlier, and I could easily monitor the soil for nitrogen, acidity, and all that. I was thinking I could get Rita to make some for me."

"And you're sure you need my help?"

"Obviously."

"Well then, let's get to work."

Chapter 19

The coming months were nothing but trial and error. The soil was too wet or not wet enough. Some plants in the southernmost patch should have been in the northernmost. It was impossible to tell if everything was going according to plan, but Seren held on to a tenuous shred of hope. Rome was not built in a day, and neither would Hiraeth Farm.

Jake had convinced her to start small. The idealistic castle in the air with fully functioning irrigation and perfect technique would have to come later. Still, Seren gave it everything she had. There were so many factors to juggle it made Seren dizzy. The failed potatoes were a haunting reminder that to err is human, but as a farmer, those mistakes cost an entire crop, money, and precious time.

By mid-June, she had to work fast. She had read about propagating plants the season prior to prepare for the next, but she didn't have a greenhouse. All she had was the land, seeds, and her hands. It took no time at all for the spinach and zucchini to die, but rather than becoming discouraged, she made things even simpler. She had an abnormal amount of luck growing beets, but they were no longer in season. Otherwise, the tomatoes seemed to be growing the best, so without a second thought, she and Jake tilled the soil and planted nothing but tomatoes.

On the nights when Seren wasn't talking to Jenna about town gossip or getting food from Otis, she spent hours watching YouTube videos, reading articles, and researching all she could about growing. In addition to learning about the efficiency of raised beds, Seren read about compost, soil nutrition, spacing, succession, plant zones, using a schedule, and so on.

It became obvious early in her research that she'd made two sizeable mistakes. First, growing in the earth, apparently, wasn't the most efficient or economical option. Second, she hadn't managed her time and money wisely. If she wanted to do things right, and she very much did, then it would come at a cost. There was a genuine possibility that she could lose all her savings, but a driving, undeniable force told her to go for it.

On July 2nd, around four in the afternoon, Seren plucked the first fully red and ready tomato from the vine. Jake stood over her shoulder as she cut it in half on the kitchen counter and gave him a half. Together, they took a bite. The tomato flesh was firm, white, and flavorless.

"It tastes like… nothing," Seren said.

"You're right," Jake agreed.

Seren spiked the tomato in the trash and bid him farewell for the night. The moment he was gone, she called Rita.

Within a few days, Rita delivered the next step toward the castle in the air. She drove into Hiraeth Farm with a truckload of large cedar planks and a few bags of wood chips. Together, they made a pair of three-by-eight-foot raised beds, pausing to high-five when they finished.

"How tall are these?" Seren asked.

"About fourteen inches," Rita said.

"Perfect."

137

There was a small garden supply shop in the next town over, and Rita graciously drove Seren to pick up vermiculite, compost, peat moss, and a large blue tarp.

When they returned to Hiraeth, Rita helped Seren spread out the tarp and unload the materials. There was no way the ratio would be perfect, not on the first attempt, but one by one, they dumped each bag onto the tarp and mixed it with pitchforks.

"What is this anyway?" Rita asked.

Seren wiped her forehead with the back of a gloved hand.

"It's called Mel's mix, I think," Seren explained. "I read about it online. The quality of the soil feeds the plants, and what I was growing wasn't getting enough nutrition just from the ground here. It's kind of a *duh* thing. I don't know why it never occurred to me before."

Though her skin shone with sticky perspiration and her limbs were dead tired, there was something about working the land that felt right in her soul, and her spirit soared with each swing of the pitchfork.

"Farming looks good on you," Rita said.

Seren looked down at herself, covered in dirt and sweat, and laughed. "That's good to hear. I guess this is my new 'look' now."

"Looks like we're almost done here."

"Yeah, but I can finish up. You've already helped more than you needed to. Thank you so much for all this. You're a lifesaver."

"Don't you worry about it. I'm just happy to see the old place coming back to life."

After Rita left, Seren filled about an inch of the raised beds with wood chips and the rest with Mel's mix. To top it all off, she sprayed a generous amount of water into the mix until it was damp. The sun was setting, but Seren kept working since she was high on the excitement of accomplishment.

She dug a hole each square foot in the two beds, equaling forty-eight potential tomato plants. The number seemed almost astronomical. Before she extracted the original tomatoes she planted in March, as well as the newly sprouting ones, she trimmed the leaves and stems from the base of each plant and dispersed the trimmings throughout the wet, raised beds. After replanting, Seren filled the last ten holes with seeds. There was no guarantee they would make it to full maturity, but if they did, she was beyond excited to taste them.

"Welcome to your newer, better home," she said.

She grabbed the hose once more, lightly sprayed the older plants, and gave the seeds a little extra water.

Moisture, heat, and nutrients, she thought.

Seren let the hose fall to the ground and placed her hands on her hips. She couldn't help but break into a wide smile and felt, for the first time, as though she were finally on the right track.

Chapter 20

Seren wished she had something smart or clever to say to Dr. Harlan to break the ice. He sat on a stool at the bar, a half-finished glass of red wine in front of him. He paid no attention to Otis or Faye, the latter of whom sat as a semi-permanent fixture at the far end of the bar for the last few hours, guzzling more beer than should be possible for a woman her size.

Seren sat in the corner of the Fig, far enough out of sight that Dr. Harlan would not have seen her when he came in. She was supposed to meet Jenna, who was late.

Like through some telepathic connection, Otis seemed to understand not to disturb her. Though her wine was dwindling, he didn't offer another glass until she indicated she was ready.

In her five months in the valley, she realized she could not predict when or where she might run into Dr. Harlan. Every time she walked past the clinic, or got groceries, or took a walk, or came to the Fig, she was taking a chance that she would have to face him. The longer time droned on and she didn't see him, the more she thought maybe her luck would last. But as she sat there, biting her lip, that luck finally dried up.

It would stand to reason that after all those weeks, Seren would have thought of some way to address what happened, but she hadn't. His demeanor that day in the clinic made her wonder if she should say anything at all. If it didn't seem to bother him, why should it bother her? But it did, and she wouldn't dare converse with him, go to the clinic, or act as though everything was normal until her lapse in judgment was cleared.

Seren took a final bite of the excellent shepherd's pie Otis had made special that evening, which sat like a rock in her stomach as she stared at Dr. Harlan.

What do I say to him? she wondered, her knee bouncing under the wooden table.

Seren checked her watch. Jenna was fifteen minutes late. As if on cue, a text came through, asking if they could reschedule. All omens pointed to Seren's fate: she would have to talk to him.

She caught Otis's eye. He had just stowed his phone in his pants pocket. He looked at her, and as he did, another text came through.

If you want my advice, just come up to the bar with your glass and strike up a conversation.

Seren looked at Otis, her face saying, *Do I have to?*

Otis leaned his head toward Dr. Harlan, who was still captivated by whatever he was reading, and nodded.

Might need your help, Seren texted back. An unspoken plan passed between them, and Seren braced herself.

"Seren? More wine?" Otis called.

Dr. Harlan lifted his head when he heard her name.

"Yes, thank you, I'll come to you," she said.

Seren decided not to acknowledge Dr. Harlan yet. First, she would get wine. She placed her empty glass on the bar.

Otis poured her a new one. "This is a good batch, isn't it? I believe you and Dr. Harlan here are drinking the same thing."

"Is that so?" she asked, trying to sound nonchalant.

"You both have good taste." When Otis finished pouring, he excused himself to the back, saying something about needing to check on the beer supply, but Seren knew he was giving them time alone.

"Miss Grinaker," Dr. Harlan said, "I didn't know you were here. I would've said hello if I had seen you."

"It's okay, I was just… over there," Seren said, gesturing to the corner. "I was supposed to meet Jenna, but she had to cancel."

Dr. Harlan nodded and closed his book.

"What're you reading?" she asked as she came closer to him.

"*The Grapes of Wrath*," he replied. Seren stared at him for a moment, then broke out laughing.

"Are you really?" she asked.

"Would I lie?" he asked as she showed her the book he'd been reading. It really was *The Grapes of Wrath*.

"Wow, I'm impressed. I think maybe I'm the one who should be reading it. I'm going through *The Alchemist* right now. It's good," Seren said.

"Maybe when we're both finished, we can trade," he offered.

"I'd like that," she said.

Dr. Harlan smiled at her and adjusted his jacket. He seemed calm and collected and, best of all, happy to see her. If there was any lingering remembrance of that night, he didn't show it.

Seren felt herself coming to a split street. She could also forget and move on. Dr. Harlan seemed to have already gone down that road. Maybe one day, it would come up organically and spare Seren the gargantuan act of courage she was saddling herself with. Or she could take the truth that was festering within her gut and bring it out into the light. The latter seemed better suited for her conscience, but the first was easier. After all, what was the big deal, anyway? It was just a kiss.

"I um—" Seren began.

"You gonna stay back there forever, Otis? Dying of thirst out here!" Faye yelled.

Just like that, Seren's courage evaporated.

"Speaking of farming, how's it going?" Dr. Harlan asked.

"It's going alright. I'm growing tomatoes, or *hopefully,* I will be growing tomatoes. I had to replant them in raised beds because the first batch was, well, tasteless, and… is this interesting?" Seren asked, feeling self-conscious.

"Very! I know it might be surprising, but we don't learn much about gardening or farming in medical school."

"No agriculture one-oh-one?"

"Not even a seminar."

They both laughed, and Seren sat down next to him to continue telling him about her plans. He listened intently as she explained all about the proper fertilizer mixtures to get tomato plants to produce more fruit, which, of course, was her goal. She told him how the trellises were holding up well despite being homemade, of the disastrous potatoes, and the contrast of the stellar beets.

"But they're apparently one of the easiest crops to grow, according to Jake," Seren finished.

"I'm glad you're helping him. He needs a good outlet," Dr. Harlan said.

"Well, I didn't really give him much of a choice. Y'know, on account of him throwing up on me and all."

"Naturally." Dr. Harlan took a sip of his wine.

"I haven't quite forgiven him yet, but it is nice to have company."

Dr. Harlan glanced down at his lap and picked a few bits of lint from his dress pants. Whether it was the wine, or the pleasant conversation, something in him shifted. "It is," he said, looking at Seren.

Otis poured more beer for Faye, who happily accepted, then came to check in on them. "How are we doing over here?"

Dr. Harlan motioned that he was finished.

"I'd love to take some of that shepherd's pie home, please, Otis," Seren said.

"Coming right up." Otis left them to pack up Seren's food.

Dr. Harlan placed some money on the counter to cover his tab. "I'd better head out. It was lovely getting to catch up, Seren. I can't wait to hear more about the tomatoes."

His abrupt departure disappointed Seren. It was still early, and there were still so many things to talk about. He had asked so much about her, and to her complete surprise, he not only listened to every word, but seemed genuinely interested to hear about everything. They'd had a good time, but as Seren watched him exit the Fig, there was a terrible quickening in her chest. There was the cliff again and the serpents below, and in that moment, a decision had to be made. Some power took over her limbs, and unable to stop her feet from planting on the ground, she hurried after him.

Her heart pounded in her ears as she jogged across the square. Ahead, Dr. Harlan was nearing the clinic, and she strove to catch up with him. Before she could lose her nerve, she called out to him. "Dr. Harlan!"

He turned to her, a surprised look on his face.

Seren came to stand a few feet away from him, her chest heaving from exertion, and she blurted out, "I kissed you."

Each word felt thick and heavy, and as she spoke, she fell over the edge. Her stomach lurched as the doctor stood dumbfounded with his half-read book under his arm, his eyes intently fixed on her.

"I remembered," she said. "It came back in bits and pieces, but I remember the walk home, and how selfless you were to do that, and then what we—" she broke off and averted her eyes before she spoke again, her face getting hot. "What *I* did. I wasn't going to bring it up, I mean, I didn't remember until that day at the clinic, and I thought maybe I could just forget about it, but the embarrassment I feel is…" She paused and slowly lifted her gaze to meet his. "I'm so sorry."

Seren felt faint. The random act of courage had come out of nowhere, but as she stood on shaky knees, her courage soured. She felt it as a long, thin ribbon of brilliant red swirling into an agitated squiggle and darting into the faraway mountains.

Dr. Harlan opened his mouth and shut it again. His silence made it hard for Seren to stand still. Then, a horrifying thought struck her. She had assumed he wasn't as drunk as her that night, but perhaps he was.

"Unless… you don't remember?" she asked, clasping her hands together.

"I remember," Dr. Harlan said.

144

"Oh."

"Best to just forget about it," he said at last. "I mean, I am your doctor, and as such, it'd be inappropriate to—" he broke off, waving his hand between them.

"I understand," she said as tears welled at the corners of her eyes. Determined not to dwell in embarrassment any longer, she abruptly ended their conversation. "Good night, Dr. Harlan."

She turned on her heels and could feel the doctor's gaze boring into her back as she walked back to the Rusty Fig. It wasn't until she reached the pub that she heard the familiar sound of the clinic bell chime and a door closing. On two occasions, she had been humiliated in the town, and it was two times too many. It had taken a lot to speak to him so candidly, but he offered no comfort, acceptance, or acknowledgment of her apology whatsoever. Who did he think he was? Maybe she had misjudged him.

Whatever, she thought, wiping away a solitary tear that fell down her cheek. She would get her food from Otis and go home. The other path was right. She should have said nothing at all.

Chapter 21

A heat wave swept through the valley. It was oppressive, relentless, and inescapable—the kind of heat that made ice melt before it could even chill a glass of water. One had to submit to it; otherwise, it was enough to drive them stark-raving mad.

Seren wiped a thick sheet of sweat from her forehead with a blistering bare hand, her t-shirt sticking to her underarms and back. Small red sores on her palms burned from wielding an axe too heavy for her slowly developing muscles, her work gloves discarded on top of a freshly cut tree trunk, useless and drenched in sweat. The heat wouldn't let up, but neither did work on the farm. She was cutting down a couple of dead trees. It was a blessing they had died because she needed the space, anyway. She was loading the last piece of chopped wood into the wheelbarrow when Jake arrived, sullen and sardonic as usual.

"How kind of you to show up," Seren said.

"You're lucky I even showed up at all on a day like this," he said.

Seren brushed off his comment and handed him the axe. "Don't get any ideas."

Jake's gloomy presence, albeit draining at times, had grown on her. He was still arrogant, morose, and perhaps one of the rudest people she had ever met, but he was also honest. Nothing got by him, either in jest or in truth. And she knew, whether he wanted to admit it or not, he enjoyed his time at the farm. He must have because he simply kept showing up. He would bitch and moan, but there was no task he wasn't up for or couldn't complete. More evidence that Jake liked coming to help at Hiraeth was that he was fine taking payment in the form of a home-cooked meal, an occasional spirit from the liquor cabinet, or simply having the distraction. Seren had never asked about Jake's life, or felt it was right to inquire, but she could tell escapism, not beer, was his true drug of choice.

"What's the wood for?" Jake asked.

"Stockpiling for the winter," Seren replied.

"It's July."

"Yes, Jake, I'm aware, but if I don't start now, I'll be shit out of luck come winter."

Seren rested the wheelbarrow and opened the door to the shed. The air inside was stuffy and smelled of old wood and metal. Fine plant matter particles floated through the still air, smelling like a warm forest floor. The remainder of last year's firewood sat in small piles against the left side of the shed. Seren pressed the back of her hand to her crimson cheek and took a deep breath.

"Help me with this, will you?" she asked.

Jake leaned the axe against the wall and started unloading the freshly cut logs into the shed. "So, are you going to tell me what happened with the doc?"

Seren nearly dropped the log she was unloading on her foot. "What?"

He shrugged. "I saw you guys yesterday. I was just getting off work. Looked pretty bad."

"I don't think that's any of your business."

Jake stopped and fixed his steely gray eyes on her. "Is this about you both leaving together that night from the Fig?"

"*What?*" Seren asked again, like a toddler whose first and only learned word became insufferable with constant usage.

"You guys dating or what? Trouble in paradise?" He was smiling as if he enjoyed how flustered his questions were making her.

Seren suddenly felt dizzy. Maybe it was just the heat. She grabbed the old doorframe to steady herself. "Jake, what is your problem?"

"Why are you so upset? If there's nothing there, there's nothing there. Just say that," he said, a drop of sweat falling from his dark hair.

"There's nothing there."

"Bullshit."

Seren threw the log she was carrying at Jake, which he caught, unphased by her outburst. On the contrary, he looked like he was having an amazing time teasing her. Irritation crawled on Seren's skin like fire ants, prickling and biting at her patience. "So, what, were you also at the—"

"The Fig that night? Yes, I was," he said. "It's amazing how little people pay attention to you when you're the town pariah."

Seren placed a hand on her hip and narrowed her eyes. "What are you, Lady Whistledown?"

"I don't get the reference."

"Whatever, I don't have time for this, anyway."

The painful blisters cracked open as Seren grabbed the axe from where Jake had left it and dumped it into the wheelbarrow, which she then wheeled back into the field. The midday sun shared no remorse, no shred of unburdening her situation, and beat down on her harder than Jake's questions. She was sure she was seeing double when Jake caught up with her.

"Okay, just answer me one thing," he said.

"What?"

"How's the sex?"

"There isn't any," Seren hissed through gritted teeth.

"That bad, huh?" Jake asked, laughing.

Seren dropped the wheelbarrow and spun around to face him. "Jake, *shut the hell up.*"

"Alright, alright. You are the one with the axe, after all," he said, playfully showing his hands as though she had caught him red-handed. His charge: being an asshole.

A powerful shot of pain parachuted down Seren's forehead like a lightning strike, and she sat down at the base of the next tree that needed to be chopped. Exhaustion overtook her like a warm summer wave.

"Did you take the payment for the raised beds to Rita yesterday?" she murmured, closing her eyes.

"No, I forgot."

"Will you please bring it to her? I told her I'd have it to her by today," Seren said.

"I think I can manage that."

"Good, now please go away. I need to… rest my eyes."

"Yeah, take a break. You look like hell," Jake said.

"Thanks."

Seren watched Jake walk away through half-lidded eyes. Her dry throat wanted nothing more than a cool glass of water, though the best she could likely hope for was lukewarm. The walk to the cabin seemed like a pilgrimage rather than a short trip, so she sat against the tree in what little shade its dead limbs afforded and dreamed of water instead.

Chapter 22

Dr. Harlan sat at his desk, a small fan blowing cool air on him. The clinic's central air was old and outdated but fought valiantly to stave off the summer heat. The fan was a precaution, as he didn't want to overtax the system. He hadn't had a worse night's sleep in years. He awoke covered in sticky sweat, and by the afternoon, he had already taken two showers. Still wanting to appear professional, he wore his usual tie and button-down that constricted his neck and trapped the heat under his shirt collar. He allowed himself one concession by rolling his sleeves up to his elbows. After his last patient, he finally loosened his tie.

The day passed with considerable haziness. The walk to and from Rita's nearly killed him. He had gone on his lunch break when the sun was at its most unforgiving, shining directly overhead on a wide-open path with little to no shade. He was lucky though, because Rita said there was no use repairing his studio's broken window unit. Instead, she had a few units for days such as today, unboxed and brand new, sitting in storage. He carried one back to the clinic and up the narrow stairs to his apartment, his arms shaking and brow burdened by hot perspiration.

Mira was lucky enough to have the day off. He was happy for her. She worked hard and deserved time away from the clinic. He wondered if she'd opted to spend the day at the beach to escape the heat and thought he might pay a visit after he closed for the day. It was unlikely, but it was a thought.

Dr. Harlan took a sip of coffee. It was old and considerably more bitter than when he brewed it a few hours earlier, but it did the trick. Coffee was coffee.

By five p.m., Dr. Harlan started to close the clinic. He was pleased with the day's work. Horace Fielder was in better spirits, as his nephew Zach had finally come to live with him and Edna. He still wasn't walking as much as Dr. Harlan recommended, but having a young, sports-loving enthusiast like Zach in the house helped. He was even eating more vegetables, too, but Edna was hard-pressed to find one Horace truly liked. For the time being, he committed to a few spoonfuls of Brussels sprouts or a couple of carrots, sometimes even a small salad with pumpkin seeds and grape tomatoes, but he always left half of every portion she served.

It's a start, Dr. Harlan thought.

There were plenty of other starts, as well. He had started working out again and admittedly felt better. Some of the women in town wanted to organize an aerobics or Pilates class every Tuesday and Thursday, and Dr. Harlan considered joining. He was used to using weights in his living room and the occasional jog around town, but he was open to trying something new.

There was also talk of modernizing parts of town, including more paved roads, streetlamps, and greenery, but that would most likely come at a later date. Mayor Doney had governed Adytown for years, and perhaps because of old age or just pure blind inspiration, he wanted to make their town an even "finer place to live". He just didn't have the funds yet. He had told Dr. Harlan all about his ideas when he came in each week for physical therapy for his arthritic knee. Together, they had successfully lowered his inflammation markers, and Dr. Harlan figured that was a good enough reason for inspiration as any.

The next day was Friday, Dr. Harlan's day off, and as such, he expected he'd spend his time the same as any other reprieve from work, putting together model planes while listening to classic radio. He was working on a beautiful model of the Wright Flyer. It was painstaking and tedious, but the craft appealed to his meticulous nature.

He wiped a bit of dust from the computer on the front desk and drew the half-closed window shades all the way down. The trash bin next to reception was almost full, mostly with crushed Styrofoam coffee cups and used tissues, but he decided he would empty the receptacle in the morning. He locked the clinic door and considered the possibility of the beach once more, but decided that unless he wanted to sweat through the night again, it was a better use of time to install the new air conditioning unit. He was about to head upstairs when he heard a frantic knocking on the clinic door. He unlocked it and saw Jake, out of breath and completely overtaken with concern and urgency.

"You've gotta come quickly, Dr. Harlan. It's Seren."

Chapter 23

Dr. Harlan and Jake ran down the path to Hiraeth Farm, kicking up dirt and dust behind them.

"When you left her, how was she?" Dr. Harlan asked.

"I don't know, fine?" Jake replied. "She was tired but fine, I think. She said she was going to rest her eyes, and by the time I got back, she was still sitting against the tree with her eyes closed."

"Was she responsive?"

"Not really. She wouldn't wake up." Jake struggled to keep up in his flip-flops.

Dr. Harlan knew he would have to act fast. Seren was most likely suffering from heat exhaustion or, worse, heat stroke. Both conditions were serious, but if it were the latter, he'd have to bring her back to the clinic, and who knows how she'd fare on the trip into town. His heartbeat quickened as he willed himself to move faster. He hoped time was on his side.

When he found Seren, she was slumped against a tree, her palms facing up on the ground. She was breathing slowly and steadily, but she looked awful. Her skin was clammy and covered in sweat. It wasn't just her cheeks that were bright red, but her entire face and neck, as well. Dr. Harlan felt for her pulse and found that it was erratic and weak.

"Seren? Seren, can you hear me?" he asked, gently squeezing her shoulder.

Seren moaned, but that was it.

Dr. Harlan scooped her up into his arms and brought her toward the cabin. "Jake, the door."

Inside, the cabin was almost as warm as it was outside. Dr. Harlan looked around and saw no air conditioning, only a small, corded fan on the kitchen table. "Grab that fan. And, Jake, in the closet by the bathroom, get a fresh hand cloth or towel and wet it. If there's ice in the freezer, bring it to me."

His plan was to bring her to her bedroom and treat her there, but before he moved ahead, he eyed the ceramic tub and changed course. He used her dangling feet to push the shower curtain to the side and lowered her into the tub. The ceramic was cool to the touch, the perfect haven for her burning body. He wanted to protect her privacy, so he brushed her shoulder, relieved to feel the unmistakable toughness of a bra strap. Supporting her head, he lifted her drenched shirt up and over her head and laid her bare back against the tub. He also removed her shoes. He didn't want to risk her potential injury by taking off her shorts, so he left them on. As he turned on the cold tap, Jake entered the bathroom with an ice tray, the fan, and a damp washcloth.

"Put the ice in the tub and give me the towel," Dr. Harlan ordered.

He pressed it to Seren's forehead as Jake twisted the ice tray with a loud *crack* and dumped the cubes into the filling bathtub. Dr. Harlan said Seren's name again, and this time, her eyelids fluttered half open. She was becoming more responsive, but slowly.

He reached into his pants pocket and pulled out a packet labeled *Electrolyte Replacer: Fruit Punch Flavor*. "Take this and stir it into a large glass of water. Bring it back here as quickly as you can."

154

"Got it," Jake said. He placed the fan on the bathroom floor and disappeared into the kitchen.

Dr. Harlan left the cold compress on Seren's forehead and plugged the fan into the wall. He placed it on the toilet lid and angled the airstream toward her. The tub had filled enough to cover her legs and lower back, and not wanting to shock her system completely, he turned off the water; the ice would do the rest. He felt her pulse again, and it was still faster than it should be, but was falling to safer levels. Dr. Harlan felt a strange sensation at the corners of his eyes. When he raised his hand to touch one, his fingertips came back wet.

"Dr. Harlan…"

His name on her lips sounded sweet and soft. She was awake. He quickly wiped his eyes and looked at Seren. Her coloring was changing, and her skin felt less warm to the touch, but she was still not quite out of danger.

"Seren," he said.

She tried to move.

"No, hey, take it easy for a little while longer," he said.

Jake came back with a full cup of red liquid and handed it to him. When he saw Seren was awake, he laced his hands on the back of his neck and rocked on the balls of his feet.

"Drink some of this if you can. I'll help you," Dr. Harlan said.

He placed the rim of the glass to Seren's lips and tilted it. She took a few short sips and gave up. The drink stained her lips. Her eyes were almost completely open.

"How are you feeling?" Dr. Harlan asked.

"Never better," she replied.

He couldn't help himself and broke into a fit of laughter. Her humor was still intact, which further indicated she was getting better. He helped her drink a little more of the red concoction and set it down on the floor.

"What happened?" she asked, still regaining strength in her voice.

"You had heat exhaustion," Dr. Harlan replied.

"Oh."

"Listen, I know there's a lot of work to do out here, but you've got to take it a little easier, at least while it's hot since you probably aren't used to it. I need you to be kind to yourself, okay?"

Seren's eyes fluttered shut again, and Dr. Harlan realized she may not be fully capable of listening in her condition, but he needed her to hear him. He was worried about her all alone out here on the farm. There were all sorts of injuries and accidents that could happen, and there would be no one around to get help. It was a miracle Jake had come upon her when he did. He knew Jake helped out from time to time, but there was no guarantee he'd always be there to be sure she was okay. If she didn't think to come to the clinic for her hand back in March or when she started to feel ill today, who knew what else she might ignore? He noticed she was considerably thinner than when she first arrived. There was no easy way to bring up a patient's weight, but one day, when she felt better, and they were on cordial speaking terms again, it would have to be addressed.

"You need to get some rest. Doctor's orders," he said.

Seren smiled at that.

"Do you feel okay enough to walk to your bed?"

"Maybe," she said.

He wrapped his hands around Seren's arms and helped her stand. The compress fell from her forehead and landed in the icy water with a heavy, wet splat. After helping her out of the tub, he wrapped a hand around her waist to support her. Jake averted his gaze and left the room, his face red.

"You can lean on me," Dr. Harlan said.

Seren surrendered her weight against him and gripped his forearm as she attempted to steady herself. Like a new fawn taking its first steps, she was wobbly at first but gradually became surer in her footing. Dr. Harlan wrapped a towel around her and led her to the bedroom. She was much easier to get into bed than the last time he was there, and at least this time, she would remember he had been there. She lay her damp hair against the pillow and wrapped the towel around her.

"I'll be right back."

Dr. Harlan grabbed the fan from the bathroom, set it up in the bedroom for her, and opened the window. The late afternoon sun was setting, and the air outside was now a little cooler and fresher. The stuffy room could use some circulation, and because she didn't have air conditioning, that would have to do. Before leaving for the night, he ducked back into the bathroom one last time and wrung out the compress, picked up the glass of electrolyte replacer, and brought them both to Seren.

"Do you feel any nausea or stomach cramps?" he asked, pressing the compress to her forehead.

"No," Seren said, settling more into the bed.

"Good. You should eat something before you go to sleep for the night. Your body needs to recuperate, so please, take it easy over the next few days."

"Mm-hmm."

Seren stilled, and Dr. Harlan figured she had fallen asleep. He left the clinic business card, which also listed his personal number, on the bedside table next to the red drink and hoped that if she needed anything, she would call or come to the clinic.

He exited the cabin and found Jake sitting on the porch steps, drinking a can of beer. Jake glanced at him and rolled his eyes at the expression on the doctor's face.

"I needed a drink after that," said Jake. "Do you want one?"

"No, thank you," Dr. Harlan said.

"I am trying, you know."

"I know, Jake."

The day Jake embarrassed Seren at the Aster Dance wasn't the only time he had seen Jake screw up. Dr. Harlan couldn't begin to count the number of times Jake had stumbled dead drunk out of the Fig at any time of day or how often he'd come to the clinic to ask for Tylenol, Advil, Excedrin, generic acetaminophen, or anything Dr. Harlan was willing to give him. It wasn't until he came and asked for prescription opioids that he stopped giving Jake anything altogether, and Jake hadn't forgiven him since. Dr. Harlan was no stranger to pain, but he would not help numb Jake's under the cold, gloved hand of prescription drugs. They had discussed therapy, changing jobs, exercising more, or anything to help him confront himself head-on, but Jake never listened. Whatever demons he had, he could not face them sober. That day, Dr. Harlan saw Jake in a different light. He was glad he was there. Without him, Seren could have died.

"Will you stay and make sure she's okay?" Dr. Harlan asked.

Jake looked up at him. "Shouldn't you do that?"

"I've got to get back," he lied, flexing his hands. "Just check in on her in a bit, and if you can get her up to eat something, she should be completely in the clear."

"Fine."

"Thank you, Jake. I left the number to the clinic on her bedside table if she needs anything."

Dr. Harlan started walking toward town but stopped when Jake spoke.

"Listen, I know it's none of my business, but I know there's something going on between you two."

"There isn't, Jake."

"Yeah? How'd you know where the towels were?"

"Jake, there isn't anything—"

"Yeah, yeah, save your breath. She said just the same, but all I know is someone isn't being honest." Jake took another sip of his beer.

"Please tell her to take it easy for a few days. Goodnight, Jake," Dr. Harlan said.

Jake didn't acknowledge his statement, but Dr. Harlan knew he had heard him. For some reason, he trusted Jake would tell her, just like he trusted she was going to be alright. For what felt like the first time in hours, Dr. Harlan took a deep, soul-restoring breath and slid his undone tie from his neck. A much-needed breeze picked up and tousled his hair. He took off his glasses and cleaned them on his shirt. The sun cast beautiful shades of orange, red, and purple on the horizon. Far-off waves crashed on the beach, looking like little more than an impressionistic painting in the distance.

She said there's nothing going on. That confirms it, then.

He took out his phone and made a call. "Rita? Hey, sorry to call after hours. Do you have another air conditioner? I was hoping you could do me a favor."

Chapter 24

The next day, Seren felt restored. Her arms and legs ached, but nothing like the first time she cleared the field in March. Time and repetition were not only transforming Hiraeth, but her body, as well. She even had some muscle on her arms, which shocked her every time the light fell on them just right. Other things were changing too. She slept better than she ever had before. She no longer stayed up until at least two and lingered in bed until ten or eleven in the morning. These days, she was in bed by ten and rose with the sun unless she and Jenna stayed up to talk and drink a few glasses of wine. She had a rhythm, a way of life in Adytown that felt right.

Seren sat on the porch with a bowl of cereal and a cup of Earl Grey tea. A few small birds flew across the sky and came to rest on sturdy tree branches in the distance. The early morning mist hadn't cleared yet, and all was still. She didn't know how she could have gone so long without experiencing the elysian beauty of sunrise. It felt like a different world, one where her thoughts became clearer and her heart rate slower. She realized how clean and fresh the air could feel as it filled up her lungs.

Yesterday had scared her. It was clear she had bitten off more than she could chew. Her body was not yet used to her work or the heat. She had never experienced heat exhaustion before, and she hoped she never would again.

Dr. Harlan had saved her. How does one thank another for such a thing? She didn't know, but she would do as he instructed. A few dead trees still needed to be cut down, but they could wait.

Instead, she painted images of her potential plans for the landscape in her mind's eye. It was mid-July, which meant there was limited time to plant much else. Most crops she researched required planting in June at the very latest. She wanted to try her hand at pumpkins but couldn't put the seeds in the soil until August. There was always corn, but she had read an endless list of factors that could go wrong with pests and parasites. Seren had also read that she should always grow what she likes to eat, though she could confidently say that her grandfather never followed that advice. He provided produce for the entire community, regardless of preference, but she was not her grandfather.

The original batch of tomatoes looked unappealing and a little orange, no doubt from the recent heat wave. The newest round was just beginning to sprout. She had intended on staggering them so the harvesting wouldn't happen all at once, but her scheduling was off.

I fumbled that one, she thought.

With one crop of tomatoes fully grown but of poor quality and the second weeks away from completion, she figured it was the worst staggering attempt in the history of farming.

Really more of a gardener, she thought. Farms were large-scale operations, and her two raised beds were a far cry from industrial.

Every crop needed different amounts of sunlight, moisture, fertilizer, nitrogen, carbon, phosphorus, and potassium. They also required varying depths in the soil, spacing, pest care, and much more. It could easily take a lifetime to become a master, and Seren didn't have a lifetime. Eventually, her savings would dry up, and then what would she have? A few plant beds with mediocre crops.

161

Perhaps the answer was focused mastery. Maybe if she perfected how to grow one crop, that would be enough. If she wasn't making money by the same time the following year, she would probably have to join Jake at Wares & More or persuade Otis he needed a second waitress, neither of which she really wanted to do.

She finished her Earl Grey tea and went to the shed to grab a pair of scissors. Then, she cut away excess stems and leaves at the base of the March tomato stalks and the very tops of the leaf-heavy plants.

"Too much nitrogen," she said.

When she finished, she scattered the leaves and stems throughout the raised beds and plucked a ripe tomato. She sprayed some water on it and took a bite.

Not bad, she thought. It seemed that replanting had made a difference in taste. She ducked inside, sprinkled some sea salt over the soft red fruit, and took another bite.

"Not bad at all."

Chapter 25

Seren was just finishing watering the peach tree when Rita's truck pulled up to the cabin. As far as Seren remembered, she hadn't scheduled any additional work with her, so the reason for her arrival was a mystery. Seren grabbed a brown basket with a dozen freshly picked peaches and went to meet her.

"Hey there, neighbor," Rita said as she jumped out of the truck.

"Good afternoon, Rita. What's up?" Seren asked.

"I've got something for ya. If you'll just open the door, I'll bring it inside."

"Oh, okay. Just a sec." Seren removed her garden gloves and tossed them on the rocking chair, then opened the front door, wondering, *what could it be?* She placed the basket on the kitchen counter and looked around the room to see if she needed to move anything out of the way or tidy up, but she realized she hadn't any idea what Rita's strange gift was, so she stood and waited to find out.

Rita carried a large white box up the cabin stairs with considerable effort. Whatever it was, it looked heavy.

"Do you need help with that?" Seren asked.

"No, no, all good," Rita huffed between labored breaths. "Where should I set this?"

"Oh, um…" Seren swept a few scraps of paper and dishes from the kitchen table. "Here."

Rita put the box down, and when she stepped away, Seren saw it was an air conditioner.

"*Whew!* Man, those things have gotten heavier," Rita said, catching her breath. "I uh…I remembered last time I was here, I noticed you didn't have one, and I had an extra in storage, so with all this heat lately, I figured you could use it."

"Oh wow, Rita, thank you!" Seren said. "This really is thoughtful. It has been pretty rough out here."

"I can imagine. I can imagine." Rita adjusted the tongue on her black sneakers.

"What do I owe you?"

"Oh, never you mind about that. Let's just say it's a gift."

Seren had learned well enough by then that insisting on providing payment after something was offered for free in Adytown was a lost cause, so she accepted the unit with grace. "Well, I can't thank you enough."

"No problem. Where do you want it?"

"Oh, um… that window should be fine." Seren pointed to a back window next to the wood-burning stove.

"Okay, I'll get it all set up and get out of your hair."

"Can I get you anything? Some water, or—"

"I'd love a few of those peaches if you're offering."

"Of course! I'll rinse a few of them for you." Seren picked up three of the beautiful pink fruits and ran them under the tap. She ripped off a sheet of paper towel and wrapped them up before leaving them on the kitchen table.

"Perfect, thanks," Rita said as she continued to work. "And don't worry about me; do whatever you gotta do."

"I was just about to head into town, but please, help yourself to anything."

"Great, I'll have it set up and cooling the place down before you get back."

Seren thanked Rita again and went into the bathroom. She looked well enough, not nearly as sweaty as the day before, but she grabbed some loose powder and patted her face a few times. Then she applied a couple of fresh swipes of mascara and tinted lip balm. It was too hot to wear her hair down as she would have liked, so she fixed her messy bun and pulled out a few loose strands to complete the look.

Chapter 26

Seren opened the clinic door, the basket of peaches hanging on her arm.

Mira sat behind reception, reading a bright blue book. "Good afternoon, Miss Grinaker. How can I help you?"

"Hi, Mira. How have you been?"

"Good, good. The summer months are the slow season, so I've got to do what I can to stay busy."

"Is Dr. Harlan in?"

"Yes. I can take you back. He's in his office." Mira stood and closed her book.

"That'd be great."

Mira flashed a friendly smile and led Seren through the hallway door. They hung a left, and Mira knocked on a door with *Dr. Harlan Beck* engraved on a small silver plate.

"Dr. Harlan? Seren Grinaker is here to see you."

She couldn't hear his voice from where Seren was standing, but shortly after, Mira opened the door for her to enter.

"Miss Grinaker," he said. "It's good to see you. Thank you, Mira."

"Can I get you a coffee or water?" Mira asked.

"I'm okay, thank you," Seren said.

Mira nodded and closed the office door behind her.

"Please," Dr. Harlan said, gesturing to two chairs in front of his desk. He swiped a hand through his hair and straightened his tie. When she sat, he leaned forward on the desk and crossed his arms. "How are you feeling?"

"Much better, thanks to you," Seren said. "I, um, brought these for you." Seren placed the basket of peaches on his desk.

"Oh, wow. I can't remember the last time I had one of Harold's famous peaches." Dr. Harlan eyed the fuzzy pink and orange fruit.

Seren settled into her chair, happy to have made Dr. Harlan happy. "I wanted to thank you for yesterday. I can't even count the number of times I've embarrassed myself in front of you over the past few months, but I'm almost certain I'm here now because of you."

"Is that what you think? That you've embarrassed yourself?"

"I know I have." She stole a quick glance at his mouth.

Dr. Harlan frowned as he leaned back in his chair.

Seren could've sworn his cheeks colored a little. *It must be the heat*, she thought.

"Let's see…" he said. "I remember that at the Aster Dance, it was Jake who threw up on you in front of the entire town when you were brave enough to put yourself out there despite knowing almost no one at all. Yesterday, you just worked yourself too hard, but it's because you care about Hiraeth, and you're doing everything you can to run it. That's all. It's nothing to be embarrassed about. And that other time… I'm the one who should be embarrassed. You stuck your neck out, but I was cold to you. I've wanted to apologize ever since, but I just didn't know how to." He seemed to collect himself and attempt to assume an air of professionalism as if he felt he had become too personal with her. "So, I'm sorry for how I acted. I just want to help you feel safe and cared for… as your doctor."

"I do."

"Good."

The energy in the room settled as if the walls had taken a deep breath and released the uncomfortable weight of their conflict.

"So… you go by Dr. Harlan and not Dr. Beck?" Seren asked.

"I figured using my first name would be more familiar and approachable in a town like this."

"Makes sense."

"How is everything on the farm?"

"Great. I'm doing as you said and taking some time to recover, though it's not nearly as hot today, thankfully. Rita was kind enough to bring by a new air conditioner. I still can't get over how generous people here have been to me."

"Good, I'm glad," Dr. Harlan said. "I just got a new unit too, but I haven't had the chance to set it up yet. It was so hot in my apartment last night I almost decided to sleep in one of the hospital beds."

"Would… would you like some help with it?" Seren asked.

Dr. Harlan looked taken aback. "You'd help me install my air conditioner?"

"Yeah, I mean, you most likely saved my life, so it seems like the least I could do."

"Well, the window does have a hard time staying open on its own…"

"Great! Then it's decided." She sensed that he felt unsure about accepting her help, but she wouldn't let him say no. Seren had a sneaking suspicion that he didn't like to ask for or accept help, and she understood why. It had never been easy for her to do the same. But, for all the kindness he had shown her over the past few months, she hoped helping him would be some small drop in the bucket to show how much she appreciated him.

"Should we go now?" he asked.

"Sure. I don't have any more chores to do. I'm taking it easy, remember?" she said. *Am I flirting with him? Maybe in some understated Serenian way.*

"Okay, let me just tell Mira I'll be heading out, and we can go," he said.

Seren stood and picked up the basket of peaches. Dr. Harlan didn't tell her to follow him into the hallway, but she did and leaned against the clinic hallway while he ducked in to speak with Mira. Seren felt a mounting excitement in her stomach. Whether it was just nerves or anticipation of being alone with the doctor outside of the sterile patient room, free from an alcohol or heat-induced stupor, she was happy to spend time with him.

"Okay, all set," Dr. Harlan said. "And you're sure you'd like to help?"

"Lead the way," Seren said.

Dr. Harlan opened a door at the end of the hallway and led Seren up a steep flight of cramped stairs. It was an easy climb for her, but she couldn't imagine it was all that comfortable for him, as his head was only an inch or two away from grazing the plaster ceiling. "I wasn't expecting visitors, so please don't mind any mess," he said as he unlocked his apartment door.

Dr. Harlan's apartment was tidy and efficient. Nothing seemed out of place, save for a few white envelopes on a small kitchen table and a few colored ties strewn over his closet door. Dr. Harlan's bed was in a corner. It was strange to see it, but there it was, small and made up for the day. Along the back wall was a display shelf full of model airplanes that were too intricate and unique to be factory-made. Seren walked toward them as Dr. Harlan hung up his dress jacket.

"Did you make these?" she asked.

"Oh, uh, yeah. It's a little hobby of mine," Dr. Harlan replied.

"They're beautiful."

"Thanks," he said with a faint smile.

"So, what can I do to help?"

"Yes, um, I was thinking this window over here." Dr. Harlan pointed to one of the two windows along the back wall. "I'll take care

169

of the insulation stuff and the heavy lifting. You can just keep the window open for me and pray I don't accidentally drop it outside."

"I think I can manage that," she said, setting the peach basket and her purse down on the kitchen table.

Dr. Harlan rolled up his sleeves and pushed his glasses up the bridge of his nose. His strong hands opened the box in one quick motion. When he kneeled on the ground to take out the unit, his tie kept getting in the way, so he undid it and threw it on the table. Once the box was emptied, he fetched a screwdriver from a kitchen drawer and started reading through the instructions. Seren watched as Dr. Harlan worked. "So, do you have a favorite airplane?" she asked.

Dr. Harlan looked as though no one had ever asked him this question before. "Hmm, I don't think you can beat a classic Douglas DC-3, or a Vickers Vimy. The B52 has a unique fuselage, but probably the Boeing 787. It's always a smooth ride. I would have loved to have flown one of those."

"If I start making model airplanes, too, will I no longer be afraid of flying?" she asked.

Her comment was in jest, but Dr. Harlan answered without hesitation. "Could be. I find it helps to know how things are put together. You're afraid of flying?"

"Terrified of it. I guess I have a hard time not being in control."

Dr. Harlan finished with the insulation materials and picked up the air conditioner.

He's strong, she thought as she watched his biceps and forearms swell under the weight. He got the unit through the window and settled into place, grunting as he held it steady and pausing for a moment to exhale and wipe a few droplets of sweat from his forehead.

Seren lost her grip on the window and couldn't catch it in time before it came down hard on Dr. Harlan's hand. She grabbed at the white wooden frame and hoisted it roughly up with one hand and grabbed Dr. Harlan's smashed hand with the other.

"I'm *so* sorry, are you okay?" she asked, mortified.

"It's quite all right, no harm done." Dr. Harlan laughed through the struggle of holding the unit in place.

Seren let go of him and placed both hands firmly on the window. *You had one job,* she thought.

Dr. Harlan extended the accordion-like slats and twisted a few screws to secure everything in place. He stepped back and wiped his forearm over his brow. "I'm just going to check outside to make sure it all looks good."

He walked to the second window along the backside of his apartment, hoisted it open, and stepped out onto the slanted gray roof, supporting the window as it slid closed behind him.

Seren stood for a moment, fiddling with her thumbs, before also opening the window to check on him. "How's it look?"

"It looks even. I have a leveler in my tool kit under the sink. Would you please grab it for me?"

Seren let the window fall back into place and got the leveler. It was easy to spot, as it was bright lemon-yellow. Warm afternoon air wafted over her as she stepped out onto the roof and handed it to him. "It's nice out here. Do you ever just come out here to sit sometimes?"

"I hadn't even thought of it," he said, checking the last bits of their installation job. "Well, I think we make a great team. Everything came out perfectly."

As Dr. Harlan gazed down at Seren, she sensed that their time together was likely almost over, but she wasn't ready to say goodbye.

"I have an idea," she said. "Stay where you are." She took the leveler and retreated inside, the window shutting with a dull thwack after her. Moments later, she returned with a pair of freshly washed peaches and a throw blanket from the back of his couch.

"Oh, careful," Dr. Harlan said as her foot grazed the window ledge as she stepped back onto the rough roof.

"We don't have to use this if you'd rather not," she said, waggling the blanket.

"Please." Dr. Harlan waved her over. He took the blanket from her and laid it on the roof.

The pair settled in, and Seren handed him one of the peaches. "Cheers," she said.

"What are we toasting?" he asked.

171

"New beginnings and new friends."

"And modern cooling systems."

"That too," she said, smiling at him.

They tapped their peaches together and took a bite. A familiar sweet, juicy, tangy, beautiful flavor filled her mouth, which Seren remembered and cherished from so many years ago. Time may have changed her, Hiraeth, Adytown, and all things, but time could not touch her grandfather's peaches. They were too perfect. A small trickle of juice ran down her chin, and she gathered the sticky, sweet liquid on her finger to spoon back into her mouth.

"Wow. These are just…"

"Incredible." Seren finished his sentence.

"Any idea how he got these to taste so good?"

"Unfortunately, no. But I tend to the tree and hope I don't screw it up. It's a good benchmark for what I'd like to achieve one day."

"You're on your way."

"I hope so."

It was pleasant outside, much more so since the sun was no longer directly overhead, and a large oak tree behind the clinic provided a generous amount of shade. It stood tall and mighty, sheltering them from the sun's gaze. A small hill leading to Rita's home obscured most of the view, and the oak tree obscured the rest. Unless there were some reason to look up, no one would know anyone was there. It was like an exclusive club or some secret hangout. It only existed for Seren and Dr. Harlan.

"I really am sorry about your hand," Seren said.

"I may never recover," Dr. Harlan teased.

She lightheartedly nudged his arm, and he laughed, taking another bite of the peach. She smiled at him, and he met her gaze, perplexed.

"What?" he asked.

"Nothing, you just have a bit of, uh…" she motioned toward the corner of his mouth.

He wiped his face and turned toward her.

"You got it."

"Thank you."

"This one time, I was on a date, and he didn't bother to tell me I had a piece of spinach stuck in my teeth. I only found out when I went to the bathroom."

"That's just wrong."

"Right? I was smiling all night and everything."

"I promise I will always tell you if you have spinach in your teeth."

"A doctor who will not only save your life and hose you down after being puked on *but also* be on spinach duty? They're not paying you enough."

"I guess I'll have to negotiate a raise. I can't have my talents undervalued, especially with such critical duties."

Seren smirked, a playful glint in her eyes. "Especially spinach duty."

"Especially spinach duty," Dr. Harlan agreed, laughing. "Sounds like he was a coward. Probably for the best it didn't work out."

"Who says it didn't work out?" she asked.

He ran a hand through his hair. "Oh, um, I'm—"

"I'm kidding." She smiled. "And he was."

They settled into a comfortable silence as the sun slowly set.

"So, tell me about you," Seren said, then took another bite of the juicy peach.

"What would you like to know?" he asked.

"Anything."

"Anything… Well, my favorite color is green. Um, I think I could live the rest of my days just eating Otis's cooking and die a happy man. I probably drink way too much coffee. I love pickled red onions—I know, it's random. I love to read. Also, I just realized almost everything I've mentioned has something to do with food or drink." He laughed.

Seren angled herself toward him. "What made you want to become a doctor?"

"Well, I didn't always want to become a doctor. I think I told you I wanted to be a pilot, but as I'm sure you can tell," Dr. Harlan fiddled with his glasses, "I have bad eyesight. I can see things close up, but anything farther than a few feet gets a bit blurry. So, I make planes now instead of flying them. As for becoming a doctor, I know it's cliché, but I enjoy helping people. I also have steady hands, so that helps."

"Let me see," Seren said.

She held her hand level, and Dr. Harlan did the same. Her index and ring fingers twitched, but Dr. Harlan's were completely motionless. He was right: they were steady.

"I'm glad the medical world has you. Based on my hands, I'd make a terrible doctor," she joked.

"You think so?" he asked.

"Oh, definitely. I also wouldn't be able to handle the pressure. I'd probably psyche myself out. Plus, I'm sure there's a fair amount of stress, like patients who don't make it or bad news you have to share with families, and I don't think I could do it." Seren took the last bite of her peach.

Dr. Harlan nodded.

"It's hard enough to lose people as it is," Seren said. "Or to have not been with them when they left."

Seren looked out past the oak and the hill toward the setting sun. Guilt suddenly gripped her heart, and the familiar melancholy threatened to overtake the moment. *Is there a point to grief?* Perhaps it was to share it with others, or to remind us of the depth at which we have loved. Maybe it was there to be used to create or inspire. There had to be someplace to put it. Otherwise, it was bottomless and could easily swallow one whole.

"This may be difficult to hear…" Dr. Harlan paused, "I don't want to upset you, but I think it could help."

Seren nodded for him to continue.

"I was with Harold when he passed."

Seren's eyes grew wide with shock as though someone had dumped a bucket of ice water over her head. "You were?" she asked.

"Yes."

"How was he… What did he…"

"He went very easily. I think he was ready to go. You should know, he loved you very much, Seren. Harold talked a lot about how he just wanted the best for you, and that you were so smart and talented but were having a tough time finding your footing. He knew you'd figure it out one day and was just sorry he wouldn't be around to see it. He wanted you to know that everything is going to be all right, and when times are tough, to always remember to be true to yourself."

Remember who you are.

"Was I right to tell you?" he asked.

"Yes. Yes, I think so," she said.

It seemed there was nothing more to be said, or if there was, it was too early to tell. Sometimes, silence is the best way to speak. Inside, Seren was a flurry of stinging questions, and she didn't have any way to answer them, but when she looked up at Dr. Harlan, she felt that was okay.

"I'm glad you didn't become a pilot," Seren said at last. "If you had, you wouldn't have been with my grandfather, and we wouldn't be here now."

Chapter 27

A stiff chill woke Seren on a bitter October morning. The first frost that year came earlier than usual. The pumpkin-covered calendar on the wall read *October 12*[th].

She rose quietly and quickly, as she had on hundreds of days before, eager to see what Mother Nature had done.

Thousands of miniature icicles covered the landscape in a vast, wintry blanket, exacting and cold. The brilliant contrast of the red tomatoes and the white, frozen dew reminded Seren of the lyrics from *White Winter Hymnal* by Fleet Foxes.

She'd read the tomatoes could withstand the frost, but not for long. They weren't quite ready for harvesting but would be soon. She had wanted to wait another five days, but if she needed to pick them from the vine a few days earlier, she would. It was a miracle they had grown at all, considering how late she planted them.

Five days later, a few tomatoes had succumbed to the frost, but there were some that came out bright, juicy, and plump. She was no expert, but they seemed healthier and richer than the first batch she planted in March. She picked what she could salvage and cut her losses. The early frost signaled the end of the growing season, and Seren felt a mixed sense of relief and disappointment. She enjoyed growing and wanted to keep going. The early change in the weather could only mean one thing: a cold and unrelenting winter was in store.

The frost also dashed any hopes of replanting the tomatoes. Come the new year, she would have to begin again, but Seren was used to beginning again.

Inside, the splendid heat of the wood-burning stove filled the cabin like a warm hug as Seren bent over the kitchen sink, rinsing the tomatoes. There was only one person she wanted to share what she had grown with, and he made the most delicious spaghetti and meatballs she'd ever eaten.

Gathering as many as she could, she set off into town with a sack of brilliant red tomatoes slung over her shoulder. She hummed happily to herself, knowing that for all the year's frustrations, she had many successes as well.

Seren threw open the Fig's door with an enthusiasm she hadn't felt in years. Her demeanor even caught Otis off guard, who stopped wiping the bar to glance up at the ruckus.

"Well, hello there, Seren. Good to see you," he said.

She plopped the sack of home-grown tomatoes on the counter triumphantly and sat. "I have something for you."

Chapter 28

Seren was getting dressed in a mauve pair of flair jeans, a fitted romantic-style top with off-the-shoulder sleeves, and high-heeled boots that had gathered considerable dust since they were last worn. Jenna had insisted that she dress up. It had been months since Seren had styled her hair or worn anything other than dirt-stained jeans and T-shirts.

"Come on, we're going to be late!" Jenna yelled out.

Sighing, Seren finished the look with her usual small, gold shoulder bag and stepped out of the cabin to join Jenna, who was pacing on the porch, checking her phone every few seconds.

"Okay, let's go, *let's go,*" Jenna insisted.

"What's the big hurry?" Seren asked.

"I don't want to miss happy hour."

"I didn't even know they had a happy hour," Seren said, struggling to keep up with Jenna down the dirt path into town.

"Yeah, it's… a new thing."

The days had been getting noticeably darker the past few days. As Seren and Jenna walked the path into town, dusk was falling fast, and with it, a proper chilly autumn evening. The air smelled of fallen leaves and a sharp crispness that was distinctly October. Seren realized she had forgotten a jacket, but at least the warmth of the wood-burning stove would welcome her home later.

"How are your art projects going?" Seren asked.

"Oh, uh, good, I guess," Jenna said.

"Are you still working on dalliance?"

"No, I gave that one up. I don't know, I keep waiting for inspiration to hit me, but it just feels so mechanical."

"What, painting?"

"No, creating."

Seren had known Jenna for just shy of seven and a half months, and she always displayed unsinkable confidence, but when she spoke of her art, that confidence sprang a leak. Jenna's countenance seemed to shield her from most of life's potential unpleasantness as if nothing could break her, but Seren wondered why, in all that time, she had never shown Seren a single piece she made. Seren knew how excruciating sharing one's creations could be. It was like turning one's insides out and serving their guts on a platter for all the world to see. If someone didn't like the creation, it wasn't just a rejection of what the person made, but a rejection of *the person*.

"I'd love to see your work someday, whenever you're comfortable," Seren said.

"Yeah, one day," Jenna said.

Jenna seemed to be in more of a hurry to get into town than usual, and Seren was out of breath by the time they reached the Fig.

"After you," Jenna said, standing aside.

When Seren opened the door, the room was dark. She was confused and wondered if Otis had taken the day off. But why was the door unlocked? "Oh, Jenna, I think they're closed."

Seren was about to turn to leave when she spotted a faint flickering pushing through the swinging doors. It was a singular

179

candle lighting a familiar yellow blouson jacket. The lights turned on, and Otis was holding a small white cake with a red candle.

"Happy birthday!" both Jenna and Otis cried in unison.

Seren covered her mouth in surprise and felt as though she could cry. "You guys! Thank you so much," she said.

"Come, sit. There's plenty more where that came from," Otis said, placing the cake and three wine glasses on the bar. Seren sat at the center of the bar while Jenna played some music on the jukebox.

"How did you know it was my birthday?" Seren asked. She hadn't told anyone and had made zero plans to celebrate outside of sitting solitarily at home in front of the fire with a glass of red wine.

"I remembered Harold mentioning it a few years ago. Steel trap memory this," Otis said, tapping his forehead.

Seren laughed. Jenna came around the bar and sat next to her. Together, the three of them raised their glasses.

"To Seren, one of the best additions to the valley and a real go-getter," Otis said.

"And one of the best friends you could ask for," Jenna added.

Seren felt as close to complete in that moment as she imagined was possible. She felt loved, supported, and lucky to have both Jenna and Otis in her life. Words did not do them justice, so she raised her glass, brimming with happiness, and clinked glasses with her friends.

"Oh, and don't forget the cake." Otis pushed it toward Seren.

"Make a wish!" Jenna said.

Her mind was blank. *I don't know what to wish for,* she thought. A new shirt, maybe. Seren blew out the candles and watched the plumes of smoke twist and rise up to the rafters.

"I'll cut this up for us in the back, but first, I have one other surprise," Otis said. He took another sip of the wine before picking up the cake and walking to the kitchen.

"So, happy hour isn't actually a thing?" Seren asked.

"No, I just said that so you wouldn't suspect," Jenna said, playfully nudging Seren's arm.

"Did Otis tell everyone not to come at this time or something?"

"Oh, no, he just knew that you probably wanted to keep things lowkey, so he told me to bring you in just before the regulars start coming at six. He wanted you to feel comfortable."

The kitchen doors swung open, and Otis returned with a heaping helping of spaghetti. He carried the plate to the bar. There was something different about the dish. Otis always put attentive care into all his food, but this was garnished with a whole sprig of basil, and he wiped the faintest stripe of red from the plate with a clean towel as he set it in front of Seren. "Bon appétit," he said.

Otis draped the towel over his shoulder and leaned against the back wall with his arms crossed. Seren sensed him watching her but brushed his odd behavior aside. Jenna sat beside Seren, sipping on the pinot.

"Oh, *wow*, Otis, this is excellent."

"You like it?" he asked.

Seren had to speak with her mouth full because she could hardly wait to take a second bite. "Yes! Is this a new recipe?"

"They're your tomatoes, Seren," Otis said.

"They're my…"

Otis nodded.

She stared blank-eyed at him for a moment, then, without warning, she raised her hands in the air and yelled as though she'd just won the lottery. She shot up off her stool and clapped excitedly. She grabbed Jenna's hand to join her, exclaiming, "They're my tomatoes, they're my tomatoes!"

Otis laughed and clapped, too, as they celebrated.

"I can't believe it!" Seren said, placing her hands on either side of Jenna's face. "Are you sure? You didn't mix them up somehow?"

"I'm positive," Otis said.

"Whew, sorry about that," Seren said, suddenly conscious of her outburst.

"Don't apologize. You should bring that Seren out more often," Jenna said, then tried a bite of the spaghetti. "Wow, this *is* good."

"I can't believe it, Otis," Seren said, her cheeks sore from smiling.

"You did it, kiddo," he said.

181

Chapter 29

Seren read the last sentence of *The Alchemist* and closed the book with weighted reluctance. It was perfect, and she was so glad she picked it up that spring day in March. She wiped her hand across the cover and felt a fondness that only a loved book could provide. Sometimes, there were worlds too difficult to let go of.

She sat on a bench overlooking the ocean, the sound of lazy waves crashing in the distance. It was getting colder as the days flew on, but Seren preferred it that way. The autumn and winter months were for inward reflection, and Seren felt that familiar sense of introversion returning. The never-ending dance between the light and dark halves of the year reminded Seren that some things are constant and eternal, like time and change.

Since her birthday—and the beautiful-tasting second batch of tomatoes—Seren had prepared the farm for the colder months. Jake stopped by from time to time to help, but he came less and less as the days grew shorter. The work was straightforward. Because Seren had raised beds, she could save the home-mixed soil for next year. All she had to do was lay down a thick layer of leaves and some hay on top of the soil to protect the nutrients she had cultivated for the next growing season. Beyond that, there was little else to do.

Jenna came by most nights for drinks and conversation. Jenna talked about Everett often. It was clear to Seren she had been interested in Everett for a long time but had never directly pursued him. Jenna told her he was always flirtatious, but it never amounted to anything. If Everett wanted to be in a relationship with her, he didn't show it, but they had their little moments throughout the years. Seren had suggested he was focused on writing his book, but Jenna countered that she had long ago stopped making excuses for men.

She couldn't argue with that.

Seren also hadn't seen much of Dr. Harlan. Mira had said the autumn and winter months were the busiest time of year, so she imagined he must be preoccupied with an influx of patients.

Maybe I should go see him and see how he's doing, Seren thought. It was the kind of promising idea she might act on, but a sudden cold breeze knocked the thought out. She needed to return the book.

The walk to the library was short. When Seren opened the door, Everett was sitting at the checkout counter, furiously transcribing on an old Royal typewriter. The end of a line reached, the typewriter stopped with a ding.

"Hi, Seren," he called out.

"Hey, Everett. How's the book coming?" Seren asked.

"Oh, you know, torturously." A tired smile spread across his face. "I'm hoping to have the first draft done in a month or so."

"How far into it are you?"

"Ah, about... sixty thousand words."

"That's amazing, Everett! Keep going." Seren set the book on the mahogany desk.

"Will do," he said, rubbing his hands together. "Ah, *The Alchemist.* That's right, I remember. How'd you like it?"

"I loved it!" Seren said. She placed her hand on the cover, not wanting to part with it just yet. "Sorry it took me so long to read it."

"Not a problem. Everyone has their own pace."

Saying goodbye to the book was like saying goodbye to an old friend, but she took comfort in knowing that if she ever wanted to return to that world, it would be there waiting for her.

"So, did you find your treasure?" Everett asked.

"I think I have."

Year Two

Chapter 1

One year.

Seren was sitting on the porch in her grandfather's rocking chair, wiping bits of dirt from her new pair of work jeans, when the thought occurred to her.

Winter had been busy, and a lot had changed. In December, Seren barely spoke to anyone. Having tasted the addicting sweetness of achievement, she decided to chase it. She sequestered herself away in the cabin, up to her ears in research and reading, determined to hit the ground running in March. Like a squirrel hides nuts in preparation for a cold winter, she hoarded information.

She was older and wiser, as the saying goes. Having mastered how to grow tomatoes and beets, she was sure she could get the potatoes right next time—she just needed to wait for the last frost and not bury them quite as deep. Her studies included how to grow and tend to garlic, onions, cucumbers, and other springtime crops. She read about the perfect nutrients for each and how much spacing was required, and refined her knowledge on crop succession, pest control, and subtle tips and tricks for how to edge out the competition. The advice she read even included how to stay organized, date keeping, and how to run a successful business. She felt confident that when the weather permitted, she could execute, grow, and tend to everything with her eyes closed.

Seren didn't buy seeds from Wares & More, as she had the previous year, but from the same nursery she visited last summer. It took thirty minutes to go there and back to Adytown, but it was a small price to pay for a clean conscience.

In mid-January, Rita helped her build a fully functional greenhouse. They contracted a deal in lieu of monetary payment: Seren would provide her access to lumber on the farm. Rita also built a large bin for hot composting and ten more raised beds made with wood directly from Hiraeth.

Seren spent all of mid-February to early March building more trellises and planting seed trays inside the greenhouse to get a head start on growing. When the weather was warm enough, all she would have to do was replant the seedlings in the soil, and voila. It was a simple solution that guaranteed no time was wasted and a higher potential harvest yield.

She had used a significant chunk of her savings to purchase supplies, but with the money she saved from the construction of the greenhouse and the raised beds, she still had enough to get her through until the summer, or early autumn if she really stretched it. There wasn't a choice in the matter. Everything before her was worth the price; she knew she needed to do it.

Mabon jumped into Seren's lap as she gazed over the monumental work she had accomplished. The soreness and muscle aches she felt when she first got started the year before felt like child's play compared to how she ached now. She could barely lift her hand to stroke the content tabby, but she did. The pain wasn't pain at all but a reminder that, for perhaps the first time in her life, Seren had used herself up in totality. She gave everything to the patch of land before her, and it felt good. It felt good to be alive, in her body, and willing to give it all to achieve something extraordinary. Before her were ninety-six onion plants, sixty-four tomato plants, sixty carrot plants, forty-eight beet plants, and sixteen cucumber plants. The last two beds were full of garlic and potatoes that would probably come out to about a hundred each in total. Seren had a bad habit of underselling herself, but not this time. She knew that this time, the numbers and work spoke for themselves.

Not ambitious my ass, she thought.

Chapter 2

Over the coming weeks, talk increased regarding how it might be time for Perry to close his business. The talk was only rumor-deep the year before, but after Seren visited him and saw how he looked—his eyes tired from sleepless nights and his countenance a faded picture of who he once was—it all but confirmed the suspicion. Seren felt that when he looked at her, he only saw the ghost of her grandfather when he asked her to help him. Even Lenora's unbothered persona faltered, and her mother, Corinne, regressed into maintaining her small herb garden and planning the town aerobics and Pilates classes.

The image of Perry's sad eyes, pleading and disenchanted, and sheer unfaltering determination propelled Seren forward. They worked out a deal that when Seren's vegetables were fully grown, she would only sell at Perry's Home & Groceries. The great gamble was in full swing.

She brought Perry a hefty shipment of carrots, cucumbers, and beets in May. He cried when he thanked her. Together, they posted fliers on the town bulletin and all over town that Hiraeth Farm was back in business, its produce sold exclusively at Perry's. It didn't take long for the residents of Adytown to prefer the taste of Seren's homegrown vegetables to Wares & More's trucked-in produce. That only added more fuel to Seren's growing fire, and she promised to deliver. All that led to one grand idea, the magnum opus that Seren had been contemplating since that October day at the Rusty Fig.

One pleasant June afternoon, Seren placed a large carton of fresh-picked tomatoes on the bar in front of Otis.

"I want us to make a sauce," she said, looking directly at him.

"You want us to make a sauce," Otis repeated.

"Yes. I'll provide the tomatoes, and you can make the sauce. We'll bottle it and sell it at Perry's."

Otis looked unsure at first, but Seren kept driving forward.

"There isn't a single person who disagrees that your marinara sauce is delicious," she explained, "and when you made it with my tomatoes, they couldn't get enough of it. Everyone would love to taste it at home in their own kitchens."

"I'm listening."

"We can start out with small batches, selling to people here in town. I'm sure Perry would love to stock it. We'd split the profits fifty-fifty, and I'm almost certain, in time, we'd grow."

Otis disappeared to the kitchen, came back wearing his red-stained chef's apron, and smiled at Seren. "I'm in."

Within a few days, they had bottled three hundred pounds of tomato sauce and started selling it at Perry's. Seren was right: everyone wanted to taste it in their own homes. One day, Joyce and her family had relatives in from the next town over for dinner, and she cooked with the sauce. The day after, Perry got a phone call from said relatives, who asked how they could get Otis and Seren's homemade sauce in their own town's grocery store. Just like that, the word began to spread.

There were still enough leftover tomatoes to sell at Perry's and pound after pound of red onions. By mid-July, Seren's second attempt at potatoes paid off. They were not a hideous mushy texture, but firm and flavorful.

All around town, people were trying new things. Mayor Doney had big plans to have a town fair where local vendors and artisans could sell their goods and services. He set the date for July twenty-eighth and invited everyone to attend, including neighboring towns. He also put up a new section on the town bulletin board for people to post anything they might need help with, and other townspeople could answer the call. It was a part of Mayor Doney's "Towns Without Borders" initiative, an idea that he hoped would grow a larger sense of community.

Marty's fishing business got a new boat with a steadier, more efficient motor and larger capacity for fish, and Rita added a showroom to her home to showcase some of her finest work. Everett added more books to the library with, of course, his own intuitive style of organization, and brought in workers to fix the roof and paint the exterior. On occasion, Gia, Theo, and even Zach—who usually wanted to spend his time outdoors throwing a baseball around—grew an interest in reading and studying together. The aerobics and Pilates classes once envisioned by Corinne and Joyce finally began every Tuesday and Thursday in the park just up the hill from Perry and Corinne's house. There was an air of meteoric expansion, and it was infectious.

Seren and Jenna sat around a firepit, once used to destroy all traces of a very different life, and drank champagne together. A small charcuterie board sat between them, covered in all kinds of cheeses, fruit, and crackers on one side. On the other were sundried tomatoes, pickled onions, and cucumbers from Seren's garden. Her small Bluetooth speaker played music from the porch, underscoring their conversation.

"Congratulations, babe! I'm so happy for you," Jenna said as they clinked their glasses together.

"Thank you my love," Seren said.

"Wow," Jenna looked over the farmland. "You've accomplished so much."

"There are times I think I dreamed this last year. There's still so much to be done, but sometimes I pinch myself just to make sure it's all real."

"Makes me wonder if I could do something this great."

"Of course you can," Seren said. "If I can do it, anyone can. Trust me."

"There're... there're a few pieces I think I may be done with. Want to see them?"

"Yes! Oh my god, *please.*"

Jenna took out her phone and opened her camera roll. "This one's *Dalliance with the Sky.* I saved it."

The large canvas was covered in brilliant swirls of different shades of blue. At the bottom was a small blue-green hill, adorned with minuscule, impressionistic bluebonnets and long reeds. A great tree stood tall with dark royal blues and midnights, while the sky beyond displayed a stark change in color and texture. Feather-light strokes of baby blue and periwinkle beautifully transitioned from one to the other. The painting gave the impressionists a run for their money, and Seren thought it was one of the most beautiful paintings she'd ever seen.

"Jenna... this is incredible," she said.

Jenna kept scrolling through a few more photos which showed other impressionistic paintings—one red, one green, and one featuring what looked like the overlook near Rita's house—and an elongated, block-like sculpture that looked like something out of a modern lifestyle magazine.

"Jenna!" Seren exclaimed, taking her by the arms and shaking her with excitement. "Why have you been hiding these? They're beautiful!"

Jenna flushed, her cheeks bright red even in the twilight. "Thank you. I don't know, really."

"What about the festival?" Seren asked.

"What about it?"

Seren gave her a look that said, *really?* She held out her arms in mild indignation. "You have to showcase these."

"I don't know…"

"Trust me, everyone's going to love them."

"You're not going to miss this one, too? Like the Aster Dance?"

"Okay, I was a little busy," Seren said, gesturing toward the farmland. "Plus, y'know, a little traumatized from last year. But yes, I will be there. I promise."

"How is Jake? Does he still help out?" Jenna asked.

"Yeah, sometimes, but I haven't been seeing him as much lately."

Jake's mood seemed to deteriorate the last few times Seren had seen him. He had come by a few times with five o'clock shadow and deep circles under his eyes, suggesting he hadn't been sleeping. He hadn't been drinking at the farm, but he sometimes smelled like beer, so Seren knew he hadn't kicked the habit. On the nights Seren went to the Rusty Fig, his usual spot against the far side of the bar near the fireplace was empty. Otis also admitted he hadn't seen Jake in quite a while, so Seren could only conclude that he must be drinking at home or somewhere he could be alone. *Isolation,* she thought. *Not a good thing. Not for Jake.*

"Well, I can't believe you let him help you after what he did," Jenna said, popping a sundried tomato into her mouth.

"He's not so bad once you get to know him," Seren said.

"You know him?"

"No, not really, I guess."

What had she and Jake talked about for almost a year? Seren couldn't remember anything beyond small talk and what needed to be done at Hiraeth. Jake shared nothing about himself or seemed interested in knowing much about Seren. She told herself he must not care about her at all, but then again, he did run to the clinic to bring Dr. Harlan the day the heat almost took her. *What was he going to do though, let me die?* she thought. *We may butt heads from time to time, but no, he wouldn't.*

"Anyway, I'd better be heading back," Jenna said, polishing off the rest of her champagne. "I'll see you at the festival."

"Yes, with your paintings!" Seren insisted.

Jenna rolled her eyes playfully as she drew her in for a hug.

Chapter 3

On the day of the festival, Seren wheeled a large cart into town. It was filled with tomatoes, potatoes, jars of pickled red onions and cucumbers, Manoa lettuce, and green beans from the summer harvest. She had wanted to bring the corn she planted in May, but it was still a few weeks away from harvesting. She was headed to meet up with Perry and Rita, who had collaborated on display bins for Hiraeth Farms' produce, and Otis, who was bringing the new and improved S&O Homemade Marinara Sauce. Jenna had made a custom label for them, and Seren couldn't wait to see it.

Seren arrived early to set up the booth. Mayor Doney had graciously scheduled the festival to take place at three in the afternoon just in case it was too hot, but the day turned out pleasant and mild, with a warm breeze wafting through the town square.

"Ah, Seren! There you are," Perry said.

Their setup was under a tree just beyond Perry's General. He and Rita had just finished stacking the wooden cartons, which Seren guessed were made of maple. She'd learned a great deal about wood since meeting Rita. The cartons were light-colored and angled to display produce for customers. Seren snapped a quick picture of the stand for posterity when they were done unloading.

Otis came out of the Fig, carrying a box of clanking glass toward the stand.

"*Ooh*, Otis, lemme see," Seren said, excitedly removing one of the glass marinara sauce jars.

Jenna's design was perfect. It was a simple white label that read *S&O* in black sage text. Underneath was a cute, singular red tomato with three bright green leaves on top. On the bottom, in small script, it read, *Grown and produced in Adytown.*

"It's perfect," Seren said.

As the afternoon wore on, more people arrived to set up their booths. Chessy advertised her animal farm and products atop three massive hay bales. She brought an adorable brown goat with her that bayed every time someone passed by. Craig had an impressive array of metal works, including large chests with iron detailing, jewelry, statues, art pieces, and, to Seren's delight, swords. A one-handed sword with a leather-wrapped hilt and a large moonstone on the pommel caught her eye, and though there was no earthly reason why, she wanted it. Rita also had her own booth with a few items of furniture displayed, and Everett was selling his short stories. A few other out-of-town vendors populated the square with a variety of crafts.

One booth was missing: Jenna's. Seren took out her phone and sent her a text that read, *I'm set up just outside Perry's. Where are you? And yes, you're coming. ;)*

A few minutes later, Seren caught sight of the bubbly redhead, wheeling a large flatbed into town that was stacked with canvases of all sizes wrapped in brown paper. The block sculpture Seren had seen at Hiraeth precariously teetered on the edge. She rushed to help her.

"You made it!" Seren said.

"I made it," Jenna echoed, out of breath.

"Can I touch this?" Seren gestured to the block sculpture.

"Yeah, just grab it from the base."

Seren helped unload all of Jenna's art in a booth across the way from her own. She placed the block sculpture on top of a table. Jenna had also brought four wire stands which she used to display *Dalliance* and the three other paintings. She leaned the rest against the table for passersby to peruse.

"I'm so excited for you," Seren said. "If there's one person who will sell out today, it's you."

"I appreciate the vote of confidence," Jenna said. "Did you get the labels?"

"Oh, Jenna, they're amazing. Thank you so much." Seren hugged her friend.

By three, the square was alive with Adytown residents and many people from other towns who had made the trip for the festival. Seren almost paid no attention to her booth because she was happy to see how many people swarmed Jenna's display. O*ohs* and *aahs* came from across the way, many from Adytown's own residents, who had no idea of Jenna's artistic prowess. Two of the paintings sold within the hour, and it looked like many others were about to, as well. Seren caught Jenna's eye and smiled at her, mouthing, *I told you so!*

Seren didn't see Dr. Harlan. It had been months since she'd briefly run into him at the Fig, and she hoped to see him at the fair. An image of his deep green eyes gazing at her, a hint of admiration present within them, flashed across Seren's mind. She must have gotten carried away in her daydream because Otis nudged her arm.

"Seren? We have someone from the city who's inquiring about our sauce," he said.

"Oh! Yes, I'm sorry; how can I help you?" she asked a long-haired man in a fashionable, short-sleeved button-down and white pants.

"Yes, I was just curious about what the process of making this is like?" the man said.

"Of course. Well, I'm the grower. I grow the tomatoes on my farm, called Hiraeth Farm, and I bring them to Otis here, who makes…"

Seren spotted Myron hanging around the booth, listening in on their conversation. He was looking directly at Seren with a peculiar look of quiet disdain on his face.

"Who makes them into the delicious sauce you see before you," Seren finished.

"So, everything is homegrown? Made here?"

"Yes, one hundred percent," Seren said, eyeing Myron, who didn't break eye contact with her.

"Excellent," the man said as he typed something on his phone. "I'll take two bottles, please."

The man paid for his purchase and walked off. Myron approached the booth and picked up a jar of marinara sauce, reading over the label multiple times.

"You seem to be doing well," he said.

"We *are*," cried Perry, his voice cracking. He stood a few feet from Myron and Seren, his chest puffed up with all the menacing gravitas of a mating pigeon.

Myron paid him no mind, his attention fixed on Seren. "Why don't you sell your sauce at Wares & More? I guarantee we have more outreach and connections than any of our *competitors*."

"So, you agree, we are your competitor," Seren said.

Myron laughed as if he'd never heard something more ridiculous. "No, I would not say you are a competitor. More like a… nuisance."

"Yet you want a nuisance's business," Seren stated.

Myron's eyes darkened, and he leaned in closer. "All I am saying is, you should be careful. Enjoy your *success* while you can. If you fall now, we will not be there to catch you. It'll only get harder from here on out."

"We'll see about that," Seren said.

Myron juggled the jar of sauce between his delicate fingers, never breaking eye contact with her. She had dealt with insects more intimidating than he was. When he finished playing with the bottle like an untrained monkey, he plunked it on the table, rattling the rest of the produce. He was the first to look away, and as he walked into the crowd, Seren stared at the greasy black mop of hair on the back of his skull, hoping it would be the last time she ever had to lay eyes on him. Perry wiped his upper lip and the side of his face with a handkerchief from his shirt pocket and looked very much like he might lose his lunch.

The festival was scheduled to end at six, but after that time came and went, there were still plenty of visitors. Everything Seren brought that day sold out. She was helping collapse the display table when Jenna came up behind her and embraced her.

"You were right," Jenna said. "I sold everything!"

Seren spun around and grasped Jenna's arms. The pair jumped up and down.

"See? I told you everyone would love your work," Seren said, pulling in for another hug.

"Except..." Jenna started.

"Except what?" Seren asked.

"I still have one, and it's for you."

Seren followed Jenna to the booth, which was empty except for one canvas covered in brown paper lying on the flatbed. Jenna picked it up and revealed it to Seren. It depicted a grassy field with a patch of tilled land, tall winding vines snaking up trellises, ripe red tomatoes, large bushes filled with flowers, and a tall tree on the right side of the canvas bearing pink and orange fruit. It was her grandfather's peach tree, and the tomatoes were the tomatoes Seren had worked tirelessly to bring into the world. The perspective was from the front porch of the cabin—her cabin—looking out over Hiraeth Farm.

"Jenna..." Seren was too touched to speak. Before she could stop herself, she was tearing up. It was one of the most thoughtful, heartfelt gifts she had ever received. "I love it," she whispered.

As Seren walked back to her booth, she glanced at the clinic. Dr. Harlan hadn't made an appearance all day, and she hoped he was okay. She'd brought a jar of pickled red onions made special for him, and had hoped to give it to him at the festival. She decided to seek him out.

"Be right back," Seren said to Otis.

She ducked behind the table, picked up the jar of pickled red onions she had made sure no one bought, and headed toward the clinic. She rounded the side of the building, scaled the narrow stairway that led to a singular door, and knocked. While waiting, she noticed a small peephole on the door and no nearby windows to see into Dr. Harlan's studio. *Better for privacy,* she thought. She heard a rustling on the other side of the door, and a stretch of a few seconds passed before it opened.

"Seren," Dr. Harlan said. His voice sounded raw and congested, and Seren realized he must be sick.

"I'm sorry to intrude," she said.

"Not at all. Is everything okay?" he asked.

"Yes, absolutely. I, um, I didn't see you at the festival, and I was worried."

A little color returned to Dr. Harlan's face. "I appreciate that. I wanted to go, but I'm getting over a cold."

Seren held out the jar of pickled red onions to him. "I remembered you said you liked them."

Dr. Harlan took the jar from Seren and held it in both hands. "Thank you, Seren."

"And you know what they say: vinegar's good for colds. I think."

Dr. Harlan laughed and turned his head to shield her from his subsequent coughing.

"Get some rest. I hope you feel better soon, Dr. Harlan," she said.

Seren returned to the booth to finish packing up for the night. She placed the wrapped canvas from Jenna into the cart alongside the display crates Rita made. It had been a beautiful, successful day, and though the night was young, she wanted nothing more than to go home and hang up Jenna's painting. She already had a place in mind:

on the back wall between the wood-burning stove and the tv, so it would be the first thing she saw when she came home.

Otis finished helping Rita load the last piece of furniture into her truck and came to stand next to Seren. "You know, when you were talking to the guy from the city earlier, I believe that was the first time I've heard you say, 'my farm.'"

"You're right," Seren said. "I suppose it was."

Chapter 4

Seren loved Halloween. If asked, she would say it was her favorite holiday. She loved the atmosphere, the otherworldly decorations, how her skin prickled when the autumn air wafted over her skin, and the eerie sense that the veil between worlds was at its thinnest. Anything was possible.

She was dressed as what she would describe as a diviner. Emelia made Seren a custom lavender and silver dress with bell sleeves and a plunging neckline. She'd tied a long, mulberry-colored, hooded robe around her neck with twisted tassels. The heavy velvet robe warmed her in the autumn chill. About her waist was a belt with faux leather pouches for 'potions' and 'ancient runes' to help offer guidance for weary travelers on the road. She painted astrological symbols and constellations along her arms and adorned her head with a simple silver crown. Emelia's sister, Olivia, helped her achieve a striking, ethereal look with her makeup which included lashes, white and purple eyeliner, and deep plum lipstick. It was one of the best Halloween costumes she had worn in years.

Jenna was dressed as a scarecrow. She wore a cute, brown, knee-length, flouncy dress with crisscrossed drawstring ties on the bodice and a red gingham, off-the-shoulder undershirt. She'd painted her nose orange and wore a tall, forest green farmer's hat.

Rita kept it simple with an all-black outfit, cat ears, and a tail.

Together, they were loading ten freshly carved pumpkins into Rita's truck. Their design was simple yet menacing. Their eyes were slim, pointed triangles, and their mouths were etched into jagged, curved smiles.

"These turned out great," Rita said, grunting as she loaded the heaviest of the bunch.

Seren had tried her hand at growing pumpkins, and though they were not as impressive as the ones her grandfather had grown, they were perfect for the spooky haunted soirée Mayor Doney promised the residents of Adytown that evening.

"Any idea where Frank wants them?" Rita asked.

"He mentioned something about the fountain, or a hay maze, so maybe there," Seren suggested, placing the last pumpkin in the truck bed.

Rita closed the tailgate, and the three of them piled into the truck to drive into town. The festivities were well underway when they arrived, and everyone was in costume. Mayor Doney had done an excellent job transforming the town square. Orange and purple lights wound around tree branches and building awnings. Glowing pumpkins and torches lined the walkways, and cutouts of arching black cats and fluttering bats framed the clinic, the Fig, and Perry's windows, backlit with orange light. A large black spider scaled the side of the Fig, waiting to ensnare unsuspecting patrons. The fountain gushed blood-red liquid that bubbled around the basin.

There were *Wizard of Oz* and Universal Monsters cutouts for people to stick their faces through for pictures. Nearby was an apple bobbing station, in which Gia and Theo took turns submerging their painted faces. Hay bales were used as seating, and Otis was selling candied and caramel Granny Smith apples, along with pitchers of regular and spiked apple cider to wash them down.

When Seren, Jenna, and Rita exited the truck, there was a quiet air of supernatural intrigue. The deep purple sky loomed like a ghostly specter over Adytown.

"Are you my pumpkin delivery?" Chessy asked. She was also dressed as a cat, though her ears and tail were white.

"Where does Mayor Doney want them?" Seren asked.

"Frankie wants—I mean, Mayor Doney wants some around the fountain and, I think, a few in the corn maze."

"Okay." Seren didn't react to Chessy's slip-up to avoid embarrassing her. She walked to the back of the truck as Rita undid the tailgate.

"Frankie," Jenna said, snickering.

The light was fading fast as the three of them unloaded seven pumpkins and inserted three lit tea lights into each. They placed some around the fountain and the rest on the ledge. When they were finished, the fountain was a macabre mixture of red, orange, and yellow, and lit up the town square like a bloody beacon.

Up the hill from the clinic was a maze. It was much taller than Seren expected, the yellow stacks of hay easily towering over her. Seren, Jenna, and Rita each carried a pumpkin and approached Mayor Doney, who stood near the entrance of the maze, pushing the corner of one protruding stack back into place.

"Happy Halloween, ladies!" he said. He wore a black suit and a tie with smiling, cartoonish pumpkins on it.

"Hey, Frank. So, where would you like these?" Rita asked.

"Oh, anywhere, anywhere," he said.

Jenna and Rita placed a pumpkin on either side of the maze entrance, and Seren placed hers just inside at the first turn.

As Seren and Jenna walked away, Rita stayed behind to compliment Frank on the swell job he'd done decorating. Mayor Doney commented on how gracious Chessy had been to loan the hay bales for the evening, and how the two of them had worked tirelessly to put the maze together. Seren imagined that wasn't *all* they were doing up there, all alone.

Seren and Jenna greeted Otis in the town square, who happily poured them two cups of spiked cider. Jenna paid him for a caramel apple and took a big bite, the soft caramel trailing long strands of sugar through the air.

"*Ooh,* a psychic," Jenna said, her mouth full of crunchy green apple. On a small patch of grass outside the Rusty Fig sat a small purple tent with a sign that read, *Psychic, Tarot, and Palm Readings, $15.* "C'mon, I want to know my future."

Seren stood outside the tent while Jenna eagerly ducked inside. She hoped that whatever the psychic had to say was helpful. Seren had once consulted a medium who told her she had known Frederic Chopin and Franz Liszt in a past life during the 1800s, and that was why she loved music so much. Seren didn't know what to make of that. She did love music, but then again, so did everyone.

There was a time when Seren would have given anything to know what the future had in store—whether she would find love, become successful, or live a long, satisfying life—but lately, her mind had become quieter. Such questions came and went, and she didn't hold on to needing to know. She had simply let go. Life was better that way. At least, that was what the last year had taught her. There was no knowing in farming, there was no knowing in fortune, there was only the audacity to try at all.

The bus ride to Adytown that cold winter night seemed more like a bad dream than reality. She recalled how she felt then juxtaposed with how she felt now, in that moment. It was as if a previously locked doorway in her mind had opened, and something clicked. She wasn't the same person, and no amount of fruitless questioning had brought her here. Living her life had unlocked the door.

"Wow, that was great," Jenna said, appearing next to Seren, the caramel apple eaten down to the core. "Are you going to go in?"

"I think I'm okay," Seren said.

As Seren and Jenna meandered back to Otis's concessions to get more cider, Jenna told her about what the psychic said. She told her she saw great success coming and that a secret admirer would make himself or herself known soon.

I could have told her that, Seren thought.

"Ah! See?" Jenna held up her phone and showed Seren a text that had just come through from Everett. "Oh, she's *good.* Are you sure you don't want to give it a try? Even if you don't want to know your future, I do."

"Okay, in the spirit of Halloween, and for you, I'll try it," Seren relented. "But don't get too excited. I'm sure she'll just say all my dreams are coming true or something cheesy like that."

Seren pulled the purple curtains to the side and entered the tent, where a woman of about sixty sat at a small, circular table. Sandalwood and rose incense swirled around her like early morning mist on a placid sea. On the table sat a deck of tarot cards, a crystal ball, and a velvet mat with amethyst and black tourmaline crystals at each corner.

The woman had a look of hardened stoicism, and her gray eyes flicked up to meet Seren's as the curtain closed behind her. "Cash first," the woman said.

Seren took fifteen dollars from her wallet and was about to set it on the velvet mat, but the woman stopped her.

"I do not allow others or their possessions to touch my tools. I cannot have their energies mix."

"Alright, where do you want it?" Seren asked.

The woman held out a long-fingered hand, and Seren gave her the money. She then pocketed it before lighting a bundle of sage. She swirled it around her temples and chest, the abundance of smoky aromas overwhelming Seren's senses. The woman snuffed the sage and told Seren to sit.

"I am Elladora. Why do you come to me today?"

"Um, I suppose to see if there's anything I ought to know," Seren said.

"You do not expect to hear an answer," Elladora stated.

"Well, I—"

Elladora waved a hand, and Seren fell silent. She picked up the tarot cards and shuffled them. Her eyes glossed over, and for a moment, Seren could have sworn her appearance shifted. *It's just the smoke getting to me,* she thought.

Elladora fixed Seren with a steely stare as she shuffled the cards, as if she could read Seren's thoughts. She then placed the cards on the table and rested her hands, palms up.

"There is a remembering. A changing. An occurring. You have not yet arrived, but you are on your way." She flipped the top card of the tarot deck. It was an unsettling depiction of two figures falling from a lightning-struck building with a black storm raging in the background. "The Tower. It could've been one or a succession of catalyzing events that brought you here." She flipped a second card. On it were three sharp swords, driven through a bleeding heart. "Three of swords reversed. Heartache. It almost took you, but you are coming out of it now." The next card she pulled had a disenchanted man standing beside a tall shrub with star-like discs around him. "Seven of pentacles. This is the present. You work hard, yet think little of your accomplishments, unaware that this life is not just turmoil and pressure. There is a light coming, even if you don't yet see it." Elladora flipped another card. It was of a woman wearing an opulent gown standing in a lush garden with a parrot resting on her outstretched hand. "This is the becoming. This is who you will be, yet it is not enough. The picture is not complete. You think this is enough. You are afraid to ask for more, but there is more." Elladora flipped one last card. "Love. This is promised in the two of cups. Do not be afraid to seek it. It is in you, and it is in this town. Someone is waiting for you to reach out and take it."

"Is… is this person here?" Seren asked.

"I cannot say for certain, but you have known them before," Elladora said.

Whatever that means, Seren thought. She left the tent feeling as though her skin were transparent. Elladora was right about everything, or at least about what had already happened. She felt as though she were being watched, perhaps by some distant, crouched figure in the shadows, keeping score, all-knowing and omnipresent. *Perhaps it was a parlor trick,* she thought, but if it was, it was a damn-near-perfect one.

"There you are. How'd it go?" Jenna asked. Everett stood beside her, drinking a cup of spiked cider.

"Um, it was good," Seren said. "Lots of good stuff coming and all that. Hi, Everett, nice costume."

"*Thank you very much,*" Everett said in an awful Transylvanian accent. He flashed a pair of long white fangs and pulled his long black cape around his throat.

Jenna laughed. "Everett, would you mind getting me another cider?"

He replied with bared fangs and a hiss, then stalked off toward Otis, apparently on the hunt for the requested beverage.

"He asked me out," Jenna whispered, bringing Seren in close.

"About damn time," Seren said, smiling at her friend.

"Really, how did it go? Did she say anything interesting?"

"Oh, well, she said that... that I'm... becoming."

"That's... *vague.*"

"Yeah, um, just that things are going to be all right. Probably more than all right, actually. She said that I shouldn't be afraid to ask for more, that when things turn out for me, I shouldn't deny myself real—"

Seren looked across the square and saw Dr. Harlan exit the clinic.

"Love," she finished

"Okay, well, that's good!" Jenna said.

Everett returned and handed her a cup of cider. "We were going to do the maze; would you like to join us?"

Seren looked across the square again but didn't see Dr. Harlan. "Yes, let's."

Seren had to hand it to Mayor Doney and Chessy—the maze was much harder than it looked. They had doubled back two times, only to find themselves at a dead-end. After reassessing and trying to retrace their steps, they reached a corridor they were marginally certain they hadn't been to before. The path diverted to the left and the right.

"I think we should go right," Seren said.

"But we've already taken two right turns," Jenna said. "I think we should go left."

"Every left turn has led to a dead end, though," Seren argued.

209

"Why don't you go that way, Seren," Everett said, "and we'll go this way, and whoever is right, just call out, and we'll meet up."

Seren agreed and turned right while Jenna and Everett went left. The path turned left almost immediately, and then continued straight. She could hear Jenna's distant laughter, and she smiled, happy they were having a good time. It grew colder, so Seren draped the velvet hood over her head to warm up. When she rounded another corner to the right, she almost ran into a familiar, broad figure.

"Oh! Hi, Dr. Harlan."

"Seren! Wow, great costume," he said, sweeping his eyes over her.

"You look…" Seren began. He was dressed in a pilot's uniform. "You look good, *captain*."

Dr. Harlan adjusted the jacket slung over his arm and straightened his tie. "It's not… sad?"

"No, not at all!" she replied.

His shoulders relaxed a little, and he looked in both directions before turning his attention to Seren once more. "Have any luck with this maze?" he asked, running a hand through his hair.

"I, um, think I've lost my party. Jenna and Everett are somewhere back there," she said, waving her hand behind her.

"Shall we find the way out together?"

"Let's do it."

Dr. Harlan allowed Seren to pass him. The paths were much narrower in that part of the maze, but they pressed on. As they walked deeper, the sweet, fresh smell of hay grew thicker, and the thrill of anticipation pitched higher and higher the more they discovered. The path became narrower still, and as they rounded another corner, Seth and Damien leaped out at them.

Seren cried out and fell back on Dr. Harlan's chest.

Seth guffawed and clapped his hands while Damien had a look of quiet amusement on his KISS-painted face.

"Got you!" Seth yelled, pointing at Seren.

"Screw you guys," she said.

"It's Halloween, baby," he said.

His boyish charm got Seren, and she couldn't stay mad at him. Damien, on the other hand, said nothing at all and leaned against the hay like he was too cool to be there.

"Who are you, Gene Simmons?" Seren asked.

"Ace Frehley, actually," he said, his voice monotone and deep.

"I'm Ace Ventura," Seth said.

"I haven't seen it," Seren replied.

"You haven't seen Ace Ventura?" Pure shock washed over Seth's face. "You gotta see it! We should get together sometime and—"

"Dude, come on," Damien cut him off and pulled him back into the maze.

Seth's jubilant protesting continued as they walked away. When the maze grew silent again, Seren realized that she was still leaning against Dr. Harlan.

"Sorry," she said as she moved away from him and smoothed her dress.

"Seems you have a date," Dr. Harlan teased.

Seren playfully slapped his arm and continued forward. The path stretched into one long corridor, the far end outlined in dark shadows.

"I think we've found the way out," she said.

They exited the maze on the far side of the park, near a rectangular seating area with two benches on either side. Seren texted Jenna to let her know the right path led her out of the maze and to double back when they could.

"So, *Captain Beck,* how are you feeling? You seem better," she said as they came to sit on a bench.

He smiled and laughed. "I like the way that sounds. I'm a lot better, thanks. I rarely ever get sick. I'm not sure where that one came from. The pickled red onions were delicious, by the way. I may or may not have finished them already."

"I'll have to make more of them for you."

"Okay, but only if you let me pay for them next time."

"If you insist."

A slight chill blew through Seren. Though the cape had kept her warm all evening, she was becoming much colder as the night wore on. She shivered and looked to see if Jenna and Everett had found their way out.

"Are you cold?" Dr. Harlan asked.

"I'm okay."

"Here, take this." He handed her a navy, double-breasted jacket. There was a winged enamel pin on the lapel and four gold stripes on the cuffs.

"Thank you," she said, draping the jacket over her shoulders.

"Seren, do you think… Would you say we've become, sort of, friends?"

"Yes, I would," she said.

He leaned his elbows on his knees and rubbed his hands together. "I… wanted to bring this up long ago, but there was no way to do it without potentially causing harm on my part. When you first arrived, I noticed you didn't eat much. And by that summer heat wave, you had lost so much weight that I was concerned about you, but now…" Dr. Harlan paused to look at Seren. "Now, you seem better. Happier, maybe. So, I wanted to ask, how are you, truly?"

"Oh, um, I'm okay," Seren said. Dr. Harlan looked at her but remained silent. "I guess there was a lot going on at the time."

"What happened?" he asked.

By the expression on his face, she knew that if she felt uncomfortable sharing, he would respect it and not press her for an answer. *I'm safe with him,* she thought. *He should know.*

"I came here because my heart was broken. I thought I had found my person, but…I guess I was wrong. But I loved him. I loved him so much. I was already dealing with losing my grandfather, and then he—Adam was his name—ended things without any warning. I couldn't take it, so I fled everything. I came here because I didn't have anywhere else to go, and my grandfather had left me Hiraeth, so I guess it helped me feel less alone to be in a place that meant so much to him."

Dr. Harlan nodded and listened attentively.

"I couldn't eat," she continued. "I just couldn't. Whenever I tried to have a proper meal, my stomach hurt, as if hot lava was eating away at my insides. It was awful, and it went on like that for months, but eventually it stopped. I recovered when I wasn't sure I would. As for how I'm doing now…" Seren looked at Dr. Harlan. "I am happy I know you, Jenna, Otis, Emelia, and so many people I would never have known if these things hadn't happened. And that the farm is doing well. I think, maybe for the first time in a long time, I'm content."

"I'm glad," Dr. Harlan said. "I'm… happy I know you, too."

The familiar sound of Jenna's laughter came from the maze, and shortly after, she and Everett emerged, their arms wrapped around each other.

"Oh, there you are," Jenna said. "Sorry, we fell a little behind."

Everett squeezed Jenna's waist, and she squirmed under his hand and giggled up at him.

"*Good evening*, Dr. Harlan," Everett said in the Transylvanian accent.

"Good to see you, Count Everett," Dr. Harlan said.

"Did you guys finish the maze?" Jenna asked.

Seren turned to look up at Dr. Harlan. then back at Jenna. "Yeah, we ran into each other near the end and found the path out together."

"We ran into Seth and Damien," Jenna said. "Seth was saying you and him have a date or something?"

Seren laughed. "Oh, no. He was just joking. He's not my type, anyway."

"What is your type?" Everett asked.

"Pilots," Jenna said without skipping a beat.

Seren gripped her nearly empty cider cup and looked at her in utter incredulity. *Did she really just say that? She did not just say that.* Seren dared not look at Dr. Harlan but felt him shifting his weight beside her.

"More cider, anyone?" Everett asked.

Seren had never been more grateful for him than in that moment. With just three words, he saved her skin, perhaps more than he realized. They all agreed that more cider was just what everyone needed, so the four of them left the maze behind and walked down the hill to the town square.

Chapter 5

A peculiar emptiness, Seren noticed, always marked the days after Halloween, as if the spirits that crossed the veil had swept across the land of the living and took a part of the material world with them. That time of year was a reminder that the unseen was just as real as the seen, perhaps never to be fully understood, but felt. Seren had always felt a connection to something, even if there were no words to describe or prove it. Call it an entity, intuition, or whatever, but that voice was a sure and steady compass and was never wrong. All she had to do was listen.

Seren liked to talk about clarity. She likened it to standing atop a mountain, the sky a crystal-clear blue, seeing as far and wide as the eye can see. There was no truth that could be hidden in clarity. The truth, she thought, was like this internal compass. If she was right with the truth, she was right on her path. The problem was her own mind. Her fears robbed her. They covered the clear sky with dark clouds, each of them blocking the light and denying her access to clarity. She'd considered letting go of the things that weighed her down, and each year the load grew lighter, but she still grasped onto fear like a lifeline, as if it would protect her.

In her near two-year stretch in Adytown, she had been saddled with an unexpected, simple choice: choose to live or choose to die. It wasn't a literal decision; she hadn't wanted to die, even though there were times she felt like she could, but it was present in a similar choice of acceptance or denial. To feel or not to feel. To love or not to love. Still, she held onto fear, and though her grip faltered, she decided to try to live.

Seren sat on the porch with Jenna, who was sitting in a new rocking chair Seren had purchased from Rita. The new, polished wood contrasted her grandfather's worn and well-loved chair, a stark example of the passage of time.

"I can't believe you said that," Seren said, shaking her head at her friend.

"What? He knew I was joking," Jenna asked. "Besides, it's completely obvious he's in love with you."

"There's nothing obvious about it! Anyway, he seemed pretty clear about wanting to keep things *appropriate*."

"Hot," Jenna said, her tone laced with sarcasm.

"He's got to, Jenna. Everyone here is his patient."

"So, what, he's just going to deny himself any kind of happiness?"

Jenna had Seren there. She didn't condone his actions, but she could empathize with them. She knew a thing or two about self-denial and sacrifice.

"We're friends," Seren said at last.

"Do friends constantly think about how hot they look in a pilot uniform?" Jenna asked.

"I dunno; I haven't worn one before. Maybe you'd be singing a different tune then," Seren joked.

Jenna rolled her eyes. "All I know is you've both been into each other since the day you met," Jenna continued, "and I think it's time you do something about it."

"I did."

"Not consciously." Jenna pointed at her. Seren said nothing, and Jenna threw her hands up. "Man, you guys are *so* annoying."

"Even if I wanted to—and I'm not saying I do, I've got plenty of other things to do. The farm is doing well. I have you, Otis, and lots of other people to keep me company."

"How long has it been since—"

"Two years in February."

"Do you still love him?"

"I think I always will, on some level, anyway. He was a big part of my life. I've tried to forget, but I'm not sure forgetting means moving on. Did I ever read you the letter I wrote him?"

Jenna shook her head.

"I started it a long time ago, but it took a while to get all my thoughts together. I wasn't sure I'd send it, but I thought it would help me just to write it. Do you want to hear it?"

"Yes, of course," Jenna said.

Seren went inside the cabin and gathered all the yellow notepad papers from the coffee table. She had edited and re-edited each passage with diligence. She'd starred or crossed out words and entire paragraphs, and written notes in red ink along the margins. Difficulty and hesitation mired the letter, but with the final draft pieced together through all the mess, Seren was sure it was done.

Seren reclined in her grandfather's rocking chair and cleared her throat. "Dear Adam, I have tried to write you this letter more times than I can count. I have struggled to decide whether I should send this to you, so if you are reading this, that decision was made. This letter will not be full of bitterness or hatred, as you might expect. I do not hate you. I love you, and I suspect I always will. You meant the world to me. There was a time I could not imagine waking up without you, not hearing your voice every day, or getting to laugh with you at the dumbest things. Having the time to do so for the last two years has been one of the hardest things I've ever experienced in my life. There were days I thought my grief would kill me, that I couldn't possibly feel so much and not spill it on everyone and everything around me, but I didn't do that. Instead, I grew things. I grew myself. I learned more about who I am, and I made new friends. I did things I did not think were possible. I used to think that I got drawn into other peoples' orbits too easily, as if the gravitational pull of their thoughts and opinions on how life should be lived outweighed and outclassed my own. I tried to find myself in others instead of looking within. When I did look, I discovered a voice that was more important than the voices of others: my own. I hope you are doing well, and please tell your father hi for me. He was always so kind. I wish you well, Seren."

Seren folded the piece of paper and laid it in her lap. Though she had wrestled with those words for longer than she ever wanted to, it felt good to have said her piece and be done with it.

"I'm proud of you," Jenna said, rising to hug her. She sat down again and settled. "What do you want to do with it?"

"I think I want to burn it."

Together, Seren and Jenna dragged the fire pit out of the shed. Seren held the letter over it, and Jenna struck a match and handed it to Seren, who held the flame against the corner of the paper. The flames licked and ate her words. She held on until the heat threatened her fingers, then dropped the blaze into the pit.

Jenna stood next to her and placed an arm around her shoulders as they watched the last bit of the letter disappear.

After Jenna left to change for her date, Seren remembered she had volunteered to help Chessy bring the hay bales from the maze to her home. It was 3:30 p.m., and the light was fading. Seren was tired from closing the season, so she wondered if Chessy would notice if she stayed home. The warm embrace of the wood-burning stove and a hot bath were calling her name, and she almost gave in.

The hay bale return didn't take long. That late in the afternoon, only Seren and Rita were left to help her, and the two of them loaded as many hay bales as they could fit in the back of Rita's truck and drove them to Chessy's.

That was the first time Seren had seen Chessy's home and animal farm. Compared to Hiraeth, it was much more modern. Her two-story brick house seemed like it could weather any storm with its sturdy, imposing frame. The adjacent pasture was equipped with a barn, stables, and three silos. Sheep, goats, and chickens coexisted around mountains of haystacks, and Seren recognized the adorable goat she'd seen at the town fair. She waved to it as it chewed rhythmically from side to side.

When the last of the hay bales were unloaded and stacked against the silo, Seren remembered that Jake lived with Chessy. She hadn't seen him in weeks at either her farm or the Fig.

"How's Jake?" Seren asked.

"Apart from sometimes catching him in the mornings on his way to work," Chessy said, "I haven't seen him much. I was hoping you could tell me."

Seren realized how little she and Jake must communicate because if they did, she would know Jake hadn't been to Hiraeth since September. "No, he, uh, hasn't stopped by in some time."

"Oh…" Chessy looked crestfallen. "Well, I'd invite you inside to say hello, but he isn't here."

"Do you know where he is?" Seren asked.

"Probably at the bar, I'd imagine."

Seren took out her phone and texted Otis to ask if Jake was there.

"Anyway, thank you so much for helping me today. If you're headed to the Fig, please tell Jake I'm making his favorite tonight—homemade pizza with mushrooms and spinach."

"I will, and it was no trouble."

Chessy smiled weakly at Seren. She could tell she was worried about Jake and had been for some time. He was a grown man and could come and go as he pleased, but Seren wanted to kick him for upsetting his aunt.

Otis texted back. *He's not here.*

Seren felt a chill go down her back, and she snapped her head to look for any sign of him, but there was nothing but farmland and trees. *Where could he be if not here or the Fig?* Seren thanked Otis and then sent Jake a quick message that read, *"Is everything okay?"*

It was late enough that Jake's shift at Wares & More would have ended. A stiff breeze blew through the trees, and for no apparent reason other than instinct, Seren walked south of Chessy's property. She had never explored that part of Adytown and didn't know where she was going. Maybe there would be a bench, or a hangout place, or *something* to give a sign of Jake's whereabouts. He frequented spaces where he could be alone, and there was no place more alone than the woods.

It occurred to Seren that it would be better if she had asked for help, but she did not want to alarm Chessy—or anyone else, for that matter—if there wasn't probable cause.

Seren pressed on through the trees. She heard and saw no one, and she couldn't suppress the mounting uneasiness that sat like a rock in her stomach. The woods seemed thicker and darker in this part of town, hardly the kind of place she would want to venture through on her own as dark as it was.

"Jake?"

Nothing.

Ahead, the light returned as she approached a rocky cliff that overlooked the ocean. The gray sky mirrored the misty, churning sea, resembling something out of a Romantic painting.

Wherever Jake was, it wasn't there. Of course, he wouldn't be there. That made no sense. *He's probably at the park. Or maybe the beach,* she thought. *Or, maybe he's at Hiraeth, looking for me right now.* She pulled out her phone, but Jake hadn't messaged her. The last bit of tenacity drained from Seren, and she decided to go home and wait to hear from him.

She was about to turn away when something caught her eye at the bottom of the cliff. It took a moment for Seren's eyes to adjust, but when they did, cold panic rushed through her. It was Jake, lying face down in the wet sand.

Chapter 6

"Jake!"

He wasn't moving.

Time was of the essence, and Seren felt pure, unadulterated adrenaline take over. There was no easy way to get to him. Jagged rocks and exposed roots made up most of the ridge, and a steep drop made up the rest. He must have fallen by accident. *Or on purpose,* she thought in horror.

"Shit, shit, shit."

She couldn't get to him, and even if she did, there was no way she could get them both up the cliff in one piece. Seren paced the ridge like a stalking lion, trying to think straight as her heart pounded so hard in her chest, she thought it would burst. The ocean below became more animated, and she realized the tide must be coming in. She yanked her phone from her pocket and tried to call for help, but she had no service so far away from town.

"Damn it!"

Marty, she thought, and she checked the time. It was almost five. *He has a boat.*

Seren took off, running through the forest as fast as she could. Hot, heavy tears almost blinded her, but she ran faster. Her ankle caught on a stiff root, throwing her racing body hard on the ground. Refusing to acknowledge the pain, she stood and ran on. She prayed it wasn't Marty's day off and that her shaky legs would get her there before it was too late. *He wasn't moving,* she thought. *Please, please don't let him be dead.*

The wooden dock echoed hollowly under her pounding feet. The beach was deserted, and Seren found no trace of Marty, and his new fisherman's boat was missing. However, a small, motorized dinghy knocked against the wet wood in rhythm with the tide.

A choice presented itself to Seren. Either she could call for Marty and pray he showed up, or she could pilot the dinghy herself and hope for the best. She had never driven one before, but every minute that passed reduced the odds of getting to Jake. The choice was easy.

Seren jumped into the dinghy and almost fell overboard. The small metal frame rocked under her unsteady feet as it hit the side of the dock. She ripped the engine cord once, twice, and three times, but to no avail.

"Why won't you start?"

She pulled again, rewarded only by a pathetic sound like a dry string screeching through frayed metal.

Is there a key? she wondered, her nerves close to being shot. She had no idea what a key to a boat like that would look like. There was no discernable ignition or obvious place where a key could be hidden.

Seren took out her phone again and saw that she at last had service, but who would she call? The only person who could help her was probably miles out on the open sea, and she had no way to reach him. She could call 911, but it would probably take emergency services too long to get to Adytown to help, and she needed to get to Jake immediately. She felt her body slip into freeze mode, where all the possible directions she could take collapsed in on her at once like toppling dominos. In her anguish, it hit her that her decision to seek Marty may have wasted precious time, and with the tide slowly rolling in, she felt a terrible, sinking feeling in her stomach that she had made a grave mistake.

She buried her head in her hands.

"Please…" she whispered.

A low buzzing approached over the rhythmic splash of the rippling water. It started low and imperceptible but grew as it came closer. Seren raised her head and saw Marty's red fisherman's boat coming closer to the shore.

"*Marty!*" Seren climbed onto the dock and wildly flailed her arms, hoping to catch his attention. "Marty! Come quick!"

He turned the steering wheel, and the boat drifted closer to the dock.

As Seren waited for him to reach her, she never stopped waving her arms, pleading for him to hurry.

The fishing boat came in for a smooth landing, and Marty threw a long heap of thick ropes onto the dock. "Seren? Seren, what is it?" he asked as he tied off the fishing boat.

"It's Jake! He fell over the cliffs," she said. "We have to go now. I don't know if he's…" Seren trailed off. She didn't want to finish the sentence.

Marty's eyes widened. He produced a coiled red cord from his neoprene pants without skipping a beat. "Let's go."

They leaped into the small dingy. Marty plugged in the safety key, whipped the cord in one strong motion, and the engine roared to life. As they backed out, Seren fixed her eyes toward the west and directed Marty where to go. The dinghy carried them over the increasingly churning water, occasionally showering them with salt spray.

"*There!*" Seren called out as she saw Jake's facedown body once more. He hadn't moved. His left hand was splayed open, palm against the Earth, and the other was tucked under his stomach. The water was lapping at his ankles, his white sneakers saturated with sand. Seren moved to jump into the water, but Marty grabbed her arm.

"Whoa, hold on! I'll bring us in closer," he said.

The tears came again, and Seren did nothing to stop them. *Please,* she thought. *Please be okay.*

Marty cut power to the engine and raised it out of the water as the boat struck sand. Seren couldn't wait another second and jumped onto the beach, soaking her boots and pants up to her ankles.

"Jake. *Jake!*"

Seren kneeled and shook him. His stubble was more pronounced than she had ever seen, and a small cut stretched across his cheek. He was still warm, and to Seren's immeasurable relief, he was breathing. She cupped a sandy hand to her mouth.

"Sern..." he mumbled, his mouth pressed into the sand.

"Yes! Yes, I'm here, Jake."

His expression was blank as he stared at the sand, his bloodshot eyes distant and cold. I don't want to be here anymore," he said, his voice barely above a whisper.

"Hold on, we're... we're going to get you some help."

They lifted Jake as carefully as they could and laid him inside of the dinghy. Marty pushed off the beach and climbed into the boat, the momentum sending them into the sea. As the boat raced to get them back to town, Jake vomited over the side, while Seren held on to him to make sure he didn't fall into the ocean. He slumped back, and his eyes fluttered shut. Blood trickled from the red cut along his cheek.

"Try to stay awake, Jake." Seren patted his arm and tried to keep his attention, but he nodded in and out of consciousness with every motion. "We have to get him to the clinic."

Chapter 7

Seren gnawed at her fingernails, her leg bouncing like a jackrabbit under the unsteady plastic chair in the clinic waiting room. She couldn't catch her breath. Fighting off the urge to cry, she fixed her chin in a permanent half-quiver. She couldn't sit still any longer, so she stood and wandered to the front desk, clinic door, far corner, and back again, her hands resting on the back of her head.

She jumped when Mira emerged from the back hall, pushing a yellow mop and bucket and holding a cup of hot, fresh coffee.

"I brought this for you," Mira said as she attempted to hand the cup to Seren.

"Please let me… let me help," Seren said, reaching for the mop.

"Oh, that's not necessary, Seren. I'll take care of it, don't worry." Mira held out the coffee cup.

"I've… I've got it."

"Here, I'll set it down for you on the counter."

When she stepped away from the bucket, Seren grabbed the mop and slopped too much water onto the floor. She tried her best to wipe away the caked piles of sand and dirt she, Jake, and Marty had tracked in from the beach, but her frenetic efforts just made it worse.

"If I could get this—if I could just get this clean."

"Seren…"

Mira tried to take the mop from her, but Seren held the wooden handle as if it was the last thing tethering her sanity to this world. Mira insisted, coaxing her to give up control.

"I've got it!" Seren whipped the handle backward and knocked the cup of coffee to the floor, covering the already dirty surface in steaming brown liquid.

"Oh, I'm sorry. I'm *so* sorry, Mira," Seren said, covering her face with her shaky hands. She crouched to the floor. Faint sobs filled the waiting room, a soft sign of surrender, as her will to be in control melted away.

"It's alright, Seren, I promise. Here, let's get you sat down." Mira crouched next to her and placed a hand on her back. They stood together. Mira led her back to the chair and made sure she took a few deep breaths. "I'll bring you another cup, okay?"

Seren nodded and felt herself disassociating. The harsh fluorescent lights made her want to scream, but there was no escaping them or the awful situation. Not yet, anyway. Not until she knew if Jake was okay.

He had been fully unconscious by the time they arrived at the clinic. He threw up again just over the bridge from the ocean into the town square and passed out shortly after. Dr. Harlan and Mira were finishing up for the day but were both still inside when Seren banged on the clinic door. Seren had never seen Dr. Harlan spring into action like he did. He immediately brought Jake back to the exam room, and while Seren had wanted to stay with Jake, Mira insisted she stay behind in the waiting room, explaining she had been through enough and needed to rest.

About twenty minutes later, a man Seren had never seen before entered the clinic. "Dr. Baylek to see Dr. Harlan," he said. Mira escorted the doctor to the back.

Marty stayed until it appeared Dr. Harlan needed no further assistance, then left to secure his boats and fish for the day. Seren hadn't wanted him to leave, but he promised he would be back before the hour was up. However, when an hour and five minutes had passed, he still hadn't returned. Minute after minute, second after second, ticked by, but still, there were no answers or comforting words to end this sterile purgatory. She slept for a few minutes before all but catapulting out of her chair the second she remembered where she was. It was the same waiting room, the same pounding heart, the same ticking clock on the wall.

Seren finished her second cup of coffee and threw the crumpled paper into the trash. She never drank coffee, and she strongly felt its effects. She could no longer tell if the jitters, sweats, heart palpitations, and slight nausea were from anxiety or caffeine.

After an hour and twenty minutes, Dr. Harlan finally walked into the waiting room. Seren rose to her feet and walked to him with her hands clasped in front of her.

"Well, it took a while to get him stable. I had to call in a colleague of mine to help, and there was a considerable mess to clean up, but he's going to be okay," Dr. Harlan said.

Seren stood there in numbed silence.

"Seren?"

"He's... going to..." she finally said.

"He's going to be just fine."

Warm tears gathered in the corners of her eyes and fell in thick droplets to the floor. She could barely contain the confusing mix of relief, elation, and shock. He was okay. She couldn't believe it. Every voice inside her head, every foreboding thought, had convinced her he wouldn't make it.

"I... I thought..." She couldn't finish the sentence.

"I know, but he's still here," Dr. Harlan said.

227

Seren brought her hands to her face as the dam burst, and tears flowed from her eyes. "If I hadn't—if I hadn't found him…" she said, hiccupping over every word.

"But you did. You *did*." Dr. Harlan placed his hand on her shoulder and rubbed her shaking arm.

Seren seized forward and threw her arms around him. She pressed every bit of herself against him, needing him more than anything. Her tear-streaked face thudded against his chest. The white fabric of his button-down felt soft against her cheek. She could hear his heartbeat quicken a little, then slow to an even beat, allowing her tired heart to fall into rhythm with his.

He didn't react at first, but as she clutched him, he wrapped his arms around her. She sobbed as he ran his thumb in small circles on her back.

"Shh, I've got you. You're okay."

As Seren calmed down, she was finally able to draw in deeper breaths. She inhaled and smelled his familiar coffee and vetiver scent. Her shoulders and arms relaxed into his embrace, forgetting everything else besides the feel of him wrapped around her. She released her tight grip on Dr. Harlan's lab coat and splayed her hands open on his back, pulling him closer. He felt so warm and safe, and she easily got lost between his arms. *He's your doctor,* she thought. *You shouldn't be holding him like this.* She released him and took a step back, hastily wiping her eyes with the back of her hand.

"S—sorry," she said.

"For what?" he asked.

Seren looked into Dr. Harlan's eyes. He simply looked right back at her. She looked at his mouth and back up at his eyes, still feeling his hands on her back.

The clinic door chimed as Marty stepped in. He was carrying a white plastic bag with something the size of a brick wrapped in brown paper inside.

"How's he doing, doc?" he asked, walking up to stand next to Seren.

"He's resting now. He had acute alcohol poisoning and a possible concussion, but he'll be much better in a few days," Dr. Harlan replied.

"Oh, good, good. Glad to hear that. He had us worried sick. Didn't he miss Seren?"

Seren nodded and smiled weakly at the old fisherman. Without Marty, his boat, and sheer luck that she'd found him when she did, there was a real possibility Jake would not be there.

But he is here, she thought. *He's here, and he's going to be okay.*

"Well, I just wanted to bring this for you, miss Seren. It's halibut, caught fresh this afternoon. After the day you've had, I figured a nice piece of delicious fish would help warm your stomach." Marty held out the bag to her.

"Thank you, Marty, it will," she said, taking it.

"I've got to be getting back. Bless you both," he said.

"Thank you for all your help," Seren said.

Marty tipped his hat and exited the clinic. The clock on the wall ticked in the silence. Seren looked at Dr. Harlan once more.

"Can I see him?"

"I think he needs some time to recover. He'll be much better in the morning," Dr. Harlan said. "Don't worry, I'll take good care of him."

"Okay," she said.

"Try to get some rest. You've been through a lot today. If you need anything, don't hesitate to call."

Seren nodded. She wished he would hold her again. His arms felt so good, so right around her, as if they were made for keeping her safe. There was nothing left to be said, but she stayed where she stood. He was so close; all she would have to do was reach out and—

"Seren?" His voice broke the wishful vision.

"Oh, yes, I, um, was just thinking about Chessy. I should go talk to her, tell her what's happened."

"I called her. She's on her way here now."

"Oh. Okay."

Walking away from Dr. Harlan was physically painful. She placed her hand on the clinic door and turned to look at him once more.

229

"Goodnight, Dr. Harlan."

"Goodnight, Seren."

The door to the clinic closed, and the bell chimed brightly behind her. It was dark, and the iron streetlamps were fully aglow. It was a misty night, and flecks of moisture laced with the scent of salty sea air speckled her face. Seren pulled her jacket around her, feeling cold and exhausted. Her right ankle was throbbing, the pain having finally caught up with her. It was as if every muscle in her body were crying out, *Go back. Go back.* She looked over her shoulder. She could still see the corner of the chair she sat in all evening through the frosted window. If she were braver or sure he was waiting for her too, perhaps she would have listened, but she did not feel brave, and she did not feel sure.

She continued along the path to Hiraeth. Just past the bus stop, where the streetlamps no longer lit the path, she was struck by the stark contrast between the light of town to the darkness of the farm. It was her home now. It was beautiful and brought her happiness. She loved her grandfather's cabin and the life she had built with all she had accomplished. She loved her friends, her crops, and, of course, sweet little Mabon with her soft headbutts and the way she purred every time Seren pet her. But there was something missing. Elladora was right. It wasn't enough.

Chapter 8

"Come on, we're going to be late!"

Seren wrapped a wool scarf around her neck and grabbed her heavy winter coat from the hook on the wall. She slung her purse over her head and fastened the gold buttons with some difficulty, her gloves clumsy and thick. The heat from the wood-burning stove flowed from the cabin as Jenna left the door open while she waited on the porch.

"Everett couldn't have picked a warmer day for this?" Seren asked, grimacing against the gust of cold winter air as she locked the door behind her.

"He's so excited, he just couldn't wait," Jenna said.

"Is it finished, then?"

"Yes! Well, almost. He's just going through the last editing phase now."

Seren adjusted her scarf tighter around her neck and rubbed her hands together. Before she could close the door, Mabon darted out onto the porch and stopped just short of the snow-covered ground. "Mabon!" Seren exclaimed. She and Jenna watched as the orange tabby stared at them and slowly extended a fluffy paw to touch the curious, cold, white substance.

"You're going to regret that," Seren said, crossing her arms.

Mabon stuck her paw into the snow, which immediately swallowed most of the cat's furry leg. She yelped and jumped back a foot or so in the air before frantically shaking the afflicted limb. Seren and Jenna laughed as Mabon darted back inside, clearly no longer curious or desirous of adventure.

Entering the town library felt like entering a Christmas card. Everett pulled out all the stops to prepare the place for an audience. He had lit the fireplace, which crackled and hissed with roaring embers. The wooden bookshelves gleamed as if they had been wiped down with teak oil, and he'd placed fake tea lights throughout, adding welcoming movement and coziness. The red Persian rug looked as though it had been freshly vacuumed and brushed. Along the back wall, Everett had laid out an immaculate spread of cheeses, olives, slices of bread, pickles, and deviled eggs. There were little paper cups and a few bottles of Seren's favorite Pinot Noir with the blue label from the Fig.

Everybody Seren knew from town was there, plus several people she didn't recognize. It was likely a mix of residents she hadn't had the pleasure of meeting and visitors from neighboring towns.

"He really knows how to throw a party, huh?" Seren asked, life slowly returning to her fingertips.

"It's impressive, isn't it? I'm so excited for him," Jenna said. "I'm warm enough. Do you want some wine?"

"Always."

Jenna walked to the back table to get them a drink while Seren noted all the faces in the room. Dr. Harlan had not yet arrived, likely tending to a certain troubled friend of hers in the back of the town clinic.

"Seren! Oh, Seren, I'm *so* happy to see you," Chessy said, coming to clasp their hands together. "Words can't express how grateful I am to you. Thank you. You saved his life, you know that, right?"

"How is he doing?"

"Much, much better. He might stay one more night at the clinic, but I'm not sure. Dr. Harlan said he was well enough to be discharged yesterday but he wanted to stay. That's a good sign, I hope." The sweet woman's face pulled into a cheerful smile.

"Yes, absolutely," Seren said, squeezing Chessy's hands back. "Dr. Harlan will take good care of him, I'm sure."

"Such a fine man he is. You know, I believe he's single. You ever think of maybe—"

"What about Dr. Harlan?" Jenna asked, handing Seren a cup.

"He's a good doctor," Seren said, wishing to put an end to the conversation as soon as possible.

"And a *bachelor*," Chessy said, patting Jenna's arm.

"Is that so?" Jenna asked, shooting Seren a mischievous glance.

Seren was relieved when Everett tapped the mic and welcomed everyone to the Adytown Library. Jenna grabbed a seat close to the front while Seren was perfectly happy to linger near the back with the assorted cheeses and deviled eggs.

"Thank you all for coming. This really means a lot to me. I started writing this novel over a year ago, mostly because I wanted to prove to myself that I could write a book. Now that it's so close to completion, I can hardly believe it."

Everett pulled out a few loose sheets of paper and cleared his throat.

"This is one of my favorite passages. I hope you enjoy it. 'Their bodies claimed a small patch of midsummer grass to the far side of town. Their hands, outstretched and untouching, reached for one another. "Dance with me," she said to him, and he took her hand.'"

The library door opened slowly, and Seren glanced over as Dr. Harlan snuck inside and closed it quietly behind him. He found purchase against the far wall near the fireplace.

"'The brilliance of the summer sky, the cool breeze, and the stringent aroma of the tall grass enchanted them. Laughing and

233

twirling and living together, they danced. She had a way of melting away his hesitance, his unwillingness to let go of the past. He knew he loved her then.'"

Seren glanced back at Dr. Harlan and caught him looking at her. Their eyes met for a moment, and then she turned back to Everett.

"'He wanted to say it out loud, his truth solidifying the string that seemed to tie them together, but he couldn't. Not yet. Did she love him? He did not know. He didn't know if he could stand it if she did not.'"

Seren sensed Dr. Harlan's eyes on her and looked back at him. She smiled and waved, and he smiled back as Everett read on.

"'*End my loneliness,* he thought. They danced still, twirling around each other, the dance seemingly like their lives. She looked up at him, her eyes filled with joy, a searching look upon her face. Her lips parted as if she had a question lingering.'"

Everett folded the papers and stepped back from the mic. The room erupted in cheers and applause.

"Thank you! Thank you so much," Everett said, bowing. "As of right now, the book is almost done. I put an email sign-up sheet in the back if you'd like updates on when it's finished."

As a few people swarmed Everett with compliments and questions, including Jenna, who ran up and jumped on him, nearly tackling him with a hug. Seren added her email to the sign-up sheet. At least ten others had already added their info, and many more lined up behind her to do the same.

An older man in a striped button-down shirt and jeans walked over to Seren from the side of the room.

"So, what did you think?" Seren asked.

"It's got potential," the man said.

Everett was unsuccessfully making his way toward the back of the room. Everyone wanted to offer their support and compliments on his work.

"Everett!" Seren called, gesturing for him to come to them.

He did his best to pry himself away from Jenna, who was somehow already quite buzzed and fawning over him. "Hey, sorry about that. Took me a second to get away."

234

"There's someone I wanted you to meet," Seren said. "This is John. He's an old friend of mine from the city who's in publishing."

"Nice to meet you," John said, shaking Everett's hand.

"Yes! Yes, thank you for coming out."

"Here's my card," John said. "When the book is ready, get in touch. We'd happily read it over and see if it's something we're looking for."

Everett's eyes widened, and he laughed nervously. "Thank you! I will."

"Good to see you again, Seren," John said before leaving.

Everett's face showed he hadn't processed what had just happened. He looked at Seren and broke into wordless, excited exclamations. "Seren!" He grabbed her and hugged her. "You did not just do that!"

"I did," Seren said, struggling to speak under the crushing weight of his embrace.

He let her go and held her shoulders. "I don't know how to thank you."

"Well, the rest of the book better be just as good."

After their private celebration, it took no time at all for more people to sweep the promising author away. He hugged and kissed Jenna, who stood by his side, beaming up at him.

Seren looked around the room for Dr. Harlan, but he must have slipped out shortly after Everett concluded his reading. She was disappointed but understood that he probably needed to get back to the clinic. It was nice enough for him to come by to offer support. Still, she wished she could have said hello.

She did, however, spot the next best thing. "Hey, Mira," Seren said.

The short brunette turned around to face her, a small plate of deviled eggs and grapes in hand.

"Off today?" Seren asked.

"Just until after lunch. I'm going in after this for a bit," Mira said.

"Would you mind bringing this to Dr. Harlan?" Seren removed from her purse a small blue and white gift bag with tissue paper sticking out of the top. Inside was a mason jar of pickled red onions and a tag wishing Dr. Harlan a happy birthday. "I'd bring it myself, but I don't have the time."

"Of course, no problem."

"Thank you."

Seren walked to the library entrance and donned her winter coat and gloves. As she prepared to leave, she spotted Jenna standing faithfully by Everett's side, beaming at all the praise he received from the townspeople. She could have joined them but didn't feel much like socializing.

Instead, she slipped out the door and texted Jenna. *If you want to hang out later, I'm free. I was very impressed by Everett's writing. Tell him congratulations from me again.*

Chapter 9

Dr. Harlan sat at his desk, rubbing his eyes with one hand and holding a phone in the other. He had just hung up as Mira knocked on his office door.

"Come in."

"Sorry to bother. I have something for you," she said, placing the blue and white bag on his desk and stepping back.

"What is it?" he asked.

"I don't know, but it's from Seren Grinaker. She asked me to bring it to you."

"Thank you, Mira."

"What was it you wanted me to help with today?" she asked.

"Jake checked out, so if you would please tend to the room he was in, and the front computer needs a few software updates," said Dr. Harlan.

Mira nodded and left the room.

The bag shimmered under the fluorescent lights, patiently waiting for Dr. Harlan to open it. At last, he dragged the bag in front of him. He reached inside, grasped what felt like metal and glass, and removed the object. It was a sealed mason jar full of pickled red onions. A length of twine was wrapped around the lid and tied in a bow. A little red card was attached to the twine. It read, '*Happy Birthday, Dr. Harlan! Seren.*'

It's my birthday, he thought. He had forgotten. His birthday had steadily dropped off in importance over the years, and no one seemed to remember it, anyway. But Seren remembered. *How did she know?*

Dr. Harlan leaned back in his chair and held the mason jar in his lap. A detail on the note caught his eye. It was a small heart. She had drawn it between the two lines of text. The simple shape was enough to set off a seismic rift in Dr. Harlan's brain.

"We're friends," he said aloud. He thought back to when they sat together on the bench outside the maze. He had asked her if they were friends, and she had said yes. "We're friends," he said again as if it were a line of text on a chalkboard he was forced to recite a hundred times.

There was a knock at the door.

"Come in," Dr. Harlan said, his voice sounding strange. He cleared his throat and sat up straight as Mira entered his office.

"I finished with the room. I just wanted to ask if you wanted me to close down for the day, too?" she asked.

Dr. Harlan checked his watch and saw it was twenty minutes past closing.

"Uh, yes. Thank you, Mira. And you can just wait to do the updates until tomorrow if you like."

"Okay, will do," Mira said. She began to close the door but stopped. "Everything okay?"

Dr. Harlan realized he had spaced out. He blinked a few times and looked at Mira, his mouth slightly open. "Yes. Yes, everything is fine."

He could tell by the slight raise of her left eyebrow that she did not believe him. He knew her well enough to know that she always pressed her lips together when she was suppressing a laugh, and she did so as she closed the door.

He raised a hand to his forehead and sighed. Folding the blue and white bag with the tissue paper, he stored it inside a narrow drawer in the middle of his desk. He decided he couldn't sit in his office any longer and climbed the narrow steps to his apartment to put Seren's thoughtful gift in the fridge, on the middle of the top shelf. The little heart caught his eye again as he closed the refrigerator door. He realized he had been holding his breath, and after taking in all the air his lungs could withstand, he walked back to his apartment door and yanked it open.

"I need a drink," he said.

The Fig was empty when Dr. Harlan took a seat at the bar. He rested his elbows on the bar and took off his glasses. He pressed his hands to his face, which were cold from the winter air.

Who would have thought that a tiny hand-drawn heart would be his undoing?

"Hey there, doc," Otis said as he entered through the swinging doors carrying a shipping box full of red and white wine bottles.

Dr. Harlan rubbed his eyes once and replaced his glasses. "Otis," he said.

Otis placed the large box on the bar and asked, "What'll it be?"

"Just a glass of whatever, and some soup, if you have it."

"Coming right up."

Otis poured Dr. Harlan a glass of Merlot and disappeared to the back. In a few minutes, he returned with a warm helping of chili and placed it in front of Dr. Harlan with a bundle of silverware. "No book today?" Otis asked.

Dr. Harlan searched himself and realized he was empty-handed. It was the first time he hadn't brought a book with him to the Fig.

"I guess not," he said. "Um… I'll go ahead and pay for this now. I doubt I'll stay long."

"It's on the house," Otis said.

Dr. Harlan's hand stopped halfway to his wallet as he looked at Otis.

The man raised a hand next to his mouth and added, "On account of it being your *birthday* and all."

Dr. Harlan left his wallet alone and placed his hand on the counter. "You remembered too," he said.

"So, she gave it to you," Otis said.

Dr. Harlan choked on the wine he was sipping. "How—"

"She asked when it was, and I told her," Otis said as he unloaded the wine bottles from the large box. He arranged them on the back bar and wiped them down with a clean dish rag.

"When?"

"When? Oh, I don't know, over the summer some time?"

He said it so nonchalantly, as if he didn't realize just how floored Dr. Harlan was. It was as if he didn't realize that one of the most beautiful women he'd ever met, inside and out, had asked for his birthday. Not only that, but she had asked and remembered months later. *Why didn't she ask me herself?* he wondered.

"You'd be surprised," Otis said.

The blood drained from Dr. Harlan's face. *Did he just read my mind?* "What?" he asked, not sure if he wanted to know what he'd be surprised by or if, at long last, Otis was revealing he had the power of telepathy, and that was how he catered to his patrons so well over the years.

"You'd be surprised how much she admires you," Otis said.

Dr. Harlan stilled in his seat. He was fully uninterested in the food and the wine now.

"Listen, doc, I know I'm taking some liberties here, but it needs to be said. Things have been a certain way for you for a long time. I've known you long enough to know you're a man of integrity, and you always try to do the right thing, but sometimes the best things for us are the things we're too afraid to ask for."

Otis's candor didn't shock Dr. Harlan. It was as if they were meant to have this conversation, as open and honest as it was, and there was no need to stand on ceremony. He wished he didn't comprehend Otis's meaning, but he did. He understood him perfectly.

"It doesn't matter what I want, Otis. I'm sure she's talked to you about everything, including bits and pieces I am shocked to know about."

"You're too hard on yourself," Otis said.

"That may be, but that's not the point. Has she told you about what happened before she came here?"

"Yes, she has."

"Then you know. You know it would be selfish of me to try. She had her heart broken, Otis. It can take months, *years* to get over something like that. I can't, in good faith, swoop in and try to... I'm her doctor. Even if I did try, if my attention wasn't wanted, it would ruin whatever friendship and trust she has in me. I'm not willing to risk that."

Otis fell silent, which was something that didn't happen often.

"Do you know how she feels? Do you have any inkling of what it is she wants?" Dr. Harlan asked.

"No, but I have my suspicions," said Otis.

"Suspicions aren't enough."

The door opened, and Everett, Jenna, Damien, Seth, Lenora, and Emelia piled into the room, obviously a little drunk from the afternoon's festivities.

"Doc!" Everett called. He broke away from Jenna, who had her arm around his waist, and approached Dr. Harlan at the bar. "Good to see you."

"I loved the reading, Everett. Congratulations on a job well done," Dr. Harlan said.

"Aw man, I didn't see you there! You stopped by?"

"I wouldn't miss it."

"That's really sweet," Everett said, tearing up. He was a bit drunk, so Dr. Harlan chalked up his sudden show of emotion to the copious amounts of wine he no doubt consumed. "Man, this has been such a great day. Seren introduced me to this publishing guy who she's friends with. I just... I just can't believe it."

The party took residence at a large table in the corner. Jenna called out, summoning Everett to join them.

"Anyway, thanks for coming, doc. I gotta get back," Everett said, shaking the doctor's hand again before stumbling off to join the group.

Dr. Harlan swiveled in his chair to look at Otis. "And you're sure it's me she admires?"

"Yes, she—"

"Hey, Otis! Could we get a round of beers, please?" Lenora called.

Dr. Harlan stood and took a final sip of his Merlot. It was clear Otis had more to say, but as the group grew louder and music started to play on the jukebox, the time for candor and honesty had passed.

"Coming right up!" Otis called to the group, who whooped and hollered in excitement. As they started to chant Otis's name, Dr. Harlan placed a twenty on the counter and slipped out the front door.

Chapter 10

Dr. Harlan closed his apartment door behind him and immediately felt guilty for feeling sorry for himself. He was completely overwhelmed. The day had not gone how he expected, and he yearned to get back to his routine. His soulless, normal, sterile routine, where the worst he ever had to deal with was getting Horace to eat more vegetables or running out of modeling glue.

It wasn't exciting or noteworthy, but at least he could sleep in peace and finish each day, only wondering what he would have for dinner or what route he wanted to take on an afternoon walk. Seren had changed everything. He hoped to see her wherever he went and always wanted to know how she was doing or how things were going on the farm. He hoped she was warm enough during those cold winter nights and had enough firewood, company, and whatever else she might want.

He leaned against the cold door frame and thought about when she held him at the clinic. He knew she needed comfort, and he was happy to give her whatever she needed. He wondered if it had been someone else, would she have done the same? Seren was kind to everyone, so why would he be special?

You've got to stop doing this to yourself, he thought. *You know she cares for you. Look at everything she's done and said. Why doubt it?*

Dr. Harlan walked to the kitchen window that looked toward Hiraeth Farm. Just beyond the trees, small puffs of smoke rose into the air, a sure sign she was home. If he were more daring, he might take out his phone and call her or march over to explain everything. Instead, he stood in his dimly lit kitchen, gripping the countertop and dreaming of things that would most likely never come to be.

He ran his hand down his face and realized he was still hungry, and opened the freezer. Inside were a few frozen dinners with peas, potatoes, and salmon. It was no home-cooked meal, but he opened one of the bright blue boxes with the too-good-looking food on the cover, punctured a few holes in the plastic, and threw it in the microwave.

He plopped down on his couch and turned on the tv. He didn't care what he watched, just as long as there was sound to keep him company. A rerun of *Seinfeld* was on.

Good enough, he thought.

He ate his meal within minutes and threw the empty container on the coffee table, unsatisfied. The episode of *Seinfeld* ended, and rather than endlessly flipping through channels as he had done on many nights just like tonight, he switched off the tv and tossed the remote beside him on the couch.

He thought of Seren again, wrapping her arms around him. She was so close to him. Any closer and they'd be—*stop,* he thought. Still, the memory of her warm body pressed against his was beginning to drive him mad. He felt where her hands grasped fistfuls of his lab coat, and how he had to will his breath from catching in his throat. He hadn't realized how touch-starved he was until then, and he wished for nothing more in this moment than to hold her again.

The memory lingered, and his mind wandered. Suddenly, they were in his apartment, and she was pushing him onto the couch. She straddled his lap, looked deeply into his eyes, and kissed him. She undid his shirt as she kissed him again, harder, and ran her hands up his chest. It was needy and urgent, the way she grabbed at him. *Harlan... please,* she whispered in his ear, and it sent hot blood all the way down to—

Dr. Harlan's eyes snapped open, and he leaned forward to perch on his elbows. *Enough,* he thought. He undid his tie and ran a hand through his hair as he tried to stave off his mounting arousal.

"What are you doing?" he said aloud.

He stood and rubbed the back of his neck as he walked to the fridge and opened it. There was nothing to drink inside besides water and a half-drunk carton of orange juice. He wished he had something stronger, but he tried not to make a habit of keeping alcohol in the apartment. He grabbed a bottle of water and started to close the fridge when the little heart on Seren's card caught his eye. At last, he surrendered.

I love her.

He felt scared and unsure, but he was completely devoted to swallowing those words for as long as he could. He did not want to imagine any future without her, so for now, he would pay the price of his love with silence.

Chapter 11

Seren sat on the couch, wrapped in a thick-knit, blush-colored blanket Edna had made for her. Somehow, news that her birthday had passed reached Edna, and being the kind, maternal woman she was, she immediately put her knitting skills to work.

"Just think of it as an early Christmas present," she had said to Seren.

It was soft and comfortable. Perfect for sitting in front of the fire on a cold night like this.

Seren had attempted to decorate for the holidays. She bought a small tree from Rita. It stood no taller than Seren's shoulders and had a few branches missing, but it fit her needs. She wove two lengths of white Christmas lights throughout its branches and fashioned a homemade star from sticks in the yard and rough brown twine to the top of the tree. It wasn't much, but it gave Seren a warm, fuzzy feeling when she looked at it.

It was 7:00 p.m., and she hadn't heard from Jenna, but Seren was perfectly happy to spend a quiet night in. She figured Jenna was still out with Everett and that the two of them must be drunk on celebration and cheap beer.

How much she had liked Everett's writing surprised Seren. It was a little flowery, but she enjoyed it. It was well-composed and left her wanting to know if the lovers would end up together. She hoped that they would.

There was a soft, almost imperceptible tapping on the front door. If the air weren't as still as it was outside, Seren may not have heard it. She checked her phone again to see if Jenna had texted her about coming over, but she had no new messages. She rose, still wrapped in the knit blanket, and walked to the door. When she opened it, Jake stood on the porch, hunched in on himself with his hands stuffed in his jacket pockets. The wound on his cheek had healed some, and he had much more color in his face than the last time she'd seen him. He even looked as if he may have shaved in the last day or so.

"Jake," she said, wrapping the blanket tightly around herself.

He stared at the wooden floorboards, looking very much like a lost child, seeming unable to look at her. She could feel his every pain and regret. When he met her gaze, his eyes did all the talking. They were steeped in sadness and guilt, and Seren felt there were no words she could offer him, no matter how much she wished she could, to relieve him of it.

"I won't be here long," he said. "I just wanted to say that I'm—" Tears cut him off. His body twitched as he seemed to strangle his emotions.

Seren walked onto the porch and hugged him. He shook as she held him, and though she wasn't sure Jake would react well to the gesture, she felt that he needed it.

"It's freezing out here," she said, her bare feet stinging from the cold. "Please, come in."

He followed her, and she shut the door behind them.

"Warm yourself up by the fire," Seren said.

Jake sat on the couch, still wearing his black winter coat, and hastily wiped his eyes with the backs of his hands. He sniffled and let out a short sigh as he leaned on his knees, still refusing to look at Seren.

"Can I get you anything? Some tea, or—"

"No," he said.

Seren adjusted the blanket around her shoulders and placed her hands in her lap. She sat with her legs piled beneath her, facing Jake, who sat staring at the fire, closed off and distant. He didn't move for a while. It was as if he expected a scolding from Seren, or that she would admonish him for being stupid, but she didn't. She gave him all the time and space he needed to begin when he was ready.

"I don't know…" he said, lacing his fingers together. "I don't know what to…"

"I'm so glad you're okay, Jake."

He looked at her then. "You are?"

"So, so glad." Seren reached forward and clasped Jake's hand in hers.

"Why?"

"*Why?* Jake, you're my friend."

"I am?"

"Yes!"

He let Seren hold his hand for a little longer before retracting it back into his lap. He looked at the fire again, his expression unreadable.

"You don't believe me, do you?" Seren asked.

"No. No, not really," he said.

"Why?"

"Because I'm not worth having as a friend," he snapped.

Seren could tell he had said those words to himself many times before, like a dark mantra that kept him away from everyone.

"Jake, what did you think? That I'd—that everyone would be happy if you were hurt?"

"Yes," he said.

"Please help me to understand," Seren continued.

Jake said nothing.

"When… When I found you, you said you didn't want to be here anymore. Did you mean that?"

"You want the truth?" he asked.

"Please," she said.

"I've wanted to die for as long as I can remember. All of this…" He gestured around the room and to himself. "I'm not cut out for it. So, yes, I got drunk and sat out there for a while, thinking I'd just… fall. I've never been very good at living, so I guess I thought I'd be better at dying. Turns out I can't even do that."

"You could have talked to me," said Seren.

"Yeah, well, no one has ever cared before," he said, anger flashing across his face. "And this thing of us being friends is news to me." Seren moved closer to him.

"I care, and we *are* friends." Seren clasped his hand again, refusing to let him shut her out.

Jake glanced at her, his face softening a little.

"Jake, I know we butt heads from time to time, but that's just how we are together. You drive me crazy, but you also make me laugh. You keep me honest. Hiraeth wouldn't be what it is now without your help, and I'll always be grateful. And I need you to know you can always talk to me. I mean it. I don't want you to ever feel alone, because you aren't."

Something shifted in him as if he was allowing someone to see him for the first time in a long time. "When I was fifteen, I found my mother on the bathroom floor. I called to her, but she didn't move." He paused as if anticipating some reaction, but she sat where she was and listened. "She was young. It didn't make any sense. Not to me, anyway. My father blamed me for it. He always thought I was useless, that I'd never amount to anything. I was never the best student, had the most friends, or had anything I was really interested in. He said I broke her heart, and that was why she died. I believed him."

"You must know, Jake, it wasn't your fault," Seren said.

"I don't know that. It is possible to die from a broken heart."

"Yes, it is, but not in that instance, and not your mother."

"How do you know?"

"Because things happen, Jake. You can't spend all your life blaming yourself for might haves and what ifs."

Jake looked as though he had something to say in response, but he shut his mouth. He turned toward the fire again.

"I lost my mother when I was young, too," Seren said. "I couldn't make sense of it. One day, she was here, and the next, she wasn't. My father walked out long before it happened. I never really knew him well, but I loved my mother. She was my best friend. I couldn't understand why. Why would she be taken from me when I needed her? I never got an answer. In many ways, I suppose I've been searching for answers ever since, not only to why she had to go when she did, but to everything. It drove me crazy, that need to know why, but I finally realized there are some questions beyond answering. Living is the answer."

"How did she die?" Jake asked.

"Car accident."

"I'm sorry."

"I'm sorry for what you went through, too."

Jake looked down at her hand as it held his. A half smile spread across his face, one that Seren had never seen until then.

"Are... are you going to get the axe if I take my hand back now?" Jake asked, laughing.

"I might," Seren. She squeezed his hand and let it go. They laughed together.

"Well then, I guess I'd better behave."

Seren's phone rang on the coffee table, but it was from a number she didn't recognize.

"It'll go to voicemail," she said.

"So," Jake said, "with all this living you're doing, did you finally ask Dr. Harlan out? Not that it's any of my business or anything."

"I thought you knew everything about that, y'know, being in the right place at the right time and everything?"

"Maybe it's time you get on that."

"Yeah, maybe I should."

There was a loud knock at the door. "Seren, open up," Jenna called out.

250

"Oh, I'm sorry. She didn't tell me she was coming. Are you...?"

"I'm fine," Jake said.

Seren walked to the door and opened it. Jenna spilled into the cabin, bubbly and smiling. "*Fuck*, it's cold out there! Hello, my love." Jenna turned around and started to take off her coat, boots, and scarf to leave by the door. "That was so great, wasn't it? And he was just telling me about your publishing friend—oh." Jenna finally noticed Jake. "I'm sorry, I didn't know you had company."

"No, it's alright, join us. Um, you know Jake," Seren said, gesturing toward him.

"Yes, of course. Hi, Jake."

"Hi," Jake said.

Seren didn't think it was possible to infuse a single word with such apprehensive coldness, but somehow Jake pulled it off. He attempted a crooked smile, but it looked more like a grimace. Regardless, she had to give him credit for trying in his own way.

Chapter 12

In the night, Seren dreamed she stood beside a large pool surrounded by plastic, maroon lounge chairs and stacks of royal blue paddle boards waiting to be used. Feathery green palm trees swayed in the light breeze, meandering without care against the backdrop of a cloudless sky. The pungent smell of sunscreen and chlorine wafted through the air, and somewhere in the distance was a low rumble of churning, bubbling water from a jacuzzi. It reminded her of some place from her childhood, though she suspected she hadn't been there in quite some time.

The pool water was still, undisturbed by occupants or the wind. Her feet burned against the hot concrete, but she hesitated to go in the water. An almost imperceptible feeling of anticipation underscored her mood, and she looked around to see what it was she was meant to anticipate, but no one was there.

The gate that surrounded the hot tub clanged as the door shut.

"Hello?" she asked.

Nothing.

There was the ship's wheel again, sitting motionless at the far edge of the pool. She remembered it from the dream the morning she had awakened, hungover and sick. Naturally, that was a signal in an illogical dream world to go into the water and swim toward it, so she did.

When she emerged from the water, with her hair slicked back and mouth dry, she saw her grandfather, just as he was the last time, standing next to the wheel.

"How long do you want me to stay?" he asked.

"Always," she said.

"I can't."

"Why not?"

"Because it's your time now."

He spun the wheel, and it made her so dizzy she awoke in a daze, the lingering sting of hot summer concrete on the bottoms of her feet.

She remembered the phone call then. Whoever it was had left a voicemail. Bunching the covers around her, she reached for her phone and played the message.

"Seren? Hi, uh, this is Jordan. Sorry about the late hour. We met at the fair last summer, and I bought a few jars of your sauce. I just wanted to call to say that my colleagues and I very much enjoyed it. I apologize for not reaching out sooner, but things have been hectic. I'm a distributor for Good Harvest, and if S&O is still in production, we'd like to sell it in our stores."

Year Three

Chapter 1

Winter had been a flurry of late nights huddled around the firepit with Jake some nights, with Jenna on others, and even Jenna, Everett, and Emelia in between. Jake steadily grew into a newer, more content version of himself. Seren knew the darkness he had seen, and she understood his temper, his disregard for people who never asked him if he was okay, and even his choices, no matter how severe they were. She saw so much of herself in him. It was strange that they were so similar yet so different in their chosen paths. She had almost lost him to the darker path, and it didn't feel right to divert toward the lighter one without bringing him with her.

So, one night in January, she somehow convinced him to join her, Jenna, Everett, and Emelia for a night in at her place. It was the first time she broke out the old board games and playing cards from the closet, and it felt so right to laugh and have fun with her friends.

Jake no longer touched beer or liquor and found enjoyment in sparkling water and the occasional soda. That night, he had insisted it was all right for the rest of them to drink. Jenna, Emelia, and Everett knew nothing of what happened the past November, and Seren promised him it wasn't her story to tell. If the day came when he wanted to share, she would be there to support him. They were surprised at the sudden change in what seemed to be a fundamental part of Jake's personality, but they accepted it. Seren could tell it was Jake's turn to learn that people were fundamentally good and would accept him as he was or as whoever he decided to become.

By spring, after many nights spent talking and laughing, it felt as though they had always known each other. Their newfound group dynamic and friendship led them to decide to go to the Aster Dance together.

Seren stood before the mirror in her bedroom, making the final touches to her hair and makeup. She didn't wear one of Emelia's creations. Instead, she found a beautiful floor-length, backless white dress in the far corner of her closet. She had forgotten it was there and couldn't remember where she had worn it before, but it was perfect. It was far less whimsical than anything Emelia would have made for her, but it was sophisticated and regal. Her hair was twisted into loose curls, half pulled up in the back, and adorned with small white and pink roses and dark green leaves. Emelia had insisted she fashion one small braid down the back of her long locks. She smelled of jasmine and orange blossom, her skin glowing and soft to the touch. She kept her makeup simple and refined, her eyelashes long and black, and her lips painted an understated blush like a single budding rose. As she looked herself over, there was no denying she felt beautiful.

Seren heard a knock at the door and walked to open it.

"Hey!"

Seren, Jenna, Emelia, and Everett hugged and exchanged compliments about each other's outfits as they scaled the porch steps to head toward the dance.

"Is Jake coming?" Emelia asked.

"Yes. He said he'd meet us there," Seren said, adjusting a stray strand of hair back into place.

It was a beautiful, unseasonably warm April evening with a brilliant pink and orange sky. The Aster Dance had been scheduled later in the season than usual. Mayor Doney decided the increased warmth and sunlight of mid-spring would be more comfortable than late March, and he was right. None of them needed jackets, nor did they need to account for the soft earth of early spring, and they could wear whatever shoes they wanted.

They walked to the dance, drunk on laughter and conversation, ready to enjoy a night of mirth and light breezes. When they reached the clearing, it was aglow with string lights that dotted the sky like fireflies. Multiple bouquets of opulent, multicolored flowers spilled over large vases throughout, and a grand, pink bougainvillea stretched up the side of a distressed wooden trellis beside the dance floor.

Lenora ran up to them, closely followed by Damien and Seth. They exchanged greetings, their voices filling the late afternoon air with excitement. Seth and Damien seemed excited to be playing a few original songs and some of their favorite classic covers from the eighties and nineties. They had practiced all year, they said, and the band was really coming together.

They passed by the buffet table, where Otis stood eager and happy as always to cater the occasion. Seren walked behind the display to hug and greet the affable chef, who had really outdone himself. There wasn't a single space of table that wasn't covered in some mouthwatering dish, including salmon tartines, finger sandwiches, lettuce cups, homemade hummus with charred ciabatta, roasted rainbow carrots, and spring caprese with edible flowers.

Seren put on her best judgmental expression as she eyed the table with pursed lips. "Not bad. Maybe next year will be better."

He yanked a white bar towel from his shoulder and whipped it against Seren's arm.

She put her hands up in mock surrender.

Jenna and Emelia joined her at the table, and Seren pointed to the large bowl of familiar, sparkly, purple liquid. If Seren wasn't mistaken, it appeared a deeper shade of purple than usual. "Midnight punch?" she asked.

"Midnight punch," Emelia confirmed, laughing. "But I modified the recipe a little. Let me know what you think."

Emelia did the honors and poured them each a cup. They raised their purple potions into the air ceremoniously and took turns toasting to their health, happiness, and the pursuit of love in all its forms.

"Mmm," Seren said after taking a sip. "Even better than I remembered."

Seren felt a tap on her shoulder and turned to see Jake, who looked dapper in a blue suit and white button-down shirt with a white rose pinned to the lapel. He'd put in more effort than she'd ever seen him attempt, and best of all, he looked happy.

"Hey!" she said as she hugged him, careful not to spill any punch on his suit. "Look at you."

"It's not too much?" he asked, shrugging.

"No! You look fantastic. Is that hair product I see?"

"Yeah, uh, just something I'm trying out."

"Hi Jake," Emelia said.

"Hi, Emelia."

"I like your suit."

"Thanks." Jake wiped imaginary lint away from his pant leg.

A light dusting of pink spread across his cheeks, and Seren realized he was happy Emelia noticed him. *Is he blushing?* She wondered.

Emelia smiled at him and returned to her conversation with Damien—something about a possible gig for him and Seth to play in the city next month. Jake watched her with a clear expression of admiration on his face. He turned to the buffet table and asked for a sparkling water from Otis.

"So, you gonna ask her to dance?" Seren asked.

"What?" he replied.

"Come on, I saw that."

"I don't know what you're talking about," Jake said, his eyes darting to Emelia.

"She loves daisies. I think I saw some over there," Seren said, gesturing toward a large white vase next to the far end of the dance floor. "Just some food for thought."

Jake's cheeks went from light dusty pink to deep crimson.

"You've got this," Seren said as she patted his arm.

The sudden sound of a guitar amp and static cut through the clearing. Damien and Seth were getting set up on the stage. Seth played a few quick riffs on the keyboard, and Damien tapped the microphone. "Good evening, everybody! How we doing tonight?"

The clearing erupted in cheers and movement toward the dance floor.

"Let's get this thing started, how about it?" Damien asked. Once more, everyone cheered and clapped, and some raised their drinks high into the air.

Seth pressed a button on his keyboard, and off the pair went, playing heavy synth and guitar riffs. Damien sang a cover of *I Was Born To Love You* by Freddie Mercury. Everyone took to the dance floor, even Edna and Horace, who held hands and swayed back and forth together.

Jenna grabbed Seren and Jake's free hands and pulled them into the action close to Lenora and Everett, who were already dancing and singing along at the top of their voices. Everyone was out tonight, including some people from neighboring towns, and all together, they jumped, swayed, and let loose. Jenna got close to Seren and sang to her with her arms outstretched, her drink almost spilling. Seren got into the rhythm of the song and sang back to Jenna. Jake danced along clumsily alongside them.

Over the next twenty minutes, Seth and Damien played more upbeat party songs. By the end of their first set, Seren could feel a light sheen of sweat on her exposed back.

"Hey, you're cuttin' it up out there," Otis said as she approached the table in between songs.

"*Phew*," Seren breathed as she wiped her brow and poured more of the midnight punch. "Thank god it's so nice out, otherwise I'd be on the floor."

Damien announced, "We're going to take a short break, but when we return, things are going to get real nice and slow."

Seren looked at Jake, who was making conversation with Everett and occasionally glancing toward Emelia, who was talking to Jenna and pointing to the string lights. Seren remembered her first Aster

Dance. Looking at Jake then, all animosity that existed between them was gone, and she had never been more grateful to be wrong about a person.

"He's changed," Otis said.

"Hmm?"

"For the better, I mean. I can't help but feel you're the reason why," Otis explained.

Seren looked over her shoulder at him.

"That day you asked if he was at the bar—something happened, didn't it?"

Seren turned to face him, glanced at her drink, and then back up at him.

Otis somehow seemed to understand and nodded. "I don't see him much anymore, or if I do, he just gets a soda and talks to Emelia when she's on shift. He seems happier."

"He is," Seren said.

"I'm glad."

"Me too."

As Otis and Seren smiled at each other, Damien and Seth ran up beside her, sweaty and animated. Their excitement was palpable after a successful first round of songs.

"Otis, my man. We need drinks, stat!" Seth said, playfully swatting the countertop. "Seren. How are you liking the show?" He attempted to run a hand through his hair-sprayed locks and failed.

"You guys sound awesome. Can't wait for more," she said, raising her cup.

"Of course, m'lady," he said, tipping an imaginary hat. Damien asked for two cups of midnight punch, and Seth asked for one. With their drinks in hand, they took off toward the stage, eager to get back to playing.

By then, it was almost fully night, and the sky was a peculiar shade of blue. It glowed the way it did in the city from the atmospheric glare of thousands of lights tightly packed together. However, the stars were still visible, and Seren traced them along the sky toward the horizon until her eyes landed on someone she had wished for all night. Dr. Harlan hadn't yet seen her, so she took the opportunity to take him in. He looked divine. The viridian tweed suit he wore looked tailor-made and fit him in all the right places. He wore brown oxfords, a brown belt, and a floral tie that Seren hadn't seen him wear before. A tie had never looked so good on a man.

"Alright, guys, this next one is an original, so make some noise!" Damien said into the mic. Seren looked toward the stage as everyone started to clap and cheer, and she added her own cheers to the chorus. The band began to play, and when Seren looked back, Dr. Harlan was approaching her. She smoothed her dress and walked toward him. Seren's heart beat a little faster as he drew closer, and the anticipation of being near him made the hairs on the back of her neck stand on end.

"Hello, Dr. Harlan," she said.

"Seren," he said, smiling down at her. "You look…" His face softened as he looked at her. "Beautiful."

"Thank you. I wasn't sure you were going to make it."

"I had a last-minute patient, but all is well. What is *that?*" he asked, pointing to her cup.

"Oh, midnight punch. Emelia made it."

"I'll have to try it."

"Not on call this year?"

"No, not this time."

The pair walked to the buffet table, their arms lightly brushing. The song Damien and Seth played was unexpectedly tender, unlike their usual fun, edgy style. "Turns out I'm not one of those people, one of those people who can be alone…" Damien crooned as Seren and Dr. Harlan talked with Otis, who chuckled when the doctor asked for a cup of punch.

"Well, alright, doc! Be prepared, though. Infused with Dionysian magic, that is," Otis said.

Seren and Dr. Harlan walked away from the table and stood just outside the dance floor. She watched him as he took a sip and eagerly awaited his reaction.

"*Oh,* wow, that is—"

"Surprising?" Seren offered.

"Yes," Dr. Harlan said, clearing his throat. "Very."

Seren watched Everett and Jenna slow dance together. She looked up at him with adoration as he brushed a strand of hair from her forehead and kissed it. More and more couples were taking to the dance floor, wrapping their arms around each other, talking, and settling into a slower rhythm. That rhythm, sweet and intoxicating, reached Seren.

"Nice song," Dr. Harlan said.

"Yeah," she agreed.

The song ended, and Damien picked up an electric guitar and slung its red strap over his shoulder.

"Alright folks, we have a special guest for this next one, but she may need some encouragement. Help me get her up here. Le-nor-a! Le-nor-a!"

After enough cheering and support, Lenora eventually pried her hands away from her face and ran up on stage to join Damien and Seth. She stepped up to the mic and sighed into it.

"Alright, alright! All I can say is, see Dr. Harlan afterward if I burst anyone's eardrums," she said, extending her open hand in his direction. Everyone laughed at Lenora's joke and turned to fix Dr. Harlan with a humorous glance before returning their attention to the stage.

"Okay, here we go," Lenora said.

Damien pulled up a stool next to her and sat. He strummed the guitar once, arranged his fingers into a starting chord, and looked at her. She breathed in, and together they started playing a stripped-down version of *Wicked Game* by Chris Isaac. Lenora's breathy, seductive voice filled the clearing as every couple came together and swayed to the music.

"Hey! Come on, you guys," Jenna called.

Seren looked at her friend, who was waving at her and Dr. Harlan, demanding they join them.

"It seems we've been summoned," he said.

"We have," Seren said. "Um…"

Her fingers felt cold against the cup of punch, and a strange chill washed over her as she dared to look at him.

"Shall we?" he asked.

"Yes," she said.

Dr. Harlan placed their drinks on the buffet table. Lenora's sultry voice filled the air as they walked together to the dance floor. Something swelled in Seren's chest that she didn't recognize. It felt like fear but it wasn't. It was too sweet, too much like coming home. The serpents were gone, and there was no force waiting to throw her over the edge. Not this time. Instead of falling into nothingness, she was falling into him and his eyes as he stood looking down at her.

He offered his hand, and she took it. Softly, like a slow caress, she slid her hand up his shoulder and found purchase there. He slid one arm around her waist and pulled her close, his hand warm against the small of her back.

"I had no idea Lenora could sing like that," he said.

"Neither did I," Seren said. "She's good."

Seren looked around to find Jake dancing with Emelia. She had both arms draped over his shoulders, a single white daisy dangling from her relaxed hand. As they turned, Seren caught his eye and smiled at him. *Good job,* she mouthed, and Jake smiled back.

"Thank you for the gift, by the way. They were delicious," Dr. Harlan said.

"I'm glad."

"I'm sorry I didn't thank you earlier. I was… uhm, I was busy."

"It's all right," she said as her thumb brushed against his neck. She didn't realize she had done it until he leaned his head toward her touch. The small gesture of care and comfort was almost unnoticeable. The look he gave her then unnerved everything she had left, and though she felt she had little courage, she looked back at him.

"Dr. Harlan—"

"Please, call me Harlan."

"Harlan."

All Seren's logic, all the thoughts that told her in a frantic frenzy to close herself, to resist and run away, dried up, and every word she might have said disappeared under a feeling of surrender. All sense of control slipped away under the warmth and safety of his touch, and in that moment, she felt complete. She felt as if she could breathe again, that she could stand still, as if there was all the time in the world.

"You know," she said, "I was just thinking. Of all the thousands of years passed, and all the people who have come and gone, how lucky I am to be here with you, under the same sky. It's sort of a miracle, isn't it?"

Lenora sang the last line of the song, and the music gradually faded out. Dr. Harlan trailed his fingers down Seren's forearm as they came to a stop.

"It is," he said. "Seren...I—"

The floor erupted into thunderous applause, with many people shouting, "Encore!" and, "We want more!"

"I trust no one needs to see Dr. Harlan after that tantalizing performance?" Seth called over the microphone. It caught Seren and Dr. Harlan off guard, and they dropped their arms as they turned toward the stage.

"None here! Ha-ha!" Faye cried, giggling and clearly under the influence of multiple cups of midnight punch, and perhaps something else. "Come on, girl, give us another!"

"Alright, boys, do we have one more?" Lenora asked. The crowd cheered as Seth and Damien readied themselves to play another song with Lenora at the helm. She flipped her hair, clearly loving the attention of being in the spotlight. She looked good in command. Seth and Damien came up to the mic to sing an opening verse, and then Lenora took over once more.

Below Dr. Harlan's waist, Theo was pulling at his pant leg. "Here, Mr. Harlan," he said, extending a single purple aster to the doctor.

"Oh, hello, Theo," Dr. Harlan said, crouching next to the little boy. "What a pretty flower! Thank you so much."

Theo looked between Seren and Dr. Harlan a few times before he took off running towards the buffet table, where Marnie and Otis stood, grinning at one another. Seren shook her head. *Very clever, you two,* she thought.

Dr. Harlan stood and turned to Seren, the flower in his hand. He smiled softly, the noise of the crowd and the music blending into a distant hum.

"Seren," he began, taking a step closer.

"Yes?" she whispered.

He gently tucked the purple aster into her hair, his fingers brushing her cheek as he did so. "It suits you," he said, his voice barely audible over the renewed music. He took a step back and placed his hands in his pockets. "I just wanted to say... how proud I am of you. You really have come into your own."

Seren felt her eyes water. "Thank you," she said.

He smiled at her.

A soft, hesitant voice spoke behind them. "Dr. Harlan?" They both turned to see Corinne, her hands clasped in front of her. "I'm sorry to interrupt, I just wanted to ask you a question about the, um—my—"

"Of course, Mrs. Williams. I'll be right there." He turned back to Seren, his eyes lingering on her a moment longer.

"Duty calls," Seren said.

"I'll find you," he said, and Seren nodded.

As he walked away, Seren touched the purple aster in her hair. The music swelled, and she watched him blend into the crowd, feeling a sense of promise and hope hanging in the air. Jenna and Emelia swarmed her then and pulled her into the throng of swaying bodies, where they danced the rest of the starry night away.

Chapter 2

It's sort of a miracle, isn't it?

Seren's words bounced around Dr. Harlan's mind like a voice echoing down a deep well. It was a miracle. There were billions of people on the planet, and only two of them. The chances were small that they'd ever meet, and yet they had. That had to account for something.

"And Horace will be here in ten minutes. Should I prepare the room?"

Dr. Harlan squeezed a red stress ball as he half-listened to Mira speak.

"Dr. Harlan?"

His eyes refocused as he blinked twice to look at Mira. She had a concerned, expectant look on her face, as if he were a sideshow attraction, oblivious to the world around him.

"Hmm? Oh, yes, Harold Grinaker. That would be fine," he said, still squeezing the stress ball.

"No, Horace Fielder, not Harold Grinaker."

"Oh, yes, of course."

"Are you all right, Dr. Harlan?"

"Yes," he said, clearing his throat. "Yes, I'm fine."

"I don't mean to pry. It's just that you've seemed very distracted recently. Sometimes I hardly know where you are, even if we're in the same room together," Mira said.

The pitying expression on her face made Dr. Harlan snap back to reality. He was embarrassed to have been perceived in that manner. He opened his desk drawer, disposed of the stress ball, and shut the door so hard that it bounced off the back panel and opened again.

"S—sorry," he stuttered as he closed the door again, propping both hands against the seam to make sure it stuck. When he was certain, he placed his hands on his desk. "Yes, I'm fine. Thank you, Mira. Please get the room ready for…"

"Horace."

"Yes, Horace."

Mira lingered in his office doorway with one last look of concern that made Dr. Harlan want to bury his head in one of the large file folders on his desk. Refusing to look at her, he reached for one and opened it as she closed the door. It was Seren Grinaker's file. He snapped the olive-green folder shut and tossed it away as if it had burned his fingers. He was grateful Mira hadn't seen him do it, or the way he then tossed his glasses on his desk and rubbed his eyes as if he had a spare set in the exam room. He took a deep breath and pinched his eyebrow ridge until he felt pressure between his fingertips, then put on his glasses. For what seemed like the millionth time that day, they slid down the bridge of his nose, and he pushed them back up. He'd tighten the screws later.

He stood and stared at the stack of files. Just knowing that hers was on top was enough to bring her image racing back, and he couldn't shake her.

Maybe I'll become a drunk, he thought. *That would do it.*

His impulse had been correct. He did need Horace's file before their routine checkup that afternoon. He'd just grabbed the wrong one. He put Seren's on the bottom and fished out Horace's file from the rest of the stack. It was thick from so many visits and complaints over the years, whether it was a headache, a shoulder that just wouldn't move the way it used to, or any little thing that Horace wanted to gripe about, including Dr. Harlan himself. He expected Horace would be no different that day, and he readied himself to give the same tired advice in a well-practiced and even-pitched tone that conveyed support and noninterventionism. Horace was the type of patient who had to feel he was doing everything on his terms, and no 'philandering, double-crossing doctor' would order him otherwise.

The thought of seeing him put Seren far enough out of Dr. Harlan's mind that he could regain composure and make his way to the exam room.

Mira opened the exam door and welcomed the Fielders inside. To Dr. Harlan's surprise, Horace looked as though he had lost weight and walked with more life than he had seen in all the previous visits combined.

"Good t'see ya, Dr. Harlan," Horace said, patting his arm as if they were old friends.

The gesture caught Dr. Harlan off guard, and he caught Mira's eye as she shut the door. She seemed as bewildered as he was.

"Mr. Fielder," Dr. Harlan said.

Edna took her usual seat against the wall and pulled out a pair of knitting needles. Dr. Harlan was making sure she was comfortable as he heard a rare sound behind him—the crunch of paper. He turned and saw Horace sitting on the examination table with his fingers laced together, patiently waiting to begin.

"Well, Mr. Fielder, you seem to be in good spirits."

"I am, doc, I am."

"Excellent," Dr. Harlan said as he opened Horace's file. "Last visit, we spoke of potentially fitting you for a cane or support of some kind—"

"Oh, that won't be necessary," Horace said.

"It won't?"

"No. I've been doing some walking, and I can get around just fine."

270

"Fantastic. That's great to hear. How is that going?"

"Oh, a little here, a little there, just enough to stretch my legs. Zach gets me out most days. He sure does love to throw that baseball around," Horace said almost gleefully, and Dr. Harlan's eyebrows raised in amazement. "I've been monitoring my blood pressure too, doc, and guess, *guess* what it is."

"Let's see, one forty over ninety?"

"Nope. Try one twenty-five over seventy."

"Horace, that's… that's incredible. Congratulations!"

He checked Horace's blood pressure just to be sure, and he was right: it was one twenty-five over seventy. Next, he had Horace step onto the scale and annotated his weight, which was another dramatic change. He weighed in at two hundred and one pounds, fifty pounds less than their previous visit.

"So, tell me, what have you done differently?" Dr. Harlan asked.

"It's that girl. She inspired me."

"Who?"

"You know the one," Edna said. "That beautiful farm girl, the one you were dancing with the other night."

Dr. Harlan looked at Edna, who gave him a knowing look as if she knew about the feelings he'd buried, that no living soul except himself had heard, but he ignored it. "Seren Grinaker?"

"Yes, that's the one," Horace said. "She brought me some beets. Damn delicious, they were. So, you don't gotta worry about pestering me to eat vegetables anymore, doc. I got a newfound appreciation for the suckers."

"She brought you beets…"

"Yeah. Don't act so surprised. I know most people hate 'em, but by God, I love 'em! Anyway, it got me thinking about the meaning of life and whatnot. I decided I wanted to be around some more, y'know? Get to know my grandkid as he grows up." Horace took out his wallet and showed Dr. Harlan what looked like a recent photo of both Horace and Edna with their arms around Zach's shoulders, who was carrying a baseball and mitt.

"What an angel she is," Edna said, placing a hand on her heart.

"Yes," Dr. Harlan agreed.

Horace's eyes glinted, and he clicked his tongue. Edna smiled and nodded as she returned to her knitting. Dr. Harlan shook his head and forced his attention back to Horace's file.

"Well, Mr. Fielder, it seems we will be seeing less of you from here on out as long as you keep at it. You've accomplished a lot. You should be proud." Dr. Harlan shut the file and placed it on the counter. "Is there anything else I can help you with?"

"Not a thing. Thank you, Dr. Harlan," Horace said as he clapped his knees with both hands and stood. "Edna, honey, I'm making us dinner tonight."

"How lovely, dear," Edna said as they shared a quick peck.

Horace opened the door with Edna's hand in his, and Dr. Harlan followed them out to the waiting room.

"Thanks for stopping by," Dr. Harlan said.

"It was a pleasure," Horace said as he shook Dr. Harlan's hand.

From behind the front desk, Mira suppressed a giggle. She and Dr. Harlan shared a bewildered glance as if they had stepped into some alternate dimension where up was down, and down was up, and where Horace Fielder was an agreeable man.

"Oh, there is one thing I might offer *you* help with, however," Horace said. "I suspect you'll be looking for a ring soon, so just a word of advice, get her a good one. Whatever she wants. It'll be worth it."

Horace winked at Dr. Harlan, kissed Edna's cheek, and the two of them left the clinic arm in arm. The bell chimed as the door shut behind them, leaving Dr. Harlan and Mira in silence.

"What was that about?" Mira asked.

"He's... feeling much better," Dr. Harlan said.

"No, not that. What about a ring?"

"I have no idea."

He must have done a good job of portraying total obliviousness because Mira seemed to let it go, but he could tell Horace's little speech would undoubtedly come up again.

"Is there anyone else on the schedule for today?" he asked.

"No, Horace was the last one, but you do have a letter here."
Mira handed him a white parchment envelope with cursive
handwriting.

"Thank you. If you'd like, you can go for the day," Dr. Harlan
said.

As he entered his office, he read over the sealed envelope. After
closing the door behind him, he sat and plopped it on his desk. It was
addressed to him from Turner Hospital. *Staffing Department* was
written under the first line, and Dr. Harlan was pretty sure he knew it
was a job offer.

Chapter 3

Seren was loading a new batch of cucumbers and carrots into a wheelbarrow when she checked her watch. It was 3:02 p.m. Seren sighed and looked toward the vacant pathway leading to town. Jake was late—again.

The past few weeks, he always came a good half hour to an hour later than he promised. A lot was happening that day, and she needed his help. As the summer season approached, there was only so much work she could do on her own. This summer would be the busiest growing season to date. Many nights, she dreamed of boxes full of rotting vegetables or fields completely dried up and ravaged by ravens and hungry earthworms, and all she could do was watch as everything succumbed to death and decay. She had brought Hiraeth back from the brink of collapse, but at the rate the farm was expanding, it was getting to be too much to handle on her own.

Seren unloaded the fresh vegetables onto a wire sheet that hung over one of two large farmhouse basins. The new addition made work on the farm much easier. She no longer dirtied her cabin floors with each trip between harvesting and washing in the small kitchen sink. She could pick, wash, and package the produce all in one place and keep her home life separate.

Not bad, she thought as she piled the last of the vegetables onto the counter. There would be plenty of cucumbers, carrots, beets, and lettuce for all the residents of Adytown and even for the next few towns over too. She had successfully staggered the crops and supplied Perry's with a springtime bounty each week. It never failed to surprise her how quickly he sold out and asked for more.

His newest thing was calling her Harold before correcting himself. He'd say, "We're sure showing that damned Myron, aren't we, Har—Seren?" and, "I can't believe it. This is just like old times, isn't it, Har—Seren?" Perry was a new man, and though his slip-ups were annoying, Seren understood. She had helped him save his store, and for that, she would gladly be the ghost of Hiraeth's past.

Seren checked her watch again. It was 3:23 p.m.

"Where is he?"

She took off her gloves and washed her hands. It was the last day she had to pick, wash, and deliver the last of the late spring crops to Perry, and prepare a shipment of S&O's Marinara for Saffron's. A delivery truck was scheduled to come no later than five to pick up the latest batch. She also told Chessy she would come by to pick up six new chicks and a brooder she purchased, although, at her current rate, there was no way she'd make it. She sent Chessy a quick text, letting her know she would need to stay at the farm until five, and that maybe she could swing by afterwards.

Seren was washing carrots when she heard shuffling footsteps behind her. "There you are! What took so long?"

Jake was dressed in a pair of ill-fitting black dress pants, a much-too-tight black button-down with a bowtie, and a black baseball cap with *WM* written in large block letters on the brim. He had a blue duffle bag slung over his shoulder that he was attempting to unzip, but the zipper kept getting stuck. By the look on Jake's face, and his pulling at the constricting collar, he wasn't happy about the outfit or the zipper.

"What are you wearing?" Seren asked.

"New uniform. I hate it," Jake said.

"Why do you have a new uniform?"

"Myron thinks it'll drive in more customers if we look more presentable."

"That's debatable," said Seren as she returned to rinsing the cucumbers, and Jake snorted.

"Thanks. I'm gonna change real quick, just wanted to let you know I'm here."

"Okay, but please hurry! You're like two hours late," Seren called after him.

Seren got into a rhythm as she waited for Jake and prepared enough cucumbers to fill one produce crate.

When he returned, he fell in line next to her and helped her work. "For the record, I wasn't two hours late. I was an hour and twenty-six minutes late."

"Oh, well, *excuse* me," Seren said.

She looked at him, expecting to see the same sly smile she'd come to expect from his teasing, but his face was humorless and grim instead.

Jake shrugged and snapped the roots from a stack of washed and dried carrots before depositing them into an empty crate. Seren had planned on giving him a hard time for being late, yet again, but something told her to approach the subject differently. This was soft Jake, the same one who needed comforting, just like the night he came to see her the past winter.

They're probably taking advantage of him, she thought. *He'd never choose to stay at W&M more than here.*

"I'm sorry they're overworking you," she said.

"I hate working there. I've given them four years of my life, and for what? Next to no pay and a shitty outfit."

Seren let him vent as they finished the last of the vegetables. He told her about how Myron "had" to cut his pay over the last few months because of a bad second quarter. "Whatever the hell that means," Jake said. He told her about the times Myron deliberately rearranged items Jake had just restocked to create more work for him, how he forced Jake to stay late, with no overtime, to fill in for tasks Myron should have been doing himself, and how everything about the place irritated him.

"You know they play the same music every day?" Jake asked.

It was clear to Seren that Jake felt he had no future at Wares & More, that every day there was a waste of time, yet it seemed he didn't know where else to go. He hadn't finished school and didn't want to go back, but even if he did, he'd have no idea what to study.

"I don't really have a passion for anything," he said.

Seren loaded the last of the crates into the same wagon she'd used for the prior year's fair. As she looked at it, she suspected she may need to invest in something larger. They hauled the wagon into town, with Seren pulling on the handle and Jake pushing from behind.

"You should get a horse," Jake said.

"A horse?"

"Yeah, so you can get a bigger wagon, and a horse could pull it. Chessy has one."

"What year is it, 1888?" Seren asked.

Jake rolled his eyes. "Anyway, I'm sorry to complain. I just—I'm lost, I guess."

"I've been there. I know it's cliché, but things will get better," Seren said.

Jake snorted and kept pushing the wagon. "I doubt it."

Seren grunted as she pulled the wagon. As they made their way to Perry's, a wheel bounced over a hole in the ground. A crate of cucumbers fell, but Jake caught it before any of them could spill out onto the ground.

"Nice catch," Seren said as she looked around to make sure there were no more potholes to disturb the rest of their journey. "I need to ask Frank if he can get someone to fix this road."

After Seren and Jake dropped off the produce at Perry's, who this time resisted calling her Harold, they arrived back at the farm with just enough time to make sure all the cans of S&O were accounted for. They had just counted the last can when a truck with *Saffron's Grocers since 1978* printed on the side door pulled in front of

277

the cabin. Seren's phone vibrated, and she saw that Chessy had texted her back.

No problem! I'll stick around here until 5:30. They're so excited to meet their new mommy. Come by if you can!

"Can you oversee this? I have to run one more errand," Seren asked Jake.

"Yeah, go ahead," he said.

Seren took off toward the south side of the farm while Jake and the Saffron's rep loaded the sauce into the bed of the truck. With any luck, she could make it to Chessy's before 5:30 and pick up the chicks. She was excited to take them to their new home. Rita had almost finished building her a state-of-the-art coop with plenty of space for them to roam. The outdoor access was enclosed with screened walls so that when they were older, they'd be protected from potential predators—including Mabon. Seren hoped the tabby would come to see the chicks as her friends, but she also knew Mabon was a cat, and it wasn't worth the risk.

The hen house itself also had ventilation and three nesting stations for when the chickens were old enough to lay eggs. The chicks were only a few weeks old, so it would be a few months before then.

Seren rounded the corner of Chessy's brick house and rang the doorbell. She checked her watch; she made it with five minutes to spare. Cows and pigs mooed and grunted as they shuffled around the pasture next to the house. Seren looked toward them and saw a beautiful buckskin horse. It swished its tail and flared its nostrils as it regarded her.

You must be the horse Jake was talking about, she thought.

Moments later, Chessy opened the door and hugged Seren. "There you are! So happy to see you. Come on in."

Chessy's home was the kind of charming old farmhouse one would expect to see in *Country Living* magazines. Everything was well kept and in its proper place, but without being too rigid or cold. A distressed wooden counter with a cash register stood in the entryway, resembling a makeshift base of operations for the farm. To the right was a long, white staircase leading to the second floor, adorned with numerous pictures of Chessy with her animals and a sweet group shot of her with Jake and Gia.

"They're right through here," Chessy said as she ushered Seren into the living room.

A large metal container sat in the center of the room, and inside of it were her chicks. Their tentative chirps melted Seren's heart, and already, she loved them.

"Aren't they precious?"

"They're so cute," Seren said as she drew closer. "Can I pick one up?"

"Of course, dear!"

Seren kneeled next to the brooder and picked up a golden chick. Her little body was covered in the softest down, and her tiny face and small black eyes peered at Seren with curiosity. She felt the strongest need to make sure they lived the happiest lives at Hiraeth.

"It's so rewarding to raise chicks. You get to see their personalities grow every day," Chessy said.

"I can't wait." Seren smiled at the baby chick and placed her carefully back into the brooder with her sisters.

Chessy briefed her on what to expect over the next few months. Chickens, as it turned out, were no more difficult to care for than Mabon. Chessy offered to help carry the brooder back to Hiraeth, but it wasn't heavy, so Seren assured her she could manage on her own. After settling payment, Chessy walked Seren outside.

"Oh, and not to pass even more animals over to you, but I've been meaning to sell miss Freya over there." Chessy jerked a thumb at the horse Seren was looking at earlier. "I think she'd be happier with a bit more space and independence. Would you be interested?"

Seren glanced at Freya, who must've heard them talking about her because she pranced toward them.

"She seems to like you," Chessy said with a laugh.

"I used to love riding, but it's been quite a while," Seren said. It was uncanny how Freya's attention was undoubtedly fixed on her, and in moments, it felt like a connection was forming. "I'll have to think about it."

When Seren returned to Hiraeth, the Saffron's rep was gone. Seren arrived just when she needed to because even though the brooder wasn't heavy, her arms had grown tired on the journey. She placed the brooder on the ground inside the coop and clipped a heat lamp on it to keep the chicks warm.

"Welcome home," she said.

The chicks scuttled around the brooder and squeaked as they bumped into each other, excitedly congregating underneath the glow from the heat lamp. They closed their little eyes and basked in the warmth, and Seren could have sworn she saw the cutest smiles on their faces.

Behind Seren, the door to the coop opened, and Jake stepped inside.

"You got chickens?" he asked.

"Mm-hmm, six of them," she said.

Jake stepped up to the brooder and kneeled beside it.

"Can I hold one?"

Seren nodded, and a look of pure excitement and wonder spread across Jake's face as he picked up a silver-colored chick.

"A lavender Orpington! They're my favorite," he said.

"A what?"

"That's the breed. These are all Orpingtons. Looks like you got a yellow, black, silver-laced, gold-laced, white, and this little girl is a lavender one. She'll grow up to look almost blue."

Jake held the chick close to his chest and let her play in his open hands. He laughed as she pecked at the strings on his hoodie, delighted at her already sweet and rambunctious disposition. Seren had never seen Jake like this. It was like he was a kid again, free from all the disappointments and difficulties life had thrown at him. It turned out that Jake did have a passion for something, and as fate would have it, that something was chickens.

"Why don't you come work for me?" Seren asked.

280

Jake paused to safely hold the chick so he could look at Seren. "What?"

"Well, you're so unhappy at Wares & More, and I'm making money now. I can afford to pay you. Better than they can."

"You mean it?"

"Yes! And anyway, sounds like they won't be around much longer."

"Yes. Yes, I would love that," he said.

Jake's smile grew wider, then returned his attention to the chick. He stroked her little head with his index finger, which lulled her to sleep.

"Would you like to name her?" Seren asked.

"How about Emelia?"

"That's perfect."

Chapter 4

Jake returned to Hiraeth bright and early the next morning with an electric heating screen. He insisted it would make the chicks happier and that the heat lamp wasn't ideal for their health. Seren, of course, had to listen to the chicken master. There was no immediate discernable difference, but Jake said they would be happier.

"They can develop vent gleet," Jake had told her.

"A-what now?" she asked.

"It's not pretty. It can happen from too much heat from a lamp—it's too concentrated, so the screen is the way to go."

Seren just nodded and listened. With Jake around, these chickens would be given the top shelf, the gold plan, the glitziest of all penthouse's standard of care.

As the season grew warmer and the next batch of brilliant, bright red tomatoes ripened to perfection, Seren remembered the scrapbook in the closet. Her grandfather had taken pictures with his crops, and so she decided to do the same. She had Jake snap a few photos of her smiling in front of the rows of tomatoes that were heavy on the vine and ready to be harvested.

She printed her favorite photo and taped it inside the scrapbook. She looked happy, and when she saw her smiling face next to her grandfather's, she felt a deep sense of pride. *If only he could see me now,* she thought. Though she hadn't known him well when he was alive, in her love for Hiraeth and in how much she had accomplished, she felt she knew him in spirit. Her feelings must have been his feelings, she thought, and in those shared moments of triumph, difficulties, growing, and learning, she felt their lives paralleled one another.

She decided then that each season she would snap more photos with each harvest and tape them in the scrapbook alongside her grandfather's memories.

Days and nights flew by, hurling the valley closer to summer. In June, a third batch of carrots, potatoes, cucumbers, beets, lettuce, onions, and tomatoes were ready to be harvested. Seren and Jake worked day and night to process the hundreds of vegetables, care for the chicks, and make plans for summer. They already had string beans, peppers, squash, and corn germinating in the greenhouse and were near the replanting stage.

Saffron's continued to pick up shipment after shipment of the S&O marinara sauce and showed no signs of slowing down. Jordan informed Seren that they would possibly expand their market and go from small batch to large batch, although that decision was far away and barely in the talking stages.

Seren was excited when the Adytown Summer Fair came back a second year in a row. Not only did she have more to offer that year, but the clinic was a stone's throw from her booth in the town square, and Dr. Harlan was sure to be there.

There were more vendors and more people from other towns, including the city. Seren noticed that the sword she'd seen at Craig's station last year hadn't sold, and so with how well Hiraeth was doing, she decided to splurge and get it for herself. By the end of the day, she had once again sold out of everything and had more inquiries about herself, the farm, whether she gave tours, and, of course, the marinara sauce. It was quickly becoming a valley favorite and, as she might dare to say, select areas of the city as well.

Myron was nowhere to be seen, and she was glad. She hadn't forgotten how he tried to intimidate her the past summer, and as she stood at her sold-out booth, she realized he had lost.

Somewhere in the blur of transactions and endless questions, Mayor Doney stopped by the booth to contribute his compliments and hand Seren a flier. "An Adytown summer bonfire!" he said. Apparently, there was enough money in the budget left over, so he was planning one for early August. "Adytown's first!" he added. "If we're lucky, we'll get to see the bioluminescence!"

Seren had never heard of the phenomenon. It sounded like something out of a biology lecture that she'd quickly forget.

By 3:00 p.m., the town square was still buzzing with activity and showed no signs of slowing down. It was hard to tell whether it was the late afternoon sun, or the throngs of people tightly packed together, but Seren had to wipe her brow as she shouldered her way past clusters of customers, who were eager to take in all Adytown had to offer. Otis had set up a large pitcher of lemon and mint water on a table next to the Fig. She texted Jenna to meet her there if she could spare a minute so they could drink together and catch up on the madness of the day.

Seren reached the table first and poured herself a hefty cup of water. It was ice cold against her tongue and just what she needed to cool down. Jenna approached through the crowd under the protection of a wide-brimmed sun hat and waved to her.

"Crazy today, isn't it?" Jenna asked.

"Craziest I've seen," Seren said.

Jenna poured herself a cup of water and took several gulps as she stood next to Seren. At this rate, Mayor Doney would have to allow vendors to use the park behind the clinic in the future if he wanted everyone to be more comfortable. This year's fair would likely go well into the evening despite the 6:00 p.m. closing time.

She was grateful for the quick break from manning the booth and took a moment to look around the square. Everyone was in good spirits except for one. At last, Seren saw Dr. Harlan, but he didn't seem quite himself. He was trudging through the crowd, his eyes fixed on nothing at all, wringing his hands together as if he was trying to work out an impossible equation. Seren tried to catch his eye, but he didn't see her. Something was wrong.

Chapter 5

It had come on suddenly. One minute, he was conversing with Joyce about Seth's post-college plans and Theo's newfound fascination with seashells, and the next, he couldn't breathe. He felt it coming when he tugged at his shirt collar and realized the world was no longer in focus. Panic announced its presence like a freight train, its horn blaring in the distance, slowly getting closer and closer until it ran him over. The tightness in his chest, the sweat on his forehead, the complete inability to think straight or to feel his feet on the ground was like a car crash.

Dr. Harlan had to excuse himself, and thankfully, Joyce hadn't seemed to notice the change in him. He walked through the crowd in a daze, unaware of where he was going or how to care for himself. His hands were moving, but the sensation felt somewhere outside of himself. *Did I do that?* he thought. His fingers shook as he looked at them, and all he could think to do was wring them together as if the repetitive action would reconnect them to his disassociated body.

"See you Tuesday, doc!" Faye said as she passed by him.

"Ah, y—yeah," he said.

She passed in a blur of muted colors and heat, and he couldn't remember her name.

His heart pounded in his chest so hard he felt he was boiling in a pressure cooker. His mind screamed, begging and urging him to run, but he couldn't, as his body forced him to stay as still as a statue and endure the storm that raged inside of him. There was no running and no escape, only the realization that he'd have to somehow wait it out.

Suddenly, Seren was by his side with her hand on his arm.

"Harlan, are you alright?" she asked.

He looked down at her and saw that her eyes were full of concern as she searched his face. Somewhere underneath the adrenaline, confusion, and extreme discomfort was remorse for making her upset.

"Harlan?" she asked again.

"I can't breathe," he said at last.

"Come on, let's get you out of here," she said.

Chapter 6

Harlan said nothing on their brief walk to the clinic and up the stairs. It was as if he were in shock. Seren never let go of his arm, even as she unlocked the door to his apartment. She must have known he was unreachable in his current state but wanted him to know, if only by a small touch, that she was there.

She closed the door and sat him on the couch. It was too hot in the apartment, so she jogged over to the air conditioner and turned it to the lowest setting. When she returned to him, he was staring out at nothing and sitting with his hands interlaced on his lap. She kneeled on the floor and looked up at him.

"What can I do to help you?" she asked.

"I… I don't…" he said.

Sweat ran down his forehead, and in his dress jacket and tie, he felt as though he were suffocating.

"Here, let's get this off," she said.

He made no moves to hinder her from removing his jacket, which she hung on a hook on the wall.

"Is it alright if I take your tie off? It looks like it's really constricting you," she said.

He nodded.

She slid the tie all the way down and tossed it on the coffee table. She then leaned over and picked up his hand. "Come on," she said.

He followed her as she led him to his perfectly made bed and instructed him to lie down. Gently, she asked him to scoot over. He was confused, but he was too tired and overwhelmed to object. His bed was in the corner of the apartment, and he pressed his back against the wall as he made room for her. It was cool against his shirt and sent a chill through him.

She lay down beside him and clasped his hand in hers. "We're going to breathe together, okay?"

They breathed in and out several times, and on the third breath, Harlan started to hyperventilate.

"S-sorry," he said between ragged breaths.

"For what?" Seren asked.

He looked at Seren, her face so close to his, and found solace there. She grabbed a clean tissue from her pocket and wiped his forehead. He closed his eyes as she touched him and felt his body relax. As his breathing returned to normal, a tranquil silence filled the room. There was no greater peace in the world than holding her hand.

"Thank you," he said, letting out a breath.

They lay together for a while. There was no need for conversation or social etiquette; they could simply lie together in the aftermath. *I could get used to this,* he thought.

"Does that happen often?" Seren asked at last.

"No, not at all. I haven't felt like that in years, not since I worked in the ER."

"What happened today?"

"I don't know."

"Well, I'm glad you're all right, Harlan."

His name sounded like honey on her lips, and he wished she would say it again. Sorrow threatened to engulf him when, instead, she rose from the bed and told him she had to get back to close her booth.

"I'll see you out," he said.

"No, hey—" Seren placed a hand on his chest. "Get some rest, Harlan. Please."

His breath hitched as he looked at her, thinking that she had to be the most wonderful woman alive. She was right; he was exhausted. He thanked her as he watched her go, and even through half-lidded eyes, he could have sworn that she lingered by the door as she closed it behind her.

Chapter 7

Seren and Jenna were walking to the beach for Mayor Doney's inaugural beach bonfire. They carried beach towels under their arms and a cooler between them containing all kinds of white wine, sodas, and beer. Seren wasn't used to wearing flip-flops, and she tripped over them as they walked.

"So, you didn't get a chance to ask him out?" Jenna asked.

"Oh uhm…no," Seren said. "There wasn't really an opportunity to."

"What do you mean? He was right there!"

"I know, but it just didn't…come up organically."

Seren decided not to tell Jenna about what had transpired with Dr. Harlan. It didn't feel right. When she met up with Jenna afterward, she told her that he had a file he needed her to update, and she bought it.

"What does that even mean? You just ask!"

"Jenna, it wasn't the right time."

"If you say so."

"It wasn't! It would've been inappropriate."

"You love to use that word when you talk about him. I don't even think you believe that. Things don't get done by being *appropriate.*"

Jenna was right. It was a boundary that Dr. Harlan had set, not her. Even though it had been months since he shut her down outside the clinic, she didn't feel courageous enough to ask him if he still felt the same way. The truth was, there were plenty of instances that were "inappropriate." He had been to her home, she'd been to his, they'd sat together on his roof and danced at the Aster, and, of course, she had *kissed* him. It didn't matter that she didn't remember it, though she remembered how cold he'd been to her when she'd tried to apologize. *That* was inappropriate. *Why did he do all those things if he really felt that way?*

"I should probably just forget about it," Seren said as she adjusted her grip on the cooler.

"All I know is it's been way too long," Jenna said. "It's giving me flashbacks to when I was waiting around for Everett to get his shit together. Someone has to do something."

"What if he doesn't have feelings for me?"

"Of course, he does! Did you *see* the way he looked at you at the dance? Because I did. I'm pretty sure everyone in town did, too."

Seth appeared out of nowhere from behind them and clapped a hand on Seren's shoulder. She jumped, not expecting to see him, and looked around for Damien, who was undoubtedly not far behind.

"Where's your boyfriend, Grinaker?" he asked.

"Um…" Seren looked to Jenna for moral support.

"Told you," she said.

"Hey, it's okay," Seth said. "I get it. He's a doctor, and I'm a musician. But you just wait. I'll come back to this town one day with accolades he could only dream of. Maybe a Grammy or two."

"He's not my boyfriend, Seth," Seren said, rolling her eyes.

"Sure, sure. Break my heart twice, why don't you?" he said as he playfully drove an invisible sword through his heart.

Damien and Lenora came up behind the trio and joined in on the conversation. The flickering glow of the bonfire came into view

292

as they drew closer to the beach. It was impressive, much more impressive than Seren had imagined. Large bundles of tree branches and planks were stacked against each other, with more wood chopped and ready to go close by. She doubted they would need the extra fuel, as the sheer size of the fire looked like it would last them until morning.

Seren hadn't realized that whatever kind of relationship she and Dr. Harlan had was cause for gossip. She knew how Adytown worked: if one person knew a rumor, everyone did. *I shouldn't be surprised. This town knows when Edna gets a new set of dentures.* Hopefully, news of this rumor hadn't reached Dr. Harlan's ears, at least not yet.

She didn't want to mar his reputation as a doctor. He didn't deserve that. Not when he'd never made a pass at her, or done anything that should call his conduct into question. She just wanted him to be happy, whatever that entailed. If he only wanted friendship from her, then she would provide it.

Seren and Jenna set up their towels close to the bonfire and sat.

There was nothing quite like August days and nights. The lazy rhythm of late summer stretched like a languid lion sunbathing on a boulder. Everything slowed down, even in Seren's world, just for a moment. She dug her toes into the warm, gritty sand and lay back against her towel. She took in the dusk sky and breathed deeply as she closed her eyes. A soft, warm breeze wafted over her face, and in the distance, wave after wave crashed against the sandy shore. Yellow and orange danced across her eyelids as the heat from the bonfire relaxed her muscles. *I could live here forever,* she thought.

Beside her, Jenna dug in the cooler for a beer and uncapped it. She drank a few long sips and lay down on her towel beside Seren.

"What're you old farts doing?" Damien asked.

Seren opened her eyes and saw him, Seth, and Everett standing over them.

"You can do that later. Come on."

Damien lent a hand to Seren, and Everett brought Jenna to her feet so quickly that she yelped with surprise. She jumped and wrapped her legs around him as he took off running to the water with Damien and Seth close behind. Lenora and Emelia were already in the water, splashing and diving under the surface.

Seren untied her sheer sash from her hips and let it fall to the ground. She walked to the water's edge and allowed the tide to wash over her feet. It was cold, and she wasn't sure she wanted to go in.

"It's better if you do it quickly," Lenora called.

Seren smiled to herself as she realized she was about to plunge. *To hell with it,* she thought. Running at full speed, she dove under the salty water. The cold liquid swept around her face and ran through her hair, her long locks swirling and flowing as she propelled herself forward. She emerged with the breath of life, her lungs filling with a sharp intake of oxygen as every capillary buzzed and vibrated in shock. She couldn't suppress a laugh when she opened her eyes again. Her friends fanned out around her in a similar state. She splashed Jenna and Everett square in their faces, which set off a chain reaction until everyone in the water was splashing each other.

It didn't matter how accustomed she was to having a community and the types of friends she had always dreamed of, or to taking risks and discovering more about herself; experiencing the euphoria that only comes from truly living never got old. As she acclimated to the water, the chill no longer bothered her. She breathed deeper, her emotions expanded, and everything was beautiful.

Everyone climbed out of the water, drenched and merry drunk, as the bonfire stretched higher into the star-filled sky. Seren's bathing suit clung to her skin as she wrung out her hair and walked back to her towel. Jenna and Everett followed close behind and joined her in front of the fire. The three of them toasted with beer and wine and drank.

"Damn, Seren, since when did you get abs?" Jenna asked.

"What?" she asked as she sat up straight to get a better look at her stomach. "Oh!"

Jenna was right. She didn't have a six-pack, but subtle lines had formed, and though she looked more toned, there was still a softness that Seren liked.

"I guess picking tomatoes has more benefits than one," she said.

"Everyone, look!" Mayor Doney cried. He was pointing toward the beach, and everyone turned their heads. When the water crashed against the shore, a brilliant blue glow lined each wave and dispersed.

"The bioluminescence!" he said.

Everyone ran toward the shore to get a better look at the alien-like water. Seren ran up on the dock to watch it splash against the wood. She looked up to say something to Jenna, but realized she was alone. Jenna and Everett were holding each other on the beach, pointing and exclaiming in delight as each wave crashed over their feet. She saw a newly arrived Jake, who was red-faced and smiling as he and Emilia also took in the phenomenon. Seren considered joining them but decided to take it in on her own.

The light of the blue water peered through slats in the wood like hazy moonlight. The shimmering patterns shifted around her as Seren sat cross-legged at the edge of the dock. Neon blue lit up her fingers and face as she trailed her hands through the water.

Behind her, footsteps thumped against the dock as they made their way closer. Dr. Harlan sat next to her.

"Hi, Dr. Harlan," she said, turning to smile at him.

"Seren," he said.

They sat in silence for a little while as the ocean glinted around them.

"How are you?" she asked at last.

"Better, thank you."

Seren noticed that he seemed preoccupied, as if there were more on his mind than usual. Maybe the rumors had reached him, but she hoped that wasn't the reason for his distress.

"It's embarrassing, really," he said. "What you must think of me after—"

Seren placed her hand over his, and he stopped speaking.

"You're human," she said. "And I don't think any less of you. Not in the slightest."

His shoulders relaxed, and Seren could tell he believed her.

"Thank you," he said.

She imagined wrapping her arm around his, leaning her head against his shoulder, and asking him to tell her about his day. It didn't matter if he deemed his day-in and day-out routine at the clinic mundane, or that something exciting happened only every so often, or that, for him, the thing he enjoyed most was working on a new model airplane, she would listen to every detail because it was *his* day. She would listen to him explain why the DC-10 has a third engine and why the 747 was the "Queen of the Skies." She would smile at him because he was so attractive to her, even if she couldn't find the right words to tell him.

The vision dissipated, and Seren realized she was still holding his hand.

"So, ever seen bioluminescence before?" she asked as she placed her hand in her lap.

"Yes, once. Have you?"

"First time. It's magical," she said. "What is it, anyway?"

"It's algae. They're, uh, a kind of organism that responds to external stimuli. They light up when the water throws them around. I guess you could say they glow when put through adversity."

"That's poetic, Dr. Beck."

"Must be the company."

Seren smiled at him and leaned her shoulder into his before pulling away to run her hand through the water again. She felt his eyes on her, and she wondered what he was thinking.

"Um… I'd better get back. I have, uh, an early morning," Dr. Harlan said as he stood.

"Of course," Seren said.

She took her hand out of the water and shook it dry. The dock felt coarse and hard under her feet as she stood, and a rush of adrenaline shot through her when she realized that this was her chance to ask him. *It's now or never,* she thought.

"Dr. Harlan," she said, "would you like to come over for dinner sometime?"

He looked back and smiled. "I would love to."

Chapter 8

"So, when are you going to see him?" Jake asked.

"I'm not sure. He's leaving town for a week or two, so probably after that."

Dr. Harlan didn't offer much information about his work trip other than he was headed to Turner Hospital in Sanborn for a medical convention that he expected to be very boring and ineffectual, but his presence was expected.

It was late afternoon, and Seren and Jake were walking through rows of sunlit corn to find fully formed husks for harvest. Seren adjusted a basket against her hip and tugged on the first whitish-brown silk she saw. When it came right off, she removed the corn from the stalk and deposited it in the basket.

"These came in really nice," Jake said as he tossed another into his own basket.

"Not bad for a first try," she agreed.

"I'm almost done with the stable, Seren," Rita called out. "If you want to call Chessy to let her know, I think it's ready enough for Freya."

Seren thanked Rita, set down her corn-filled basket, and called Chessy to tell her the news.

"Yes. Yes, it's looking like it's ready. I'll be here. Thank you, Chessy!"

When she hung up, she had to suppress a laugh as she looked at Jake, who was clearly dumbfounded.

"You just don't stop, do you?" he asked.

"It was your idea!" she said.

Thirty minutes later, Chessy rode in on Freya's back from the south side of the farm. She had a western saddle and reins, which were Seren's preferred riding style. Freya's long mane flew behind her as she cantered. In all Seren's life, she'd never seen such a beautiful horse.

"*Whoa*," Chessy said as she pulled back the reins, easing Freya to a stop. "Good to see you, Seren! Where do you want her?"

"There's an entrance in the gate right over there." Seren pointed to a small segment of wooden gate on the western side of the farm.

"Sounds good," Chessy said. "Unless you'd like to take her yourself?"

Seren hadn't ridden in years, but since Freya was hers, and with the open expanse of untilled farmland to the south, she couldn't resist.

Chessy dismounted and handed the reins to Seren.

She stood before Freya and stroked her regal, yellow-gold face and whispered to her as Jake and Chessy stood by the fence and talked.

"Shall we go for a ride, Freya?"

Seren stuck one foot in a stirrup and threw all her weight over Freya's back. She settled into the saddle and adjusted the reins. As if she and Freya's minds worked in tandem, they mutually decided to go. Freya leaped forward, gaining speed as she pounded her long legs against the ground until they were running at full speed. The world whizzed by in blurs of greens, browns, and blues as Seren leaned forward and tightened her legs around Freya's powerful body. It was as if they were racing the wind itself, and nothing could stop them.

Chapter 9

By early October, the last batch of tomatoes was almost fully ripe, as were the beets, broccoli, carrots, peas, and spinach. Seren put aside a few beets to gift to Horace, even though he assured her he always bought them from Perry's whenever he saw them. Still, she insisted, as it had become a little tradition between the two of them. She would deliver the beets, and she, Horace, and Edna would sit on their couch, and she'd listen as they recounted long-remembered stories about their lives in Adytown.

Seren had grown fewer pumpkins, as she only wanted them for decoration on the farm. It was her favorite time of year again, and as the leaves changed and the air grew colder, she was pleased she had placed the pumpkins close to the cabin so she could enjoy their deep orange color every morning as she sat on the porch and drank her Earl Grey tea.

Seren scaled the porch steps with fresh tuna from Marty and feta crumbles from Chessy. That night, Dr. Harlan was joining her for dinner at Hiraeth. She'd already prepared a fresh beet salad with sauteed spinach and peach slices, and she planned to prepare the mashed potatoes and tuna when he arrived. It was one of the easiest meals to make, but it was one of her favorites.

She opened the fridge and took out a large bowl containing the beet salad, dusting it with feta crumbles. With two large wooden spoons, she mixed everything together, sprinkled one last pinch of sea salt over the dish, and stored it in the fridge with the rest of the ingredients.

It was 5:30, which gave Seren plenty of time to shower and get dressed. She looked around the cabin and was pleased with how everything looked. A fire crackled and hissed in the wood-burning stove, every surface was clear and cleaned, and Edna's knit blanket was draped over the back of the couch, adding a nice pop of color to the room. She played her favorite music and swayed to the rhythm as she rifled through her closet. It was hard to decide what to wear. Was it a date? A cordial get-together with an old friend?

She didn't want to try too hard or be too casual because either suggested one answer over the other, so she decided something simple and elegant was the way to go. She laid out a dark navy wrap dress on her bedspread and took a quick shower. When she finished, she swiped mascara through her eyelashes, applied concealer, blush, and her favorite rose-colored lip tint, then spritzed her favorite perfume along her wrists and collarbone. She let her hair hang long after she brushed it, falling where it may over her shoulders.

For all that Seren had grown, there was still a part of her that struggled to allow herself to be seen. At times, she didn't think herself worthy of affection, care, or tenderness, no matter how many people said she deserved not only those things but more. She had lived a life in quiet, not daring to make herself or her talents known for some misperceived notion that someone else would always be prettier, smarter, or more talented. Yet she pushed forward for no reason other than some light inside herself told her to reach. She had reached for Dr. Harlan on the dock through some act of courage she wasn't sure was entirely her own. Perhaps it was the magic of the glowing blue water or how his comforting presence inspired her to try, but somehow, she had done it. After so much time, and all she had grown to feel for him, she was excited to have him in her home, no matter what came to pass.

The sun dipped ever closer toward the horizon as his expected arrival grew nearer. As a final touch, she lit one of her favorite candles scented with sweet tonka bean and woodsy cedar. The table was set, and the wine was chilled. All she needed was his company. As the clock ticked closer to seven, she wondered if he was as nervous and excited as she was. Had he wondered what to wear or what they might talk about? She hoped that her invitation had made some of her feelings known, even though she still didn't know how to articulate them. She realized she was holding her breath as she heard steady footsteps ascend the porch, followed by a knock on the door.

She would see him in a few moments, and her excitement carried her forward to open the door.

He stood in a pair of well-fitted, pleated slacks and a white, collared shirt with a maroon sweater layered on top that looked softer than Oxford down. She never grew tired of the rush of remembering how attractive he was each time she saw his face. He held a bottle of wine tucked under his arm.

"Hello, Dr. Harlan," she said.

"Seren, good to see you," he said.

"Come in."

Seren stepped aside and welcomed him into her home. As he walked inside, she eyed the bottle of wine with interest. The familiar blue foil gave it away.

"Is that—"

"Rombauer," he said as he held it up for her to see.

"You remembered," she said as he handed the chilled bottle to her. "I haven't seen this in ages. Where did you find it?"

"At a pitstop on the way back to town, if you can believe it."

She gazed at the bottle with delight. It had been years since she had the chance to drink such delicious wine, and her joy brought a smile to Dr. Harlan's face.

"Should we have some now?" he asked.

"Absolutely."

They talked about his trip, and from his account of the experience, it proved to be as boring as he predicted, though not altogether ineffectual. He offered details about the panels and meetings he attended, but Seren took little notice. She was so happy to uncork the wine, pour a glass for each of them, and sit down with him at the table. As she listened to him speak, she forgot all about her self-taught misgivings and ill-perceived shortcomings. They were not welcome there, not with the man who made her feel like she could be herself in all forms and colors.

When she brought out the tuna and home-grown russet potatoes for cooking, he stood and kept her company in the kitchen. Nothing could deter him, even her protests that he needn't help her, so she relented.

"Fine, okay, I'll peel them, and you can cut them," she said, laughing.

"Good, okay. I think I've got that covered," he said.

Seren playfully rolled her eyes and took a sip of wine. In a short time, they had each finished a glass and were on their second. She handed each peeled potato to Dr. Harlan, and he cut them into small sections.

"Very good," she teased.

He smiled as he cut the potatoes and glanced at her. "Told you I've got it."

When the last potato was ready for him, she handed it over, leaned against the counter, wineglass in hand, and watched him. He must have sensed this because, after the first slice, he turned to her with worry spread across his handsome features. "What?"

"Nothing, just looking at you."

He stood up straight and cleared his throat, apparently about to put on a show since the lady of the house was watching him. He cut the potato slowly and checked with her for her approval after each section, then jokingly wiped his brow with relief when she gestured for him to continue.

"Okay, now what?" he asked.

"We'll drop them in that saucepan and boil them."

"Got it," he said.

"Seriously, it's okay if you sit down. I can take care of it."

"No, no. I've got to earn my keep," he said.

He slid the potatoes into a black saucepan and then, to her surprise, filled it with the right amount of water. She took over, fired up the gas burner to high, and placed the pan over the flames.

"And now?" he asked.

"Now, you take your wine and relax," she said as she handed him his glass.

He raised his hands in lighthearted surrender and took his seat at the kitchen table.

When the potatoes were boiled and seasoned and the tuna seared, she retrieved the beet salad from the fridge and delivered the feast to the table. Conversation and wine flowed freely as they ate, and Seren had to admit, it was one of the best meals she'd ever made. The earthy beets, salty feta, starchy potatoes, and succulent, sweet peaches clinging to sautéed spinach leaves elevated the fresh, tangy flavor of the tuna. They drank their wine as the sun set below the horizon. The warm, flickering fire chased up the cabin walls, bathing the room in orange and yellow light.

Seren felt an unfamiliar sense of pride as she sat and looked over their empty plates. Everything had been cultivated, caught, and created right there in Adytown, mostly by her own hand, and it was a delight to see Dr. Harlan satisfied with the food she had prepared. She watched him take his last bite and sink back into his chair with luxurious conclusion. She poured them both another glass of wine and sat with her feet crossed beneath her as she gazed at him. While he was away, she missed him, and though they had gone much longer stretches of time without speaking or seeing one another, his absence from town somehow made it worse. Adytown wasn't Adytown without Dr. Harlan, and she was so glad that he was back.

She noticed the change in his body. His shoulders and arms looked bigger. She wondered what he'd done differently over the last few months, and tried not to stare as she listened to him speak.

"Enough about me, though. What about you?" he asked. "How are things here?"

"Things are good. Excellent, actually. I met a rep at the fair last year, I think you know."

Dr. Harlan nodded.

"They really like our sauce, and it's been selling well, so they might want to expand from small batch to large batch."

"Seren, that's fantastic!"

"I'm terrified," she said as she laughed. "It'll mean a lot more work for me, Jake, and Otis. I'm not sure we'll be able to keep up."

"The good news is you have time to figure that out. You have what they want. Make them bend to your terms," he said.

"You're right. Care to be my life advisor?" she joked.

"I think I have my hands full with the clinic," he said as he laughed and took a sip of wine.

"You've done so well there. Everyone loves you."

Dr. Harlan's mood shifted, and Seren thought she could detect some tinge of sadness or resignation across his face.

"I'm glad you think so. Sometimes, I think they resent me, you know, for having to dole out diagnoses and recommendations on habits they should change to live healthier lifestyles. People don't want to be policed. It can be isolating."

Seren understood how he felt. They had lived different lives and had different professions, but isolation and loneliness were common amongst her experiences. It wasn't until she moved to Adytown that everything changed. As she listened to him speak, it occurred to her that she hadn't seen him with anyone, whether that was at the Fig, at the beach, or at festivals throughout the year.

"Do…" she began, second-guessing what she was about to say. "Do you think that you do that to yourself?"

"Could be," he said, nodding.

She was relieved that he didn't bristle at her question. He instead was open and convivial, as though he wasn't too good to admit his own faults and vulnerabilities.

"There's this… expectation in my position. I am the authority, the one who has all the answers, the one people can rely on to help them. There's not much room for mistakes or being too friendly. So, I've learned to live alone. It's not glamorous or exciting, but it's worked for me."

"You're not alone now," she said, looking him dead in the eye.

"You're right," he said.

She wanted to reach forward and grasp his hand, just as she did that afternoon in his apartment or when they sat together on the dock, but before she could give it another thought, he spoke again.

"Oh, before I forget…" He reached into his pocket, pulled out a small brown box with a red bow, and slid it across the table to her.

"What's this?" she asked.

"Open it."

Seren untied the ribbon and glanced up at him once before she coaxed the lid off the box and looked inside. Beneath a small sheet of silver tissue paper was a gold ring.

"It was your grandfather's," Dr. Harlan said. "There was an old mine just up the way from Adytown, and he had Craig fashion that ring from a few pieces of gold he found there. Or at least that's the story he told me. He gave it to me for safekeeping a few months before he passed. I guess he felt I would look after it while he got his affairs in order. He never asked for it back, and since it's almost your birthday, well, I think it should be yours."

"Dr. Harlan this is—this is really special. Thank you," she said.

He rose from the table and brought their dishes to the sink. As he worked behind her, she slipped the ring onto her thumb. It was made for much larger fingers. Craig would have to resize it for her.

Regarding the ring with reverence, she turned it around her finger as it glinted in the candlelight. She swiveled in her chair to watch Dr. Harlan rinse the dishes, completely oblivious to her observance. She imagined walking up to him and sliding her arms around his waist.

"Dr. Harlan…"

He stowed the last plate and turned to her.

"Please, I meant what I said. You can call me Harlan," he said. "At least when we're outside the clinic."

"Harlan…" she said.

The weight of total vulnerability took a toll on Seren. Whether it was the wine, the beautiful gift, or the desire for him that seemed too much to bear, she found she wanted nothing more than to tell him everything. She wanted to tell him how mixed up and confused she was, that for the first time in a long time, she felt her heart thaw and open, and how terrified she was at the prospect that it could break again. He had shut her down once, and there was no guarantee he wouldn't deny her again.

"Do you… do you think that…?"

"Yes?" he asked.

Please, just read my mind, Harlan, she thought desperately. *Please help me say what I want to say to you.*

"Um… sorry. All that fancy wine."

Dr. Harlan nodded and smiled at her. "I'd better go," he said, checking his watch. The moment was gone. He seemed to hesitate, as if he, too, had something he wanted to say but didn't.

Seren saw him to the front porch.

"This really was delicious. Thank you, Seren," he said.

He towered over her in the flickering porch light, and in the half darkness, Seren thought she saw a trace of something that made her wonder if he wanted to stay.

"You're welcome," she said, stepping closer to him.

Whatever Seren thought she saw was gone as he stared down at her. *Please. Stay.*

"Goodnight," he said.

"Goodnight, Harlan."

She watched him go as she twirled the ring on her finger. It could've just been a trick of the light, but she was sure she'd seen him steal a glance at her mouth and lean in slightly before he left.

Chapter 10

The following Monday, Seren met Mayor Doney at his house. It was quaint and only moderately messy, with all kinds of fliers and corkboards throughout his living room, covered in thumbtacks and pieces of paper with *"Brainstorm!"* written at the top. He explained they were future plans for Adytown and that he did his best work with all his thoughts pinned up all around him. Seren admired his enthusiasm.

Mayor Doney had spearheaded a lot for Adytown in the last year, and though she hadn't thought him capable, she was glad he proved her wrong. Not that she disliked or mistrusted him, but he was older, and she figured he would've thought about retiring. After seeing his hard work since the first fair, she understood there were enough ideas and fire left in him to last another decade. She hoped that fire would extend to fixing Roseleaf Way.

"It'd make things easier. I have to bring carts full of produce to Perry's all the time, and Rita stops by in her truck often. The ground is a bit uneven, too, so sometimes I drop things. Would you consider it?"

"Hmm, I see your point. However, I'm much more partial to the idea of keeping the natural beauty of Adytown alive. The thought of a big slab of tar running through there doesn't sound appealing," he said.

Seren nodded and understood his point. It would be the only paved road in town, and it would stick out like a sore thumb. Still, the road was a nuisance, potholes and all.

"What about some resurfacing?" he offered. "We could add in fresh gravel, cover up any divots and slopes. Would that work better for you?"

"Yes! Yes, absolutely."

"Alright. Well, I can't promise the work will be completed any time soon—there are a few other projects that are at the top of the list—but I'll see what I can do."

"Thank you, Frank," Seren said as she shook his hand.

"So, how are things on the farm?" he asked.

"Couldn't be better," she said.

"I'm glad! And I know Perry is just beaming from ear to ear. I don't think his shop has done better, not in a long, long time. Harold would be proud."

Seren thanked him and shook his hand once more, then turned to leave. She had just reached for the handle when he stopped her.

"Oh! I almost forgot. Do you happen to know of any doctors from the city who might be looking for a change of pace?" he asked.

"What do you mean?" she asked.

"Dr. Harlan is transferring to Turner Hospital."

Seren felt as if someone had punched her stomach. "What?"

"We'll get another excellent doctor to fill his place, don't you worry. I remembered you brought your publishing friend to Everett's reading, and I just thought you might know somebody. How's his book going, by the way?"

"Um… good, I think. It'll be published soon."

"Excellent! If you happen to hear of any candidates, please refer them to me."

Seren nodded but had no intention of referring anyone, no matter the circumstance. No one could take Harlan's place. No one. Her mind was racing as she turned to leave.

"Good day!" Mayor Doney called behind her as she closed the door.

She hadn't meant to ignore his goodbye, but she couldn't think straight. *He's leaving? He can't be!*

The road home wasn't a straight path, as she kept walking towards the clinic. She had a mind to break down his door and confront him. To ask him why in the world he hadn't mentioned it, or how he could even think of leaving Adytown after so many years. Or, on a deeper level that she didn't want to acknowledge, to ask him how he could think of leaving *her*. He had said he hated working in a big hospital and that the last time he worked in one was the last time he'd had a panic attack. *Is that why he went to the convention? To see if he'd move there?* she thought. Turner Hospital might not be as large as a city hospital, but it was still unfamiliar and far away. He knew everyone in Adytown, had relationships with them, and had trust with them. Nothing about it made sense.

Seren needed to clear her head. Even though her feet kept bringing her toward the clinic, she resisted. It wouldn't be good to speak to him then, not without calming herself first.

She hurried home to Hiraeth and sat under the shade of the peach tree. She wanted to cry, but the sheer shock of it all prevented her.

"This wasn't meant to happen; this wasn't the story. It can't be," she said.

The trees on the far side of the farm drew her attention. Just as they called to her that first winter she arrived in Adytown, they called to her again. She stood, dusted off her pants, and hastened toward the forest. The tall pine trees towered over her as she entered, bearing witness to her disquiet. Heat radiated off the forest floor, and birds fluttered overhead from tree branch to tree branch as she walked deeper. She looked around the trees as if she expected to see a wise sage materialize and tell her what to do and think. Balling her fists, she looked up toward the blue sky above and waited for something, anything, to offer guidance.

"*Well?* Where are you?" she called. "I heard you. You spoke to me then. Why won't you speak to me now?"

The trees swayed in the wind, and clouds meandered through the sky above. Birds sang in their nests. Seren stood in the middle of it all, expectant and patient, but there was no voice. Perhaps there never was. Suddenly, she was crying again, and no matter how hard she tried, she couldn't shake the feeling that it was all going to end. It always did—her relationships, her homes, her neighborhoods, and any sense of belonging and peace. In the face of losing someone she cared for once again, she felt she was in danger of losing what had kept her going: her resilience. What chance did any storm have against that resilience? She could weather anything, even if everything fell away in the end. At least she had herself and that feeling, but what if that fell away too?

No, she thought. *This time it's going to be different. Things have changed.*

Chapter 11

The next morning, Seren tended to Hiraeth as she would any other day. She watered what needed watering, petted and played with Mabon, and started plans for closing Hiraeth for winter. By three in the afternoon, she was checking in on the chickens to finish the day. She fed them some treats as Butter, the golden Orpington, watched her intently. Seren stood with her phone in her hand, the slow, blinking cursor tormenting her as she stared at the screen.

Say something, she thought. *You can do it.*

"Boy trouble," Seren said. The hen cocked her head and clucked. "You guys are lucky; no roosters to bother you here."

After petting each hen and making sure they had enough food and water, she took a long, hot shower, scrubbing every inch of herself, then toweled dry. The plan was to meet Jenna and Everett at the Fig that night, but she told them not to wait for her.

Shaking her head, she looked at herself in the mirror. She'd been in a pensive mood all day, and that worry had etched ramifications between her eyebrows and in the corners of her lips. She practiced smiling to try to appear happier than she was, then rifled through her closet and decided on a simple t-shirt and jeans and spritzed her favorite perfume along her collarbone and wrists.

It was almost four o'clock. *Are we going to eat there?* she wondered. Regardless, she made something quick to eat.

When the dishes were washed, and she could find nothing else to distract her, she sat on the couch and pulled out her phone again. She hesitated for a moment, wondering if what she was about to do was a good idea.

Anxiety propelled her back to her feet, and she paced back and forth by the coffee table, her heart beating faster as every moment went by. She hated confrontation, and she hated delayed confrontation even more.

She had just typed *Hi Ha* when there was a knock at the door. "Wha…?" she muttered. *Who is that?* Taking out her phone, she read over Jenna's invite again to be sure she hadn't misread it. It said, *Meet us at the Fig at 7.*

Seren walked to the door and listened. She couldn't hear anyone outside, and she had never wished for a peephole more in her life.

"Who is it?"

"Seren, it's me."

The voice sounded familiar. Its cadence and inherent smile behind the words reminded her of someone, but who? The part of her mind that hadn't heard that voice in a long time played the words again. *Seren, it's me.* Then, the truth came hurling forward from a long-forgotten memory, and it clicked.

Adam, she thought.

She opened the door, and there he was. That familiar face, smile, hair, eyes, body, and spirit she had once loved so deeply, thinking it would be hers forever. She stood with her mouth agape, and her heart shoved so far up her throat she thought it'd fall out.

"What are you doing here?" she asked.

"Hi," he said.

"What are you doing here?" she asked again.

"Um…" He flashed that toothy grin she knew so well.

There had been many times she'd imagined that exact moment: how he'd come back to her and stand on her porch just as he was now, get down on his knees, and beg for forgiveness. But that was before she'd moved on, before she ripped out the parts of herself that she wanted to heal.

She stood her ground. He was on her property, unannounced and unwelcome, and he would answer her question.

"Can I come in?" he asked.

"No."

He played off her coldness in the same way he always treated all instability, bad news, or hardships: with ease and a smile on his face. He stepped back and leaned against the porch railing as he looked out over the farm. "This really is beautiful, Seren. You've done a lot."

"What world do you live in?"

He drew his eyebrows together, apparently confused at her question, all the while looking at her like he used to. He hadn't changed. He was still carefree and maddeningly attractive in his cotton hoodie, the one she had bought him for his birthday four years ago. She'd searched all over the city to find it for him, and he loved it. There was no end to how personable he could be, even facing her after over two years of radio silence.

"It's impressive, really. The delusion," she said.

"I wanted to see you," he said.

"How am I supposed to respond to that?"

"I don't know, Seren. It's the truth."

She drummed her fingers against the door frame and felt a tight knot in her stomach that grew tighter the longer he stood there looking at her. It angered her how completely unaffected he was, and she questioned how he could be real. How could he not feel the utter absurdity of the situation, remorse for what he had done, or be so cavalier with her feelings? It was cruel, and though the smile on his face protested otherwise, she could hardly bear to be near him any longer.

"I have somewhere I need to be," she said.

"If... if we could just talk," he said as he took a step forward.

She knew what he wanted, to get her inside the cabin, but she wouldn't allow it. A fire lit inside her, and she slammed the door behind her.

"*No!* What we are *not* going to do is go in there and entertain any of this *bullshit*. This is *my* home, and how dare you think you could just show up here and expect us to have a normal conversation?"

"I thought—"

"No, that's the problem, because you didn't *think*. If you did, you'd see how clearly everything has been done on *your* terms. You left me. You left me when I needed you most, and you ended everything when you were hundreds of miles away. I hadn't seen you in weeks, Adam, and what you—you decided to break up with me *then*?"

Adam's face transformed into quiet remorse. If Seren had been weaker, that would have been enough to call off the war and let him inside, but she continued.

"You couldn't wait to do it, could you? You couldn't wait until you were home with me to talk things over. Everything was done on your terms then, and everything is on your terms now. You didn't care if you hurt me then, and you don't care if you hurt me now."

"Seren—"

"You have *no idea* how hard I tried, how long it took me, to pick myself up off that floor and somehow imagine myself with anyone else, *anyone* at all that wasn't you. That spot was yours, and you *threw it away.*"

The silence was deafening, and for once, Adam seemed speechless.

As he looked at her, a brilliant clarity rushed forward through the emotional fog. Seren knew she no longer wanted a single thing from him. "I have to go. When I get back, you'd better be gone," she said as she ducked inside the door to put on a pair of flats and fling her bag over her shoulder.

Adam didn't say a word as she locked the door behind her, marched off the porch, and didn't look at him once. As Hiraeth faded in the distance and she passed the bus stop on the pathway into town, her heart racing so hard she had to stop walking. She placed a hand on her chest and crouched on the dirt road. Dark spots pulsated with every beat and clouded her vision.

Everything is okay, she thought.

Seren took a deep breath and continued walking to town. She eyed the clinic as she passed by and wondered if, by chance, Dr. Harlan would come outside. She knew he was still there, as the clinic stayed open later during the summer, but the door didn't open. It was too early to go to the Fig, and Seren didn't feel like conversing with anyone yet, anyway. Instead, she rounded a corner and walked to the bench that overlooked Adytown.

Adrenaline still coursed through her veins as she sat down. *I can't believe him,* she thought. It was absurd for him to come here like that. She wondered why he had taken the trouble of coming all this way instead of just calling. She hoped the two-hour drive was worth their five minutes of conversation.

With some distance between them, her body relaxed. As she looked over Adytown, she wondered how long it would take him to leave. *You have a chance to end things the way you always wanted. Don't waste it.* She hadn't heard those words outside of herself, nor did she think them of her own accord. The message came from somewhere, and in that moment, she knew there was one more thing she needed to do.

Chapter 12

When she saw that Adam was still sitting on the porch steps at Hiraeth, she said nothing. He was asleep against the banister, softly snoring with his arms crossed. She scaled the porch steps, got a bottle of wine and two glasses from the kitchen, and sat against the banister across from him. As she sat down, his eyes opened, probably jostled awake by the sound of clinking glass.

"Do you want a drink?" she asked.

"Yes," he said.

Seren poured them each a glass and corked the bottle. They drank in silence, both aware of the heaviness of time that had passed since they last saw each other.

"I know you told me to leave, but you asked me why I came here. I'd like to give you an answer," Adam said.

Seren settled as she crossed her legs and waited for him to continue.

"When I went to Saffron's, there was this great display at the front, showcasing some sauce I'd never heard of. I would've normally passed by, but there was a picture of you standing here on the farm. You looked happy, and the farm—it looked fantastic. I felt so proud of you. Then I realized the sauce was yours. I meant what I said earlier: you've really come into your own. And…"

"And?"

"I felt bad. I felt bad for saying the things I said on the phone. You didn't deserve that. Since I did it so wrong the first time, I wanted to do it right the second. So, I'm here, in person, to apologize. I hope you can accept it."

Seren considered his words carefully and took a sip of wine. "I'm glad you said it."

Adam cocked his head and waited for her to elaborate.

"I just mean… I might've never made the life I have without those words. I may have never turned into who I am. The pain was considerable, I will say that. It was hell, really, but I got over it. So, I guess… I'm grateful."

"Well then, my work here is done," Adam said, laughing.

"I still did all the work, mind you, so don't let your head get too big."

"Oh, of course. I would never."

She laughed with him, and for a moment, things were just like old times, when they would laugh together over the dumbest joke or find equal footing in their silliness and conversation. However, they both knew that would never happen again.

"I want you to know I wish you well, now and always," she said.

"You too," he replied.

Seren knew then that she had forgiven him. Through some act of fate well beyond her understanding, she'd been given what most would beg, borrow, and steal for: closure. Adam wasn't a bad person. She had loved him for five long, beautiful years, and despite how it ended, she was grateful for the time they had. She believed that those we love or have loved never truly leave us, and if she was right, she was happy that Adam had been one of them.

"So, is he a good guy?" Adam asked as he finished his glass.

"Who?"

"You know who."

"He's a very good man."

"Good. Well, he's a lucky guy."

Seren didn't know how Adam knew, but he did. She could tell he was happy for her and so very glad that they could end things in a better light. They said their goodbyes, and this time, he promised he would go and not come back.

When Adam had gone, she returned to the text she began before his unexpected arrival. She watched the cursor blink, and the more she thought about it, the more her plan didn't feel right. She didn't want to wait any longer.

Rising from the porch, she stowed her phone and walked the path back into town. She'd never been surer of anything in her life, and this time, she didn't resist where her body wanted to take her. Ahead, Mira left the clinic and walked around the corner. Seren's heart raced as she stepped up to the door and knocked. There was no turning back, and as Dr. Harlan opened the door, seeing him only strengthened her certainty.

"Seren, what's—"

"I don't feel good, Dr. Harlan," she said, cutting him off.

"Oh, please come in then," he said, asking her to follow him to the back.

They pushed through the inner door, down the hallway, and into an exam room.

"So, what kind of symptoms are you experiencing?" he asked as the door shut behind them.

She wasn't sick, but she definitely had symptoms of something. "My heart keeps racing, my stomach feels like it's doing somersaults, and I can't seem to focus on anything."

He picked out her file from a stack against the back counter while she sat on the examination table and placed her hands on the sanitation paper. Before he could open her file and ask her more questions, she spoke.

"I need you to kiss me. Now, please."

Dr. Harlan froze. She could almost see the hairs stand up on the back of his neck, and as he turned to look at her, time itself lost all direction. He dropped the file and walked to her. He placed his hand against her cheek and gazed down at her. She reached up and clutched his lapel, his face mere inches away from hers. His breath was hot against her mouth, and as his lips came closer to hers, she closed her eyes.

"Seren... I—"

"One more thing, Dr. Harlan. Do we—" Mira opened the door and froze.

Startled by her sudden arrival, Dr. Harlan stepped back and placed a hand over his mouth. Seren's fingers grew white as she gripped the examination table.

"*Oh,* I'm sorry," Mira said. "I didn't realize you had a patient." She started to close the door.

"What is it, Mira?" he asked.

"Um, well, I forgot to ask: Do we have any more items we need to order from the distributor? I told them I'd have a list by morning."

Through the extreme discomfort and absurdity of the situation, Seren found her voice and spoke. "Well, I should probably get going. We were just finishing up, anyway. Finishing with my... physical," Seren said, hoping by some miracle that her face, which she was sure was bright red, hadn't given her away.

"No, S—Miss Grinaker, it's alright, Mira and I will—"

"No, no, I insist," Seren said. She cleared her throat and looked around the room for her bag until she realized she hadn't brought one. "I'll just, uh..." She pointed to the door. "Thank you again, Ha—Dr. Harlan."

Seren felt a distinct feeling that both he and Mira were watching her leave. After she passed through the front door, she slapped a hand to her mouth. She couldn't shake the feeling that she had just made things a lot more difficult for Dr. Harlan.

What have I done? she thought.

Chapter 13

Over the next few days, Seren waited for Dr. Harlan to call her, but he never did. She replayed what happened in her head again and again, and after each time, she was certain that if Mira hadn't interrupted, he would have kissed her. She remembered every detail—the way his hand felt against her cheek, the color of his lips, the smell of his freshly laundered shirt—and as she thought about it more, other details took shape. There had been shock and awe on his face when he turned to her, but there was also something else, something *pained*. Seren didn't know what that meant, but despite the confusing circumstances, she knew one thing: he *wanted* to kiss her.

Life in Adytown and at Hiraeth didn't slow down despite what happened. Though Seren always had her phone on her and always kept a watchful eye on the path to town just in case he called her or stopped by, she was glad for the distractions.

On her birthday, Jenna and Otis threw her a party at the Rusty Fig. Almost everyone in town came to celebrate, and by the end of the night, Seren was so full of homemade cake that she thought she would burst.

By Halloween, Seren's pumpkins had grown considerably. She, Jenna, and Emelia carved them together in the front yard, drinking one of Emelia's new creations and eating takeout from the Fig. The weather was mild, and by evening, Seren lit up the carved pumpkins with small tea lights and arranged them on the porch. Afterward, she walked the path to town without a costume or the intention of staying long. When her friends asked why, she told them she was too tired.

That was true. She hadn't quite processed Adam's visit, what happened at the clinic, or the aftermath. Mira didn't seem to look at her differently, and as far as she could tell, no one in town knew about it. It was a real gossip-free first for Adytown. Seren hoped it would remain that way, but if it did get out, she would explain. *It was my fault,* she would say. *I came onto him, not the other way around.*

Dr. Harlan was notably absent from both her birthday and the Halloween festival, and he still hadn't called. Her plan had failed. She thought that maybe if she threw herself at him, in a way that was so obvious what her feelings were, that maybe he would turn down Turner Hospital's job offer and stay in Adytown. Stay with *her.* His silence was all the response she needed. She tried not to let it bother her, and even more so, she tried not to think of it. Instead, she focused all her energy on closing Hiraeth for her third winter in Adytown.

Jake was a great help in clearing the raised beds and salvaging whatever crops could be replanted in the greenhouse for next spring. They had worked together long enough that they could work as one mind. Jake knew the schedules, the rhythms, and the intentions Seren had for Hiraeth, so she hardly had to explain or tell him what to do. If she had to replant tomatoes in the greenhouse, he already had pots and trays ready. If she finished combing through a bed of soil, he'd scatter leaves and straw to preserve it for the next year. When they were finished, they sat on the porch, drank sparkling water, and talked.

"I finally worked up the courage to ask Emelia out on a date, and she said yes," Jake said.

Seren swatted his shoulder. "That's great! Where are you taking her?"

He was buzzing with excitement. "We're going to the city to catch a basketball game. Can you believe it? I've wanted to ask her out for so long, but I was afraid to. I can't believe she actually likes me, too."

"Well, I think you've come a long way. You used to be an asshole…"

At that, he jabbed his elbow into her side. "What do you mean, 'used to'? I have a reputation to maintain, you know."

She laughed and shook her head. "Well, regardless of your amazing Squidward impression, you're actually a nice guy."

"Oof, not a '*nice guy.*'" He cringed.

"You know what I mean. You're… fine."

He quirked a smile and took a sip of water. "So, if I bring her a bouquet of flowers, would that be *fine* too?"

The thought of Jake presenting anybody with flowers was both heartwarming and absurd, and Seren couldn't help but chuckle. As soon as she did, she slapped her hand over her mouth.

"That bad, huh?" he asked.

"No, no! I'm sorry. It's just… you with flowers. Yes, it's fine. More than fine. I think she would love that. Definitely bring her flowers." She jabbed a finger into his chest. "And you better tell me how it went. I want all the juicy details."

He laughed as he set down his glass and stood up. "I will, I promise, but no juicy details. I'm a gentleman, after all."

Seren stood up and hugged him. "Who are you, and what did you do to Jake?"

He stepped back, scowled, and shrugged.

"There he is. Anyway, I'm so happy for you." She couldn't help but beam with pride. He was a new man, and though Seren had saved him, Emelia had brought him back to life.

After they said their goodbyes, a heaviness pooled in Seren's chest. The trees were barren, and all signs of life were drying up.

Though she was surrounded by wonderful friends, she couldn't help but feel alone. Jenna had Everett, and Jake had Emelia, and she could even say that Lenora had Damien and Seth, as the three of them mostly hung out with each other. *I can always talk to Otis, too,* she thought. The point was she had more people to talk to than she ever had before, and she was happy, though not happy enough. She felt spoiled. Hiraeth was thriving and provided her and hundreds of others with beautiful produce. She had friends who she loved and who also loved her. The natural beauty of Adytown was unmatched, and there was never a shortage of things to do in town, not since Mayor Doney had revitalized everything. The chickens said hi to her every morning and provided her with fresh eggs, and Freya and Mabon provided a special kind of companionship when she tired of the company of people. She had everything she ever thought possible, yet...

A tear shot down her face and landed on the ground beneath her. It formed and fell from her face so quickly she had to feel her cheek to confirm it had happened. Sure enough, it was damp, and when she looked at the ground beneath her, a small, almost imperceptible spot of moisture broke up the dry dirt.

Mabon approached with her tail held high and chirped at her as she padded closer. The cat brushed against her shins and rubbed her face against Seren's open hand.

"Hi Mabs. I'm okay," she said.

Mabon looked up at her and meowed, and when Seren didn't talk to her again, she jumped onto her lap and lay down. Her soft, fluffy body warmed Seren's legs, and Mabon purred as she petted her.

Everyone should be so lucky, she thought, *to have loved and lost, and come to find the light again.*

Chapter 14

In early December, Everett triumphantly announced through town that his book had been published. His elation fueled a party to celebrate, and he insisted that Seren stop by.

"Please come. It would give me great happiness if you attended," he said in the usual flowery tone he liked to use when he was artistically inspired. "The book would not have come to be without you."

Ultimately, his charm won her over, and Seren conceded that one night spent out of hibernation at Hiraeth wouldn't hurt.

It was cold, and Seren wrapped her wool scarf tighter around her neck as she made the trek to the library. She didn't give the clinic a second glance and quickened her pace to avoid anyone who might meet her as they exited. She'd given up on hearing from Harlan. He was probably furious at her for putting him in a compromising position.

Snow crunched under her feet as she walked by the Rusty Fig. The delicious aroma of sauteed garlic and onions wafted through the chilly air. Seren hoped Otis was making soup.

The library was warm and inviting. The fireplace was lit, and the decorations gave an air of sophistication and cozy academia. She sidestepped around Craig, who was standing with an expectant smile under a sprig of mistletoe with white berries and a red bow hanging just shy of the door, so she wouldn't have to talk her way out of kissing him. He shot her a scowl. Seren made a silent vow to go nowhere near it, at least not until it was time to leave and no one was coming in or out.

"Seren!" Everett walked toward her in a bright red suit and green waistcoat that made him look as if Santa Claus had de-aged a few decades and modeled for J. Crew. "So happy you could make it!" He handed her a cup of red wine. He knew her well. Jenna wasn't far behind, and she ran up to Seren and hugged her.

Seren felt claustrophobic, as most of Adytown and other friends of Everett's were tightly packed together inside the small space.

The afternoon unfolded like Everett's reading had, with grand spirit and good-natured merriment. He had a knack for creating an atmosphere that seemed more akin to a gala rather than a small-town get-together, and Seren was convinced that somewhere in the rows of bookshelves, magical fairies were dusting the pages with Daliesque substances that wafted undetected through the air.

There were two more readings, both of which Everett theatrically delivered. The crowd bellyached and begged him to read them more when he finished.

Two hours later and three cups of wine down, Seren thought about heading home. It was close to four o'clock, and the light was fading fast. She wasn't scared to walk home alone; she just wanted to make it to the Fig and back before it was pitch dark. Seren was gathering her things when the sound of clinking glass got her attention.

"Everyone, there's one last announcement I'd like to make," Everett said. He stood by the library entrance with a flute of champagne. "I just wanted to thank you all for coming. It's been quite a wild ride. There were times I thought I'd never get my book done, but here we are, a year later, and I have the book in my hand. And hopefully, all your hands soon, as well."

The room buzzed with light laughter, and some people proclaimed that the book was slated to be a *New York Times* Bestseller. When the room quieted down, Everett spoke again.

"I would not have achieved this dream without Seren Grinaker," he said as he gestured toward her, and everyone in the room turned to look. "So, if we could all raise a glass… to Seren!"

"To Seren!" everyone echoed.

"You have my undying thanks, now and always," Everett said.

Seren raised her empty cup to Everett and coaxed the last drop into her mouth.

"I also could not have done this without someone else," Everett added. "Jenna, you inspire me every day, and I thank you for being by my side as a fellow artist, and the woman I love."

Jenna wiped a tear from her eye, her other hand clasped in front of her chest as she mouthed *I love you* to him.

"I have some mistletoe here. How about it, Jenna? Will you do me the honor?"

Everyone's voices combined into muffled *oohs* as Jenna walked forward to kiss Everett under the mistletoe. Not a moment after they finished their kiss, Everett descended to one knee and pulled a small, velvet black box from his pocket. Jenna's hands flew up to her mouth when he opened it to reveal a beautiful, ornate ring.

"Jenna, will you grant me the greatest pleasure of making me your husband?"

"*Yes!* Yes, of course I will!" she said.

The room erupted into applause and spirited cheering as Everett stood and hugged Jenna close. Her eyes were bleary with tears as she pulled away, and Seren couldn't help but join her in that happiness.

The room swarmed them both. When Seren got her turn with the happy couple, she draped her arms around Jenna's shoulders and hugged her as more and more of Everett's friends ventured forward to clap him on the back and congratulate him.

"I'm so happy for you!" Seren said in Jenna's ear.

Jenna nodded and hugged her back. More people wanted their time with Jenna, so Seren backed away. "If you want to stop by later to celebrate, my door is open."

Everyone was so distracted by the proposal that the people Seren passed under the mistletoe paid her no mind as she stepped out into the cold.

Chapter 15

Seren sat in front of the fire with an empty bowl nestled between her crossed legs. After she left the library, she stopped by to pick up some soup from the Fig. Otis had made French onion, which was one of her favorites.

They had talked for a little while about Hiraeth's closure for the season, how things were at the restaurant, and how their sauce business was growing. When that was done, Seren delivered the happy news of Jenna and Everett's engagement. Otis was beside himself with glee and promised that when the happy couple came by, a bottle of champagne would be chilled and waiting for them.

All warmth had long faded from the once-scalding-hot bowl as she sat and stared off into space. She propped her head against her palm on the back of the couch, with the other resting on her thigh.

There wasn't much to do on dark winter nights except catch up on a show or read, but Seren had seen most shows she had any interest in seeing, and there wasn't a book that captured her imagination enough to pick up. Instead, she listened to the sound of the clock ticking on the wall and imagined being happier than she was. Of course, she was overjoyed for Jenna and Everett. They deserved each other, and it couldn't have been clearer that they belonged together. Seren's unhappiness was an unwelcome visitor, but she fed and clothed it from the cold.

Somewhere around eight, Jenna called her. She and Everett and many others from the library had migrated to the Fig for food and drinks, and she mentioned the fantastic champagne Otis gifted them for the occasion.

"Are you sure you don't want to join us? It's not as much fun without you," Jenna said.

In the background, Seren heard someone tell a joke and an eruption of laughter afterward. She couldn't hear Jenna for a moment, but when the cacophony died down, she responded. "I'm just so tired. But come springtime, we'll have a big engagement party at Hiraeth. Invite everyone. No number is too many. I'll make it happen."

"Do you mean *everyone?*" Jenna asked.

"Of course."

There was a pause at the other end of the line. "I didn't see Dr. Harlan at the library today," Jenna said.

"Oh, really? I hadn't noticed," Seren said. "Anyway, Jenna, I told Otis I'd pay for dinner for you two. I hope you guys have fun tonight."

Jenna thanked her, and after they hung up, the silence in the cabin washed over Seren once more. The fire had died down, so Seren added two more large logs to keep it going through the night. Their conversation hadn't lasted long, and Seren found herself once again wondering what to do. Mabon slept beside her in perfect relaxation, her orange fur rising and falling against the soft knit blanket. Seren decided Mabon had the right idea, so she turned in early.

Three hours later, Seren still hadn't slept. It started snowing somewhere in those three hours, and Seren watched it fall silently past her window. It was peculiar to lie in bed with no thoughts flying through her head and no discernable cause to keep her awake. She simply couldn't sleep.

She rose from bed, got dressed in double layers, and covered her ears. The thick wool socks she stretched over her feet felt snug when she stuffed them into her winter boots. Gloves were also a must. Winter was never kind to her hands, and they often cracked and bled from the dry air.

Mabon was still sleeping soundly on the couch when Seren entered the room, and she did her best not to disturb her. The warmth and glow of the fire flickered and stretched across the floor, washing over Seren's bundled body as she walked through. When she stepped out into the cold night air, she brought nothing with her.

Freya perked up as Seren entered the stable. After she brushed the mare's back, she fitted her with a pad, saddle, and reins, then tightened the straps for riding. When everything was secure, Seren led her into the pasture and climbed onto her back.

Freya gained speed as Seren kicked her sides to propel her forward. Cold snow rushed past and stung Seren's eyes as they cantered faster into town. They passed streetlamps that illuminated snowflakes as they drifted past their wrought iron glow. They passed dormant trees that didn't look like trees at all, but dark figures of winter stillness. As the world passed by, a sense of calm control seeped into Seren's veins. The ride was exhilarating, and the cold air that rushed into Seren's lungs with every breath made her feel alive.

She wiped the snow from her eyes as they pressed on and around a corner. Freya carried Seren up a hill and down the pathway that led to Rita's house. Just beyond was a thick expanse of uncharted forest and mountains, and Seren guided Freya there. A large, fallen log proved no match for Freya, who jumped and cleared it with ease.

When they approached the forest, Seren pulled on the reins to signal Freya to turn. Dark branches whipped and whistled past them as they flew by. Seren had an impulse to let go of the reins and reach out. The strap landed against the saddle horn, and as she extended her hands, she closed her eyes. She put absolute trust in Freya, who carried her onward through the wind and snow.

Seren picked up the reins and signaled for Freya to turn. They ran back down the path toward town and turned to the right. They were closing in on the park, and at first, Seren assumed it was deserted. However, as her eyes focused, she saw a familiar figure sitting on a bench.

Seren pulled back on the reins, and Freya came to a complete stop.

"Harlan?" Seren asked.

She slid off Freya's back and threw the reins over her head to hold her steady. He acknowledged her with a tired nod, and she walked a little closer. It was surprising to see him, as she expected to see nobody out so late, least of all Dr. Harlan.

"I couldn't sleep," he said, reading her mind.

"I thought you left," she said.

"Left?" he asked.

Seren clutched the thick strap of material between her gloved hands and floundered. She didn't know what to say to him. He seemed too slack in her presence—as if she hadn't barged into the clinic months prior and asked him to kiss her—and too friendly to not remember they hadn't spoken or seen each other in all that time. Was he playing dumb about the job offer? She waited for him to say something, but he didn't, and when the silence became too much for her, she felt everything she'd kept inside boil over.

"Why didn't you tell me that you're leaving?"

"What are you talking about, Seren? Where would I be leaving to?"

"To Turner Hospital."

A look of bewilderment spread across Dr. Harlan's face, then he took a step forward. "Who told you that?" he asked.

"Frank. He said you're transferring."

"Oh," he said. "Well, I did get an offer, but I turned it down."

Seren loosened her grip on the reins as his words soothed her like warm honey. *He isn't leaving. He never was.* She was so relieved she wanted to cry, but there was still so much that she didn't understand, so many things that were left unanswered. She did her best to keep her composure.

"Then… why would he say that?"

"I don't know," Dr. Harlan said as he laughed. "But as he's said himself, he's either the last to know or knows nothing at all."

"And… after that day in the clinic? Why didn't you call me?" she asked.

"You didn't call me either. I couldn't… I can't just be some fling you want out of impulse," he said.

"Some… *fling*?"

"Yes. I heard he—the one you told me about, I can't remember his name—had come to see you that day, and that he'd stayed the night."

"And who told you that?"

"Faye said she brought him in on her bus route, but she didn't bring him back. She… came to the clinic the day after. Believe me, everything I heard was not from asking."

Seren couldn't believe what he was saying. Of course, it had been Faye. It all made sense. Having answers should have made her feel better, but all it did was anger her. There had been so much wasted time and so many miscommunications that should never have carried on without confirmation that any of it was true.

"I just want you to be happy," he said.

"You want me to be happy?"

"Yes, and if that's with him, I can accept that."

"And you thought—what? That you mean so little to me that I'd use you like that?"

Seren could see from the pain in his eyes that he did think that, and it had wounded him. The way his hands twitched, and the way it became so quiet she could hear the snow falling, seemed to answer multiple questions, but in barely perceivable, complicated ways. There was no universe, no reality in which Seren would ever want to use Dr. Harlan, and she hoped he didn't genuinely believe her heart was that cold.

He swallowed a few times and found his voice again, though it was careful. Strained. "This has been… very hard for me, Seren."

"What has?"

"Everything. You can't imagine the anguish I've felt, day in and day out, trying to manage how I feel about you. From knowing that one false move could cost me my license or forfeit your trust, to telling myself you felt only friendship for me, to wanting your happiness above all else. I saw who you were when you first came here, Seren. If I tried then, when I knew how hurt you were from what you'd gone through, I couldn't forgive myself. I wanted to help you, not only because you are my friend, but because I…"

Dr. Harlan stopped. He stared at Seren as though he needed her to reach out and help him get the words out, but she stayed rooted to the spot.

"There were moments," he continued, "many of them when I thought maybe you felt something for me too, but I put them out of my mind. It wasn't worth losing one of the best things that has ever happened to me."

Seren looped Freya's reins around a low-hanging branch and stepped closer to him.

"He didn't come back to me, Harlan. He came here to apologize."

He looked at her with his lips parted. Something shifted in him as he listened, as if whatever narrative he'd told himself about Adam's visit had vanished. They stood there, looking at each other, as Freya softly neighed nearby, and snow fell silently around them.

"And you…" she said, hesitating to gather the courage to let the words spill out. "I can't imagine my life without you. I didn't come to the clinic because I wanted some—I don't know, fling, I guess, as you put it. The thought of you leaving Adytown for that job at the hospital terrified me. I came to stop you because I was tired of waiting. I came because I finally knew what I wanted, and that's you, Harlan."

He watched her intently as she spoke every word.

"I think I've always known," she said. "But I wanted to be okay on my own first."

"And are you?" Dr. Harlan asked, taking one tentative step forward.

"I am," she said, gazing up at him.

Everything was out on the table. There wasn't anywhere else to hide, and though every atom in her body longed for him to touch her, her heart beat steadily as she waited for him to speak. She wiped snowflakes from her eyelashes and shook her head.

"Why couldn't we have just talked?" she asked, as much to the universe as to him.

"It wasn't that simple, Seren, you know it wasn't."

"What do you want, Harlan?" she asked.

His breath billowed in front of him as he looked at her. She waited for him to answer, but after everything that was said, and after everything that had come to light, he didn't answer her. Seren nodded and slowly backed away to the tree where Freya was tied. She untangled the reins and climbed onto her back. Seren felt Dr. Harlan's eyes on her as she rode away, back toward Hiraeth Farm.

Chapter 16

As Seren ascended the porch steps and entered the cabin, she decided then and there that was the end of it. *No more,* she thought. She had said her piece, and that was enough. The entire situation with Dr. Harlan had drained her, and with all the words spoken, she leaned against the door frame and sank to the floor. The heat from the wood-burning stove gradually thawed her frozen fingertips. She peeled off her gloves and tossed them against the back of the couch. When they splatted against the floor, Seren wrapped her arms around her knees and closed her eyes.

Is he a good man? she heard Adam ask her.

Memories of Dr. Harlan played across her mind in rapid succession like a Rolodex, one fitting into the other just like her hand in his. He removed the splinter from her hand with tenderness and care. From beneath a sun-scorched tree, he lifted her and nursed her back to health. They sat together, talking, and he listened to her. At dinner, he laughed and then presented her grandfather's golden ring.

He held her after she discovered Jake's twisted body lying motionless on the shore. His face grimaced in agony in his bed, and she gripped his hand in her own as they breathed together. His face inches from hers in the clinic and at the Aster Dance. Throughout those memories, there was one constant: he was looking at *her*. She saw care and admiration, fondness and yearning. As she saw his green eyes again and again, she realized he was telling her how he felt all that time, not in words, but in his actions, with his eyes ever looking in her direction.

Yes, he is. One of the best men I've ever known.

Seren wiped her eyes with the back of her hand. She shed her coat and boots and kicked herself for being so blind. *I have been such a fool,* she thought. She wanted to go back and speak to him again, to tell him she didn't want to waste another day without him. She rose to her feet and wondered what she should do. There was no doubt he'd still be awake. *What would I tell him?* she wondered. There was only one last thing she could say. *I'll tell him that I—*

Footsteps broke Seren's train of thought, and she quieted herself to make sure she'd really heard them. Sure enough, they were real, and when they came to a stop, there was a knock on the door. She opened it and saw Dr. Harlan, out of breath and covered in snow.

"Ask me again," he said.

Seren stood there for a moment, unable to speak, gazing into green eyes that burned with a fiery intensity. Finally, she murmured, "Ask you…?"

"Ask me what I want."

"What do you want, Harlan?"

"You."

Seren's breath hitched in her throat as Harlan closed the distance between them and pressed his lips to hers. The kiss was slow and intentional, his touch reverent and careful as his fingers grasped the nape of her neck. His mouth felt right against hers. As her heart beat faster, she wished to always remember this moment in resplendent detail.

Seren felt his body relax, tension draining away, as she kissed him back. The corners of his mouth pulled into a contented smile.

Their lips separated, and he looked at her with all signs of anguish and hesitation gone from his eyes. "You are everything to me," he said.

Seren felt as though her heart could burst with happiness. She had always hoped that one day she might meet the man of her dreams, but she never truly believed. Yet, here he was, standing before her. As she regarded his handsome features and felt the warmth and strength of his body, a hunger stirred deep inside her.

"Harlan…" She gripped his shirt, her breath growing ragged as she yearned for him. "I need you to touch me."

Harlan's eyes darkened. She tugged him closer, and he kissed her again. She opened her mouth, inviting him in, as he kicked the door shut. They stumbled back, tangled up in each other. Seren didn't know or care where they were going. They collided with the kitchen table. Without skipping a beat, he gripped her thighs and lifted her onto it.

They broke apart, breathless and chests heaving. He planted sweet kisses along her neck and breathed in her scent. Seren threw off his coat and fumbled over his shirt buttons. His shirt opened to reveal his flushed broad chest. He snaked his hands under her shirt and lifted it over her head. He paused and stared, seeing her bare before him for the first time.

Harlan shivered as Seren ran her hands over his unshaven pecs and moved upward to cup his face. "You're so handsome," she said.

That broke his mesmerized stare. He lifted his eyes to look at her and laughed so infectiously that Seren couldn't help but join in. She found purchase on the slope of his neck as he leaned forward to hover his mouth over hers.

There was nothing accidental or clumsy about Harlan's touch. His large hands gripped her waist and pulled her closer. Slowly, he slid a hand up her chest to cup her breast. Seren's breath hitched as his thumb brushed over her nipple.

"Harlan… please," she begged against his lips.

He grinned as he kissed her forehead, temple, and chin. He brushed his lips over the tip of her nose and around to her other cheek.

He undid her jeans and slid them down to discard them, the wood-burning stove casting flickering orange light over the hardwood floor. He paused there, kneeling in front of her, to plant a kiss on the inside of her knee.

He rose to meet her once more, recapturing her lips with his. Slowly, he slid his hand down her stomach to cup her through the thin white fabric between her thighs and grunted in surprise.

"F—fuck. Is that all for me?" he asked.

"You have no idea," she said.

When he took his hand away, Seren nearly whimpered in protest. Instead, she felt him grasp her hips to pull her closer.

"Do you feel that?" he asked close to her ear as he pulled her flush against him.

Seren gasped as she felt him hard against her. The ache between her legs was almost painful the longer he held her there, and she became delirious from wanting. "Yes," she breathed.

"Can I…?" he asked.

Seren nodded furiously.

He lifted her off the table as if she weighed nothing and carried her to the bedroom. When he set her down, she threw the covers back. Harlan stripped to his undergarments and climbed into bed with her.

Seren reached between his legs and wrapped her fingers around him. An involuntary, low moan escaped from Harlan's chest as she stroked him. He closed his eyes. She loved the noises she coaxed from him. He breathed her name as if in prayer, with perfect adoration.

Her underwear slid against her soft flesh as he pushed the small patch of cotton to the side and dipped his fingers into her. She was dripping wet, and she held nothing back so he'd know how good he was making her feel. Her moans grew louder and more depraved the more he teased her.

As if he could read her thoughts, he sat up and slid the last barrier between them down her legs. She propped herself up on her elbows as he kneeled between her legs. He looked at her as he slid his underwear down to his knees and kicked them off to the floor. He was perfect.

"Condom?" he asked.

"I'm on birth control, remember?"

He lowered himself to hover over her as he laughed, his breath warm against her mouth as he looked deeply into her eyes.

"If you're sure..." he said.

"Yes."

He slid into her.

Seren's eyes rolled back in her skull as he filled her with wave after wave of pleasure. She grabbed a fistful of his hair and moaned against his mouth as all sense of time and space slipped away. There were only the two of them, and nothing else mattered.

"Look at me," he said.

She snapped her eyes open as he drove into her harder. His name spilled from her lips. Their bodies glistened with sweat that was sweet on Seren's tongue when she kissed his neck. She was swept up in him—the way he smelled, how he sounded, and how his body felt on top of hers. She knew with every fiber of her being that this was *it*. This was the feeling she'd been searching for her entire life.

She rolled him over and climbed on top of him. As she placed herself over him, he watched her, red-faced and sweaty. He inhaled sharply as she lowered herself onto him.

"*Seren,*" he rasped, bringing a hand to his temple as if his rational mind couldn't compute the sheer pleasure coursing through his body.

She spread her legs wide and pressed her sensitive spot firmly against him as she leaned over.

"Don't move."

She hovered over him, grinding her hips against him as she softly kissed his lips. He groaned underneath her, sending waves of electricity down to her groin. She pressed herself upward and gripped his pecs as she rode him harder and faster. The mounting pleasure between her legs grew tighter, and she neared the edge.

"I'm so close," she whined.

She clawed at his chest, unable to stop herself, as she ground into him. Harlan sat upright and pulled her hips onto him, gripping her waist while she climbed closer to release. "That's it, that's it, Seren."

Orgasm washed over her in rapturous euphoria, her moans spilling out of her in sinful release as she perched high on a cloud, one that she wasn't sure she'd ever come down from. Not when he felt this good, and she could have pleasure like this.

"Seren, I'm…I'm going to—"

Harlan's hips drove upward a few more times before he, too, fell over the edge and buried his face in her neck, her name a whisper on his lips.

He lay his head against her chest, and she stroked his hair and kissed his forehead as they descended together. In that silence, she didn't know if he was thinking the same thing, but being thoroughly spent and ravaged after the night's turn of events, it was enough to think it. Despite everything that came before, they had found each other. Their souls intertwined and bonded as they were always meant to. They had come home, and no act of fate or time could ever part them again.

Chapter 17

The haze and bird song of early morning crept through the frosted windowpane as Seren opened her eyes. The faint yellow dawn rose on the eastern horizon, peeking through the leafless trees and filling the room with dim sunrise. Seren's senses came slowly back to her as she glanced through the window. The snowstorm had passed, and the sky was clear. Harlan's arm was wrapped around her, and her body was warm and relaxed under the security of his embrace. She smiled as she remembered the night before. She was in no danger of waking from a dream. He was there, and she contentedly traced her fingers over his palm as he stirred beside her.

"Good morning," he said.

She twisted around to face him. His eyes were closed. She giggled at the state of his hair, which was twisted and tangled against the pillow. He had evidence of her handiwork all over him, from his messy hair to the faded scratches on his chest. There was a look of absolute contentment on his face, which she was happy to consider was her doing.

"Good morning, Harlan."

She moved a stray strand of hair from his forehead, and he opened his sleepy eyes to look at her. She moved closer to kiss him. He placed a hand on her waist and pulled her to him. Her bare chest brushed against his, and she felt in that moment that she could spend the rest of time just like that, fully wrapped up in his scent, his touch, his everything.

"You are so beautiful," he said as she ran her hand down his chest.

He shivered at her touch. He drew in a shaky, shallow breath as she ran her hand over him. She kissed his neck, coaxing every low, restrained sound from him.

"Harlan…" she whispered.

His hair stood on end as her teeth grazed against the soft skin below his ear. The wet sound of his excitement slipped through her fingers. With each stroke, he grew harder in her hand, and every muscle in his body tensed under her.

"Seren, I'm—"

She let go of him and hitched her leg over his thigh, warm and flushed, brushing against his arousal as she told him to take her. She grabbed a fistful of his hair. His movements were slow and sensual, and she closed her eyes in perfect bliss, breathless and enraptured by the feel of him. His chest swelled under her. She moaned his name and squeezed him with her thighs. She was in too deep, but she didn't care. She would happily drown if she were drowning in him.

His hips sputtered as he came down, and she kissed his forehead as he settled. She collapsed, spent, beside him, her body flushed and glistening.

They spent the remainder of their morning showering and talking over a simple breakfast of eggs and toast that Seren whipped up. Harlan was due at the clinic at eight, and even in the winter, there was no shortage of farm work Seren had to attend to. She joked with him about the state of his hair, which was in desperate need of a combing. He told her he'd stop home before going to the clinic but that, ultimately, he didn't care who saw.

"Mira isn't suspicious?" she asked him, twirling her fork over a bit of egg as she watched him.

"No, I don't think so. Or, if she is, I haven't heard anything from her," he replied.

Seren had been concerned that she jeopardized Harlan's position because of her impulsivity that day, but if he had heard nothing, she could let it go. She was relieved. She knew how important his job was to him, and she didn't want to get him into any trouble.

"To hell with it, though," he said. "I want them to know."

Seren cleared their plates and washed them in the sink.

Harlan stood behind her and wrapped his arms around her waist. He kissed her neck as she dried her hands and leaned into him. "Will I see you tonight?"

"Please," she said as she turned to face him. "I think Jenna and Everett are going to the Fig. We should join them."

"Perfect." He leaned in and kissed her, and she raised onto her toes to wrap her arms around his neck. "Seren, I am…so happy," he said.

"I am, too," she replied, kissing him. "See you tonight."

"Can't wait."

Harlan released her and walked to the door to leave. It was hard to watch him go, but she knew he had to. He had lives to save and all of that. She smiled as she watched him, and though their night and that morning were beyond her wildest dreams, she still couldn't believe it'd happened. He was there, in her home, not just as a doctor or a friend, but simply hers. The reality of that would carry her through the day on a bed of roses. Then, a thought occurred to her.

"Harlan?"

He stopped and looked at her.

"Do you still have that pilot uniform?"

Chapter 18

The day passed with a considerable sense of lightness. After Harlan left, Seren dressed and walked onto the porch wrapped in the knit blanket from the back of the couch and thick wool socks that saved her feet from the cold. It was a clear day, and she could see farther than she ever could before. The sun gleamed off the fresh, untouched snow that turned Adytown into a winter wonderland. Far in the distance, she could see the dark blue sea and detect the faintest smell of salt spray as the deep water crashed against the rocks.

As she took in the expanse of the Earth and sky before her, she had an irrepressible urge to dive headfirst into the snowbanks. Ducking inside, she threw on snow pants, a coat, and boots. Without hesitation, she ran down the porch steps and kicked through the snow, sending it flying in front of her. She bent over and threw handfuls of it into the air and let it fall against her, not feeling the cold. Laying down and rolling over, she made snow angels and laughed. She felt like a kid again, happily prancing and playing without a single care or worry in the world.

Freya whinnied in the distance, and Seren made her way toward the stable to let her run free with her. After placing a warming blanket on her, she opened the door, and Freya rushed out.

Seren ran through the open pasture, checking over her shoulder to see if Freya would follow. When she did, she laughed and clapped as the horse charged forward. Her strong legs made the frozen earth sound hollow as she cantered past Seren, who marveled at her strength and beauty. She would let Freya have free reign of the pasture for the day, for as long as she wanted.

Seren scaled the fence and sat at the top. Her lungs filled with cold winter air as she breathed from the exertion and excitement of running with Freya. The horse came to say hello, and Seren patted her neck for a while before she swiveled herself over the fence and jumped down.

She walked along the forest edge, brushing snow off the great pine trees as she passed. *This is where it all began,* she thought. She remembered how she cried and demanded to know why she had been given the circumstances she found herself in. Her throat had been raw from screaming as she ran, desperately wanting to be heard in her grief. She likened herself to a ghost, or whispers, or a stranger in a strange place, but none of that was true. Adytown had made of her more than she ever thought possible. Before she'd even begun, she counted herself out.

Then, with the sun shining above and all the monsters gone, she entered the forest. Where there was fear or anger before, there was only peace. The light stretched and shone through the trees as she pressed onward.

There had been dreams, voices, and omens to guide her. She believed something, or someone had spoken to her, that the universe itself planted little moments or signs to show her the way. Her grandfather had come to her in her dreams. The voice she heard when she arrived wasn't his; it didn't sound like him. But he had been there, and she couldn't escape the feeling that, somehow, he always would be. An overwhelming sense of gratitude overtook her, and she hugged her arms to herself as she looked up.

"Thank you for everything," she said.

Seren pushed open the door of the Fig in a flurry of evening snowflakes. The outer cloud cover of the prior night's storm passed over Adytown to bless them with a light dusting. She took off her gloves and spotted Jenna and Everett at a table near the bar. They called to her, and she waved back as she made her way over, glancing around at the many faces surrounding them. The warmth inside the Fig quickly refreshed her, and as she sat down, she could feel her toes again.

"Who're you looking for?" Jenna asked.

"Hmm?" Seren replied. "Oh, no one."

She looked over her shoulder to see if Harlan was passing through the door each time it opened. It was a Friday night, and most of Adytown had piled into the Fig for a helping of hot soup and drinks.

The door opened again, and Harlan stepped inside. He smiled and waved at Seren and made his way to their table. Jenna and Everett looked at each other with puzzled expressions.

"Hello," Harlan said as he sat down. "Jenna, Everett, good to see you both."

"Good evening, doc—"

Everett stopped dead in his tracks as Harlan wrapped an arm around Seren and kissed her.

"No way," he said.

"Wait, *wait* a minute." Jenna sat upright, clasping her hands together as she stared at them both. "Are you guys…?" She pointed to them both.

Harlan looked at Seren, and she nodded and squeezed his hand under the table. "Yes, we are," he said.

Jenna squealed in her seat so loudly almost everyone turned to see what the ruckus was. Seren wondered if the sudden influx of attention would bother Harlan, but he didn't flinch. Jenna jumped up and ran to Seren to hug her, then hugged Harlan, too.

"*Finally!*" she said.

The four of them laughed and talked together, Seren and Harlan answering as many of their questions as they could without spilling the x-rated bits. Their happiness garnered the attention of one disgruntled patron at the bar, who didn't seem too impressed with the two of them together.

"I thought you weren't supposed to *fuck* your patients!"

If a pin dropped, every person inside the Fig would have heard it. They all turned to look toward the bar to see the source of such a vulgar, confrontational comment, and when they saw who it was, no one was surprised. Craig sat at the bar with a pint in his hand and glared at Seren and Harlan. Seren held her breath as her face grew hot. She hadn't felt this way since everyone stared at her when she arrived at her first Aster Dance. She looked to see Harlan's reaction, but he sat tall in his seat, his face even and unflustered. He squeezed her hand beneath the table, then stood.

"Pardon me?" he said.

"I *said*, I thought you weren't supposed to f—"

"No, you misunderstand me. I heard what you said. You embarrass yourself, Craig."

Craig's face turned red with anger as he looked around. No one seemed to be on his side.

"Well, I don't think—"

"Ah, give it a rest, Craig. Just 'cuz you're miserable don't mean the rest of us need to be, too," Faye said from the end of the bar. She laughed and took a swig of beer. Her voice pierced through the tension. "Hey! I'm happy for 'em. To Seren and Dr. Harlan!" she called as she raised her pint into the air.

Everyone in the Fig drank, and to Seren's surprise, some people turned in their seats to nod and congratulate them. It made her wonder, *Did they know long before we did?* She didn't want to answer that

347

question. Instead, she turned to smile at Harlan, who sat back down in his chair and pulled her close.

"I'll speak with him," he said after enough time had passed and everyone was no longer paying their party or Craig any mind.

Craig hunched over another pint, and his shoulders collapsed in on himself. Harlan was right. He had embarrassed himself. No one seemed to mind that Harlan was with her. If anything, they were pleased. Everyone knew him as an eternal bachelor, a solitary figure in a small town, always attending town events alone, with no indication he would come out of his shell. They probably saw how Seren had changed him, and for that, they likely felt nothing but happiness for them both.

When Harlan finished talking to Craig, the two of them shook hands. Seren felt relief swirl around the pit of her stomach as Harlan patted him on the back and turned toward their table. Before he was halfway, Otis appeared from the back kitchen and walked toward them with his phone inches away from his ear.

"Seren!" he called.

"What is it?" Seren asked.

"I just got off the phone with Jordan. He says they want to expand!"

"What? Really?"

"We did it, kiddo."

Seren rushed forward to hug him.

As soon as she let go, Harlan picked her up to twirl her around. "That's fantastic! Congratulations!" He cupped her face and kissed her.

Jenna and Everett stood and clapped excitedly.

They had done it. All that was left to do was celebrate.

Otis popped three bottles of champagne and distributed them to everyone at the restaurant. "Gather 'round everyone! Grab a glass!"

Everyone quieted to listen to Otis, their attention flitting back and forth between him and Seren, who was standing with Harlan. Each of them held a full glass of champagne.

"As you all know, Seren Grinaker came to us almost three years ago. Who was this woman? No one knew. Oh, there were rumors that there were! There was talk through town that Harold Grinaker's granddaughter herself had returned to Hiraeth Farm. I think I can say for not only myself but for each and every one of you here tonight, everyone loved Harold. He was a good man. He brought so much joy and life to this town." He paused and turned to look directly at Seren. "Seren, after having the privilege of getting to know you these past three years, I can say for certain you are every bit as influential and admired."

Seren wiped a tear from her eye, but Harlan's hand on the small of her back anchored her. It seemed there was only so much happiness a person could experience before it became too much and flooded out. Her body had held so much grief for so long, and she wondered why she couldn't hold just as much joy.

Jake and Emelia came in from the cold and sequestered themselves against the wall. Confusion played across his face as Otis continued, but it didn't take long for it to change to a look of realization.

"Seren came to me with a new venture last winter. We would make and bottle my famous marinara with the tomatoes she grew at Hiraeth. Most of you here, I know, have tried it."

"Delicious!" Rita called out.

"Best I've ever had," Joyce said.

"We've just gotten word tonight that Saffron's wants to not only continue business, but they want to expand the market and make way for a bigger partnership with S&O!"

The room erupted in good-hearted cheer, with some people setting their glasses down to applaud their success. Seren caught Jake's eye, whose mouth had fallen open in surprise, then broke into a wide grin.

"And so, everyone, raise your glasses. To Seren!"

"To Seren!"

Chapter 19

Seren and Harlan stumbled through the door of the cabin drunk on champagne and celebration. She shrugged out of her coat and boots and ran to the bathroom to fetch her Bluetooth speaker.

She emerged with it tucked under her arm, red-faced and animated, as she rifled through her phone to choose a playlist. "We will have music!"

Harlan hung up his coat, out of breath from their brisk walk home, and laughed.

"Got it," she said.

She set the speaker down on the coffee table. A catchy, upbeat song filled the cabin as Seren added more wood to the fire. She shook her hips and spun around, enjoying one of the best nights of her life. She turned around and looked at Harlan, hoping he felt the same way. "Hey! Dance with me."

She grabbed his arm and pulled him into her, spinning and swaying, determined to coax him further out of his shell. Harlan obviously wasn't a dancer, but her unbridled surrender seemed to light a flame inside him. He danced with her, his body relaxing under her touch. His hands found hers, and they spun around in a circle until she was dizzy. She sang to him, getting closer and closer, her hands running down her hips. He clasped her hand and spun her around, dipping her low to the ground and lifting her back up again. All the while, the champagne buzz prodded her to continue as the song changed. It was lower and downtempo, the perfect opportunity to press herself close to him and sway in place.

As she lay her head against him, Harlan said, "I love you."

Seren raised her eyes to look at him. "You do?"

"Yes."

She didn't think she could ever love again. After all, how often does one find that kind of treasure in one lifetime? She had loved once, and she thought that was her one stroke of good luck. That even though it had ended, at least she could love once. So, she closed her heart and told herself it wasn't worth the risk, but when she met Dr. Harlan, even if she didn't know it, her heart began to thaw. She held off from admitting how she felt, running away from it as far and wide as she could, desperate not to fall again.

But as she looked at him, she felt that feeling. The one that, until then, had only felt fleeting and unattainable. With him, there was no vulnerability in joy. They could ride the train together, ticket or no ticket. With him, she could stand still with all the time in the world.

"I love you, too."

Epilogue

"Okay, everyone, gather 'round!"

Every resident in Adytown congregated in the town square, dressed in their best. Mayor Doney had invited everyone to celebrate the new and improved Perry's General. Perry took over the old Wares & More building and gutted it from the inside out. As usual, Seren delivered fresh produce once a week, and he stocked his newly constructed shelves with pride. He and Rita worked tirelessly to design the space, and she lent her carpentry skills to make the store fit Adytown's natural charm and beauty.

There were talks that Dr. Harlan might annex Perry's old space to the clinic as more people moved to the valley and his patient list grew. He'd even mentioned hiring a second doctor and a nursing assistant, so he and Mira wouldn't be so overworked.

It was a beautiful spring day, and after the ribbon-cutting ceremony at the new Perry's General, Seren asked if everyone wanted to be in a group shot. Perry loudly proclaimed that it was just like old times. Seren couldn't count how many times she'd heard him utter that phrase, but she appreciated his enthusiasm.

"Press in closer," she said as she set up the timer on her camera. "Okay, perfect. Here I come!"

Seren took her place at the center of the shot. Harlan wrapped his arm around her as she fit into the line. The camera flashed, and then Seren ran to check the photo.

"Perfect," she said. "Thanks, everyone!"

Seren had the photo professionally developed and framed. When it arrived in the mail a week later, she knew just where to put it.

She'd slipped the group shot of her grandfather from the scrapbook, with all of Adytown's residents inside a frame, and hung it against the back wall near the wood-burning stove. Next to it was Jenna's original artwork of Hiraeth, with an open space on the other side of the painting for the new photograph.

Seren sat on the couch and slipped the new photo out of the manila folder. She unwrapped the bubble wrap-covered frame, careful not to touch the glass. When she turned it over, everything was perfect. She went down the line of faces one by one, noting the differences from the first photo to the second. For one, Jake's smile was unforced and real. He looked so happy with Emelia by his side, her hand placed against his stomach. Mayor Doney still wore the same newsboy hat, and Chessy still only had eyes for him. Jenna and Everett stood wrapped around each other and beamed at the camera, the two of them matching in dark blue and maroon. Rita, Joyce, Mira, Darius, Damien, Seth, Perry, Corinne, Lenora, Marty, Craig, Zach, and Edna were all there, smiling. Even Horace, who wasn't fond of having his photo taken, looked glad to be there. Gia and Theo huddled around Chessy's feet, doing their best to look at the camera. There were so many faces that Seren had come to know and love. And at the center of it all was herself standing next to Harlan, with his arm wrapped lovingly around her, and her grandfather's gold ring glinting in the sun.

She fetched the orange scrapbook from the closet and set it down on the coffee table. She turned through its pages in search of the last thing to top it all off. At last, her fingers landed on a thin piece of parchment paper, grayed from time and smudging, and unfolded it. It was the will her grandfather had written before he died. She read over his words again.

To my granddaughter, I give you Hiraeth Farm. Take care of her, and she will take care of you.

Seren traced her fingers over his penmanship and felt a distinct feeling that, somewhere, he was smiling down on her. She taped the will to the back of the frame and rose to hang it on the wall. She looked at the old photo and smiled at her grandfather, then at the new photo with herself smiling back, and felt complete.

This is what it was all for, she thought. *Love.*

Her grandfather was right. She had taken care of Hiraeth, and through everything, it had certainly taken care of her too.

Acknowledgments

I'm currently sitting in a popular Los Angeles café, drinking a matcha latté, and writing this section. I began writing this book in 2022 after going through a traumatic personal experience. I needed to take that pain and channel it into something, and this book is the result. I wanted to write something that would not only alchemize that pain but could also be an escape for readers. Books have always been such a beautiful part of my life. The characters and stories I've come to love over the course of my lifetime have shaped me, and knowing how special books can be, I hope that in some way, this book gave you a bit of comfort if you are going through tough times, or that you saw yourself here.

I have many people to thank, but first off, I'd like to thank myself. You did it, Kate. You wrote a book! You took something difficult and turned it into something beautiful.

This book would not have been possible without the amazing contributors to my Kickstarter campaign, who singlehandedly made it possible for me to publish *Under the Same Sky*. First, I have to thank my mother for her endless support and willingness to provide feedback and read through the early drafts. I also must thank my stepfather, Ron, for his incredible support and excitement for this project. I also have to send special thanks to my friend Tanner Gordon. It was his donation that officially made publishing possible. Thank you for collaborating with me on making this beautiful cover! I have loved our unique hangouts, whether they're on top of a mountain to try to see the northern lights or walking the streets of London. I am so glad we met and first bonded over classic 1930s-style typewriters!

I also have to send my sincerest thanks to Adam Elenbaas (my Elden Ring buddy! And wonderful collaborator and friend), Tim Wilson, Bodhi, Benjamin Patterson, Mary Trube, Mark Takata, Robert Munguia, and M.A. Batten (who is also an author—you should check out his books!). Thank you all so, so much! Again, this book would not exist without all of you!

I have to thank my amazing editor, B.K. Bass, who helped me polish *Under the Same Sky* to a fine sheen and was always available to answer any and all of my questions.

I also must sincerely thank the Threads and TikTok online communities I have cultivated over the years. I have rarely encountered such genuine support as I have from strangers on the internet. I remember when I first mentioned I was writing a book on my TikTok account in the summer of 2022. I had barely begun writing then, and the road seemed so long ahead, but day by day, word by word, *Under the Same Sky* took shape. I can't believe we're finally here!

Thank you so much to anyone who has ever believed in me, whether you are seen or unseen. You are amazing. Thank you to everyone who, throughout the years I was writing, told me in passing, whether that was online or in person, that you couldn't wait to read my book. Your support doesn't go unnoticed.

And to you, the reader, thank you so much for spending some time with *Under the Same Sky*. May you always have the ripest tomatoes and love knocking on your door.

Songs I listened to while writing
Under the Same Sky

1. *Lover,* Taylor Swift
2. *High Hope,* Patrick Droney
3. *Finally // beautiful stranger,* Halsey
4. *Simply the Best,* Billianne
5. *Montana,* Daya
6. *August,* Taylor Swift
7. *Slow Hands,* Niall Horan
8. *I'll Be By Your Side,* Patrick Droney
9. *Moonlight,* Ariana Grande
10. *Invisible String,* Taylor Swift
11. *Tennessee Whiskey,* Chris Stapleton
12. *Guilty as Sin?* Taylor Swift
13. *I Found a Boy,* Adele
14. *Cardigan,* Taylor Swift
15. *Rose Colored Lenses,* Miley Cyrus
16. *All Of The Girls You Loved Before,* Taylor Swift
17. *Next to You,* John Vincent III
18. *I'm In It With You,* Loreen
19. *I Won't Fight It,* Andrew Belle
20. *All the Things,* Trevor Myall
21. *You Mean the World to Me,* Freya Ridings
22. *Hard to Do,* Gavin James
23. *Never Enough,* Loren Allred
24. *Wicked Game,* Jessie Villa
25. *Lost in Your Love,* Colyer
26. *Evermore,* Taylor Swift

Kate Hill

Kate Hill is a Los Angeles based actor and writer. When she isn't reading, writing, or dreaming of fantastical worlds, she is shooting archery, hanging out with friends, voraciously researching, and enjoying a glass of wine. Under the Same Sky is her first novel. Keep up with Kate and all her future projects on Instagram, Threads, and Tiktok: @itskatehill

Printed in Great Britain
by Amazon

54410848R00209